MW01701166

ELVENER'S LEGACY

Book Two of the Amoran Chronicles

Debra Koehler

~ Crescent Place Press ~

Copyright © 2026 by Debra Koehler

All rights reserved.

No portion of this book may be reproduced, stored in or introduced into a retrieval system, or transmitted in any form, or by any means (electronic, mechanical, photocopying, recording, or otherwise) without the prior written permission of the copyright holder, except as permitted by U.S. copyright law.

NO AI TRAINING: Without in any way limiting the author's [and publisher's] exclusive right under copyright, any use of this publication to "train" generative artificial intelligence (AI) technologies to generate text is expressly prohibited. The author reserves all rights to license uses of this work for generative AI training and development of machine learning language models.

This is a work of fiction. The story, all names, characters, places, brands, media, and incidents are either the product of the author's imagination or are used fictitiously. No identification with actual persons (living or deceased), places, buildings, and products is intended or should be inferred.

Cover Design: Ebooklaunch.com
Edited by: Raquel Brown Editing Services

E-book ISBN: 979-8-9907429-3-2
Print ISBN: 979-8-9907429-2-5

~ Crescent Place Press ~

Praise for *Amoran*, Book One of the Amoran Chronicles

"*Amoran* begins in a perfectly ordinary New England household and expands into an extraordinary multiverse. Koehler weaves in classic fantasy motifs, but grounds them in modern emotional realism. It's this juxtaposition, heroism amid domestic practicality, that makes *Amoran* stand out in a crowded genre."

— Jessica Fahey, San Francisco Book Review

"Original, deftly crafted, and a fun read from cover to cover. With a genuine flair for the kind of imaginative and humor laced storytelling that will appeal to fans of fantasy, romance, and unlikely heroines drafted to save the universe."

— Midwest Book Review

". . . feel-good portal fantasy. Readers looking for a fun, comforting story with an enjoyable heroine, a warm tone, and light romantic tension will likely have a great time here."

— Fantasy Book Critic, Self-Published Fantasy Blog-Off

". . . a heroine's journey in the best sense. We travel with Kerrin as she navigates a world so beautifully described, I want to vacation there."

— Marlene Cullen, The Write Spot

". . . Debra Koehler does a great job showing us both worlds and how Kerrin gradually comes to terms with her place in each of them. The story engaged me to the point I finished it in two days."

— Sheri McGuinn, Author & Screenwriter

To Barbara Rose Brooker

Who believed in my writing before I did.

Chapter 1

"Paper or plastic?" the cashier chirped.

I lifted my eyebrows and pointed at the reusable sack I'd already given her.

She laughed. "Sorry. That's just my way of saying 'cash or credit.'"

"Ah." I smiled. "Plastic it is. I need the points."

"I'm with you there. Earned enough for a free trip to visit my grandkids in California."

I inserted my card and began punching the endless procession of buttons. "I've always wanted to see California. The Golden Gate Bridge. Japanese Tea Garden. Redwoods."

The cashier leaned over the counter and winked at me like a co-conspirator. "Life's too short to put off what you really want. I moved here a few days after that huge storm last November. You know the one I mean?"

I nodded. Boy, did I.

"What a mess," she went on. "Homes lost. Folks hurt. And that poor woman they found half-naked, sunburned, and dead in her backyard! That was pretty weird."

"Sure was," I mumbled, glad she didn't recognize me as the formerly dead woman with an unexplainable sunburn. Lucky for me, I'd only departed the land of the living for a few minutes, and the sunburn cleared up in a couple of days. As for the naked part? Being blown out of an exploding tunnel of energy isn't easy on the wardrobe.

I poked the last OK button, then steered us back to a safer topic, one that would not conjure up painful memories of my last moments in the

Seventh Vortex. "I'll get to California someday. My daughter wants to go to school near San Francisco, so who knows?"

"How old is your daughter?"

"Twelve." I rolled my eyes and sighed. "Going on twenty."

"I had a kid like that." Her expression grew thoughtful as she handed the bag to me. "I'll say it again. Life's too short. You want to see redwoods? Go straight home and book that flight. Just do it. Don't wait. For some, like my husband—God rest his soul—it's too late when they finally get around to following their dreams."

A chill rose up my spine at the clerk's candid admission. I left the store and headed toward home, her advice looping through my brain like an earworm.

Life's too short. Just do it. Don't wait. Life's too short . . .

I was well acquainted with how short life can be, seeing as I'd actually died twice last year. The Foreseers brought me back from the dead the first time, allowing me to complete my mission as a Vortex Guardian. But repairing the vortex to save Earth and Amoran from annihilation had cost us. We'd lost—and I mean that literally—my Twin Light, Ashi, in the process. It was my job to find him, a task currently on hold due to a decree from the ethereal Foreseers that I reintegrate into my Earth life. In keeping with their penchant for vagueness, they hadn't said how long that would take. I'd been confined to the Earth side of the vortex for ten months now, and I wasn't at all pleased by the delay in returning to Amoran.

Thanks to the faulty air conditioning in my prehistoric car, I reached my small New England town of Glenwood Falls with little rivers of sweat slinking down under my tank top. Not a fan of heat, humidity, or sweating, this trifecta of discomfort called for an emergency stop at the convenience store for a crushed ice drink and free cold air.

I bing-bonged my way past the heavy glass doors, waved at store manager Gary, then filled a "small" twenty-four-ounce cup with a frosty strawberry treat. To prolong my stay in the welcome chill, I roamed the aisles tossing bags and boxes into a handheld shopping basket while sipping the icy concoction destined to turn my tongue pink for the rest of the day.

When I had sufficiently cooled off, I made my way toward the register, lost in thought as I pondered whether to put back some or all of the comfort food I'd impulsively chosen. Considering how much I missed Amoran, I figured I should probably buy more. Might as well drown my emotions in salt, sugar, and fat. It's the American way, after all.

"Meiri?" a resonant voice sounded behind me.

I whipped around, heart thudding as the basket slipped from my fingers.

"I'm sorry," Gary said. "I didn't mean to startle you."

I drew in a shaky breath. "Why did you call me Meiri?"

Gary shook his head. "I didn't. I asked if, now that the kids are back in school, you were 'making rather merry.'" Retrieving my basket from the floor, he handed it back to me.

Oh. *That* merry. Same sound. World of difference in meaning. My Earth name is Kerrin, but Meiri is my Amoran nickname. And the baritone Gary had affected sounded just like Master Guardian Eliasser's deep voice. Although now that I was paying attention, I caught the English accent, then blinked as recognition dawned.

"You were quoting *A Christmas Carol*?" One of my favorite holiday stories.

"I was indeed. Guess which part I landed in the Glenwood Falls Holiday Play series?"

This was, as the saying goes, a no-brainer. I'd known kind, gentle Gary since high school.

I smiled. "You'll make a great Bob Cratchit."

He beamed at me. "Thanks. I certainly hope so. Now, can I ring that up for you?"

I nodded and set the basket on the counter as Gary took his place behind the register. He rang in the drink, then lifted one eyebrow while scanning the potato chips, pretzels, chocolate bars, vanilla ice cream, a large bottle of root beer soda, and two blue boxes of mac and cheese. Not my usual fare.

Pursing his lips, he pressed his hands to the counter and leaned forward. "Not that it's any of my business, Kerrin, but is everything all right?"

I glared at my antidepressant fodder as if it were somehow betraying a deep, dark secret. Then I blew out a sigh. "I suppose I can't say 'yes' and get away with it."

He grinned. "Not with this smoking gun."

Come on, Kerrin/Meiri. Buck up. You didn't stay dead ten months ago. And you have a pretty great life on Earth. That counts for something.

"I'm okay, Gary. Honest."

Just to be sure, I tossed another bag of chips on the pile.

It was lunchtime when I arrived at my house in a more rural section of Glenwood Falls, my mouth watering for mac and cheese, a mound of chips, and a root beer float. I slid the key in the lock, pushed open the front door, then froze. Someone was banging around in what should be my empty kitchen.

A smart person would call 9-1-1. I even had the chief detective, a close friend, on speed dial.

Alas, I have never been crowned Queen of Smart Things to Do.

More like She Who Acts on Impulse.

Without making a sound, I placed my bag and frosty drink on the floor, then tiptoed down the hall. Pulse thrumming in my throat, I peeked around the corner right as the intruder straightened up and muttered, "Where has she put that tea strainer?"

I gasped. "Ari?"

Amoran's resident elf jumped in surprise, hand on his chest. "For the love of the Light, Meiri, don't sneak up on me like that."

I threw my arms around him. "Oh my God! I'm so glad you're here."

Ari hugged me back, then held me at arm's length. "Better yet, you'll be there soon. I wanted to surprise you with a little tea for two before we go, but you moved everything around. The tea's brewed. I just need the strainer."

I didn't bother to ask how Ari knew when I'd be home. He had ways of keeping tabs on me.

"Thanks for the tea, but I'd like to leave now."

I gathered up my stuff from the hallway and shut the front door, then dumped the frosty drink in the sink, stowed the ice cream in the freezer, and spun around.

Ari stood in the same spot, head bowed. His blond hair, which always looked like he'd just exited a wind tunnel, poked out in all directions. We were the same height—five and half feet—and his visual age was close to my thirty-seven years. His actual age I didn't know, but it was more than a thousand years. Probably a lot more.

He glanced up, his doe-brown eyes too serious for the fun-loving elf I knew and loved.

"Sit down, Meiri. We need to talk."

Ah, geez. I hate it when my stomach feels like I've swallowed a rock.

"Is everyone okay?"

Ari hesitated, then shrugged. "For the most part."

I tried not to think too hard about the qualified response.

"Ashi?"

"Still no trace of him."

"Then whatever it is will have to keep. I've been stuck on this side of the Seventh Vortex for almost a year. I'm not waiting another second."

Despite the Foreseers' decree that I remain on Earth, I had tried to open the vortex portal early on in my forced sequester. But the Guardians know me too well, and had sealed it shut. My daily attempts dropped to once a week, then once a month. I hadn't bothered since June and it was now mid-September.

I strode into the family room and thrust my hands into the air. Focusing on the invisible gateway above me, I took a deep breath, visualized the result I needed, then thought, *Open,* as I brought my arms down with a slight twist. After a few tries, the ceiling vanished. A shiver of excitement rippled through me as I gazed up at a sea of sparkling blue. My ticket home. To my other home. My *original* home.

Ari gripped my arm. "I need to tell you something before we go."

I shook him off. "It's been ten long months. Can't it wait?"

The blue light energy spiraled down from the gaping hole in my roof.

Ari sighed, then gave a resigned smile. "I guess it will have to."

He clamped his arms around my waist as the glimmering twister yanked us skyward.

Chapter 2

"Let . . . go. Can't . . . breathe."

Ari lessened his hold. "Sorry. Things are different now."

The shimmering blue energy dispersed as we soared up through a white-walled tunnel of light, the first stage of vortex travel.

"Looks the same to me," I said.

"The energy signature is altered somehow. Don't you sense it?"

I should be able to, and not just because I'm a Vortex Guardian. My soul came into Being inside this magnificent spiral of energy. But before I could give it another thought, the vortex slammed on energetic brakes I didn't know it had. Our ascent stopped so fast, it seemed like my feet wanted to exit through the top of my head.

"Oh, wow," I cried out, "I see what you mean."

"You ain't seen nothin' yet, Earth-girl."

"What do you—"

"Wait for it . . ."

"Wait for what?"

"Three . . . two . . . one . . ."

The white tunnel stretched side to side, formed itself into a hollow sphere with Ari and me at the epicenter, then snapped out of sight like a balloon popping. And there, all around us, was the rainbow of light that made up the vortex. But instead of swirling in a constant pattern, as it had before, now the energy moved sideways, then up, then down, then circled around and around, catching us up with a colorful tailwind and pulling us through—horizontally?

"Ari," I cried out again.

"I've got you," he called over the crackling of the vortex wind.

A few minutes later, the wind ceased and the Amoran portal materialized beneath us. We dropped through the opening into the cavernous Main Chamber of the Guardian Sanctuary. Located deep inside a mountain on Amoran, the Sanctuary contained healing rooms, meeting rooms, recreation areas, rooms for eating, special rooms for celebrations, galleries for art, a conservatory for music, and even a school.

The blue light energy returned, rotating more gently around us, blocking our view of the ground as it carried us to the bottom. When we touched down, a wave of dizziness rolled through me. I gripped onto Ari for support.

"You okay?" he asked.

"I think so. Guess I'm not used to interdimensional travel anymore."

"Well, get used to it," a voice barked through the haze.

The blue light plumed upward, then rolled away, revealing the Master Healer of the Seventh Vortex—a short, gray-haired woman who regarded me with storm-gray eyes, one of them narrowed.

"Ashara," I said evenly.

"Meiri," she said, copying my tone. Then, she snapped, "Go on. Greet your fellow Guardians."

That was so like Ashara. I'd only just arrived and she was already ordering me around.

And because it was Ashara, I obeyed her command and turned to my left.

Danaeus's cheeks went tomato red, then he lowered his gaze. "I don't need any of that hugging you like to do," he mumbled.

Faker. I knew for a fact that he loved my hugs. I wrapped him up in my arms and kissed the top of his head, which was easy to do since he only came up to my chin. Danaeus hailed from the Dwarf world—name unpronounceable, he'd once told me—and had arrived on Amoran by accident, never able to return. Most closely resembling the dwarves in the Lord of the Rings, he was stout with thick, coarse brown hair and a long, bushy beard.

"Really now," he blustered, but gave up the false protest with a grin as I moved on to the vortex Master Technician.

Balthasarre drew me into a good, solid embrace. Unlike most Amorans, and especially those who dwelt beneath the Mountain, Balthasarre liked physical contact. But his hug went on longer than usual, and my intuition picked up an unsettled emotion emanating from him.

I pulled away and searched his silver-gray eyes. "What is it?"

His smile, framed by a close-cropped, medium-brown beard, faltered. "You have been sorely missed, Meiri."

Was that what I'd felt? That he missed me?

"I wish I could have been here. You'll have to catch me up on all things vortex."

"With pleasure," he said, his warm smile back in place.

I turned to his teenage son. Minus the beard and sprinkling of gray at Balthasarre's temples, Anders was a younger version of his father. Same silver-gray eyes, shoulder-length, medium-brown hair, and skin the color of unblanched almonds.

He folded his arms across his chest and stepped back. "Thank the Light you are here. You can make up for all the turns you missed gathering *nemestes.*"

I laughed. "Is that all I am to you? Nemestes relief?" Harvesting the thorny plant, whose roots seemed to run to the heart of the planet, was a prickly pain in the butt. Sometimes, for real.

Anders blushed worse than Danaeus had. "Well, I might have missed you a little."

Ari snorted. "A little? He kept track of the days until your return."

Anders tightened his arms, but said nothing. Within the Guardian Sanctuary, commonly referred to as "the Mountain," aging crawled by at a snail's pace. His father looked to be in his mid-forties, just as he had before the Reparention—the official name for the vortex repair job that had spared Earth and Amoran. But Anders? He should still be the equivalent of about fifteen on Earth, yet something was different. I studied him before venturing, "Have you grown taller?"

He straightened his spine and smiled. "I will match Eliasser's height soon."

Eliasser. The pain in my heart during my confinement on Earth had been most pronounced where the Master Guardian was concerned.

With a slight vibrational difference, Eliasser was as much my Twin Light as Ashi. So why was Eliasser absent from my welcoming committee?

"Where is he?" I asked Ashara.

"Busy," she huffed. Locking onto my eyes, she telepathically dug into my brain, retrieved whatever information she wanted, then withdrew—all within a matter of seconds.

I held my hand to my aching mind-probed head. "Was that necessary?"

Ignoring my question, she pulled me into an embrace as warm and strong as Balthasarre's had been. Stunned by what for taciturn Ashara was an emotional outpouring, I returned her hug. She patted my shoulder, then said gruffly, "You are called to the Glen."

"So soon?" I wasn't ready for an encounter with the Foreseers.

A hint of sympathy graced Ashara's well-lined face before her no-nonsense demeanor slipped back into place. "You will have to see them eventually, Meiri."

Eventually, yes. But I had hoped to settle in for a bit. A few weeks. Maybe months.

Wanting to buy time before I faced them, I glanced down at my jeans and tank top. Hardly the conservative two-piece outfit normally worn in the Guardian Sanctuary.

"I'll just change first."

Ashara shook her head. "Go now. Use the Forest Portal. They are waiting."

Oh, lucky me.

The Foreseers reside in their own realm, which exists "out of time, out of space." I'd received that explanation when my spirit was pulled into their dimension the first time I died saving Eliasser's life. I had pushed him out of the way of a lethal shower of toxic light, taking the fatal blow instead. Insisting that I had not yet fulfilled my promises to the One Light, the Foreseers returned me to the land of the living so I could take part in the Reparention.

That visit to their domain had been a onetime affair. They usually met me in their Glen, a lovely intermediary space located deep within the Guardian Forest where the Foreseers could interact with those of us in physical bodies. The Guardian Forest is two hours away on foot, making the Forest Portal—a room within the Mountain that acts like a teleportation device—a much faster way to get there.

I traveled down a myriad of stone corridors in a confusing series of twists and turns, especially considering that all the passageways were made of identical gray-brown stone with no visible doorways anywhere. It had taken me quite a while last year to find my way around.

At the portal room location, I waved my hand in an "s" shape while filling my mind and heart with the feeling of "open." When an arched doorway appeared, I activated the portal itself using hand movements and mental commands similar to the way I'd accessed the vortex portal in my home. However, the effect here was instantaneous, with none of the jarring effects of vortex travel. The walls of the small room vanished and I stood on a sunlit path deep in the forest.

I sniffed the sweet-scented air. Jasmine? It seemed to change each time I arrived. Somewhere in the distance, a bird crooned a low series of notes. Nearby, another responded with a lighter, airy refrain. I pulled in a breath and let it out slowly, taking in the painter's palette before me. Like an English country garden squeezed into the woods, flowers of all shapes and sizes bloomed everywhere, not just from the ground up. Low bushes topped with tiny lavender buttons lined the forest trail. Blossoms sprouted out of tree trunks. Tulip-like flowers shot up into the air on slender olive spikes. Thick, flowering vines in rainbow hues cascaded like feather boas from the trees' high branches. That was different. The last time I'd last seen the vines, they were only in shades of blue and yellow.

"How I have missed you, my lovely woods."

As if in response, the tree limbs dipped down, then up. Yet, there wasn't even a slight breeze. Had the forest returned my greeting? I sighed with contentment, awed by the sheer magnificence of my other world.

I followed the path for a quarter mile to the stream, where I paused to appreciate the petite, five-foot-high waterfall sparkling in the sunlight.

Turning left, I continued on, slowing my pace while dreading the ethereal beings I had to face.

The Foreseers know the past, present, and future, including a person's thoughts and what resided in their hearts. Therein lay my problem. They must know how I felt about them after the Reparention. How angry I'd been. Still was, in all honesty. While they would never view what they'd done as deception, their habit of omitting key points, or phrasing things obliquely, made misinterpretation of their meaning almost a certainty. Case in point: they'd predicted my demise in the vortex during the Reparention, yet neglected to share one important fact—I wasn't going to stay dead. On the other hand, they'd never said a word about Ashi's fate, just stated that I would one day guide him out of "darkness." What kind of darkness wasn't clear. And they hadn't specified when "one day" might occur. Since time meant nothing to them, Ashi's return might be years in the future.

I moved down the trail, scanning left and right for the landmark entrance to the Glen—a pair of enormous trees that, like the Glen itself, appeared when and where necessary, and to whom the Foreseers chose. I usually came across the Glen about a hundred yards past the waterfall, but I'd already gone beyond that. Puzzled, I bent over to re-tie my sneaker, then straightened up and shook my head in wonderment. The two leafy giants were now right in front of me, straddling the path, their enormous trunks jammed together.

Assuming things still worked as they had before, I brushed my fingers over the smooth bark. The trees parted only a few inches. Not enough room for me to squeeze through even if I hadn't indulged in an excess of comfort eating during the past year.

Remembering how I'd entered the Glen on my first encounter with the Foreseers last fall, I placed a hand on each gray-green trunk and leaned forward. A *whoosh* of air sucked me inside as though I were no bigger than a kitten and tumbled me onto my knees. I rose up, brushed the soft grass from my jeans, then looked ahead, my heart nearly exploding with affection.

Eliasser stood in the center of the Glen as six of the seven Foreseers moved in a wide circle around him. Their misty forms glimmered with a soft radiance, each Foreseer a different color: red, orange, yellow, green, blue, and pink. Typically, only one or two Foreseers showed up at a time. This many signified an important event. They glided counterclockwise around Eliasser as he rotated the opposite way. Eyes closed, he seemed to be praying. Sleek, snowy hair fell to his shoulders, blending into the pure white caftan that draped his slender frame. But neither his hair color, nor his youthful, unlined face, indicated his true age. Master Guardian Eliasser had been alive for many thousands of years.

The Foreseers stopped circling, aimed their palms at his chest and sang, their etheric voices rolling out in surges of palpable energy. Even from this distance, the vibrational impact set me trembling. Eliasser, directly on the receiving end of all this input, shook visibly and stumbled. I sprinted ahead and was almost to him when I bounced back as if I'd struck an invisible force field. Which, in a way, I had.

The seventh and last Foreseer—the Elder—made her appearance by materializing in front of me. Peering down with a tinge of amusement, she floated several feet above the ground.

"What do you wish to do, Meirashannar?" she asked, using my full Amoran name.

"I wish to help him," I replied, pointing beyond her.

"Observe." She wafted her silvery form to the side.

Upright and smiling, Eliasser now seemed fine. His face brightened as our eyes met. Unable to speak around the sudden lump in my throat, I pressed my palm to my chest, then held my hand out as though I were offering my heart to him. Expression softening, he nodded.

"Come," the Elder said to me. "It is time to for you to strengthen your Second Twin Light."

Me strengthen the Master Guardian? Hardly. "Don't you mean that the other way around?"

"I always mean precisely what I say," she replied, motioning me to stand in front of Eliasser.

"Could have fooled me," I muttered under my breath.

She waved her hand in front of Eliasser and his eyes closed, his breath at once slow and steady. I recognized the signs of a deeply meditative state.

The Elder kept her eyes on the Master Guardian.

"Meirashannar, will you honor your promise to serve the One Light, no matter what the task?"

That was quite a blank check request, one I didn't recall agreeing to sign. Considering how I'd been misled by the Foreseers in the past, I took a page from their playbook and made my reply true, but vague. "I will do my best to serve the Light in all ways. But I cannot promise you now that I will perform some unnamed task in the future unless I know what that task is. To say otherwise would be dishonest." And not too bright, either.

A smile lit up her ethereal face. "You will honor all of your commitments. Your answer has shown us that."

I didn't see how. Yet a weight seemed to lift from my shoulders, followed by relief, on the heels of which came a flash of irritation.

"You never told me I would survive my death in the vortex! And what about Ashi? He's not in the actual Darkness, is he?" It was my understanding that nothing could survive inside the dense gravitational field of the vortex's dark energy component.

"Darkness has many manifestations, Daughter of the Vortex."

I shook my head in frustration at the non-answer. "You know all and see all. Don't you know where he is? Can't you help me with this?"

"You alone are tasked with guiding your Primary Twin Light from darkness, however that is not your only purpose or task. Indeed, you have many."

I opened my mouth to protest another oblique response, but she held up her hand, the universal sign for "stop" on any world. "We may speak of this another day if you wish. Now it is time to enter communion with your Beloved. You must be clear to do so." She touched her misty silver palm to my forehead and peace saturated my Being, washing my anger away.

"The Master Guardian is prepared," the pink Foreseer said to the Elder, who indicated with a wave that I should move closer to Eliasser.

"What about me?" I asked.

The Elder smiled again. "I have just prepared you."

"But . . . I haven't meditated recently." That was stretching the truth. After the Reparention, I'd gone to the other extreme and hadn't meditated in months.

"How curious," she said. "How you are is how you should be. It is what your sweet king needs from you. Do you understand?"

"No," I replied quietly, taken aback by her use of my private nickname for Eliasser.

"Understanding will come," she said, with such kindness and compassion that I experienced her Love as a warm glow in the center of my chest. "Now. Say the Vortex Prayer."

Eliasser's eyelids fluttered open. "Foreseer?" It was as much of a question as he could ask in his current state. The Vortex Prayer is a powerful incantation in any case, but the effect of speaking it in the Foreseers' Glen could be exhausting; the aftermath, unpredictable.

"Yes, Master Guardian," the Elder affirmed. "The Vortex Prayer. Begin."

Eliasser stretched his arms straight out to the side, palms up. I matched his movements, then we chanted together:

Born inside the spiral of Light, within the vortex spinning.
Born of energy, born of Light, as in the beginning.
To return is to go forward, to leave is to come home.
To love is to remember, you are never here alone.

Eliasser continued on alone, his breath coming in short bursts:

Light of my Light, come into your Knowing.
Light of my Light, to keep the Love growing.
Light of my Light, the Dream you are sowing,
Light gives to Light, our Gift overflowing.

We aimed our palms toward one another. Light poured from our hands, shooting back and forth between us. I stumbled backward from the impact, then regained my footing. It was my turn to speak alone, but I wasn't sure I could manage. It seemed to take all my strength just to remain vertical.

The gift of your Light, which gave me my start,
The gift of your Life, of which I am part,

The gift of your Love, which flows through my heart,
In Light and with Love, we are never apart.

We pressed our hands together, the intensity of the energy we now shared hot and vibrant as we gasped out the most powerful part of the prayer together.

To Light, I will lead you.
In Light, I become you.
As Light, I release you.
For All are One.

My mind buzzed and it felt like my heart had grown so large that I lived inside it, like existing in a love bubble. Physically? Every muscle in my body shuddered from fatigue. I knew I was energetically out of shape, but surprisingly, Eliasser's condition was even more pronounced as he swayed in place.

"Again," the Elder said.

"Again?" Eliasser wheezed. "Is that wise?"

"You doubt me, Master Guardian?" she asked, once more with that hint of amusement.

He closed his mouth and shook his head.

"Then begin."

Eliasser's hands shook as he held them out to the side. We made it through another recitation, but by the time we reached the end, I was so overwhelmed by the energy coursing through me, I could barely speak.

"Again," the Elder said.

"What?" I rasped out. I pointed at Eliasser. Bent over at the waist, gasping for air, he was in no condition to defend himself. "No! He'll never make it through."

"Remember where you are, Meirashannar," the Elder said. "Indeed, remember who you are." She waved an ethereal hand in front of Eliasser. As if he'd been given a reviving draft, he straightened up and his arms shot out to the side. But when he began the prayer, his voice was still little more than a whisper. I forced my hands into position like

I was pushing them through churning water and caught up with him mid-sentence.

When we uttered the final words, Eliasser's eyes rolled back in his head and he sank to the ground. I dropped down and pulled him to me, cradling his head in my lap.

The Elder spoke. "We have vibrationally enhanced each word of the Vortex Prayer to provide you both with added strength for the tasks ahead. You will return to the Glen at sunrise for the next seven days and perform this ritual three times."

"Three times? Seven days? We'll never survive it."

She turned away as the red and blue Foreseers wafted forward, each carrying a small silver chalice. "You will be refreshed," the red Foreseer said, handing one to me.

"I certainly hope so." The cool blue liquid tasted like water with a slight sweetness. True to her word, I began to feel better.

I returned the empty chalice to the red Foreseer as the blue Foreseer offered me the second one. "For the Master Guardian."

I propped him up and held the cup to his lips. When he didn't react, I dipped my finger into the liquid and placed a drop on his lips. He roused for a moment, pulled the chalice to his mouth, and drained it in several gulps. Flopping back, he closed his eyes. I gazed at him lying in my arms, my heart feeling as if it might burst.

The Elder still had her back to me. "You have great love for your Second Twin, yes?"

"Yes." She'd used the official title that defined our Twin Light relationship. But the labels were meaningless to me. No matter what name or designation—Second Twin, Master Guardian, sweet king—my affection for Eliasser was boundless.

"In truth, you love him more than any other Being, including Makashannar, your Primary Twin," she said, using Ashi's full name. "That is as it should be. You have a long journey to take with the Master Guardian, one that may at times be perilous, even heartbreaking."

"What do you mean by heartbreaking?" I asked, showing where my priorities lay.

The Elder faced me. "All points converge when and where necessary. Despite hardship, you will ultimately prevail. This I have foreseen."

My arms, still holding Eliasser, broke out in goose bumps. Forget the hardship reference, never had any Foreseer referred to herself in the first person. It was always "we this" and "we that." They might appear individually, but they seemed to operate as a single entity.

"Care for him," she continued. "Give to him that which he needs."

I beheld Eliasser's sweet, but tired face. "Sleep heads the list at the moment."

"What nourishes him most is your pure, all-encompassing love. Do you know what a rare gift that is? To love another so deeply, yet with no expectation of what you will receive in return? Indeed, more than once you have offered your own precious life in exchange for his."

The second time I'd saved Eliasser was during the Reparention. His Life Force nearly spent, I'd injected as much of my own Life Force into him that I could, then pushed him toward the Amoran portal. With no time left to make my own exit to Earth, I'd resigned myself to the death the Foreseers had predicted. But right before the stabilizing explosion occurred, Ashi came out of nowhere, fed me *his* Life Force and pushed *me* to safety just as the center of the vortex erupted. No one had seen Ashi since.

"Your love gives the Master Guardian great strength."

"I thought the One Light gives us everything we need."

I was being prickly, but the Elder just smiled.

"Yes. All things do come from the One Light. But the One Light also gave you each other. Dwell on that, Meirashannar." With those final words, all seven Foreseers floated, one by one, through a circular opening in the trees at the far end of the Glen.

Eliasser's head was still in my lap. I brushed a few stray hairs away from his face, humming tunelessly as I continued to stroke the white, satin-soft strands. When the ashen color in his face returned to its normal light bronze, I lay back on the grass, overcome by exhaustion.

CHAPTER 3

"Welcome home, Meiri."

A smiling Eliasser gazed down at me. We had somehow traded places, and it was now my head resting in his lap.

I sat up slowly. Whether it was due to the Vortex Prayer marathon, the intimacy of caring for the staid Master Guardian before I also succumbed to fatigue, or just knowing I was back "home," my emotions threatened to spill out in tears—a "condition" not common to the Guardian community.

"Thank you," I replied as evenly as I could. "It's good to be back."

To compose myself, I looked out over the Glen, appreciating anew its tranquil beauty. Grass that felt like velvet carpeted a round area half the size of a Little League field. Bordering the open space were short bushy trees, so tightly packed together it was hard to tell where one ended and another began. Three precise rows of blue, yellow, and pink carnation-like flowers grew beneath the trees, forming a second perimeter ring.

At the opposite end of the clearing from the entrance soared another pair of trees, not as tall as the entry giants, but more luxuriant. Spaced about twenty feet apart, the trees' lush branches grew espalier-like into the gap between them, intertwining above and below to create a leaf-rimmed hole in the center. Through this aperture, the Foreseers came and went from the Glen.

"Are you feeling all right?" Eliasser asked.

He must have picked up on my emotional state. I drew in a breath as his brilliant aqua eyes studied me with an intensity that was both embracing and unnerving.

"Mostly okay. You?"

"Quite well."

He seemed to have recovered better than I had. I wondered if he'd heard any of my conversation with the Elder. "What do you recall after the third time we said the Vortex Prayer?"

He shook his head. "Nothing at all until I woke a short while ago."

Leaving out most of what the Elder and I had discussed, I let him know we had to repeat this scenario daily for the next week.

"Oh, dear Light." He stroked his beardless chin. "I had no idea."

I snorted. "Gee. I am so shocked the Foreseers kept you in the dark."

Eliasser's snowy brows lifted, but he didn't comment on my sarcasm as he glanced at the sun's position. "We should go. Evening Meal will soon be ready."

"Really? It was early afternoon when I arrived. That was some nap we had." I rose to my feet. "Has time-stretching held up since the Reparention?"

He nodded. "We began it as soon as you and Ari entered the vortex."

The Guardians were able to elongate time when I was on Amoran, a necessity when I could only be absent from Earth for brief periods. I'd left at noon and needed to be back by three. Since an Earth hour equaled about five time-stretched days, I had two weeks to spend on Amoran.

"I'd like to change out of my Earth clothes first."

"Of course."

Eliasser and I made our way to the Forest Portal. Most portals were accessed by a combination of thought, feeling, intention, and physical motion of some kind—typically a hand wave or finger movements. Eliasser didn't miss a beat, didn't need to close his eyes and concentrate, like I had to at times. A casual flick of his wrist and the portal room materialized around us. I accessed the exit doorway—a much easier feat to accomplish than opening a portal—and stepped into the passageway.

That's when it hit me. In order to change out of my Earth clothes, I would have to go to my room. Ashi's room was around the bend from mine. I leaned against the corridor wall for support and took a deep breath to steady myself. When the Foreseers made me stay on Earth to fully reintegrate to my life there, I'd done the best I could—which meant I had to compartmentalize my grief over Ashi's violent disappearance during the Reparention. Today, with the excitement of returning to Amoran, then spending time in the Glen with Eliasser, I'd managed to avoid confronting that aching loss.

Not wanting to be alone right now, I asked Eliasser to accompany me. He regarded me thoughtfully for a moment, then nodded. We arrived at my quarters, where the outfit worn by most Mountain residents was waiting for me. Referred to as a "tunic," the two-piece ensemble consisted of a long-sleeved top that draped to mid-thigh over matching leggings in a heathery pastel blend of blue, yellow, and white.

I perched on the edge of my sleeping stone—"stone" for short—and held the soft but sturdy garment to my chest as I glanced around my room. Nothing had changed, although why would it have? Wall hangings covered nearly every conceivable space, their varied geometric patterns barely discernable, their colors muted. A single touch from my hand would illuminate them for a short time, however, I preferred them subdued. Along the entire back wall was a deep counter with drawers of all shapes and sizes tucked underneath. A table with two chairs rested near my sleeping stone, which was a little right of center in the room. The stone was firm, yet pliable—a bit like memory foam. It offered exactly the right support, including shaping itself into a pillow if required. I allowed myself a brief smile over the simplicity of life in the Guardian Sanctuary. Even names for things were simple. Sleeping stone, Meal Room, Celebration Hall.

Eliasser took a seat at my table and looked at me expectantly.

"Right," I said. "Evening Meal. I'll just be a minute."

I headed for the ancillary, a small enclosure off the main room that was the Mountain equivalent of a bathroom/dressing room. The only visible items were a short counter and a stone bench. When needed, the toilet rose up out of the floor, while the sink—an oval basin that sprayed light, not water—pushed out from the wall above the counter.

I "closed" the doorway, used the toilet, and "washed" my hands in light, shaking my head at the wonder of it all. A wonder I'd easily become accustomed to last fall. Shedding my Earth clothes, I pulled on the tunic leggings, then donned the top. As I left the ancillary, my hand reflexively touched the empty spot at the center of my chest and I blinked back sudden tears.

"What is it, Meiri?" Eliasser asked.

"Ashi's amulet. It's at home. In a box. I *had* to stop wearing it. I mean . . . I couldn't any longer when I needed to . . . when John and I . . ." I trailed off, feeling anew the immense guilt I'd experienced over my love for Ashi.

Eliasser came to where I stood, eyes brimming with compassion.

"I know this is hard for you to understand," I continued, "since no one in Guardian Lands has the desire to . . . uh . . . there is no need for—"

"Physical connection of an intimate nature?" he provided helpfully.

I nodded, still unable to fathom the total lack of interest Mountain residents had toward making love. The type of energy that permeated Guardian Lands, and particularly the Guardian Sanctuary, curbed what little libido Amorans possessed. Even expressions of general affection were primarily nonphysical. Before I showed up a year ago, they didn't even hug. And a friendly kiss? Unheard of.

But it went even further for some. Eliasser and Ashara possessed bodies incapable of sexual desire, regardless of where on Amoran they were. Ashi had too, until I accidentally infected him with my Earth energy during a healing ritual he'd performed on me. And because of our connection as Twin Lights—similar to, but far more intense than what people on Earth think of as soul mates—it was only a matter of time before we became attracted to each other in an unstoppable way.

"Were the potions I brought to you after the Reparention effective?" Eliasser asked, referring to the seven tiny vials of potent elixir that Ashara had crafted to help my energy patterns realign with Earth.

"They worked great. Got me back in sync with my Earth life like they were supposed to."

"And your husband; you and he were all right in that area of your relationship?"

I smiled at the delicate way he'd put it, then wound up blushing.

"That part turned out fine."

More than fine. John and I had always been a little rabbit-like. After Ashara's potions, things got even more so for us. Not that either of us complained.

"Yet, you are not fine now. I sense this is not just about missing Ashi. What troubles you?"

I did my best to explain, but it was like we were speaking two different languages.

"John is the only man I had ever been with that way until I made love with Ashi."

"But Makashannar is your Twin Light."

"But John is my husband," I countered. "What I did was wrong."

Eliasser shook his head. "I am the last one to comprehend this drive to connect physically, however, what good would it have done to deny yourself? When you and Ashi were gifted one night together by the Foreseers, we believed you were destined to die in the vortex. Never to have another opportunity to 'make love,' as you call it, with either Ashi or John."

On some abstract level, he had a point. But I still couldn't accept it.

"I will never know if I would have remained faithful to John without the pressure of my impending death—a death that didn't last too long," I added with bitterness, not because I survived, but because the Foreseers knew I would and chose not to tell me. Whatever reason they had for withholding that information, it had given me the final impetus to risk my own life to save Eliasser in those final moments in the vortex—but their deception still stung.

Eliasser's forehead puckered. "On Earth, you are not allowed to love two people at once?"

"You can, but most of us commit to only sharing physical love with one person. That's what I promised John when I married him. I betrayed my husband by making love to Ashi. I can't undo it and I can't seem to live with it. And that guilt weighs on me." To complicate things further, I felt I had also betrayed Ashi by reuniting with John, even though Ashi would never see it that way.

Eliasser frowned. "This will not do, Meirashannar. This emotion, this 'guilt' is quite unhealthy."

I lifted my hands in mock surrender. "I welcome your help in getting rid of this unhealthy guilt. Right now, though, I could use a nice, quiet dinner. Lead the way, my sweet king."

At the sound of my nickname for him—called a fond-name on Amoran—Eliasser graced me with a look of such affection, my breath caught in my throat. Before I'd been sent to Earth a thousand years ago, then wound up living ten incarnations as an Earth dweller, I was like Eliasser and Ashara—and Ashi, until our healing mishap—incapable of sexual desire and with no interest in even casual physical contact. But when I returned to Amoran last fall, along with having no memory of my previous Amoran identity, I was in a fully equipped Earth body. In addition to liking sex, I enjoyed friendly hugs and kisses. Over the course of what was only a month on Earth, but with time-stretching equaled seven months on Amoran, I'd managed to change a few minds about the benefits of physical touch. My greatest accomplishment? Turning the non-demonstrative Master Guardian into a hug-junkie.

The man was a natural. He wrapped his long arms around me, and I rested my cheek over his heart. "In truth?" I sighed. "I have missed you more than Ashi."

Eliasser kissed the top of my head.

"Your return today, my Meiri, is like a long, sweet drink for my tired soul."

Eliasser had said it was time for Evening Meal, so I was curious when we bypassed the Meal Room and continued down the corridor. Several turns later, he stopped in front of the blank wall which concealed the entry point to the Celebration Hall.

"We're eating in here?" I asked.

Eliasser pointed at the wall. "Would you please?"

Once again, I filled my mind and heart with the thought and feeling of "open," and gave a small S-shaped wave of my hand. The doorway appeared, I strolled through, then turned back to Eliasser, who smiled at my astonished expression. "Surprise, Meiri."

Surprise indeed. The Celebration Hall was decked out like a cross between a wedding reception and a birthday party. Glowing silver and gold banners draped from the ceiling, rippling as if moved by a slight breeze. Ether Lights—sentient, colorful luminescent orbs the size of softballs—floated around the room. A feast of Amoran delicacies rested on a side table festooned with garlands of *vallius* vines. The red flowers and bright green, heart-shaped leaves lent a Christmas touch. Milling about in the area reserved for dancing stood what must be the entire population of the Guardian Sanctuary, including the children of the Guardian school. About eighty people total, give or take.

The musicians halted the subdued tune they were playing and the room went still as all eyes focused on me.

"What's going on?" I asked Eliasser.

"You were not able to be here when we celebrated the Reparention's success. We are rectifying that now."

"By throwing another big party?" I was deeply touched, although it hardly seemed warranted. It wasn't their fault I'd been stuck on Earth.

"This 'party' is to honor you for your help in securing the vortex and for saving my life during the Reparention. And the entire Mountain community knows you are tasked with bringing Makashannar home. They wish to offer you their support."

I let my gaze wander over the crowd gathered—the healers, teachers, energy workers, musicians, and artists, to name a few—who kept the Guardian Sanctuary running smoothly. During the months before the Reparention, I'd been isolated to protect my energy field, and so hadn't met most of them. I hoped to change that this time around.

Judging by the silence, I figured I needed to say something, but speeches are not a strong suit of mine. Besides, they deserved more than my usual ramblings. On inspiration, I asked the One Light to guide me—something I was sorry to say I hadn't done for nearly a year.

And of course, the One Light came through. It usually does if you listen.

"I am overwhelmed with gratitude for this wonderful festivity. I understand you wish to thank me for helping repair the vortex and keeping the Master Guardian at his post. However—"

Applause and cheering cut me off. Eliasser was a favorite of everyone under the Mountain, not just me. When the group settled down, I continued.

"However, it is I who thank and honor you. All eight Guardians were needed to set the vortex right, but without your help we would have failed." I held my hand over my heart. "The Foreseers say that I will guide Makashannar out of darkness. But I can't do this alone. We all have a role to play in what will unfold over time. I promise to do my best to live up to your faith in me, and to find our beloved missing Guardian."

An even louder cheer followed. The musicians struck up a lively tune and the "party" officially began.

I piled appetizer-type food, a meal in itself, onto a plate, then made the rounds. After the first dozen or so folks, I wished I'd brought some "Hello! My Name Is . . ." tags from Earth to slap on their tunics. It might have been easier if they had Earth names, like Dave or Sarah. But with monikers like Mikellan, Sandashanna, and Esteven, I gave up trying to remember them all.

As the evening wore on, I began to tire. At the far end of the room, Eliasser was gathering the Ether Lights for their return to the unseen substance of the universe where they lived and needed to recharge. One by one, the colorful globes dropped onto his outstretched hand and vanished.

"Boo, Earth-girl!"

Flinching, I let out a yelp.

Ari moved beside me, smiling. "Still twitchy, I see. Nice to know some things never change." His tone was light, but underneath was a layer of tension I could feel.

"What's up, Ari?"

He sighed. "I'm sorry to be the bearer of bad news, but Eliasser's been leaving Amoran for 'meetings' or 'appointments' as he calls them. At first, it was an occasional day here and there, but it's been increasing. Last time he went, he was gone for a week."

"A whole week?" Having only just returned to Amoran, I wasn't wild about the idea of Eliasser disappearing for days on end. "Where does he go?"

"He won't say. No one knows except Ashara, and she's not talking."

One energetic blue Ether Light refused to be sent "home" to recharge. Unlike its more sedate companions, it had spent the evening zipping around the Celebration Hall like a fly on speed when it wasn't trailing after me. Now it hurtled out of Eliasser's hand and darted behind the musicians, making me smile.

Wishing I could go somewhere to recharge, I turned back to Ari. "Walk me to my room?"

He scanned my face. "Are you as pooped as you look?" I nodded. "Okay. The rest of what I have to say can wait."

"Thanks, my most favorite elf," I said without thinking, then cringed. I'd made up the pet phrase for Ari last fall before I'd relearned the story of Elvener's destruction, something my Amoran self had been well acquainted with. Eleven hundred years ago, Ari's homeworld faced impending destruction through vortex implosion. Their vortex was too far gone for a repair job, so we were making ready to bring the entire population of Elvener to Amoran. Just as we were about to begin transport, the Fifth Vortex imploded, sucking Elvener inside and crushing the planet like an empty eggshell. Ari was the only one spared. Everyone else died, including Maya, his Eternal Companion—Elvener's name for a Twin Light.

"I'm sorry. I guess I should stop saying that."

"Don't. I like it." He grinned. "Besides, I *have* always been your favorite elf, so it works."

I poked him in the ribs. "I'll have to take your word for it. I still don't recall most of my life here before I left to become an Earth dweller. That includes any time I spent on Elvener."

"Well, then," Ari said, as he offered me his arm. "Let me tell you about all the wonderful things you used to say about me."

Chapter 4

I met Eliasser at the doorway to his quarters the next morning so we could begin the seven-day ritual I'd dubbed our Odyssey of Prayer. Holding a finger to his lips, he motioned me inside and pointed. There, floating above the counter that ran the length of the back wall, was the hyperactive blue Ether Light from last night.

"You brought it back?" I asked.

Eliasser shook his head. "It never left. After returning the rest of the Ether Lights to their domain last night, I could not find this one."

"I didn't think they could exist in our dimension this long."

"Normally, they cannot. This determined Ether Light is long past its need for energy. I have a suspicion, though. Get as close to it as you can."

I inched forward until I was nearly touching the glowing sphere. Its color deepened as it bounced up and down.

"How curious," Eliasser said. "Move out of sight."

I went into the ancillary and hid around the corner, but left the doorway open.

The Ether Light zipped in after me, circled my head several times, then hovered at my side.

"Well, hey there," I said. "What's new with you, Blue?"

It brushed against my cheek, the tickle of its energy field making me laugh.

Eliasser leaned against the ancillary doorway and stroked his chin. "Offer it your hand."

I did, and the Ether Light settled onto my palm and rolled back and forth.

"Oh, you are so cute," I gushed, holding it to me in an approximation of a hug.

"And you are full of surprises, Meiri. Ether Lights are impartial to their surroundings, but it seems this one has attached itself to you."

"How odd," I said, really thinking, *How adorable!* "I wonder why?"

"That is a mystery we will have to solve another time. We are due in the Glen at sunrise. This Ether Light must go back now, for it will not survive much longer without recharging."

Eliasser reached out, but the Ether Light scooted away and hid behind my back.

I laughed again. "Apparently, Earnie doesn't want to go home." The Ether Light's energy tickled again as it floated up to rest on my shoulder.

Eliasser cocked an eyebrow. "Earnie?"

"It just popped into my head. Maybe because he's so earnestly trying to avoid having you send him back where he belongs."

Eliasser raised the other eyebrow. "I am not aware that they have a gender."

I'd thought the same thing until the words popped into my head.

I shrugged. "I only know what I feel. Meet Earnest, fond-name Earnie."

As if to underscore my declaration, Earnie moved directly between Eliasser and me and glowed brighter, his color shifting to red, then purple, then back to blue.

Eliasser's jaw dropped. "Never have I seen one alter its color! And unless I am mistaken, he is trying to protect you. However, it is he who needs protection."

I smiled at the Master Guardian's quick adoption of the gendered pronoun.

Eliasser reached out again. "If I promise to bring you to Meiri later, will you return now for replenishment of your energy?"

Earnie tilted side to side a few times, as if weighing his options, then dropped onto Eliasser's palm and faded from view.

Our sidetrack with Earnie had put us behind. We scurried down the corridor to the portal room, transported to the forest, and set out at a rapid pace. On this fine pre-dawn morning, the Glen of the Foreseers wasn't hard to find. A little past the waterfall, the towering trees rose majestically into the brightening sky. We squeezed between the massive trunks as the first sliver of sunlight graced the top of the leaf-rimmed aperture. Through that gateway, the red Foreseer made her entrance as we scrambled to the center of the Glen.

"You may begin," she said, without preamble.

"No prep?" I asked.

She made no reply, her expression noncommittal.

"Guess that's a yes." I lifted my arms to the side. "Here we go again."

Eliasser smiled and raised his hands to match mine.

I woke from my post-prayer nap lying on my side facing Eliasser, our heads resting on a pillow of some sort. It was midmorning, judging by the position of the sun, which meant we'd been out for several hours at least. I didn't recall anything after the second recitation.

I stretched and rolled over. The red Foreseer floated in the air holding two small goblets.

"Come and partake of this *tamonos.* It satisfies both hunger and thirst."

I wasn't hungry, which surprised me; I do like my food. I rose on shaky legs, wobbled over, and relieved her of a cup. Green, thick, and lumpy, the contents promised to be nauseating. A cautious sip proved otherwise. Tamonos tasted like eggnog, something I happened to love.

Eliasser opened his eyes as I handed my empty goblet back to the Foreseer. He stumbled to his feet and helped himself to the second cup. When he finished, he returned the goblet, then keeping his eyes on the Foreseer asked, "Is there someone to accompany Meiri?"

Oh, hell no. "You're not coming back with me?"

"Arrien is waiting outside the Glen," the Foreseer replied to Eliasser, using Ari's proper name. "Be advised. You should not travel far or for long until this process is complete."

Eliasser nodded. "I am aware of that. However, this appointment is unavoidable."

"What appointment?" I demanded. "Ari said you keep disappearing, but I didn't think you'd leave now when I've just returned to Amoran."

I was laying it on thick, and I wasn't particularly proud of it. Didn't matter, though. They continued to ignore me as the Foreseer stared into Eliasser's eyes. I knew from experience that they were carrying on quite the mental conversation, one meant to exclude me.

"Before nightfall," Eliasser said to her.

"Indeed. Tomorrow at sunrise." She wafted to the aperture and floated back to her realm.

Eliasser finally looked at me, took in my disgruntled expression, and graced me with one of his heartwarming smiles. "I must go . . . elsewhere now. Enjoy your time with Ari, but do not tarry long. Ashara needs to begin your retraining today."

"What retraining?"

I didn't get an answer because Eliasser vanished right before my eyes.

Ari was sitting on the path as I exited the Glen. "What's this early morning meeting with the Foreseers all about?" he asked.

"It's an intensive prayer session meant to strengthen Eliasser and me for unnamed tasks which await us. We have to say a vibrationally enhanced version of the Vortex Prayer, three times in a row, each day for a week."

"Three times? Seriously?"

I smiled. "Yes, Earth poser. Seriously. And it wipes me out. I guess that's why they think I need an escort back to the Mountain."

"In that case, I know the perfect way to spend the rest of the morning. If we take the long way back, we can catch up, especially since you passed out on me last night. Some date you are!" He rolled his eyes and I laughed. We'd barely made it through my doorway the previous evening before I collapsed onto my stone, face down. I was asleep in seconds.

The long way back involved a trek through the forest, a hike across the valley, then crossing the Mindsail Lake in a boat that ran on thought. Normally, I'd jump at the opportunity.

"At the risk of giving you a complex, what part of 'wipes me out' was unclear?"

"We'll take it slow, and rest if you get tired. It's a beautiful day. Why waste it?"

I shrugged. "I don't know." Something nagged at me. It wasn't this nebulous retraining Eliasser mentioned, but I couldn't place what it was.

"You don't *know*? What have they done to you in there?" He pointed to where the Glen had been. No sign of it existed now, not even the mammoth trees that marked the entrance. "On the off chance you lost your Earthly marbles, let me restate; I'm suggesting we go forest-walking, valley-hiking, mindsail . . . uh . . . sailing, and then"—he pretended to beat out a drum roll on a nonexistent instrument—"swimming in the Garrammon Lake."

I gave my goofy elf friend a fierce hug. "God, how I've missed you."

"The feeling is mutual." He pulled back. "Well?"

My resolve was weakening. This didn't match Eliasser's request that I not tarry long. Wondering if it was even possible to "tarry short," I made an executive decision. I'd been gone for nearly a year. What more could a few extra hours mean in the scheme of things?

"Okay. Count me in, Elf-boy," I said, using a nickname I'd given him once.

Ari smiled. "That's my Earth-girl," he replied, using mine.

We strolled along the sun-dappled path toward the valley. "I see what you mean about Eliasser's frequent traveler deal," I said, after telling Ari about the Master Guardian's disappearing act.

"Interesting. I didn't think it was possible to ethermove out of the Glen. He must have been in a real hurry. The question is, where was he ethermoving to?"

"Haven't a clue." Some Guardians could disassemble their molecular makeup and reassemble it at another location. Sort of like the transporter in *Star Trek* without the machinery and sparkles. Here one moment, gone the next. I couldn't ethermove, but Ashara had transported me with her once last year. The adrenaline rush nearly made me pass out. I had no desire to experience it again.

We left the leafy, flower-filled canopy of the forest and struck out across the gentle hills of the small valley between the Guardian Forest and the Mindsail Lake. When I questioned why there were fewer flowers in evidence, Ari explained that our area of Amoran was entering its colder time.

"I forgot Amoran had a cold season," I said. "Everything always seems so perfect here."

Ari loved to gossip and wasted no time filling me in on the past ten months of Mountain news, including his observation—with raised eyebrows—that Balthasarre's son Anders and Meilee, a girl from the Guardian school, had struck up quite the friendship of late.

I stopped and stared at him. "What are you implying?" In Guardian Lands, where libido was nonexistent, their friendship shouldn't mean anything at all.

Ari shrugged. "Just seems like they feel more than they ought to."

"Wow. That would be something."

Ari met my eyes. "It's what I've been trying to tell you. Things have been different since the Reparention, not only in the vortex, but under the Mountain as well. The energy patterns have shifted somehow. Most of the variations seem minor, but as an elven energy worker, I learned to respect any alteration in vibrational magnitude."

"I assume you've mentioned this to the other Guardians."

"Of course. No one else has noticed a difference." Ari kicked at a clump of grass.

"But you're worried about it anyway."

He nodded. "Unless we identify what's changed and why, we could be in for a problem."

Ari's somber mood was a change in itself. I decided to cheer him up with some Glenwood Falls gossip as we continued our journey to the Mindsail Lake. I'd been mistaken in thinking Ari had been keeping tabs on me this past year. Just like I'd been locked out of Amoran, he'd been barred from traveling to Earth, which had frustrated him to no end. As the only Guardian who could spend unlimited time on that world, Ari had watched over me during nine of my ten lifetimes there. I hadn't known that at the time, of course. Like most Earth dwellers, I'd been born with no knowledge of my past. As a precaution, he had always disguised himself, but it really wouldn't have mattered. The past life amnesia worked all too well.

At the lake, Ari asked if I wanted to pilot the mindsail, a watercraft that resembled an overgrown rowboat, but ran on a combination of thought, feeling, and desire—no oars, paddles, or sail necessary. I declined. Mindsailing takes a lot of concentration, and while the fresh air and walking had perked me up a bit, I was still too tired from my prayer session in the Glen to attempt something so mentally challenging. Ari, on the other hand, was naturally skilled in all forms of energy manipulation, not to mention his elven energy worker training. Within seconds the boat was cutting a slow, steady path across the water.

The lake mirrored the turquoise sky, while sunlight created sparkles across its surface. I rolled up the sleeves of my tunic and leaned against the back of the boat as Ari resumed filling me in on life since the Reparention. Relaxing into the cadence of his speech, my mind wandered back to last fall, when Ashi and I had traveled this same route by moonlight. I'd felt increasingly drawn to the reserved Guardian, and as a happily married woman, that troubled me. But when he later shared that our two "souls" were created from a single point of Light energy, making us energetically linked forever as Twin Lights, that growing connection I experienced with him made sense. That wasn't all, though. We'd essentially been formed from the condensed energy of the Seventh Vortex itself, making us Vortex Lights—a very rare phenomenon. It was that point of origin, and our interconnection as Twin Lights, which had allowed us to perform our roles in the Reparention.

Curiously, though, the bond I felt with Eliasser was even stronger than what I experienced with Ashi, which didn't add up. To my knowledge, there was no closer relationship than the one energetically linking Ashi and I as Primary Twin Lights.

My thoughts continued to drift as the gentle rocking of the boat, the warm sun, and Ari's pleasant voice lulled me with their soporific effect.

"Am I boring you?"

My eyes popped open. I didn't remember them closing.

"Sorry. It's odd. This thing Eliasser and I are doing to strengthen us actually leaves me drained of energy."

"Not so odd. Processes to increase your energy can initially have the opposite effect."

A chill blew across my arms. Caught off guard by the abrupt temperature change, I rolled my sleeves back down and asked Ari if it was due to the cold season approaching.

"No." His eyes narrowed. "You felt that, too?"

"Does that surprise you?"

"It concerns me." He glanced at the sky where no clouds were evident, then at the willowy trees lining one shore. They were as still as if they'd been frozen. "These random chills began a few months ago. They never happen on the same day of the week or at the same time of day."

"In other words, there's no pattern to them. Do you feel it anywhere else?"

"Only when I'm on the Mindsail Lake in this general area. I'd say it was just my elven makeup, but now that you've felt it . . ." He trailed off as we reached the small beach on the opposite side of the lake, abutting the Garrammon Meadow. As we jumped out and secured the boat to the mooring post, I felt another chill, this one internal. The type of willies you get when something isn't right. Or is about to go very wrong.

"I'll have to take a raincheck on swimming," I said, suddenly uncomfortable about ignoring Eliasser's request that I not tarry long. "I think Eliasser wanted me back by now." Or was it the retraining Ashara had planned that weighed on me? What if it was important to finding Ashi?

"We could take a shortcut," Ari said, pointing toward the sprawling grassy area. "We'll be able to take a quick swim and still get back to the Mountain in the same amount of time."

"I thought we couldn't go that way because of the *glazzien*."

The Garrammon Meadow was populated with sentient, cranky flowers that nipped at you if disturbed. To avoid the meadow, we would have to travel the path toward the Mountain for a mile, then double-back at the fork in the trail until we reached the Garrammon field. The Garrammon Lake was on the other side of a steep hill beyond the field. All told, close to an hour's journey. Crossing the Garrammon Meadow, which lay between the Mindsail Lake and the Garrammon field? About ten minutes.

"The glazzien are hibernating now," Ari said.

"You're sure about that?" At this end of the meadow there were few glazzien in evidence. But up ahead, their distinctive flower heads were visible in abundance, something that did not bode well for our feet, ankles, and knees if the sentient flowers got too grumpy to let us pass by.

He hunched up his shoulders. "I think so."

"You *think* so?"

"Okay. I'm sure. I came this way a few days ago. No bites. Come on, Meiri. It'll be fine."

I tried to sense what was bothering me, but the chills and the willies were gone. Maybe I was just overreacting. "I'll take your word for it, but I'm making you run interference."

Ari tweaked my nose. "You're so cute when you're being neurotic."

I pushed his hand away. "Lead on, you bratty elf."

Chuckling, he forged ahead, pumping his arms military style for my benefit.

Twenty feet in, he dropped to his knees with a screech.

"Hey, watch out," I cried, as I almost ran into him. "I told you they'd bite. Now get up and—*Ari?*" His pale elven skin was completely white. I knelt in front of him. "What's wrong?"

"My legs," he wheezed out. "They're being pulled into the ground."

His legs looked just fine to me. This had to be one of his practical jokes.

"Come on," I whined. "This isn't funny."

Ari clutched at his throat. "Air . . . air . . ." His eyes glazed over, and he pitched forward.

Fear spiked through me. Even Ari wouldn't kid like this.

He sucked in a ragged breath. "Sphere . . . hurry . . ."

"You want an Ether Light?"

"No . . . in my . . . pocket."

I dug into his tunic pockets.

"Hurry . . ." Ari rasped out.

I removed a tiny golden ball and held it up. "This?"

"My . . . mouth," he whispered.

Heart hammering in my chest, I pushed the little ball into his mouth. He had barely enough strength to press his lips together, then his head sank to his chest.

"Ari!" I grabbed his shoulders. His thin body was ice cold. I held him to me and tried to picture energy moving from my heart to his. When Eliasser does this to me, my entire body fills with healing energy. But my paltry attempt only produced a vague buzzing sensation, not enough to do anything.

Ari pushed me aside, held a hand to his mouth, and coughed the little ball into his palm. Seeming none the worse for wear, he held the sphere up to the sunlight and examined it as it changed color several times before returning to gold.

"Hmph." Ari put the ball back into his pocket.

"Hmph? That's all you have to say? I nearly had a heart attack. What just happened?"

"It's complicated." He stretched out on the ground. "And exhausting. I need a nap."

A *nap?* I was trembling from an adrenaline rush almost as bad as ethermoving.

I hugged my knees to my chest, trying to calm myself. "What's in the sphere?"

"An antidote to dimensionally variant energy."

"Right." I rolled my eyes. "Like I know what that is."

"Sorry." He managed a weak laugh. "I'm really good at sensing when a dimensional abnormality is about to occur, but that also makes me more vulnerable to its effects. The sphere was designed to protect me by resetting my vibrational patterns if I encounter a disturbance."

I decided to point out the obvious. "If I hadn't been here, the sphere wouldn't have done much good when you couldn't get to it yourself."

"Well, I usually receive some warning before an anomaly hits."

"Unlike this time. I rest my case. Why do you think it happened?"

"I'm not sure, but—" Ari bolted upright and slammed his hands over his ears. "Noooooo—"

Oh. *Shit.* "Do you need the sphere again?"

"Aagghh. Make it stop."

"Make what stop?"

Like the entire world had been switched off, the sky went blacker than a starless, moonless night. Fear of the dark is primeval. Utter darkness falling with bionic speed? Unimaginable.

"Oh my god. What's happening?" I yelled into the abyss.

"Calling . . . they're calling . . ." Ari's disembodied voice raised my flesh into little mountains.

With a suddenness defying logic or science, morning careened back like a time-lapse film.

"Stop them," Ari pleaded. "Please . . . *please* . . . aagghh . . ."

Daylight speed-raced into night, then catapulted into day before plunging back to night. I pulled Ari to me, his screams resonating in my chest, blending with my own terror as I clung to him in the dark.

As abruptly as it had started, the day/night merry-go-round lost speed and the sun hiccupped to the midday position. And stayed put.

Ari's vacant eyes rolled back in his head. My vision grayed out and a different kind of darkness engulfed me.

"Meiri."

The voice in my head seemed familiar.

"Who are you?" I thought back.

"Meiri."

"Where are you? It's so dark, I can't see."

"Meiri," the voice called once more, then faded away.

"Meiri."

Determined to find out who kept calling my name, I pried my reluctant eyes open, then snapped them shut when I realized I was flat on my back staring up at a blinding sun. I turned over, shielded my face from the wattage, and braved my eyelids apart once more.

"Eliasser?"

"Wake Ari." The Master Guardian spoke in measured tones from about ten feet away.

"Uh. Okay." Like I'd swallowed a tranquilizer, the absolute terror was gone, replaced by a sluggish calm that made it hard to move and difficult to think. I nudged Ari gently, then with a little more force. No luck.

"Hurry!" Eliasser's voice was losing its steadiness. "You both must come to me *right now.*"

What was the rush? The planet had stopped spinning. Besides, I wasn't sure how to revive an unconscious elf. I sat up, pondering a solution. But my thoughts were becoming even more jumbled as that drugged feeling increased.

"Try again," Eliasser urged.

"Why don't you wake the elf yourself?" Unaccountably, I snickered at the rhyme.

"Meiri, *please!* You are in danger!"

"All right, hold your horses."

I shoved Ari, then pinched him a few times. Nothing.

When Eliasser pleaded with me one more time to *please hurry*, I considered slapping my elven buddy awake. Only seemed fair. It was his fault we were in this mess. Then, I got the most brilliant idea *ever.* Why not jolt him with a kiss? The difference in our energy fields should do the trick—provided it didn't kill me first.

I planted my lips on Ari's.

Any remaining calm vanished from Eliasser's voice as he yelled, "Stop!"

Stop? I did not. Hell, I was just getting started. Sure it was risky. Elves could only be intimate with other elves because their energy field could zap the Life Force out of you—for good. But I wasn't going to make love to him. Just kiss him a little. Like Sleepy White.

Snowy Beauty?

Whatever.

Bad girl that I am, I didn't kiss him a little. I kissed him a *lot*, enjoying every intoxicating minute of it, thank you very much, until he started to kiss me back. My heart rate doubled, my body convulsed, and Ari did in fact wake up, barely in time to keep from killing me.

"Ari," Eliasser shouted frantically. "Bring Meiri to me. Now!"

Ari half-dragged, half-carried me to Eliasser, who wrapped his arms around us both and ethermoved us away from there.

Chapter 5

"I told you to return promptly to the Mountain," Eliasser exclaimed as he paced back and forth across the Healing Room floor.

"You did not. You only said that I shouldn't tarry long so Ashara could start my retraining, whatever that is. Nothing about that sounded urgent."

He accepted a potion goblet from Ashara and, eyes narrowed, handed it to me as I sat cross-legged on a healing stone, Amoran's version of a hospital bed. "You know what I meant, Meiri."

To avoid his prolonged stare, I dropped my gaze to the small cup of brown, smelly gunk, took a sip and gagged.

Ari, on the healing stone next to mine, went bug-eyed. "I feel fine. Don't need any of that!"

Ashara's eyes flashed as she came back with a larger goblet for Ari. "You may feel fine, but you are not. This will, hopefully, repair the damage to your body. Now, drink. Both of you."

I forced myself to drain my cup, then handed it to back to her. Ari, complaining between sips, did likewise.

Eliasser placed a chair between our healing stones and sat down. "I need you to recount your movements from when you left the Glen until I found you in the meadow. Leave nothing out."

This meant that Eliasser wanted excruciating details, including everything we'd noticed, felt, or been exposed to. How many clouds were in the sky? How hot was the sun when we crossed the Mindsail Lake? Did the glazzien notice us at all or just keep sleeping? What were we thinking and feeling every step of the way?

Ari and I took turns giving him the minutiae he required, including the random chill we'd both encountered out on the Mindsail Lake. When Ari tried to expound on his concern about the intermittent bursts of cold air, Ashara waved him off. "Our cold time approaches. More important to us is how long you were in the meadow before you were affected."

"Less than a minute," Ari said, glancing at me.

I nodded. That was my impression, too.

Ashara and Eliasser traded a look. "Why did you enter the Garrammon Meadow?" Eliasser asked. "You know it is not permitted."

I cut my eyes to Ari. "It's off-limits?"

"Of course not," Ari grumbled. "At least, it wasn't before. I saw no harm in using that shortcut to get to the Garrammon Lake so we could fit in time for swimming."

Eliasser shuddered at the swimming reference. Amorans had a weird relationship with water. In some ways, they considered it a sacred substance, but other than it being mixed in with potions, they never drank it straight. I thought Eliasser was going to lose his lunch the first time he saw me splashing around with Ari in the Garrammon Lake. Amorans not only didn't swim, they treated the idea as if it were toxic.

"What happened to us?" I asked.

Eliasser drew in a deep breath and let it out in a long sigh. "You encountered a highly localized energy anomaly. It opened a temporary portal between our realm of existence and another, one which we have not yet been able to identify. In essence, you and Ari occupied two different dimensions simultaneously."

"That's impossible," Ari said.

Eliasser frowned. "It should be. Corporeal form is designed to inhabit one dimension at a time; it is the nature of temporal existence. However, Ari's experience of being pulled into the ground was truly happening, although in another spatial reality."

"But I saw his legs," I protested. "He wasn't being pulled anywhere."

"They were phantom images of what you expected to see," Eliasser explained. "Time then propelled itself forward to balance the inequity and return you both to your own dimension."

My brain was going fuzzy around the edges. "In English, please."

Ari's expression turned grim. "A time warp, right?"

Eliasser nodded. "You were in the meadow for three days."

"No! It was ten minutes at most until we passed out," I said.

Ashara rubbed her hand across her face. "It may have appeared that way. But for those of us looking for you?" She shook her head. "When I could not sense your Life Forces or energy signatures, I sent out search parties. Finally, I summoned Eliasser to return to Amoran."

"By nightfall, we were frantic," Eliasser said. "The Foreseers were unavailable—"

"Or unwilling to help," Ashara snapped.

Eliasser shot her a look before continuing. "We utilized every possible method to find you, without success. I even had Balthasarre check the vortex, and then I went to Earth myself to see if you had gone back there. It was not until time slowed down again in the area of disruption that we could detect your energy signatures. I ethermoved as close to you as I could, with only moments to retrieve you before you would be forever damaged by the energy imbalance that continued to permeate the meadow. It was much reduced by then, but I could not enter or I might have become susceptible to the same aberration of mind as you were, Meiri. I had to revive you both and convince you to leave." He paused, the toll those three days had taken evident on his pinched-in face. "When you kissed Ari—"

"I was out of my mind at that point. I thought I could do anything, including kissing an elf. Although, during my lifetime as Hannah, I kissed Ari a lot. It was only when we actually—"

I broke off at Eliasser's grimace. He didn't like hearing about my past lives on Earth. In this case, Ari, tasked with watching over me, had fallen in love with the person I'd been then. Equally enamored of the man she thought was merely a traveling cobbler, Hannah had suggested that they consummate their affections. That's when Ari learned the real reason why elves were not supposed to make love to anyone other than another elf. His energy stopped Hannah's heart, but not before she'd experienced just how accomplished a lover an elf can be.

"That was different," Ashara said. "Hannah's brief, tragic love affair with Ari occurred in Earth's vibrationally lower environment. Amoran poses a greater risk for that sort of thing. Even a single kiss here might have killed you."

That was a sobering thought.

"The Garrammon Meadow has returned to normal," Eliasser said. "However, no one is to leave the Mountain until the Foreseers are able to give their blessing. In the meantime, you both need to get plenty of rest. Do not skip meals; you need the balancing effect of food." He rose from his chair and looked at Ashara. "I would like a few moments with Meiri."

Eliasser waited until we were alone. "Given your impetuous, strong-minded and sometimes quarrelsome nature—"

"Hey!"

"You disagree?"

Oh boy. "Well, if I did, I'd be proving your point."

He managed a smile at that. "Exactly. Which is why I must extract a promise from you."

"I get it," I said, waving him off. "I'll try to listen better from now on."

"Try?" The snowy eyebrows lifted as he shook his head. "No, my Light. You *must* listen. But that is only the first step. Swear to me now that you will always heed what I ask of you."

Always? I couldn't give that assurance to the Elder, and she was a Foreseer. But as the words, *my Light*, bathed me in waves of our mutual love, it was getting harder to hold my ground. The endearment was unique to those of us created in the Seventh Vortex, and was far more powerful than saying the words *I love you.*

"I'm sorry, but I can't make you a promise on a generalization."

We locked eyes for several moments. When he opened his mouth to speak, I beat him to the punch. "That's the best I can do." I slid off the stone and pressed my hands over his heart. "I love you too much to lie or pretend otherwise."

At the inexplicably sad look on his face, I started to weaken. But any thought of giving in to Eliasser's demands flew right out of my head when he grabbed my forearms so quickly, I let out a yelp of surprise.

"You do not understand," he exclaimed, the emotions on that beautiful face sliding from sadness to despair to . . . was that fear? "You *must* obey my requests. And you are never to rescue me again. Do you understand what I am asking of you?"

"No! I don't." I wrenched free and pulled in a shaky breath. "Why are you being like this?"

I waited for an explanation. As his Twin, I *felt* his turmoil, yet the specifics eluded me.

Instead of answering me, he snapped his jaw shut, raked his hands through his hair, and strode from the room.

Ashara felt that Ari and I needed to be protected from larger gatherings for the time being, so we ate Evening Meal in the Guardian Meal Room, a smaller, more intimate setting than either the Celebration Hall or the Main Meal Room. Except for Ashi, the other Guardians were all present: Ashara, Eliasser, Balthasarre, Anders, Danaeus, and Ari. It broke my heart to see that empty chair between Ari and the Master Healer.

Eliasser and I had no interaction during dinner. Due to our close relationship, and the fact that we typically sat next to each other, this did not go unnoticed. No one commented on it, though, as if the unusualness held their tongues in check. But the preponderance of furtive glances said it all. Danaeus, in particular, kept looking from Eliasser to me and back again, his curiosity not masked in the slightest. I was surprised that it was my friendly neighborhood dwarf who seemed the most affected. Emotional cues had never been a strong point for him.

When we finished eating, I broke the silence between Eliasser and I with a reminder that he'd promised to bring Earnie the Ether Light back to our domain "later," which was now three days ago because of Ari's and my mishap in the meadow.

"Quite right," Eliasser said, steepling his hands. He'd avoided my gaze throughout the meal, but now he stared sideways at me. "And I prefer to never break a promise."

I stared right back. "I agree. That's why I won't make one I know I can't keep."

The room went still as Eliasser and I held each other in an eye-lock.

It was Ashara's turn to break the silence. "Promises take many forms," she offered quietly. "You must both keep that in mind. Especially you, Master Guardian."

It was rare for Ashara to be as oblique as the Foreseers. I didn't know what she meant, but Eliasser must have. He sighed, looked away, then brought Earnie and six of his luminescent friends to the Guardian Meal Room where they entertained us with a glowing rainbow light show. Earnie stole the spotlight when he played peek-a-boo. He'd pop into view, scurry up my arm to my neck, drop down behind my back, then peek out from my side. Slowly retreating, he'd peek out from my other side. It was not only certifiably cute, but hysterical as well. Earnie's antics had everyone laughing, including the Master Guardian. By the time we decided to call it a night, the tension that had accompanied dinner was gone.

Eliasser gathered the lights together. Six of them went directly back to their realm. Earnie, however, whizzed around the room like a crazed bee, then zipped out the doorway.

"I believe I know where he is going," Eliasser said. "Come with me, Meiri."

We traveled to my quarters, where we found the wayward light in my ancillary. Earnie flew past us into the main room and ducked behind my sleeping stone.

"He is attempting to hide from me," Eliasser said with a smile.

I walked around my stone and crouched down. Earnie pulsed brighter. "I don't want you to come to harm. If you go back now, maybe I can convince Eliasser to teach me how to send you back and forth. What do you say?"

Earnie did that thing where he bounced side to side, as if considering my proposition. Then he "kissed" my cheek, floated over, and settled onto Eliasser's palm where he disappeared.

"Can you? Teach me?" I asked Eliasser.

"We will see. So far, I am the only one who has been able to access their domain."

Eliasser idly sketched circles with his finger on my table. "I apologize if my behavior in the Healing Room frightened you. I have things weighing on me. Burdens I must carry alone."

"Why alone? Share that load with me; maybe I can help."

He favored me with a gentle smile. "Some of what troubles me cannot be divulged to anyone but Ashara. As for the rest? I am sorry, but I simply do not want to share it with you. And before you decide to argue the point, I have my reasons. Please respect that."

I did. And I gave him a whopping big hug to prove it.

The Foreseers cleared it for Eliasser and I to resume our Vortex Prayer intensive the next morning, provided we continued to go directly to the forest via the Forest Portal. As the week progressed, we required less sleep. By the seventh day, we barely napped. Ashara, in deference to how the prayer sessions affected me, postponed my "retraining" until my next visit the following Friday. Before the Reparention, it had been necessary for me to come five days a week. But stretching time to that extent placed a significant strain on the energy balance in both dimensions. Since we were no longer on an urgent deadline, weekly visits were the most that could be risked. I was okay with that. As much as I loved being on Amoran, the effects of near-daily trips last fall had almost ruined my Earth life.

When the end of my fifteen-day visit arrived, I journeyed through the vortex and touched down in my family room, relieved to be back. I was out of practice for long stints away from my family and had really missed them.

I did a meditation to reorient my energy patterns to Earth, then took a few minutes to consider what life would be like now that I'd be traveling to my other world on a regular basis. Certainly nothing as eventful as last November. That had been one wild month! Seven months counting the time-stretched days I'd spent on Amoran trying to regain skills to fix a vortex that had been slowly spiraling out of balance for hundreds of years.

I was still living on Amoran in my original body when we discovered that the Seventh Vortex was on a thousand-year path to implode, crushing Earth and Amoran the same way Elvener had been destroyed. The only way to fix the problem? The Guardians had to transform into pure energy (called light-bodies) and channel massive amounts of power while inside the vortex when implosion was just a few hours away.

Ashi and I had a more perilous role—one that only we, as Primary Twins created in the vortex, could fulfill. We had to absorb all that power, then shoot a concentrated bolt of energy into the vortex center when collapse was imminent. The only way we could manage that much power was to merge our light-bodies into a single entity.

While Twin Lights long to merge under normal circumstances, the energy training and Life Force augmentations Ashi and I underwent to prepare for the Reparention amplified that longing a thousandfold, putting us at risk for an early, spontaneous merging. If that happened, our drive to return to the One Light—where all life ultimately came from—would be nearly impossible to withstand. And without Ashi and me, the Reparention would be doomed.

When the painful decision was made to separate us, I was the one sent to Earth on a short-term basis. I'd only been there a few months when I suffered a violent death that pulled me into Earth's cycle of reincarnation. Forced to remain there until the Reparention was close at hand, I lived through ten incarnations as a bona fide Earth dweller—each new lifetime a fresh start, experienced without the hindrance of past life memories, including Amoran. When I finally arrived on Amoran last fall, I desperately needed those seven time-stretched months to catch up.

But that came at a cost. I began to radiate Amoran energy, even on Earth, which affected my husband in a bizarre way, turning him angry and mean-spirited. We were on the brink of separation when the Reparention happened. Afterward, with John no longer at the mercy of invisible energy currents, he returned to normal and wanted us to be a couple again. My grief over losing Ashi made that impossible. Only when Ashara's special potions reset my energy patterns, was I able to rekindle my relationship with John.

I'd never stopped loving Ashi, though. Just shoved the grief deep down and went on with my Earth life. So much so, that I'd made a difficult decision. I would find my Twin Light and bring him back to Amoran from wherever he was. But Ashi and I could never again be lovers.

I'd been worried how my trips to Amoran might affect John now, but Ashara had assured me that with the Reparention behind us, he and I were no longer subject to the discordant energy that had nearly destroyed our marriage.

The grandfather clock in the hallway interrupted my revery as it pealed out three bongs.

Three? Yikes! In the excitement of being back on Amoran, I completely forgot about hosting Cootie tonight. Like Bunco, the adult version of Cootie is played using paper, pencil, and dice. Eleven of my friends and I met once a month at a different host's house. After a light meal of appetizers and desserts, with wine glasses at the ready, we played two dozen rounds of the fast-moving game.

The three Earth hours I'd spent on Amoran this afternoon had come out of my Cootie prep time. I had cleaned the bathroom and kitchen yesterday. Now I speed-walked the vacuum cleaner through the downstairs, swiping a dust cloth over the more obvious accumulations on the furniture as I breezed by. That accomplished, I took a long shower, not because I needed to get clean after two weeks on Amoran, but because their version of a shower was an energy cylinder that appeared in the ancillary when needed and cleaned by spraying intense light. I assumed it killed germs—if germs even existed on Amoran, no one ever seemed to get sick. However, the energy shower was nowhere near as satisfying as hot water.

I brushed out my long, dark brown hair, threw on some fresh clothes and headed back downstairs to make my contribution to our potluck Cootie repast. Hot artichoke dip and bread cubes. Not original, but always tasty and quick to make. Especially now that I was so far behind.

My kids—Kiley, twelve, and Ryan, fourteen—rode the bus to and from school now, a departure from last year's partial carpools. This made it much easier for me to get to my job at Pierson & Todd on time, where I was employed by my childhood friend, Tom Pierson, and his business and life partner—now husband—Dave Todd. It also allowed me to put in full days as needed—a boon to our flailing finances, especially since I only worked Monday through Wednesday.

Today, Kiley was going directly to a friend's house for a sleepover. After a club meeting, Ryan took the late bus and got home right as I was sliding the artichoke dip into the oven.

"I know, I know. Cootie," he said without preamble, pushing his dark hair out of his eyes. "I'm going to get my stuff and head over to Jake's for the night."

"Again?" Jake's family was new in town, and he and Ryan had quickly struck up a friendship.

"Yeah. I told you about it yesterday."

Right. That was one of the problems with time-stretching. I'd lived through two weeks on Amoran since noon on Earth. Definitely made for a skewed sense of time. "Okay. But be home by ten tomorrow so we can go shopping for your Back-to-School Dance outfit."

Ryan stared at the floor. "Um . . . Jake's parents are taking him to the mall tomorrow. They said I could go with them. Can't you just give me the money and I'll buy it myself?"

My friends consider me an anomaly among women because I hate to clothes shop, even for myself. Being relieved of a duty I despised should have had me reaching for the champagne. But something didn't feel right.

"Not this time, Ryan. Your dad and I will pick you up at Jake's house."

"Aw, Mom. That's not necessary. I'll just walk home."

"No. We'll get you. Ten o'clock."

Ryan opened his mouth as though to argue, but at the determined look on my face, he sighed, nodded, and trudged upstairs. I hadn't met Jake's parents, which violated one of my cardinal rules of parenting. I'd at least vetted them through the Glenwood Falls grapevine. So far, they'd checked out. But that wasn't the same as a face-to-face meeting.

A few minutes later Ryan descended the stairs, a bulging backpack slung over his shoulders. I offered him a ride, which he declined. That wasn't unusual; Jake lived a half mile away and Ryan often walked. But I was getting the impression he didn't want us to meet the Hansens.

I was loading the last of the dishes into the dishwasher at the end of the night when John walked in carrying a bottle of champagne.

I eyed the expensive label. "What's the occasion?" Much as I loved the bubbly, we could only afford the cheaper stuff.

"I ran into Tom and Dave at the movies," John said, referring to my bosses and our longtime friends. "Dave got this from one of your clients, the—"

"Mini-mall developers," I cut in, recognizing where I'd seen that bottle before.

"Right. Anyway, Tom and Dave—"

"Don't like champagne, which of course means they're crazy, because who in their right mind doesn't love bubbles?"

John rolled his eyes. "Can I finish a thought? Or would you rather read my mind?"

"John," I breathed out as realization dawned. "Both kids are at sleepovers."

My handsome husband tilted his head to the side. "Both of them? All night long?"

"That is the definition of a sleepover."

"Huh. That means we're all alone in this big old house. All by ourselves." He wiggled his eyebrows while working the cork out of the bottle. "Are you reading my mind yet?"

"I certainly hope so," I said, using my best Lauren Bacall voice.

The next morning, John and I treated ourselves to breakfast at our favorite café. As we ate, I filled him in on my concerns about our eldest child, unloading for five solid minutes while John worked on polishing off the remainder of his meal.

"Now that I think about it," I said. "Ryan's been acting funny for the past month, ever since he began spending Saturday nights at Jake's house. And he never wants Jake to come to our house. Don't you think that's strange?"

"I'm sure he's fine." John emptied the mug decorated with a ring of prancing roosters and held it out for the waitress to refill.

"But haven't you noticed how quiet he is now? Like he's hiding something."

John shrugged. "He's a teenager. What do you expect?"

With that oh-so-helpful response, my normally well-mannered husband skewered the last skinny sausage link and stuffed the entire thing into his mouth.

"That's gross," I said, shaking my head at him while biting back a smile.

He had enough decency to chew and swallow before whispering, "I'm hungry and it's all your fault. I haven't had that much aerobic exercise in months. Nothing like a night of marathon sex." John grunted and thumped his chest. "Gave the old ticker a good workout."

I rolled my eyes. "What are you, a caveman?"

"Caveman," John mused. "We can try that next time. I get to wear the leopard skin, though."

"Stop," I hissed, barely able to keep from smiling.

"Stop?" He leaned closer. "That's not what you said last night. Not once as I recall."

I nearly choked on my tea as I gave in and laughed. "Enough already."

"Enough?" John grinned. "You didn't say that either. I believe 'more' was the operative word." He took in my reddened face and relented, relaxing back in the wood slat chair. "I love it when you play straight man for me." I pointed my knife menacingly at him. "Okay, I'll behave," he said. The devilish smile reappeared. "Not that either one of us did."

We snickered and made googly eyes at each other as a couple with seven kids in tow entered the restaurant. When it registered who one of those kids was, John and I shot a look at each other, then turned to acknowledge the entourage as it approached our table. I figured the couple had to be Jake's parents, followed by their six children. Ryan hung at the back of the pack, his eyes fixed on the chipped linoleum floor.

"Hi," the petite woman said amiably enough. "I'm glad to finally meet Ryan's parents." Her blond, curly hair bounced with each syllable she uttered, a trait I found oddly annoying. She introduced herself as Sue Hansen, her husband's name was Richard, and I lost track of the kids' names, as there were so many of them.

After John and I introduced ourselves, John asked, "Are you here for breakfast? They do wonderful sausages."

Sue tinkled out a laugh. "Oh goodness, no," she said, as if the idea was preposterous. Then again, with six kids, the cost of one meal at a restaurant probably equaled my family's grocery bill for a week. "I came by to collect my check for the muffins I bake each day."

"You make these incredible muffins?" I asked, impressed despite my reservations about her. She seemed friendly enough, but for some reason, my BS-detector had shifted into overdrive.

Sue let loose with that wind chime laughter again. "I do. And thank the Lord I've been able to sell them around town." She patted her abdomen. "We'll need the extra income, what with another one on the way."

Richard stroked Sue's hand, which was now resting on her barely rounded tummy. After giving birth to six kids? That alone was reason to dislike her.

"We abide by God's commandment to be fruitful and multiply," Richard boomed.

I narrowed my eyes at the two of them. In a flash, John's foot pressed down on mine with such force I almost cried out in pain. It was his way of letting me know that whatever I was thinking should remain between my ears and not spew out of my mouth.

I kicked his boot away. "Be fruitful and multiply. Huh. Wasn't that before there were billions of people on the planet, half of them starving?"

Sue's expression tightened momentarily, then settled into a frosty smile. "The Good Lord takes care of His own."

Whatever that meant. My mouth opened again, but this time John nearly broke my instep. In the face of bodily injury, I gave up and asked

Ryan if he wanted to get his things from Jake's house before we took him to the mall.

Richard answered for my son, fueling my growing irritation with the Hansens.

"Why, Ryan is packed and ready to go," Richard said, as if the Red Sea had just parted. "He asked that we drop him off at your house, which we are more than happy to do for him. That's quite a fine young man you've got there, but I'm sure you already know that."

Richard's hearty chuckle didn't match the look he turned on us, which suggested he didn't believe we realized what a prized son we had.

Sue picked up the exaltations. "Yes, such a wonderful boy. So kind and attentive. And he's so good with the little ones."

I gulped some cold tea to keep from retorting, *You have enough of them to choose from, he's bound to like at least one.*

But Sue wasn't done extolling Ryan's virtues.

"And he's been such a big help at church every Sunday."

My fingers tightened around the handle of my mug as I caught John's eye over the rim. Ryan shifted side to side and wouldn't look at either of us. John blinked several times, his face assuming the same bright shade as the maple leaves outside the café window. In an unusual role reversal, my foot came down, good and hard, on top of his.

John threw down his napkin, snatched the bill, and went to pay our tab, leaving me to deal with the Hansens. Remarkably, I'd been thrust into the role of good cop for a change. Will wonders never cease.

"Thank you for having Ryan over so much," I said with fake cordiality. "It was good to meet you Sue, Richard, and"—I waved at the rest of the family—"kids."

I hadn't lied. It was a good thing we'd finally met. Now to deal with the fallout.

Out in the parking lot, Ryan retrieved his belongings from the Hansen's commuter-sized van, then got into the back seat of our modest Subaru wagon, which looked like a Matchbox car by comparison.

I pulled John aside before we got in. "No matter what's going through your head right now, we need to hear Ryan out. He isn't you, and you are not your father."

John squeezed his eyes closed. "I know," he said, face contorting as he struggled to get his emotions under control before facing Ryan, who only knew that his father disdained all organized religion, but not the reason why. John had never wanted to burden his kids with the truth about his childhood.

John took several slow deep breaths and opened his eyes. The anguish reflected there all but broke my heart. Too upset to drive, he handed me the keys, slid into the passenger seat, and called over his shoulder, "I love you, Ryan. Let's talk about this later, okay?"

"Thanks, Dad," Ryan said. "I love you, too."

John pressed his lips together and stared out the window all the way to the shopping center.

Chapter 6

"I like going to church!"

"Why?" John demanded. He and Ryan had been arguing for a while, and John was at his limit with Ryan's newfound love of church, God, and the Hansens.

Ryan squirmed. "I don't know. It just feels good."

John scowled. Church had never felt good for him. John's father had dragged his family to a house of "worship" where they prayed, knees pressed to a rough stone floor, for the redemption of the inherently vile congregation. This mostly meant the women and children, whose sins were greater due to their presumed innate weakness. The men then reinforced each week's lesson at home by physically impressing it into the flesh of their inferior family.

"What's it to you, anyway? Why do you care that other people believe in God?"

"I care because there is no God," John shouted, unable to hold back any longer.

"That's blasphemy," Ryan shouted back. "You'll go to hell for that."

John clenched his fists. "You think I'm going to hell? Well, there's one place you won't be going from now on. I forbid you to go to any church, ever again." John stormed out the back door, slamming it shut.

Ryan bolted up and flung the door open again. "I don't care what you say, I believe in God, and it's still blasphemy!"

"You sure about that?" I asked.

Ryan spun around, his expression defiant. But I saw a hint of uncertainty in those hazel eyes.

"Maybe it's only blasphemy to the Hansens," I continued. "What about Buddhists? Hindus? Muslims? What about anyone who believes in God in a different way than the Hansens? Are they wrong? Or do they just have a different belief?"

"But what the Hansens believe in is true," Ryan protested, taking his seat again.

"Is it? How do you know?"

"Because . . . well . . . the Hansens say Jesus is the only one who—"

"Stop." I held up my hand, knowing I couldn't go there. Not since Amoran. "I don't care who the Hansens think Jesus is. I want to know what you think, what you believe because you feel it in your heart."

He folded his arms and glared at me. "I have a right to believe what I want."

"Yes. You do. I'm not trying to dissuade you from believing what feels right to you, but I'm not impressed by hearing you parrot what the Hansens think, or anyone else for that matter. What do you feel deep in your heart? Because that, my wonderful son, is where you will find your truth. Not the Hansen's truth, but your own."

Ryan gave a frustrated shake of his head. "I don't get what the big deal is. Why don't you and Dad come tomorrow and see for yourselves? It's not a cult. It's just church."

Ah, and there's the rub. For John, there was no difference between the two.

When John finally returned home, I shared the conversation I'd had with Ryan, including his request that we attend church with him the next day.

"Are you crazy?" John thundered. "Absolutely not. I swore I'd never set foot in another church and I'm not changing my mind now. It was clear after all I experienced that there couldn't be a God. No 'supreme being' would ever allow such abuse to occur in his name."

Or her name, I thought automatically. I considered how different things were on Amoran, where all Life was seen as a blessing of the One Light and violence was unthinkable. The Guardians wouldn't know what to make of spirituality on Earth where the idea of a supreme being was expressed in so many ways it was almost as dizzying as a trip through the vortex.

I waited for John to collect himself, then asked, "Are you quite sure there's no God?"

"Oh, please. How can there be?"

"That's not what I asked you. Are you certain that no such thing or being exists?"

John clamped his jaw shut and frowned. I was skating dangerously close to the edge. During the four Earth weeks leading up to the Reparention, I'd talked in my sleep about Amoran and the One Light. At Thanksgiving, I'd even said a blessing, something we'd never done before. John knew that my views on this subject had changed. But since we'd agreed to put that time behind us as though it had never happened, my altered position had never been discussed.

He unclenched his jaw. "Yes, Kerrin. I am sure there is nothing out there."

"Okay. That's fine for you. But Ryan has a right to pursue his own idea of how the universe is put together. Can we really prevent him from believing in God? Do we even want to? Wouldn't we be a variation of your father, trying to enforce what we believe on him? Ryan has a right to make up his own mind. Just like you did."

In the charged silence that followed, I held my position, while John seemed to be deciding if he needed to defend his. When he finally spoke, it was in a small, tired voice. "Ryan can go to church. But if anyone harms a hair on my son's head, I won't be responsible for my actions."

The following day, I settled into a folding chair next to Ryan at the back of one of those modern churches with an electric band, informal atmosphere, and a Bible translated into plain, everyday language. A few minutes to eleven, the Hansens strolled in, single file and all smiles, and took up an entire row toward the front.

The service was pleasant enough, lots of singing and praising God, and the sermon centered on unconditional love. No argument there, and I gave them points for having a female minister.

When we arrived home an hour later, Ryan again asked, "Why does Dad hate church?"

John came through the back door at that moment, glanced at me and raised his eyebrows.

In answer to John's unspoken question, I said, "It's a beautiful day. Why don't you two take a walk. Some stories are best heard in the open air and sunshine."

John nodded somberly, put his arm around Ryan, and they left the house.

"Our kids have been free to form their own opinions because they haven't had a specific belief forced on them," I said later in bed as we talked it out. "I'm not saying that's necessarily good, but it is how it happened."

"He just seems so . . . passionate about it, it scares me."

"We'll keep an eye on things. I remember someone else having passion as a teenager."

John leered at me, and I snickered. "You had plenty of that sort of passion, too, but I'm talking about your days as Magic Man."

John and I met through his sister Nancy when I was in eighth grade and John was a sophomore in high school. Nancy and I became best friends, and John and I got together soon after. Throughout high school and college, John had worked as an amateur magician.

He shook his head. "You know? I miss doing magic."

I poked him in the ribs. "That thing you did Friday night would qualify."

He laughed, then grew thoughtful. "Maybe I'll get out the old box of tricks and see if I've still got what it takes."

I walked my fingers down his chest. "I can assure you," I breathed in his ear, "you've still got what it takes."

He smiled and rolled over on top of me. "Guess what I can make disappear."

I rolled my eyes. "You are, without a doubt, the King of Clichés."

Eight hours later, I did my Monday morning stumble downstairs to start breakfast.

John was already up, examining the contents of his beloved old magician's chest.

The next few days went by uneventfully. John and I put off telling Kiley about our new family development as we debated what and how much to divulge. Our hands were forced when Ryan was tagged in a church photo on social media, his hazel eyes shining as he smiled into the camera. I guess he really did like church.

We sat Kiley down and gave her an abbreviated version of John's past, Ryan's decision to attend church, and that they were each free to come to their own conclusions about religion and spirituality.

Kiley rolled her eyes, the same cornflower blue as John's, and guffawed. "Good one, Mom. Like I really care about religion. I mean, what kind of a wuss needs to go to church? It's for no-mind sissies. I'm a Rationalist all the way."

John's hand covered his mouth, but his eyes were dancing.

I shot him a warning look, then announced to our daughter, "You are entitled to your opinion, however, do not confront your brother about his in this particular area."

John's jaw tightened. "I don't agree. I think it's healthy for them to debate the issue." Kiley smiled and gave him a fist bump. She was daddy's girl, for sure. And Daddy had a point.

"All right. You can debate it all you want. Civilly. No name-calling or you're grounded."

Kiley bestowed me with her signature withering look as she pulled her long, blond hair into a pony tail. "Where's the fun in that?" And she flounced out of the room.

John stared at me, his expression blank. Had I crossed a line by defending Ryan too much? Sticking up for the side of spirituality? Did I need to be more careful about what I said and did now that Amoran was back in the picture? Amoran, and its principles, had a way of sneaking into my life on Earth.

John sauntered over and kissed the top of my head. "Don't worry. The kids will work out their own relationship. Nancy and I did. We're no worse for it."

Nervous excitement pricked through me on Friday as the shimmering blue light spiraled down from my family room ceiling, wrapped me in its tingly embrace, and drew me into the vortex. The ride was beautiful and uneventful until I touched down in the ten-foot-wide Golden Circle that lay directly beneath the portal and slumped to my knees, swallowing hard to keep from throwing up.

"Uhhh . . . dizzy . . ." I wheezed out.

Ashara pushed a goblet into my hand. "Drink. Then we work."

I chugged it, not caring about the vile taste, only wanting to end the vertigo that occasionally accompanied interdimensional travel. A few moments passed until I was stable enough to stand up. Ashara's potions really are remarkable.

I eyed the Master Healer. "When you say work, you mean—"

"Retraining. Come!" And she stalked off.

I hurried across the enormous mandala that covered most of the Main Chamber floor. The intricate design was an amazing work of art created by thousands of tiny tiles in a dazzling array of colors, all with an energetic significance I didn't fully understand. Eight dark brown rays, like the spokes of a giant ship's wheel, overlay a succession of nesting circles including the Inner Circle—a two-foot-wide band in shades of blue, green, and magenta—and the Outer Circle in purple, yellow, and orange hues.

I practically had to run to keep up with Ashara. "Will this retraining help me find Ashi?" I panted, as I crossed the far edge of the mandala.

"Tell me, Meiri," she called over her shoulder. "How do you propose to locate him?"

"Hey! Slow down!" I was stable enough to stand, not run a marathon. With an audible sigh she lessened her pace. I caught up to her, and we continued side by side.

"Thank you," I said. "As to your question, I haven't a clue. This task came from the Foreseers with no instructions."

Ashara harrumphed, her usual response to anything the Foreseers said. "It would seem you must discover this on your own." She changed the subject. "The potions Eliasser brought to you after the Reparention; were they effective in reacclimating you to Earth?"

"Very. My husband doesn't know it, but he has you to thank for getting our marriage back on track." I narrowed my eyes, suddenly wondering if those tiny vials of elixir had been a little *too* effective. "Ashara, what haven't you told me?"

She frowned. "To fully resume your life there, your body had to be reset to match Earth's energy frequency, which also meant removing much of the energetic progress you had made in order to fulfill your role during the Reparention. Now, to enable you to move forward and accomplish the tasks set before you, you must regain skills and abilities that were quite natural to you before you left Amoran a thousand years ago."

"Like what?"

She ticked them off on her fingers. "Piercing intuition. Ether-moving. Manifesting."

I stopped short. "I'm sorry. Did you say manifesting? Like the way Eliasser and Ari can make objects appear out of nowhere? As for ethermoving . . ." I trailed off, not sure I ever wanted to be able to do that—not that I believed I ever could. To me and my Earth body, ethermoving felt like instantly downing twelve cups of coffee, then going on the teacup ride at the county fair.

"Come along, Meiri," she snapped, pulling me by the arm. "We must not waste what little time you have this trip."

"What are you talking about? I have almost a month beneath the Mountain."

"Not nearly enough," she complained as we reached the blank wall concealing the entrance to the Healing Room. With an impatient flick of her hand, the doorway appeared. She bustled inside and patted the nearest healing stone. I lay down on my back so she could perform an energy scan. Holding her palms above me, she ran her hands the length of my body.

"Excellent. The Vortex Prayer has given us a good base to work from. But there is still much to do." She moved to the potion table and began mixing another yummy brew. Oh joy.

I sat up, wishing I'd changed into a tunic. It always feels strange to be on Amoran in my Earth clothes. I picked at the hem of my T-shirt, carefully formulating my next question as I watched Ashara shake drops from various containers into a goblet.

"My intuition seems to have held somewhat, but aren't ethermoving and manifesting too advanced for me in my Earth body?"

Ashara wheeled around, eyes blazing. I shrank back, startled by the sudden change in her.

"Do you have any idea how critical your energy signature is *because* you are in an Earth body? I am loath to admit this, but the Foreseers were right to send you to Earth, where the vibrational essence of who you are has blended Earth and Amoran energy. Know this; you are tasked with far more than the Reparention or finding Ashi. And Eliasser—"

"Ashara!" Eliasser stood, hands braced against the sides of the open doorway, eyes on fire. "What in the name of the Light are you doing?"

"I thought you had an *appointment*," she snapped.

"I am leaving now. What have you told her?"

"Nothing of consequence, although not by my choice."

It was like I wasn't in the room. I held my breath hoping they'd continue speaking out loud. No such luck. For a full minute, they stared at each other, communicating silently until Eliasser finally said, "You know I disagree. They know I disagree. It would be a mistake."

"What would?" I demanded.

They looked at me as if surprised to find I was there. Since I'd caught them off guard, I pressed my advantage.

"Didn't we go through this last time? Secrets and all? What haven't you told me? Because keeping me in the dark may be the real mistake you're making."

Ashara glared at Eliasser. "She is right. Consider her feelings in this. Not just your own."

"That is quite enough," Eliasser said in an ominously quiet voice. Then he ethermoved right out of the doorway without even saying goodbye. Or hello, for that matter.

Ashara refused to talk about what had just happened. Instead, we spent the morning crafting potions, elixirs, and drafts. At one point I interrupted her instruction to ask what making potions had to do with the trio of skills she'd mentioned earlier, or with finding Ashi.

"Not everything I teach you is for the express purpose of locating your Twin. But everything you learn will help you to do so."

Clear as mud, as the saying goes.

By the end of the morning, my head was so full of substances and quantities, I didn't think I could stuff in another thought. But we only stopped briefly for Midday Meal, which we consumed in the Healing Room. Alone.

"Why can't we eat with the others?" I asked, trying not to sound petulant.

"You must remain focused." She pointed to my plate. "Finish, so we can get back to work."

"I really need a break. Can we do something else for a change of pace?"

Without answering, she busied herself pouring a glowing golden liquid into a large goblet.

"Drink," she commanded. I thought about resisting, but judging by the look on her face, resistance would be futile. I downed the oddly textured, sour mixture and made a face. She laughed, breaking the somber mood that had permeated our morning.

Six hours later, I dragged myself into the Guardian Meal Room for Evening Meal.

Ari let out a low whistle. "You poor thing. Ashara won't let any of us near the Healing Room. Probably afraid we'll break you out of jail for a well-deserved game of Garrammon."

"I would love nothing better than to go several rounds with you, but the Headmaster from Hell won't let me out of her sight. Besides, this ball and chain attached to my leg would make it impossible to leap into the air to field a pop-up."

Danaeus's chocolate brown eyes widened and he slowly lowered his head to peek under the table at my feet.

Ari and I laughed.

"Just an Earth saying, my favorite dwarf," I said, causing Danaeus to blush.

"Hey!" Ari pouted. "I thought I was your favorite . . . Oh, yeah. I guess he can be your favorite furry, grumpy, pudgy dwarfish . . . ow! Danaeus! When did you start pinching people?"

Danaeus folded his arms across his chest. "You are my first. Thanks to Meiri."

I choked back another laugh as Ari shot me a wounded look.

I held up my hands. "He wanted to know why people on Earth pinch, so I told him. I didn't expect him to put it to such good . . . I mean put it to use." I turned to Danaeus and smiled. "Timing is everything, my friend, and you timed that just right."

Danaeus smiled back and wiggled his caterpillar eyebrows. I'd taught him that, too.

Ashara, Balthasarre, and Anders entered during my last comment and took their usual places, Balthasarre and Anders to my left, Ashara two seats to my right with Ari and Danaeus now next to her on the opposite curve of the C-shaped table.

The chair between Ashara and I remained depressingly empty.

"Isn't Eliasser coming to Evening Meal?" I asked.

"As you said, Meiri. Timing is everything. Eliasser will join us when the time is right. Until he arrives, you are to remain within the Mountain."

"Well, that was rude of him," Ari said.

We were alone in Ari's room after Evening Meal. I'd just filled him in on Eliasser's odd behavior earlier and how he'd ethermoved out of the room without even acknowledging me.

"It's not the rudeness that bothered me, Ari."

"I know. I'm just trying to help you vent."

I smiled. "Thanks. But I'm more confused than upset. I expected things to be different this time, but here we are again with secrets."

Ari tapped the table and a chocolate bar the size of my hand appeared.

"Holy fat calories, Elf-boy. Is that for real?"

"Nah. I can't make chocolate here. Not sure why. I promise it will taste good, though."

I broke off a chunk and nibbled the edge. "You're right. It doesn't taste at all like chocolate, but it's great." I took another bite. "Is it another of your elven treats?" Ari had manifested an amazing dessert once, which I had to admit was better than chocolate.

"It is." He helped himself to a hefty chunk, sampled it, and then sighed, his expression wistful. "In a way, these treats I manifest are all that's left of Elvener."

"I'm so sorry. I wish there was something I could do. But you're wrong about all that's left of Elvener. There's you. We haven't lost your whole world, because we still have you."

He snorted. "That's me. Arrien Etan. The last of the elves. Elvener's legacy," he added with a bitterness uncommon for my funny, fair-haired friend.

I spent the next three days having Everything You Always Wanted to Know about Drafts, Potions, and Elixirs, But Never in Your Right Might Intended to Ask pounded into my brain. I'd been half-joking when I referred to Ashara as the Headmaster from Hell, but it was no laughing matter now. Strict, demanding, and unforgiving of inattention and error, she structured my retraining like the fate of the planet depended on it . . . tomorrow. Every night after Evening Meal I crawled to my room and passed out. I was still so exhausted the next morning that an Assistant—a designation assigned to pretty much all Mountain residents who didn't have some other title—had to be sent to wake me up. Late in the afternoon of the fourth day, I hit my limit as Ashara scolded me yet again for some minor infraction.

"Pay attention, Meiri! Vallius nectar must be used raw in constructing the base for the Mind Link potion. Put the refined back."

My hands, aching from fatigue, trembled now with repressed frustration. The vial slipped from my shaking fingers and shattered on the floor. All I could do was stare as the precious liquid spread out from the shards in a spidery pattern.

"Well?" Ashara barked. "Get the wiping cloth and clean it up."

"No."

Ashara's voice dropped to a low, threatening pitch. "Get the cloth, Meiri."

"Go to hell, Ashara. Didn't you figure out last fall that you can't remake me into the Meiri who left here a thousand years ago? It remains to be seen whether I can concoct potions to your perfect standards or ethermove to the other end of the planet. But if I can, I will do it with Kerrin's brain in Kerrin's body. If you wanted Meiri's brain or Meiri's body, you should never have sent me to live on Earth!"

Ashara flinched as if I'd physically struck her, and my heart compacted into a tight ball of remorse. But I didn't know any magic powerful enough to let me cram my thoughtless words back into my stupid head where they should have stayed. Ashara had made the arrangements for me to live on Earth—with the Foreseers blessing. While they maintain that "everything happens as it should," Ashara had never forgiven herself, or them, for the fact that I had died a horrible death not long after arriving on Earth. It was a deep, ugly wound I'd just poked.

"I'm sorry," I whispered. "I should never have—"

"Leave me!" she hissed, and bent down to clean up my mess.

I spent an hour roaming the halls within the Sanctuary, avoiding contact with others while trying to think of a way to make it up to Ashara for my outburst. Eventually, even that relative freedom became claustrophobic. I'd been cooped up inside the Mountain for days now, most of that time spent in the dimly lit Healing Room being scolded. I couldn't stand it any longer. I needed to be outside. Breathe fresh air. Feel the sun on my face.

At the end of a long corridor, I opened a doorway to the protected natural courtyard leading to the Outer Grounds. Curving stone walls as high as a house grew directly out of the Mountain, then met about twenty yards ahead at the Main Gate—a waist-high, metal-slatted contraption that creaked whenever it swung open. Beyond the gate, a stream bubbled out from a channel in the Mountain and flowed straight ahead for about forty feet before meandering to the right toward the western plain. A dirt path ran parallel on the left side of the stream for the same distance, then turned sharply away from it. Just beyond where the path and stream split were the Resting Stones. Some of the large gray and brown boulders provided chair-like seating, while others tilted at an angle perfect for leaning against to watch the water go by.

I strode across the courtyard, intending to defy the mandate to stay within the Mountain. I wanted to fling open the pretentiously named Main Gate and run free, even if it was only as far as the Resting Stones. I couldn't explain it, but I felt certain that I'd be safe. All I had to do was avoid the Garrammon Meadow.

Hand on the latch, I debated with myself. Should I follow my intuition, which told me I'd be all right? Or obey Eliasser's mandate and go stir-crazy? He and Ashara had been devastated when Ari and I "disappeared" during that time warp/dimensional anomaly thing. I never wanted to worry him like that again.

The debate became moot. Past the gate to the left, blocked by the sheer wall of the Mountain, a deep voice hummed a happy, bouncy tune. Then Eliasser came into view. He stopped his song at the sight of me and gave me his sunniest smile.

"Good news, my Meiri. I have a temporary reprieve from my . . . meetings. And we are all released from our restrictions."

"All? I thought I was the only one confined to quarters."

He looked aghast. "You have not spent this whole time in your room, have you?"

I smiled. He and Danaeus took me so literally at times.

"No. Although, in a way, it was worse. I've been held captive in the Healing Room while Ashara attempts to transform me into something I'm not."

I'd tried to make light of it, but the sharp edge to my voice didn't escape his notice.

"Shall we talk about it on our way to Evening Meal?"

"No," I said, thinking better of it. This was between me and Ashara. "I guess I just needed a break from my studies."

As we walked arm in arm to the Main Meal Room, Eliasser explained that he had sent word ahead to Ashara to assemble the entire Mountain community for a celebration of sorts. I wasn't aware if anyone else in the Guardian Sanctuary could communicate wordlessly like Eliasser and Ashara. Those two have an industrial strength telepathy that can span miles, even dimensions. Ashi and I had been able to do the same thing right before the Reparention. We'd even carried on a mental conversation while he was on Amoran and I was on Earth, although I didn't know if that level of connection would hold once he returned.

Eliasser and I passed through the open doorway to the Main Meal Room, where the full complement of the Mountain waited for us. This room was much larger than the Guardian Meal Room, but not as big as the Celebration Hall. The C-shaped tables—closer to a semi-circle than a true letter "c"—were positioned so that few diners, if any, had their backs to another person.

Eliasser led me to the only exception, a table against the wall opposite the doorway that was longer and fashioned in more of an open, gentle arc. Unlike our arrangement in the Guardian Meal Room, he had us switch places, indicating that I should sit at the center while he took the seat to my left. This put Ashara on my right, with Ari and Danaeus next to her. Balthasarre and Anders filled out the remaining chairs beside Eliasser. Ashi's chair was missing.

There was a festive feel in the air, which magnified when Eliasser ordered the newly fermenting stash of fairybee wine to be opened. While the non-alcoholic beverage was not intoxicating, it did produce a deep, pleasurable relaxation. The fermenting wine would not have the same intensity, but would be enjoyable, nonetheless.

When all goblets were filled, Eliasser said the blessing, then raised his cup. "To freedom."

The Master Guardian could usually be counted on to say something like, "to the One Light," or "to the Love which fills the universe," so this dedication prompted some curious looks.

"Why freedom?" Balthasarre asked.

"A very good question," Eliasser responded, then he took a large bite of his meal and chewed thoughtfully. It did no good to hurry him when he was processing his thoughts—or his food—which he did with as much love and devotion as every other task he tackled.

Ari and I grinned at each other, but Ashara said, "We should all appreciate Life as much as Eliasser does. To live from the depth of our Hearts."

She stared out at the room, which gradually filled with the sound of clinking dishes and mealtime chatter. But her words, now, were only for me.

"Your retraining must happen. However, we need not destroy your spirit in the process. Or your very necessary Earth body, for that matter." She allowed a slight smile to grace her face before resuming her serious demeanor. "But be forewarned; I will push you beyond what you think is your limit, as that is what I must do. And I will not coddle you, as that is not my nature."

Eliasser tapped a spoon to his goblet, and the room settled down.

"To answer your question, Balthasarre, I speak in praise of freedom because it appears that the anomalous energy disruption, which nearly cost Ari and Meiri their lives, was an isolated event. No other dimensional abnormalities have been detected by"—he cleared his throat—"have been detected. We are now free to go anywhere in Guardian Lands." A loud cheer ensued, but Eliasser held up his hand for quiet. "And to celebrate, we will hold a Garrammon tournament in three weeks." He broke into a broad smile as the room erupted again.

I looked over at Ari and raised my eyebrows in question.

He grinned. "You're so gonna love this."

Eliasser and I took a walk each evening just as the stars were beginning to wink their way into the darkening sky. Sometimes we discussed philosophy, sometimes he asked me to tell him more about current day Earth. At other times we walked in a silence so companionable it felt like my heart would burst to be near him like that. No matter what we did, we always ended up at the Resting Stones where we sat, side-by-side, gazing out over the stream and the plain beyond.

Ashara was true to her word about not coddling me, although I only spent mornings now under her tutelage. Afternoons found me at the Garrammon field practicing for the tournament.

As the sun rose each day, I dragged myself to the Healing Room to mix up concoctions that would turn a person's hair gray. Some quite literally. Even though I found creating potions, elixirs, and drafts boring, there came a moment when I began to sense the right ingredients and their quantities. Pretty soon, it was no longer necessary for me to read from the Master Book Ashara kept by the mixing table.

When I corrected her recipe for a special reviving draft one afternoon—a day I willingly skipped Garrammon practice to complete a difficult elixir assignment—she breathed an enormous sigh and grabbed both my arms. "Thank the Light. This part of you is back."

And for some reason, I started to cry.

Chapter 7

The day of the tournament dawned sunny and bright like it always did on Amoran. I was still getting used to the chilly part. With our breath forming little clouds in the cold, early morning air, the entire population of the Guardian Sanctuary arrived at the Garrammon field.

The grassy field was bordered on three sides by steep, tiered hills—a perfect natural stadium. Tournament seating was on the incline farthest from the Mountain. On the other side of that hill lay the Garrammon Lake, a rather ambitious name for what was barely a pond. But it was deep enough to allow swimming, and it was in this "lake" that Ari and I liked to do just that. We didn't swim in the Mindsail Lake, though. Ari said it was too "electric" to tolerate. It was one of those rare times when I didn't press for an explanation.

The basics of Garrammon were simple enough. The square field was divided in half, with each team of two players occupying a side. Using handpieces—glove-like contraptions that strapped around the wrists—the teams volleyed the baseball-sized Garrammon ball across the center line until one of them missed. A typical scenario for a "court" type game. But, as they say, the devil is in the details. The Garrammon ball could disappear, then reappear somewhere unexpected and on a completely different flight path. Plus, with no net—just a line dividing the team sides—missing a play was that much easier. Anything over the line was considered in bounds, even if the ball was only an inch high in the air when it got there. Many a bruise had been tended to in the Healing Room by a desperate player who dove to the ground to field such a play. Then there was the requirement to doff the Garrammon handpieces at key points in a match and field the ball bare-handed. Ouch.

I had played surprisingly well last fall. But a lot had happened since then, including the return of my energy balance to Earth standards. Based on my practice matches these past few weeks, I wasn't looking forward to today.

I settled in the second row of the stadium seating with Balthasarre and the children from the school and began chatting with Clarisanna, a former food Assistant turned healing Assistant, and one of the few non-Guardians that I had spent time with before the Reparention. As we waited for Eliasser to announce the beginning matches, Meilee claimed a patch of grass on my other side, her light brown face glistening. This was not surprising as she had elected to run the whole way from the Mountain to the field, a move met with frank stares by the rest of the Mountain inhabitants. No one on Amoran ran for the fun of it. In fact, I'd never seen anyone run at all, except during a Garrammon match. But that was Meilee. Besides Ari, she was the only person I'd encountered on this world who would fit right in on Earth.

"Where is Anders?" she asked.

Something in her tone gave me pause. I pointed him out at the end of the first row, then watched as her eyes followed my outstretched finger. Her cheeks, flushed from exercise, went even darker when she spotted him. Ari had mentioned he thought something was up between Anders and Meilee. On Earth, her reaction wouldn't raise an eyebrow. A girl, approximately fourteen, blushing over a boy? Happened every day. Here? It shouldn't happen at all.

Eliasser stepped onto the field, held his hand up for silence, and the crowd quieted down.

"I am pleased to preside over our first tournament in many years. We will have the usual prizes for first, second, and third place teams, as well as our own special Guardian Sanctuary prize for Best Overall Player."

I caught Ari's eye and mouthed *BOP?* He just smiled and shrugged.

"As a reminder," Eliasser added, with a glance at me, "all six players from the top three teams play against each other. The last player standing wins the tournament and the best player designation."

I turned to Meilee. "Last player standing? Sounds insane, not to mention grueling."

She smiled. "To some, it is a matter of honor. The stories of you and Makashannar on the Garrammon field are legend. One time, after eliminating the other four finalists, you and Makashannar kept at it. As I heard it, you were both exhausted, but would not give up. The Master Guardian finally demanded that one of you concede. But neither of you would allow the other to win Best Overall Player, so you called the only tie in Garrammon history." She laughed. "Then, you collapsed on top of each other."

"I can't believe we were that competitive." Although, I'd seen that spark in Ashi last fall, when my Garrammon ability seemed to come rushing back to me. I could only hope I'd do us, and our fabled antics, proud.

Eliasser explained that there would be several breaks throughout the day, including Midday Meal served on the other side of the hill in the grassy area facing the lake. Depending on the speed with which the elimination matches progressed, it was expected that the top three teams would be awarded their prizes by mid-afternoon. After a short rest, they would compete in the final event to determine Best Overall Player, followed by a gala feast in the Celebration Hall.

My foursome was up after the first morning break. So much for doing Ashi's and my Garrammon legacy justice. I may have been a top-notch player at some point in the past, but that was then and this was now; and now, I barely made it through the match. It was only the skill of my teammate that kept us in the game. Apologizing to him afterward, I said I hoped he had better luck being partnered for the upcoming cycle.

When all forty-eight players had competed, we took a second break as the remaining twenty-four were re-shuffled. I was paired with Clarisanna, another excellent player, who was solely responsible for moving us to the next level. Then, thank the Light, it was time for lunch.

Ari found me by the food tables. "Good news. You and I are first up after Midday Meal."

"Good news? You've seen me play, right?"

He smiled. "You'll do fine."

"Uh-huh."

Ari cautioned me to limit my food intake so I wouldn't feel weighed down during the final matches when high leaps into the air were expected and necessary. This advice was wasted on me and my Earth appetite. While Ari arranged the equivalent of carrots and celery on his plate, I loaded mine with the Amoran version of turkey, mashed potatoes, and gravy. Our selections made, we settled out of sight behind a thick cluster of tall shrubs a little ways up the hill.

We were nearly finished with our meal when voices on the other side of the bushes told us we had company. It was Mikellan and Esteven, two food Assistants. They must not have seen us through the gnarly wall of green vegetation as they launched into some idle chatter. Ari held a finger to his lips and smiled. My dear elven buddy was as bad an eavesdropper as I was.

"This is a great tournament," Mikellan said. "I wish we could have done this years ago."

"When you were in better shape?" Esteven replied, and they both laughed.

"I never saw Makashannar compete," Mikellan continued. "Did you?"

"Yes. You missed something grand. He was a marvel to watch back then."

"Was she also a marvel to watch?

"From what I understand, before she went to Earth, the two of them were virtually unbeatable. Not like now. He so loved the game; I think he would have found this unbearable."

I shot a look at Ari, who frowned and tossed his last "celery stick" down.

"Do you think she will be able to find him?" Mikellan asked.

"If Makashannar has fallen into the Darkness, there is no hope. Can you name one person who has suffered that fate and ever returned? And even if he could be rescued, how likely is it that she will be able to do that?"

My teeth clenched. Negativity aside, *she* has a name!

"But she is his Twin Light," Mikellan objected. "If anyone can find him, it would be her. And they successfully performed the Reparention together."

Esteven snorted. "Not so successfully, eh? She is alive and he is not. Besides, she is in an Earth body. And you know what is said about Earth bodies."

Ari's face darkened and he made a movement to rise. I knew he'd put an end to their gossiping, so I grabbed his arm and mouthed, "Wait."

Mikellan let out a low whistle. "If her Garrammon playing is any indication, you may be right. Do you think she has been paired so well to keep her spirits up?"

"I do. Like I said, what can we expect of an Earth person? Come. I would like more."

Once they'd gone down the hill, Ari leapt up and said we should report them to Eliasser. I was upset, too, but I shook my head as my mind replayed Esteven's callous statement. *What can we expect of an Earth person?*

And the Earth equivalent?

She's a woman, he's black, they're gay, old people are so . . .

It took me a moment to work out that my anger wasn't about the way they'd insulted me, personally. It was about every time a decision was made about someone's worth based on what was on the outside, or where they were from, or who their parents were, or who they shared their bed with.

Esteven and Mikellan were right about one thing, though. My Earth body would never perform the same way my Amoran body had. That just made me more determined to win this game for all the people who had ever been told they wouldn't amount to anything because of what side of the blanket—or vortex—they'd been born on.

"Elf-boy?" I rose slowly to my feet. "You know that Earth saying, the one that goes something like 'doing well is the best revenge'?"

"It's 'living well is the best—'"

"Close enough," I cut him off. "You and I are going to win this one. For Ashi."

Ari pressed his lips together, narrowing his eyes as he studied my face.

"I mean it," I said. "We got this."

He broke into a smile and gave me a bear hug. "You go, Earth-girl."

There was a little time left before the final rounds. On impulse, I walked to the shore of the lake, kicked off my shoes and dove in, shocked by how cold it was. When I resurfaced, Ari was right next to me, grinning. "I assume you have a good reason for this," he said, teeth chattering.

"Not really. I'm running on pure instinct at this point."

An astonished crowd gathered on the narrow stretch of white sandy beach. Ari and I swam through the bracing water to the opposite shore—a minute or two at most—then back to the tiny beach, where we moved onto the grass. Using a bit of Ari's magic I referred to as the drying dance, we rotated in a circle while asking the sun to remove the water from our tunics and return it to the lake. As the water wicked away from my skin, I grew warm all over. And peaceful. So . . . peaceful. Gentle tingling pulsations tickled their way through me—ebbing, flowing, ebbing, flowing . . . .

Someone shook me and I woke as if from a dream, the phrase "use the power of intention" rolling through my mind. I lay on my back, a glittery pink mist swirling above me so thickly, it was like I'd drifted into a blizzard of sparkling cotton candy. I never knew when the mist would visit me. Its appearance was random and rare, and came only when I was in the proximity of Ashi or Eliasser. In fact, the first time I'd encountered it was with Ashi at this very lake. But why had it come now?

The pink mist rose into the air, then dissipated. I rolled over and sat up. The group on the shore no longer stared like I was nuts. They seemed outright alarmed.

Ari crouched down next to me. "You okay?"

I nodded, my eyes still on the crowd. "Why are they backing away?"

"They're scared. Frankly, so am I. The mist extended all the way to the Garrammon field."

"It did?" I didn't know what to think. The mist had never spread that far.

Eliasser stood on my other side, his pensive gaze fixed on the ground. I didn't want him to prevent me from competing, so I sprang up and brushed the grass off my tunic.

"Let's go," I snapped at Ari. "We're up."

Ari's expression clouded. "I don't think you should play. You passed out for a full minute."

I glared at him as Eliasser crossed his arms and said my name in that flat tone he used when I was about to be called out on something.

"Meiri."

No way was I getting benched. Turning my back on the Master Guardian, I grabbed Ari's arm. "I'm fine. We have to win this for Ashi, remember?"

Eliasser raised his voice. "Meiri."

I whirled to face him. "I'm doing this no matter what you say."

But my sweet king surprised me. "What is the Earth phrase you use when someone is going to perform? It is a terrible sounding thing, but actually means you are wishing them well?"

"What do you . . . oh . . . you mean . . . break a leg?" I'd used it on Danaeus last fall, and the Guardians had nearly passed out from shock until I explained it.

Eliasser shuddered, then composed himself and smiled. "Break two."

I laughed all the way to the field, now determined to show our doubting Assistants just what a little old Earth person could do. Remembering how I'd improved dramatically last year during a single game when Ashi tutored me, I called the "heart" feeling of my Twin—the very essence of him—into my own heart, soul, and body. And I did use the power of intention. I set the intention to do him proud.

Maybe the pink mist had something to do with it as well, but as strength infused my legs and arms, my body seemed to wake up and physically remember how well it had played Garrammon last fall. And apparently still could. Even for an Earth person.

There were quite a few surprised folks as I leapt high into the air to return the volley that won Ari and I a spot in the Best Overall Player match.

But none quite so surprised as Mikellan and Esteven.

"I know Mikellan and Esteven are gossipy, but I didn't think they were mean," I said the following night. I'd been quickly eliminated from the BOP match, but Ari hung out until the last two, losing to a musician with leaping skills that boggled the mind. We were in my room for our daily catch-up, which we'd missed the day before when the post-tournament celebration ran into the wee hours of the morning. I really valued our time together. Aside from the fact that he was rocking good fun, my friendship with Ari seemed to ground me during my bi-world journeys.

"That's what I've been trying to tell you." He frowned. "The energy is changing, and people are changing along with it. And not always for the better."

"Different doesn't necessarily mean worse." I told him how I'd seen Meilee blushing when she laid eyes on Anders. "It was sort of sweet."

Ari shook his head. "For you and me, that wouldn't be a problem. We're made that way."

"Amorans are made that way, too, even if they only want to have sex once a decade."

He laughed. "A little more than that. But that's my point. With an inherent low sex drive, Meilee and Anders shouldn't be feeling that at all in Guardian Lands."

I took a bite of another elven treat Ari had manifested—cookie-like rounds that were crunchy, sweet, sour, and spicy. Amazing on the taste buds. Ari sipped at one of Ashara's potions, which she claimed would help even out his moods. Anders and Meilee weren't the only ones who had changed. My elven BFF was emotionally all over the map these days.

Which made me wonder. "Who else do you think has changed?"

He counted on his fingers. "Balthasarre snapped at Anders yesterday before we left for the Garrammon field. He never does that. Clarisanna? I thought I saw tears in her eyes the other day, but she denied it when I asked her."

That was troubling. Clarisanna was one of my favorite people.

"You already know that Eliasser is absent a lot, and distant or moody when he is here."

I held up my hand. "About that. You remember that strange interaction he had with Ashara, about not telling me something?" Ari nodded.

"Twice now I've caught them arguing about the same thing. Eliasser isn't just distant, he's worried. There's something he doesn't want to have happen that Ashara does want to have happen, and it has to do with me." I took a breath. "Do you have any clue what it might be?"

"I'd tell you if I knew. And even if I wasn't supposed to tell you, I'm so lousy at secrets that you'd twist my arm and I'd give in anyway."

That had me laughing. "So true. I love you, you pushover."

"Yeah, well, just don't kiss me again."

We stared at each other for a long moment, then looked down at our snack, each shoving a handful into our mouths at the same time.

Ari chewed, swallowed, and snorted. "At least you can get some."

"Gee. That was crass! And if I could help you out, I would. You've got skills, Elf-boy."

Shoot! What was wrong with me? I should never have said that.

Ari didn't seem bothered by my lapse in judgment as he winked and did a thumbs-up.

"So do you, toots. You're a ten all the way."

A thrill shot through me. I laughed uneasily. "Uh . . . thanks?"

Ari clamped his jaw shut and gulped while I mopped sweat off my brow.

"Okay, Ari. I gotta ask. Are we being affected by the changing energy?"

He sighed. "I hope not. I love our uncomplicated friendship just the way it is."

"Amen to that, brother. If it helps, I didn't notice anything until I kissed you in the Garrammon Meadow. It's like it triggered something."

He nodded somberly. "Same for me." We shared another long look.

"Change of subject," I blurted out. "Where is Danaeus? I haven't seen him since the night Eliasser announced the Garrammon tournament. Ashara said he's away on a trip, but I'm surprised he left without saying goodbye."

"Off-world visitors appeared on the other side of Amoran while you were still imprisoned in the Healing Room. They were described as looking a lot like Danaeus."

"You're kidding. We have a bunch of dwarves on Amoran now?"

"That's what Danaeus went to find out."

"If they didn't come through the vortex, how did they get here?" Unexpected visitors to Amoran usually arrived via an accidental trip through the vortex. Those occurrences were rare.

Ari shrugged. "Unknown. Could be a dimensional variance. That's how Danaeus wound up on Amoran in the first place. You don't remember that?"

I shook my head. "I only know because Danaeus told me last fall. My life before I left Amoran to become an Earth dweller is hazy, like a dream you only remember in snatches." I licked my finger and sponged up some cookie crumbs. "Isn't Elianna trapped inside a dimensional variance?" I asked, referring to Eliasser's Primary Twin Light.

"Yes, but hers is different from the one Danaeus slipped through. There are so many kinds of dimensional variances, each one is like a person with its own personality and quirks. In Elianna's case, being trapped was a blessing. Without it, she would have perished."

Like Ashi and me, Eliasser and Elianna had been created within the Seventh Vortex, which meant they were also Vortex Lights as well as Twin Lights. In addition, Elianna was a Vibrational—a trait we had shared. The energetic makeup of a Vibrational makes it possible for them to exist more easily in other dimensions. That's why Elianna was selected thousands of years ago to assist the Guardians of the Thirteenth Vortex with their energy imbalance. She was nearing their vortex when it imploded without warning, and Elianna was presumed dead. We learned later on that the shock wave from that implosion forced her into a dimensional variance where she entered a type of stasis.

Then, right before the Reparention, she began to appear to me—and only me—as a silvery energy form. It was my Earth body that allowed her to reach me, and me to perceive her. I'd always loved that touch of irony, considering that some people saw my Earth body as a drawback. As the energy in our vortex grew more volatile, it became easier for her to access me. Finally, I acted as her channel, allowing her spirit to fully inhabit my body for a brief time so that she could visit with Eliasser, Ashara, and Ashi. We'd had no contact with her since, and I hoped it was only because the tear in her dimensional variance had closed up again, and not something worse.

I sat up straight. "Could Ashi be inside a dimensional variance? Maybe he was even pushed or pulled or however it happens, into the same variance as Elianna?"

"Unlikely."

"If Elianna is in one, and a dwarf can slip through one, couldn't the same be true for Ashi?"

"Not all dimensional variances remain in a static location. Some are like conduits that fluctuate in space. If Ashi wound up in one, he could be halfway across the universe, or in a completely different dimensional reality than the one we're in."

"What about that anomaly thing we encountered in the Garrammon Meadow?"

"That wasn't the same as a dimensional variance."

I sighed. One more thing I didn't know. "I guess I'll start attending classes with the kids."

"They don't usually teach about dimensional variances in the Guardian school. I learned most of this as an energy worker on Elvener." He paused. "Eliasser is the only one on Amoran, besides Balthasarre and Anders, who truly understands them."

"And no one has thought about investigating a dimensional variance for Ashi?"

Ari looked thoughtful. "First, a variance is impossible to detect unless it makes itself known, either by altering its energy signature or when a tear develops, as happened with Elianna."

"You make it sound like it's alive."

"In a sense, it is. Second, we know from survivors that variances aren't dark—not when you are inside. They are brilliant and beautiful and impart a sense of well-being."

"That doesn't fit, then. The Foreseers said I would lead Ashi from darkness. What does that leave, Ari, except *the* Darkness?"

Ari's expression turned grim. "Nothing that I can think of."

Chapter 8

Over the next six weeks, I settled into my bi-dimensional life.

On the Earth side of the vortex, John polished up his magic act and began volunteering at hospitals and schools. Kiley landed a role in a children's theater production, part of the Glenwood Falls Holiday Play series. While she hadn't snagged the lead, something she was certain was a mistake, her part was pretty substantial for someone with no experience.

Ryan continued to go to church with the Hansens. One day, while putting a basket of clean laundry in his room, I noticed a sheaf of papers and the edge of a book poking out from underneath his bed. Curious, I took a peek. The book was a Bible and the papers were notes he had made, presumably during Sunday service as each page was clipped to a bulletin for a specific day. One of the "notes" read like a sermon. I couldn't help it, I laughed out loud. My son was writing a sermon? Why that struck me as funny, I'm not sure. When I heard the front door slam, I stuffed everything back under the bed, resolving to find a way to ask him about it without admitting I'd been snooping.

I continued to make my weekly journey to Amoran on Fridays, using every minute I could while the kids were in school. With time-stretching, that gave me over a month beneath the Mountain, where intuition—especially locating lost objects—was now the main focus at Ashara's Boot Camp.

Her plan was simple enough; she hid items in various places, then ordered me to find them—no training, no help. In typical Ashara fashion, she barked that I was perfectly capable of mastering this because I had the innate ability to sense, to feel, to . . . well . . . intuit.

I may be able to sense emotions and feelings at times, but objects? I wasted hours combing the corridors, practically sniffing like a bloodhound. One day Ashara threw her hands up in the air and stalked off, muttering under her breath. So much for innate.

Back on Earth, I happened across an article in a magazine that talked about how everything is alive with some form of consciousness; in fact, everything *is* a form of consciousness. That concept was nothing new on Amoran, but for some reason, it struck a much deeper chord in me now. Unable to get the idea out of my mind, I pondered the many ways consciousness might express itself as I took my daily hike in the woods behind my house.

My property is nestled at the base of a small mountain. A short path at the edge of my backyard leads through a thick forest of maple, pine, oak, and birch to the main trail, which then winds upward for a quarter mile before reaching a flat open area. The trail continues on from there, but I usually stop at the clearing with its natural stone benches—a present from the last ice age—and a breathtaking view of the southern, more rural part of Glenwood Falls.

Gazing out over the vista before me, I wondered; what exactly is consciousness? If everything is conscious, does that also imply feeling? Emotion? Thought? What would, say, a chair's consciousness feel like to me? Was there a way to sense it by the energy frequency it vibrated at? Turning the notion inside out, can that same chair feel me? My emotions?

I ran my fingers over the stone "bench." Could it feel me sitting on it? Did it mind the extra couple of pounds I'd gained this past year? I found myself smiling at the idea of having a conversation with this wide slab of granite.

At length, thinking about this became as mind-bending as contemplating infinity or imagining eternity. My mental process just froze. So I took a deep breath, turned my face to the weakening late October sun and gave thanks that I live in such beautiful places on both worlds.

Returning to Amoran, I decided to put my musings to work. It was not as simple as I had hoped, but I earned the fruit of my labor late one evening. Ashara hid a bowl from the Healing Room, then requested that I bring it to her. Instead of trekking around the passageways of the Mountain complex, I closed my eyes—and felt for it. The color, warm. The energy vibration, muted. The love surrounding it—recognizable.

Opening my eyes, I matched Ashara's steady, intense gaze with one of my own and said, "Get it yourself. It's in the school beneath the library table. But it's not the glazed bowl as you suggested, it's the marble one Eliasser gave you as a gift."

She stared at me, stone-faced. I sighed with frustration, thinking I'd gotten it so wrong that she was stunned speechless by my continued lack of progress. But then, the stoic Master Healer of the Seventh Vortex broke into a broad smile, gave me a rough hug, and exclaimed, "Next? Ethermoving!" And she stomped away, rubbing her hands together.

I decided to add Ashara to my list of people and things that were "different."

When I wasn't training with Ashara, I turned my attention to finding Ashi. I had gone back to wearing his amulet, but only when I was on Amoran, leaving it on my back counter when I left for Earth at the end of each visit.

The brushed silver pendant necklaces with raised tree of life designs had been given to Ashi and me when we left the vortex after our creation. Two days before the Reparention, the Foreseers held a special Joining ceremony for us in the Glen. They blessed our amulets, then had us exchange them, which meant it was Ashi's amulet that I wore during the Reparention. Wherever Ashi was, I hoped he still possessed mine.

Holding onto the amulet, I spent hours trying to sense my Twin's energy signature. As his complementary vibrational partner, I thought this would be the most productive avenue. So far, I'd come up empty. It was time to mix it up. Literally. Using my Healing Room training, I created a potion to increase my ability to sense people, then drank it while focusing on Ashi.

Nothing.

Next, I tried my hand at making a Wiccan location spell I read about in one of my cozy mysteries back on Earth.

Again, nothing.

On a whim, I drank the sensing potion, used the location spell, and topped it off with a few drops of straight vallius nectar.

Still, nothing. At least, not what I was aiming for. I got violently ill and had to be treated in the Healing Room for several days. Ashara barred me from the potions table for a month and told me to try something else.

So, I did. I put on my aqua dress tunic—Ashi had a matching one, and we'd been wearing them at a celebration dinner last fall when I first realized I was in love with him. Then I did the meditation on Love taught to me by the Foreseers, and followed that up by downing an entire carafe of fairybee wine. Since that beverage was only relaxing, not intoxicating, I wasn't worried about overdoing it. I figured the more relaxed I became, the easier it would be to "let go" and reach out to my Twin.

This turned out worse than my potions fiasco. Danaeus came looking for me when he returned from his trip "down under" Amoran. He had a funny feeling I was in trouble and was drawn to Ashi's room on a hunch, where he found me comatose. Danaeus, who claimed to have never had an intuitive feeling in his life, saved me by a funny feeling and an impulse.

I added Danaeus to my Folks Who Are Different roster.

The weird thing was, I didn't remember going to Ashi's room. I'd wanted to ever since I returned after the Reparention, but every time I got near his invisible doorway, I broke out in chills, and not the good kind. I'd pushed past my reticence on only one other occasion, figuring that being in his quarters might somehow afford me a stronger connection to him. Instead, I'd been swamped by a sense of foreboding so strong, I left at once.

That experience, and my strong reaction to being there now, concerned Ashara. As a precaution, she sealed his doorway using an extra strong energy lock until she could do a thorough vibrational assessment, and ordered me to stay away.

She didn't have to plead with me on that count. I was laid up in the Healing Room for a full week after Danaeus rescued me. At least I had Eliasser to keep me company for part of it, once I came to. He was so upset by what happened to me that he canceled his numerous "meetings"—which had resumed soon after the Garrammon tournament—and planted himself at my side. I let him hold my hands, feed me energy, and generally fawn over me. And I didn't feel the least bit guilty about it. Whatever these trips were for, I wasn't the only one tired of his absence. Even calm, gentle Balthasarre grew testy when the Master Guardian went away.

As for the dwarf-like people Danaeus went to see? They were non-physical travelers from a dimension three universes removed from our own. With all their expertise at "reality-jumping," as they called the way they moved from one place to the next, they could not explain how they wound up on Amoran. Once here, they adopted the physical shape of beings from a world they'd recently visited; beings who bore a strong resemblance to dwarves. But right before Danaeus arrived, the travelers said they could no longer maintain corporeal form in our reality, transformed into amorphous blobs of glowing light and got sucked through something that looked like a tiny vortex. Poor Danaeus never had the chance to ask about what had to be his homeworld. Disheartened, he had taken his time traveling back to us.

Two weeks before Thanksgiving, I made my usual Friday trip through the vortex. I had a few extra Earth hours to spend, as both kids were occupied until early evening and John was in the city doing a late afternoon volunteer magician gig at a children's cancer ward.

Ashara or Eliasser—sometimes both—made it a point to greet me when I arrived. This time, the Main Chamber was empty. My first inclination was to change into a tunic, then check the Meal Room. Instead, an inner prompting sent me to the Outer Grounds, where the sun was barely visible through an overcast sky. I even felt a few drops of rain as I crossed the courtyard and unlatched the gate. While Amoran's cold time brought a chill to the air, it wasn't supposed to alter the rains, which arrived on schedule every evening around midnight. Usually.

I headed toward the Garrammon Lake, unsure what propelled me in that direction. The darkening clouds held their moisture and I made it to the Garrammon field without getting wet. Wind whipped at my

Earth clothes as I scrambled up and over the stadium hill. Down below, erratic gusts blew across the water, crowning what should have been a placid lake with whitecaps.

The Master Guardian stood at the shoreline, muttering. I didn't want to interrupt if he was praying, yet something felt wrong. With growing apprehension, I made my way down the hill.

Eliasser kept his back to me as I stepped onto the narrow beach.

"I knew you would find me, Meiri."

Was this another test of my intuition?

"You will always find me," he continued, voice trembling. "No matter where I am, where I go, what form I take. You will always find me. Why can you do that for me, but not for Makashannar, your Primary Twin?"

Shocked by what I took as blatant criticism from the person I love more than Life Itself, I sank to my knees and stared at my hands, flexing and shaking them as if they were at fault.

"I'm sorry," I said, forcing words through my constricted throat. "I've tried so hard."

Eliasser spun around. Our eyes met and his face paled. He scooped me up from the ground and hugged me to him. "I am the one who is sorry, my Light. I know how hard you have worked to find Ashi. I did not mean to hurt you. I will never mean to hurt you."

With a suddenness that made me lightheaded, I was now fully exposed to his raw emotions. Pain . . . sadness . . . fear . . . dug at my heart as if his feelings were my own. No longer able to control myself, heaving sobs choked my airway as I pressed my hands to his chest.

"What is happening to you?" I cried out. Beneath my fingers, his heart throbbed wildly. "Tell me what is wrong. Tell me how to help you!"

The answer did not come verbally from Eliasser, but wordlessly from me. A swell of pure Love energy jettisoned from the depths of my Being, then poured out through my palms and straight into Eliasser. As if I were physically linked to the energy, I actually felt it find its way home. When that Love reached Eliasser's magnificent heart, we both sighed in relief. The sweetness of our connection prompted my tears to come even faster.

"I don't know how I did this," I whispered while crying. "Do you want me to stop?"

Eliasser shook his head, covered my hands with his own and curled his fingers around mine. He sighed again, then peered into my eyes like he could see my very soul. I knew he was silently asking my permission for something, but even with my intuition humming, I couldn't tell what it was. But . . . it didn't matter. Whatever Eliasser wanted of me, my answer was yes. Except for his mandate that I never save him again, my answer would always be yes.

I shivered in anticipation and nodded.

He pulled us together, heart-to-heart, and crossed his arms behind me. As if it couldn't hold back any longer, energy burst forth from his heart into mine, where it intensified before surging back into his, then magnified even more as it began cycling between us. Looping in a circle, it picked up speed with each revolution. Eliasser had done something like this once before, when he'd learned I was destined to die in the vortex during the Reparention. At the time, it was a way for us to deal with our immense grief.

The energy quadrupled, enveloping the core of who we are in a sphere of Love. This was far beyond what he'd done previously. I lost a clear sense of my physical body, of my location in space and time.

There was one more giant surge of Love energy, and then my heart and Eliasser's beat as One. Loved as One. My tears transformed into those of sheer release.

Eliasser touched his forehead to mine, and the energy centers residing there communed in some wordless fashion. We stayed that way, heart pressed to heart, forehead to forehead as the energy flowing between us subsided to a soft hum.

"Let her sleep," Eliasser whispered.

I tried to open my eyes, but it was like they'd been glued shut. The last thing I recalled was Eliasser and I standing on the shore of the Garrammon Lake embraced in a peace so complete words could not do it justice.

Ashara didn't bother to lower her voice or hide her dismay. "You did this, and with no warning, yet you balk at the Foreseers' request?"

"Wrong . . ." Eliasser wheezed out. "We . . . should . . . not . . ."

"It is not wrong, and you know it!"

His smooth hands cupped my chin; his thumbs traced across my cheeks. "Must . . . go."

"Have some decency. Do not leave now, for your own sake as well as for hers."

Lips touched the center of my forehead in the gentlest of kisses followed by footsteps across a stone floor.

Rough hands now encased my own. "We will get through this, Meiri," Ashara said softly. "All of it, I promise. And you will be the richer for it."

Unable to form words, I tried to *think* to Ashara that I was all right. Wonderful, in fact. Eliasser hadn't left me at all. Our hearts, still connected, let me feel him as an Assistant helped him to the Main Chamber. I was surprised that he entered the vortex, then saddened when I could no longer sense him. But just before that happened, I learned a strange thing. Wherever Eliasser went, he got there through the vortex. And he enjoyed his meetings. Save for one small, dark area of sadness, he was happy.

"He gave you a great gift," Ashara said the next day. "Although I question why he did it so impulsively. Heart Coalescence can open many pathways within your consciousness, not just in your heart, and should not be undertaken lightly. Be advised, it is also a private matter that should be discussed with no one. Not even Ari."

Heart Coalescence. The incredible joining of our hearts had a fitting name.

"When can I speak?" I asked, my voice as hoarse as Eliasser's had been when he left.

"Anytime you like," she huffed. "But it will take a week for you to be able to talk properly." She handed me a flask. "Stay hydrated. Rest is essential. Remain within the Mountain until—"

I touched her age-worn hand. "Why are you angry?"

She held my gaze for a long moment, her expression slowly softening. "He should have consulted me first. There are other things that are more important."

I didn't think Eliasser had a choice in the matter. I had the unshakable feeling that we both wound up at the Garrammon Lake specifically so that we could coalesce our Hearts.

Eliasser stayed away for two full weeks. I finally understood something he said before our Heart Coalescence. *I will never mean to hurt you.* True, he would never intend me harm. But hurt me, he had. To experience something like Heart Coalescence and then have him leave for that length of time was painful. When he returned, looking exhausted and pre-occupied, he avoided my eyes and headed straight to the Foreseers.

"I don't understand," I said to Ashara, trying not to take it personally.

She stared after him as he retreated down the corridor to the Forest Portal. "Neither does he, I am afraid."

"Get it," Danaeus shouted. "Get it, get it, get it . . . ohhh."

I laughed as Anders threw down his handpieces and chased the dwarf around the field.

Ari came up behind me, slung his arm over my shoulder, and pretended to smoke a cigar.

"Hey, sweetheart. Nice gams."

I looked down at my "gams" which were completely covered by my leggings. "Say what?"

"You know . . . gams. Legs."

I fake-punched him in the chest. "I know what gams are, doofus. I don't get the context."

"The way you sprang into the air to field that last pop-up? Sweet!"

"Watch out," Anders yelled.

Ari and I swiveled his way, then hit the deck as the Garrammon ball shot directly at us.

"Holy crap, Anders!" I yelled from the ground. "Were you aiming for us?"

Danaeus sprinted forward wearing a sheepish grin. "Sorry. That was me. I was trying to hit *him*." He pointed at Anders, who trotted up, his expression pure smug satisfaction.

"Not surprisingly, he missed!" Anders gently roughed up the dwarf's hair in a tame version of a noogie. Since I hadn't taught anyone that, I could only assume it already existed on Amoran.

I so loved these guys. "Another round?"

Anders actually rolled his eyes. "You need to ask?"

We'd been playing for over an hour, enjoying the bright sun, a rarity lately. Cloudy days were the new norm in Guardian Lands, however the word from "on high" was that while the recent climate change wasn't part of Amoran's cold time, it was temporary and not harmful to us or the ecosystem. "On high" was, of course, the Foreseers, backed up by whomever Eliasser took his meetings with. They seemed to have as much clout as the ethereal beings in the Glen, so the verification was doubled-down genuine.

We swapped partners and took our places.

Ari opened with a serve that whizzed past Danaeus's head. The ball hit the path next to the field and bounced into the Garrammon Meadow. I jogged to the edge of the path, shielded my eyes from the sun and looked around for the ball.

"Just go in and get it," Ari called out. "It's fine, remember?"

"You said that the last time we set foot in the meadow and look where that landed us!"

The ball had come to rest only a few feet in. I stepped between the hibernating glazzien, bent over to pick up the ball, and the world went dark.

"Meiri."

There was that voice again. Familiar, yet unfamiliar.

"Ashi?"

"Meiri."

"Who are you?"

"Meiri . . ."

"Is she going to be all right?" Ari asked.

"She will be fine," Ashara said. "Help me to sit her up."

"But she's still unconscious."

"No . . ." I breathed out as I opened my eyes. "I'm back."

"Back?" Danaeus said. "Did you go somewhere?"

I smiled.

"We must return to the Mountain," Ashara pronounced.

"Seriously?" Ari tilted his face to the sky. We all followed suit, probably thinking the same thing. When would we have another sunny day?

Ashara crossed her arms. "Now."

She held me back as the rest of the group went on ahead. "Have you been hydrating?"

"Well, sure. Not like I was after the Coalescence, but it's been three weeks already. Do you think that's why I passed out? Not enough liquid intake?"

"Tell me what happened."

Accustomed to the fact that Ashara often ignored my questions when it suited her, I relayed the incident, including hearing a voice calling my name three times.

"Only your name? Three times?"

I nodded. "Just like when Ari and I got caught in that time warp anomaly mess. Here's the really odd thing, though. I'm not sure why I think this, because the voice doesn't *sound* the same. But it could be the same person who called to me during the Reparention, when I nearly succumbed to the Darkness." That voice had counseled me to not *fight* the Darkness, but *bless* it for its part in keeping balance in the universe. The advice helped me break the hold the Darkness had on me, saving both me and the Reparention. "I don't think it's anyone I know," I added, "yet, he feels familiar somehow."

Ashara looked thoughtful. "That is odd."

We continued in silence for several minutes, then I asked, "How long was I out?"

"Ari summoned me at once and I ethermoved to you right away."

"Summoned?" The first time Ashara used that expression was when she had "summoned" Eliasser to return to Amoran after Ari and I were caught in that time warp anomaly thing—sheesh, what a mouthful. I assumed she'd physically gone to get Eliasser. Now I was thinking it meant something else entirely.

"Summoning is a form of direct mental contact with a person when they are urgently needed. Ari made the right choice."

"Who else beside you and Ari can summon?"

"All Vortex Lights can do this naturally."

"So, you, Eliasser, and Ashi. What about me?"

She hesitated for a moment. "You could before you became an Earth dweller."

Another skill I'd lost along the way.

"Do you think my passing out had something to do with the meadow?"

She shook her head. "I did not feel anything unusual emanating from there."

"Then we can still play Garrammon tomorrow?"

"I did not say that."

I sighed. "Mind telling me why?"

She smiled. "I do not mind at all. We can finally begin your ethermoving lessons. That will require your full attention for"—Ashara was the one to sigh now—"however long it takes."

CHAPTER 9

Ashara pulled me off my sleeping stone at the crack of dawn, claiming that early morning on an empty stomach was an ideal time to learn ethermoving. I spent the next four hours attempting to disassemble my atoms and reassemble them someplace else. And failed miserably. Following a late Morning Meal, I slept the afternoon away. Seemed ethermoving—or in my case, trying to learn how to—consumed a lot of energy. After Evening Meal, Ashara made me review what we'd done that morning, then led me through a series of meditations to increase the speed at which my cells vibrated. It was similar to what we'd had to do for the Reparention when we transformed our bodies into light energy. But without the increased Life Force augmentations or the ramped up vibrational output of the vortex as the Reparention neared, I couldn't even feel a flutter.

Two weeks into this delightful schedule, Ashara seemed to think I'd made some progress. I didn't feel any difference other than in my overall energy level. I only needed to sleep half the afternoon to recover from that day's lesson.

The next morning's session was even more arduous, prompting me to ask a question I'd put to Ashara early on in my ethermoving practice; one she'd ignored at the time.

"What are the dangers in ethermoving?"

She narrowed an eye. "What makes you think there are dangers?"

"The fact that you sidestepped my original question and are obfuscating now."

She waved a hand in dismissal. "You are so far from accomplishing this, it—"

I cut her off. "I don't care if I can't ethermove until hell freezes over. I'm not going to continue with these lessons until I get my answer."

We had one of our staring contests. When I folded my arms across my chest and began tapping my foot, she relented. Sort of.

"I do not want to—how would you say it? Put ideas in your head. Or frighten you off, because the only real danger is something so rare, I have never witnessed it happen."

"Great," I snorted. "Based on my track record, I'm sure to experience it."

She smiled at that, then sobered. "You need not concern yourself. When you are closer to a successful ethermove, we can discuss potential problems."

Problems? Plural? I opened my mouth to protest further, but the expression on the Master Healer's face told me it would be useless, so I let it go.

It was time for our late Morning Meal, but I wanted to change into a fresh tunic, so I headed to my quarters. Deep in thought, I overshot my destination, hung a sharp left, then stopped short when I realized I was standing outside Ashi's room.

Ashara had done several assessments of his quarters since my most recent debacle landed me in the Healing Room. However, she had not been able to determine why I had such a strong reaction to being there, or account for my intense sense of foreboding. But she did agree that something was off vibrationally, and his room had remained sealed until she could do further testing.

I was about to backtrack, when a flash of blue light dashed by me and burrowed straight through the section of wall containing Ashi's invisible doorway.

And then, things got even weirder as the wall did a slow dissolve. Ashi's room, which Ashara had sealed with an extra strong energy lock, was now open.

Zip. The flash of blue whizzed out of Ashi's quarters and down the passageway.

"Earnie?" I called out in surprise.

Whoosh. Earnie buzzed past me again, rocketed around inside Ashi's room, then bounced off several walls before coming to a halt above the sleeping stone.

I followed him into the forbidden zone.

"What are doing here, my little friend?" I hadn't seen him for several months. Eliasser was away, so he hadn't brought the Ether Light here.

Earnie took off around the room in another burst of dynamism, then settled above the back counter where a blanket shrouded a row of lumpy objects.

Unaccountably, my heart rate bumped up and my breath came faster.

Earnie sailed forward, "kissed" my nose, then glided back and forth above the row, pulsing brighter, softer . . . brighter, softer.

A picture formed in my mind of what Earnie wanted me to do. Chills crawled up my spine in response. Whatever these objects were, I sensed that viewing them would be painful.

I hugged my arms to chest and shook my head.

Earnie approached me again, nestled against my neck, then went back to the first lump hidden by the cover.

"Do I have to?" I whispered. My intuition prompted me to acquiesce; however, it also cautioned me to be careful.

Earnie pulsed pink twice, then remained pink.

I didn't need to speak Ether Light to know that was yes.

I licked my dry lips, joined Earnie at the counter, and inched the fabric back to expose the first item. As soon as I laid eyes on the polished ovoid stone, I simply knew that all these objects were relics of my past lives on Earth. But why did Ashi have them? They held a special meaning for him; that much I could feel. Was that why I was here now? Would they somehow bring me closer to locating Ashi?

Last fall, I'd recalled the short time I'd lived on Earth as Meiri, when I went straight from Amoran to a small village in a part of Europe where I was killed soon afterward. That was the death I'd suffered that Ashara couldn't forgive herself for. Other than that, I had only recalled one of my previous incarnations—also last fall—as Hannah the midwife. That was the lifetime when Ari and I had been lovers. What would I learn now?

I took a deep breath, steadying myself for whatever might come. When I lifted the stone from the counter, the information came to me at once.

"I used this as a paperweight; it was a gift from my father," I said to Earnie. A mental image of myself with blond hair in ringlets breezed by before fading. "I was the only child of a wealthy lord, spoiled by privilege. I wasn't the nicest person." I grimaced at the understatement. I'd been demanding, impatient, and entitled—exactly the type of person I couldn't stand in my current life. Hoping that was the worst of it, I replaced the stone and uncovered the next item.

Before I could even touch the bracelet of colorful beads, I was plunged into a vivid recall of such potency, it was if I were physically there, being chased across a savanna somewhere in Africa. The broadness of my smile grew wider as my pursuer's hand grabbed my shoulder and we fell to the ground in a heat of love and passion so intense it took my breath away. My lover's face, dark as a moonless night, shone with perspiration as he spoke softly to me in another language; one which I somehow understood perfectly.

As if a giant cord yanked me back to the present, I was again in Ashi's room, staring down at the bracelet I had been given that day so long ago. It was a gift from a man who had promised in that life, as well as in this one, to always love me. John.

I basked in that love for a moment, then exposed the next relic.

Tears streamed down my cheeks. The tiny funereal headpiece made of feathers, shells and beads was for my young son, a victim of one of the diseases brought by white settlers. I could almost feel his small body as I held him to my chest in that life, grieving. The soul of that little boy was also known and loved by me in my present incarnation: Tom—my oldest friend, current employer, and the man who was more a brother to me than my own flesh and blood.

Moving on to the next object, I gently folded the blanket back to reveal a small mixing bowl, one I instantly recognized. This had been my favorite vessel in which to craft remedies during my life as Hannah. It was also in this bowl that I had intended to grind a lethal mix of herbs to end that life before my swiftly growing cancer did it for me. But I was spared that demise. When Ari and Hannah finally gave in to their love, his energy stopped her heart—but not until they'd both enjoyed the fruits of that passion.

I wasn't clear on the order of these lifetimes, but I knew the leather pouch next in line was from my first full life after I'd been pulled into Earth's reincarnation cycle. I'd lived a simple but peaceful existence in a small town surrounded by a large, close-knit family. Although death arrived when I was still young, my passing was gentle and without much suffering.

My fingers trembled as I uncovered the next item—a colorful silk pillowslip. With tender devotion, I held it to my face, experiencing the love it represented. Barely fifteen, I'd been sold in marriage to a cold, angry man who needed to produce an heir as quickly as possible. Each night for months, he spent himself as quickly and roughly as he could, then left me alone.

My maid was a young girl about my age. Contrary to proper form in our culture, we became fast friends, sharing our hopes and dreams—and our despair that we would never know the kind of love we wished for. One evening, she found me crying after yet another harsh and loveless coupling. My husband had taken out his anger over my inability to conceive on my body. At the sound of his carriage retreating into the distance, Marisah picked up my hairbrush and began to work it through my long, black locks.

"Why are women so hated?" I'd asked her. "Why must we suffer without love as though we are not worthy of anything but to be bought and sold?"

The brush stopped moving. "There might be a way for us . . . if you are willing." Her hands caressed the sides of my arms as her lips kissed the top of my head.

I could barely breathe. When I turned around, the shock must have shown on my face.

She looked down quickly. "I am sorry," she whispered. "I beg of you, please do not tell on me."

But Marisah had misread my surprise. I grasped her hand and held it to my face. "*If* I am willing?" From that night forward, we never again worried about love.

I set the pillowslip down, then bared the final relic—a plain, clay pot.

"Oh!" Brutal images bombarded my mind. "Earnie, I don't think I can do it."

Earnie left his post above the artifacts and moved to the center of my chest. Then, he moved *into* my chest. I looked down at the pink glow emanating from my sternum, amazed not only that he could do that, but that it provided me the strength to go on.

"We were wretchedly poor," I said. "My father was a drunk, my mother a prostitute. He beat her when there was no money for his ale, and he beat me when beating her did not satisfy him. And when she did not satisfy him in other ways, he turned again to me."

The scenes continued to speed by. Two small pots, the one resting on Ashi's counter and its companion, were given to me by a potter on market day—as a gift! These were magnificent treasures for a young girl living a dismal life. But a short while later, more drunk than usual, my father discovered them hidden beneath a basket near my sleeping mat. Demanding to know where I'd gotten them, I finally confessed. A fist will often have that effect on truth telling.

"Whore," he shouted. "Just like your slut of a mother."

He smashed one of the pots, then flung me to the mat. But before he could pin me with the weight of him, I rolled to the side. *Never again*, I thought as a strangely quiet determination took hold of me. *Never again will you take from me what is not yours to take. I would rather die.*

Clutching my remaining treasure, I bolted from the house and straight into the potter. A potter who always seemed to be nearby. I thrust the clay pot at him. "Keep it safe for me."

My father lumbered through the doorway waving a stick of firewood above his head. Heedless of the thunder of approaching hooves, I ran as fast as I could away from him.

"No, Meiri!" the potter shouted. Even if I had responded to the strange name impulsively misspoken, the warning came too late. My foot caught in a pothole and I flew forward into the street just as the first horses bore down on me. I felt an instant of blinding, excruciating pain. Then peace. Total peace.

I sank to the floor of Ashi's room. Emotionally and physically exhausted, I had one thought before I slipped from consciousness. How many times had Ari been forced to watch me die?

"You should never have viewed them all at once," Ashara said.

I looked up at her from the healing stone where I'd just awakened. I was beginning to think they should assign me a permanent bed here.

"How was I supposed to know that? I didn't even know they were there!"

"But you were in his room before the Reparention."

"Only that one time. And I was so nervous about telling him I was in love with him, that I didn't notice much else." I thought for a moment. "Whatever is going on now, that energy wasn't there then."

Her expression grew thoughtful. "When we found you, the mementos of your past lives were emitting a strange, humming vibration which quieted soon after. But that unusual, discordant vibration remained."

"Which is why you should not have gone in there," Eliasser snapped. I watched him try to control his emotions. He reminded me of Ashi right now. Hands balled at his sides. Lips pressed so tightly together, there were spots where no color showed.

"Yet I managed to get inside. Doesn't that tell you something?"

"Like what, Meiri," Eliasser said through clenched teeth. "What does it tell us?"

"That I needed to view them. And you can stop scolding me, because it was Earnie's idea."

Ashara and Eliasser looked like they'd seen a ghost.

"Earnie?" Eliasser whispered, his voice almost a squeak.

I told them who had unsealed the entrance to Ashi's room, and how the Ether Light had encouraged me to view Ashi's collection. Omitting all the rest, I merely added, "When it was time for the last relic, I couldn't face it. So Earnie helped me out by moving inside me." I tapped my chest to indicate where Earnie had resided temporarily.

Eliasser's lips parted, he held his hand to his forehead, then stalked across the room where he planted his palms on the potions table and hunched over.

I tore my eyes from him to look at Ashara. She did not seem upset by this. In fact, her expression was more . . . appreciative? Calculating? Maybe both.

"I did not think such a thing possible," she said. "Perhaps we do not know the Ether Lights as well as we think."

Still hunched over, staring at the floor, Eliasser demanded, "I want to know the details."

"About Earnie going inside me?" I asked.

"About what you viewed."

Ashara and I traded a worried look. "Unwise," she warned, making me wonder if she already knew the details of my past lives.

Eliasser straightened and slid his gaze to her. "Do not attempt to oppose my wishes. Meiri will tell me what she viewed. And bring Ari here at once. He is the one who brought those objects to Ashi."

"At Ashi's request," Ashara snapped.

"And against my wishes," Eliasser shot back. "Ari has something to answer for."

Ashara patted my hand. "Use your judgement," she whispered, then left the room.

Eliasser insisted that I start. I began with the most benign life, the one I'd lived right after being pulled into Earth's reincarnation cycle. Next, I glossed over my life as spoiled minor nobility, and was completing my African savanna life when Ari strode into the Healing Room, followed by the Master Healer.

"They made me promise, Eliasser," Ari exclaimed. "You are never to know the details."

Eliasser's face went bright red. "I care not one bit for what Meiri's past life counselors made you promise. I am hearing it all. Now."

I had past life counselors?

"There are good reasons why they—"

"Now!" Eliasser thundered.

"Who are they?" I asked Ari.

Ari shook his head. "I can't."

"I am waiting, Meiri," Eliasser barked.

"Give her a minute," Ari shouted. He perched on the edge of my healing stone, facing me as he tucked strands of my hair—which resembled tangled yarn at the moment—behind my ears. "This is *quite a mess,*" he breathed out with peculiar emphasis. "I think we can *clean it up,* though." His gaze met mine and he blinked twice. "Let me tie your hair back, so we can *clean this up.* There's no need for *all of it* to be *messy.*"

Ah. Message received. "Thank you. I agree. It is quite uncomfortable the way it is. Maybe Ashara has a hair tie you can use."

Ashara had been listening. Along with a hair tie, she gave Ari a hairbrush. Positioning himself behind me, Ari began working the soft bristles through my snarled mop.

Choosing my words with care, I continued with my past life recitation. Eliasser already knew about my incarnation as Hannah, so I skipped that. He was saddened by the death of my young son in my Native American lifetime, but the silk pillow life had him furrowing his brow.

"You loved two people physically at the same time during that life," Eliasser said, "yet you cannot do that now with Ashi and John?"

Curiously, Eliasser made no comment that one of those people was a woman. Even more curious, I thought, with a bit of chagrin considering who my oldest friend on Earth is, I had never thought to ask about same-sex relationships on Amoran.

"It was a different time," I said vaguely. "Different circumstances."

"Why? How?"

Ari halted his brushing. "Keep it simple," he whispered in my ear.

"I didn't love my husband. I just had to accept his . . . attentions. But I loved Marisah."

Eliasser's back stiffened. "What do you mean you 'had to accept'?"

Unsure why Eliasser wanted me to go into this, I searched for words that would satisfy his need to know. "Once I was married to him, I was . . . I had to . . . do what he told me to."

Eliasser turned to me. "He was unkind. I hear it in your voice. Why did you marry him?"

I licked my lips, then opened my mouth. But I couldn't say it.

Ari put his hands on my shoulders. “She had no choice. Leave it at that.”

“Why did she have no choice? Why did she have to do what—”

“You really think you need to know this?” Ari rasped, his voice tight with anger.

“Yes!”

“Don’t say I didn’t warn you! She was sold, Eliasser. Sold to a man who hated her. She became his property. He owned her. And for years, he did to his property whatever he—”

“Stop!” Eliasser’s voice trembled. “I cannot hear any more.” When he finally met my eyes, his were moist with unshed tears. “I do not understand Earth at all. I am sorry that you ever had to go there.” He pinched the bridge of his nose and left the room. Thankfully, I was spared having to tell him about the worst life of all.

I didn’t see him again until the last day of that elongated visit. I’d spent most of the time working on ethermoving, with dubious progress; I could now practice without having to sleep at all afterward, and there was the faintest buzz in my body when I attempted to disassemble myself.

I tried to get Ari to tell me who “they” were, the ones who didn’t want Eliasser to know about my past lives. For once, he kept silent. I only knew it wasn’t the Foreseers as Ari had no relationship with them.

But my past life memories weighed on me; Eliasser’s reactions, even more so. I mentally reviewed the lifetimes I’d witnessed, but only counted nine, including my current life and the very brief one when I’d first left Amoran to live on Earth.

What was the tenth life? And why didn’t Ashi have an artifact from it?

It didn’t occur to me until I was in the Main Chamber getting ready to call the vortex that our Heart Coalescence may have been to blame for Eliasser’s insistence on hearing about my past lives, as well as his emotional response when he did.

“Wait, Meiri,” Eliasser called out as he made his way across the tiled floor. “I will be more available from now on. My meetings . . . where I go . . .” He paused and took a breath. “I have told them I am needed here.”

What I was about to say surprised me. "The Foreseers maintain that all things happen as they should; that there is a purpose to everything." I pressed my hands to Eliasser's chest. "You should do what is deepest in your heart to do. And only that." I let my eyes meet his. "I am fine. Whatever my past lives brought me, I am here now, in this body. Back with you."

"As it should be," he said softly.

I smiled. "As it should be."

I didn't understand why we'd said that, but I experienced the rightness of our assertions as a heightened vibration throughout my total Being.

We held each other beneath the portal, then I called the vortex and returned to Earth.

Chapter 10

The Thursday before Thanksgiving, John slept in. He'd taken the day off so he could do a magic show for the kids at a children's hospital south of us. After Kiley and Ryan left for school, I peeled off my sweats and crawled back into bed to give my husband a proper wakeup. Later, as we enjoyed a mid-morning breakfast in smiling silence, rain began to patter on the roof.

I checked the weather app on my phone. "This storm wasn't expected until tomorrow."

John finished off his waffles. "I'd better be on my way. I'd like to get there by eleven to unpack and set up."

I helped him load his gear into his Jeep Cherokee, then ran my finger along the aging weather stripping on the back window. "We need to get you a new vehicle."

"Nah. I'm happy with the old beast. And the window doesn't leak much unless it rains super hard. I'll get around to fixing it. Maybe this weekend. Oh, can I borrow your car charger?"

"You lost another one?"

He gave me a sheepish grin and a palms-up. "I lent it to one of the guys at work."

I shook my head, retrieved my charger, and handed it over. "I want mine back tonight."

"Yes, mistress," he said with fake meekness. "Your wish is my command."

I smiled. "You got that right, buster."

Between work and our family activities, John and I rarely had a morning to ourselves, and never mid-week. All I wanted at the moment was to do these last few hours over again. John must have been having similar thoughts, because he bent under my umbrella and whispered, "How about I get a local job with a four-day work week. I could get used to this." Then he kissed me so thoroughly my lips went numb. "Consider that a placeholder for tonight's activities."

I giggled and pushed against his chest. "You're home when?"

"Three at the latest. I like to visit with the kids after the show, grab some lunch, and then, if the rain isn't too bad, I may stop to pick up Kiley's new bookcase."

I eyed the back of the Jeep. "It'll fit?"

"Yep." He pulled me in for one last kiss. "It fits just fine."

Holy moly. "What's got you so randy, Andy?"

He slid into the front seat, waved his hand up and down indicating my body, then drove away, leaving me with a dopey grin on my face in my rain-drenched driveway.

I'm okay with solitude. In fact, copious alone time is something I need to keep sane. But when I returned to the house, it felt too empty. The sound of rain on my roof—another thing I normally love—just made me lonely. At odds with the weather, and life in general, I left at one o'clock to do "errands"—my code word for retail therapy with a practical purpose.

A few hours later, I headed back to Glenwood Falls to pick up the kids from their respective schools. Kiley and Ryan still took the bus home most of the time, but Thursdays were now loaded with activities that required a car and a chauffeur. Thankfully, they were both on time and I didn't need to text "Where are you?!?"—which would have been impossible because my cell phone died. And the only way to revive it was the car charger I'd lent to John.

I drove to one end of Glenwood Falls to drop Kiley off at play rehearsal, then back across town to deposit Ryan at Nancy's house so he and his cousin Robert could work on their health project. The rain was now coming down so hard, I considered staying in town until the kids were finished. But with a dead phone, I couldn't read an e-book while I waited, so I headed toward home, barely able to see through the sheets of water straining my wipers.

Nightfall came early this time of year, and the storm only hastened things. I had just hit a long, dark stretch of Farnham Road South, the road I live on, when the downpour transformed into frozen golf balls bouncing off the windshield. There was no place to pull over, so I slowed to a crawl. Heart racing, I kept the double yellow line in sight as I crept forward for the sixty seconds the hail slammed down.

When the hail turned to sleet, I knew I should have stayed in town. I drove the last half mile with my hands clenched on the steering wheel as I slid first one way, then the next. I was shaking all over when I finally pulled into my driveway—right behind my friend Rebecca's maroon Honda. Crap! Had I mixed up the day I'd promised to meet her for the library fundraiser? I jumped from my car and peeked in the sedan's windows. No Rebecca. Where was she?

Right. John said he'd be home by three. He must have let her in.

Adrenaline still pumping from my frightening ride, I dashed up the stairs, opened the front door and stepped into the darkened house.

A finger of light poked down the hallway from the kitchen. My mother moved from the shadow of the dining room into the entryway, clutching the spare key I had asked her to keep in case we locked ourselves out or she needed to get in for some emergency.

"We just arrived," she said quietly. "Where are the kids?"

"Ryan's at Nancy's and Kiley's at rehearsal," I replied, shivering. "Why are you here? And where's Rebecca?"

Mom looked confused. "Rebecca?"

"Yeah. Her car's outside."

"Rebecca's not here," Mom said.

"But her car's here," I protested.

If Rebecca wasn't here, that meant her husband, Dan, was. And if Dan was here . . .

"Nothing's happened to her, has it?" I asked. "Rebecca's okay, isn't she?"

Mom's expression turned guarded. "Rebecca is fine."

A light switched on in the family room. I took a step forward. "John?"

John didn't answer. It finally sank in that I hadn't seen his Jeep in the driveway where he'd been parking it lately because our garage was too filled with junk.

Dan, one of our closest friends and the detective I brag I have on speed dial, exited the family room and shuffled toward me like his legs were made of lead.

A split second is all it takes for your life to change forever. But right before that split second is a splinter of time which hangs in eternity in blissful ignorance of what is to come. In the fractional silence before me, I willed the Earth to reverse its direction, for time to go backwards.

Time did not obey. My heart began a rapid descent through the bottom of my stomach.

Dan reached me, red eyes rimmed with pain. "I . . . there's been an accident."

"Please . . ." My throat tightened. "No . . ."

Dan held me, his professional demeanor slipping as his voice broke. "I'm so sorry, Kerrin. Oh, God. So . . . sorry."

Rebecca arrived a few minutes later, dropped off by a squad car. She sat on one side of me, my mother on the other. Dan pulled a hassock up to the coffee table so he could sit directly across from us. He'd been off duty when the call came in. He'd insisted on coming to the house to tell me in person. When he couldn't get me on my cell or at home, he'd called my mother, and then Rebecca, who showed up right after Dan delivered the news to me.

"What John did is nothing short of heroic," Dan said, after giving me the details.

"Selfless," Rebecca added.

I sat on the edge of the family room sofa with my mother's crazy patchwork afghan wrapped around me. I couldn't think what to do except nod in response. John had rescued a half dozen girls and their Scout leader from a crashed minivan. He'd gotten them safely to his Jeep, then—according to the troop leader—went back to get the cell phone he'd dropped inside the minivan after calling 9-1-1. At that moment, a pickup came around the bend, spun out on an ice patch and slammed into John and the minivan at the same time.

The troop leader and her charges were physically unharmed.

John was not. John was dead.

"Yes, I guess it was," I finally whispered, quelling a sudden, savage wish that John hadn't been such a nice guy, a selfless person, a *hero.*

"No guessing about it," my mother said. "Imagine what would have happened if John hadn't been there, and the pickup driver slammed into that van full of kids?" She shook her head.

"We just got word," Dan said, looking up from his phone. "The pickup driver died at the hospital."

I pulled the box of tissues closer and took another long swig from the Irish coffee Rebecca had placed in front of me. I hate coffee and I hate whiskey. But Rebecca had ordered me to drink it, so I did. The way it burned going down my throat actually felt good. John would be impressed that I was drinking hard liquor.

Would have been impressed. Now, he'd never have the chance to be impressed by anything.

I stumbled up the stairs to my bedroom to get the wool sweater John had given me three Christmases ago. Even though the heat was blasting, it felt like the chill would never leave me.

My eyes strayed to our bed. I'd neglected to make it, an unusual omission for me. The covers were rumpled, and the bunched up down pillows still held the impression of our heads. Less than twelve hours ago John and I had reveled in the mysteries of each other's bodies, then lay there talking like we had our whole lives ahead of us. John had even confessed to feeling early empty nest syndrome. He'd asked if I ever thought about having another child. I'd laughed at the idea. Now I wish I hadn't.

Forgoing the sweater, I slipped between the flannel sheets. Goofy snowmen, like cartoon characters. Like you'd see on a kid's bed. John had insisted. I'd thought he was nuts. They'd become my favorite sheets. That was John. He somehow always knew what would work, what was right, what to do.

Tell me what to do now, John. I'm not strong enough for this.

I fit my head into the depression in his pillow, thinking . . . maybe . . . *maybe* I'm asleep. Yes! That's got to be it. I'm dreaming. One of those crystal clear, lucid dreams. All I have to do is wake up. Of course, that's it. Has to be. Because this can't be happening. How could John be perfectly fine this morning and dead now?

Has to be a dream . . . has to be . . . just a dream.

Mom's voice drifted up the stairwell, asking Dan if he would go with her to pick up Ryan and Kiley. And should they wait to tell them until they got home?

That's when the beautiful dream in which John was still alive ended, and the nightmare of reality dug its icy claws into me, unrelenting in its infliction of cold, hard truth.

I cried freely the night of John's death, then my tears curiously dried up and disappeared as shock set in. The emotional paralysis traveled from my heart to my brain, numbing my tongue along the way, which turned out to be good. Discretion is called for to deal with the things people say to you in their own discomfort and denial when someone has died. I'd had my first real experience with that a few years back when John's mother had died suddenly from a heart attack. Helen had left her abusive first husband when John and his sister, Nancy, were still in elementary school. She soon met and married George, a kind, compassionate soul. John's stepdad, with his usual quiet dignity, had gracefully received comments like, "You're still young enough, George. You can always remarry," and "Better to go quickly than to linger." And my personal pet peeve, "She's in a better place now."

George arrived at my house the following morning and planted himself next to me. My friend and coworker, Megan, claimed my other side, alternating with my mother. They kept me moving through the steps required of a widow during those incomprehensible first days. It was as if a giant drill had removed the center portion of my body and what remained was propped up with toothpicks. I don't know how I would have made it without their help, as dealing with my cantankerous family, never a walk in the park, turned into an obstacle course.

Friends and relatives came and went. Rebecca and Dan. John's sister, Nancy, and her husband, Bob. My parents. My sister Sarah with her latest boyfriend. I was surprised that my cousin Camryn—my personal nemesis who'd had the hots for John for over two decades—was absent, until Sarah let me know that Camryn had finally found the true love of her life and was in Europe on an extended vacation with him. In her place—and not particularly welcome—were Sue and Richard Hansen, who claimed they were "moved by the Lord" to make sure that Ryan's spiritual needs were taken care of.

My brother Michael showed up Saturday morning, and a tussle ensued between the believers and the nonbelievers. Michael, decidedly in the latter group, claimed it was his duty to watch out for John's best interests.

I gaped at him. "I think John's main interest would have been staying alive."

"Oh, but he is alive, Kerrin dear," Sue Hansen oozed in that officious voice that grated on my nerves. She shot my atheist brother a superior look. "And he is in a much better place."

"*Excuse me?*" I hissed. I'd had enough of her using John's death to proselytize. "If you say one more time that 'John is in the hands of the Lord,' or that he's 'happier because he's in a better place,' or anything else relating to where he is now or how he might be feeling, I will ask you to leave. It's hard enough helping my kids deal with their dad's death, without you telling them that he's basically happier now that he's gone."

Sue managed to look contrite and she shut up for a while.

Saturday morning wore on. More people came and went. Hot food was placed on the kitchen table at lunchtime. When there was clearly more than anyone could eat at one sitting, Megan took charge of depositing the rest into my refrigerator and freezer.

Condolences were offered. Minutes ticked by in an anguished blur.

At a friend's prompting, John and I had long ago taken care of all the legal arrangements should one or both of us die. But we'd only discussed funerals in that cavalier manner that younger people not facing death can afford to do. I mostly knew what he wouldn't want.

It was finally decided to hold a memorial service at the community center. My father—a card-carrying Episcopalian—objected to the non-religious setting, but I insisted. John had made it clear that he never intended to enter another church in his life. I planned to honor his feelings.

"He's dead, Kerrin. How will he know?" my father said, proving that he could at times be as blunt as my mother. "Besides, he probably would have come around eventually."

The heat rose to my face and pushed out through my voice. "I'm not going to disregard John's wishes just because he's dead. Whether he would have eventually 'come around' is a moot point. We'll never know, will we?"

So many things we'll never know, never experience. My throat tightened, but my eyes remained oddly dry. Me—the crier in the family, the "emotional" one, couldn't shed a tear.

I was mostly ignored as the debate started up again. George tried to mediate, while Megan went to open a bottle of wine.

"They don't get it, do they?" I whispered to my mother. "I need to take a walk. Can you keep them from killing each other until I get back?" *When I just might do it myself.*

Mom patted my arm. "Don't worry. I'll take care of the circus animals while you're gone."

"Thanks, Mom. I love you."

"Of course, you do," she said with a small smile.

I motioned to Kiley and Ryan to follow me. When we left the room, no one but Mom seemed to notice our departure.

"Get your coats. Dress warmly. Wear boots," I said to my kids, my words clipped. Tellingly, they didn't question where we were going or offer up a protest. I think they needed to get away as much as I did.

We hiked up the mountain on that cold November afternoon to the clearing where we'd held many a family picnic. I had a purpose in mind for this sojourn. After breaking the news to them Thursday night, we'd cried on and off for hours. Ever since then, they'd seemed unusually quiet and withdrawn. Like me.

We settled together on one of the large, natural stone benches. I had planned a number of things to say to my kids, but now that we were here, I simply sat, breathing in the healing presence of trees, open sky, and sunshine.

After several moments, I pointed to the center of the clearing.

"Remember when the four of us tried to play soccer and your dad kicked the ball so hard it went flying over the edge?"

"Yeah," Kiley said. "He had to go get it because we'd borrowed the ball from the team."

Ryan laughed. "He looked so funny when he climbed back up that steep hill."

I smiled. "He could barely walk for a week, his muscles hurt so much."

"But he never complained about it. He made it into a joke," Kiley said, blue eyes wide with awe. Complaining came naturally to her. "He's the best, ever."

Ryan clenched his jaw. "*Was* the best. Best Dad, best friend . . ." Tears began to stream down Ryan''s face.

Kiley threw her arms around me, crying. "Why, Mommy? Why did my daddy have to die?"

Twelve-year-old Kiley's descent into childlike pleading skated across the icy wasteland of my feelings providing a temporary thaw and the bittersweet release that only tears of grief can bring. "I don't know, Kitten," I cried, using one of her dad's nicknames for her. "There are no reasons for a tragedy like this."

Ryan swiped at his tears. "The Hansens say it's just God's will and we should never question that. But why would God want Dad dead?"

He finally let go, sobbing openly.

The three of us cried and talked—about John, about death. Finally, like they had an automatic shut-off valve, our tears stopped. For now.

As we made our way back to the house, I counseled them again on what to expect in the coming days, particularly at the memorial service and just after.

"People react to grief and loss in different ways," I said. "Sometimes they say things that make no sense, or even seem heartless."

"Like Uncle Michael and Grandpa Martin fighting about the memorial service," Ryan said.

"Like the Hansens saying Dad must be happier now," Kiley snapped, curling her lip. Ryan shot her a look but said nothing.

"Like that," I agreed. "Sometimes worse. Grandpa George says everyone means well. They don't intend to be hurtful; they just feel so strongly that they have to say something, and anything's better than nothing. Maybe they think it will make us feel better if we believe John's happier, or in a better place." We went through the gate at the back of our property and walked toward the house. "No matter what they say, it's probably best to respond with something like, 'Thank you for your kind thoughts,' or 'I appreciate your concern.'" Ryan nodded, but Kiley rolled her eyes. Right. What was I thinking? So not her style.

"A simple thank-you will also suffice, dear daughter. Although, as the consummate actress I know you to be, you should be able to pull off flowery language." And I rolled my eyes right back at her. For some reason, the three of us giggled. We were still giggling when we entered the kitchen. Thank goodness for George's excellent and thorough counsel. Grief giggles, he called them. I'd warned Kiley and Ryan about it, but apparently Sue Hansen had never encountered this phenomenon as she entered the kitchen and stood there, horror struck.

"How can you laugh at a time like this? What kind of example are you for your children?"

This from the woman who thought my husband was happier now! "What kind of example am I?" I stopped as the argument being waged in the family room grew louder. Richard Hansen and my father were debating which minister would be more appropriate for the memorial service; Episcopal—my dad's choice—or the Hansen's version of Christianity. Shouting over them both, my brother Michael expounded, "This is ludicrous! John didn't believe in God. Why call in a clown-of-the-cloth now?"

It became all too clear why my emotions kept going into deep freeze.

I looked Sue in the eyes. "You and your husband need to leave. Now." She opened her mouth to say something, but I pushed past her into the family room. The argument, instead of stopping, got even more heated.

"Enough!" I yelled. The room went silent. "I understand that you want to help, but I need time alone with my kids. I'd appreciate it if you would all leave us for a few hours." I turned to Megan, George, and my mother. "Except for you three."

"But what about the Episcopal priest for the service?" Dad asked me.

"I am capable of making that decision on my own, thank you."

"Tom suggested the minister at his church," Megan said tentatively.

"Tom and Dave are back from their trip?" I asked.

She nodded as the doorbell rang. "That might be them. They called while you were gone. I let them know what had happened."

My throat stung with the effort of holding back tears. Tom's first partner had been killed in a violent accident not unlike John's. The memory of that loss collided with John's death as my knees buckled and my ears began to ring. Conversation came to me like snatches from a dream—Megan asking me if I needed to sit down; Tom's muffled voice talking to Kiley and Ryan in the entryway; footsteps down the hallway; my father asking Megan what church Tom attended. When Megan responded, Sue and Richard gasped in unison.

"That's not a Christian church," Sue said. "It's one of those New Age-types."

"If you can even call it a church," Richard said with disgust. "And I think the minister is a . . . a . . . *homosexual.*" He spit the word out as though each of the letters burned as it passed between his lips.

Tom now stood in the doorway, one arm around Kiley, the other around Ryan, with Dave behind him, his hands protectively on Tom's shoulders. All four had tears streaming down their faces as they stared in disbelief at Richard Hansen.

My mother rubbed her hands together. "Well, that settles it. The gay vicar it is."

I burst out with a laugh and hugged her. "Way to go, Mom. John would have loved this moment." Then, in a hiccupping transition, my laughter became a series of choked sobs.

Mom handed me over to Tom, who rocked me gently from side to side. The man who was more a brother to me than my own flesh and blood didn't say anything. It wasn't necessary. Because Tom had been there, too. To the place no words can ever reach.

Chapter 11

The euphemisms for death baffle me. Passed on. Lost. *Lost? Really? Try and find them!* Crossed over. Made his transition. That last one sprang from the lips of Matt Morris, the minister at Tom and Dave's "New Age" church. Matt stopped by on Sunday afternoon to discuss a memorial service with me. Something about him seemed comfortable, almost familiar. I took an instant liking to him, so I forgave him the catch phrase, but it still rankled.

Perceptively picking up on it, he offered an apology and an explanation.

"I'm sorry. I don't mean to trivialize your experience. In our tradition, we believe that the soul continues on after death of the physical body. So, when we say someone has made his or her transition, we are referring to their soul, which is still living."

Matt and I were alone at my kitchen table. Megan had taken Kiley and Ryan to her house for a few hours. Tom and Dave were in town to pick up my favorite Chinese food which they thought they could force me to eat. George was taking a nap. Everyone else was gone.

"I agree with you in principle, Matt, but from where I sit, John Scott is dead. The soul who became John Scott in this lifetime may be floating around somewhere getting ready for his next life, but he won't be John anymore. The man who shared my life and could make me feel that all was right with the world just by holding me is gone for good."

Matt nodded appreciatively, but a distant sadness framed his eyes. Something pulled at my heart, making me wish I'd held my tongue.

"Forgive me, Matt. What my mother calls honesty, I call blunt, bordering on rude. Unfortunately, I seem to be carrying on in the family tradition."

He shook his head and smiled. "I find your honesty refreshing. And you wouldn't believe some of the things I've heard at funerals."

"Try me."

By the time Tom and Dave returned with the Chinese food, I could barely breathe from laughing so hard at Matt's stories.

"Well, another point for me," Tom said, pulling the little white cartons out of the bag. "I knew you two would hit it off."

Dave opened a carton and began spooning broccoli beef onto my plate. "No arguments, young lady. Eat."

I smiled. "Thanks, Daddy Dave."

"Daddy Dave?" Matt chuckled. He had the habit, I'd already noticed, of tilting his head back when he laughed. His perfectly straight, dark brown hair was cropped at the ears, almost like a Beatle bob. His eyes were a pretty light brown and ever so slightly almond shaped, a fact that was barely noticeable until the black, wire-framed Harry Potter glasses slipped down his nose. His cheeks were sprinkled with freckles, while his skin was a lovely shade of medium brown. All in all, the completed picture was of a human being whose DNA probably hailed from all four corners of the globe.

"Stop staring at the poor man," Tom exclaimed. "I apologize for my friend, Matt. Must be the grief. Although, come to think of it, she's usually worse."

I flushed. "How rude of me. I just find your face fascinating." I frowned. "That didn't come out right. What I mean is, you're good looking in a different sort of—oh good lord! That was no better." I pretended to smash my face into my plate of food to end my embarrassment.

Matt flashed perfectly white, perfectly straight teeth at me. "I already told you; I like your honesty. It's amazing what people think they can't say around me because I'm a minister. Or what they expect me not to say for the same reason. It's nice to be treated like a regular person."

"Even if it's by an irregular person?" I was poking fun at myself, but then I realized another way that "irregular" could be taken, and I went red in the face all over again. "I . . . uh . . ."

Matt laughed and shook his head. "Better quit while you're ahead."

George entered the kitchen. I introduced Matt to my father-in-law, then pulled out the chair next to me. "Would you like some Chinese food, Dad?"

George sat down and replied in a weary voice, "Yes, please. The nap helped, but only a little. I've had so much trouble sleeping each night that I wind up leaving the den to lie on the family room couch with the TV on to distract me. I doze occasionally, but I'm still exhausted."

"I know what you mean," Tom said. "When I finally do get to sleep, my dreams are all over the place, and I don't mean in a good way."

George looked thoughtful. "I don't usually recall my dreams, but I had one Friday night that's stuck with me. Not really a nightmare, just very odd."

"How so?" Matt asked. "If you don't mind a stranger asking you such a personal thing."

George smiled at Matt. "Not at all. I dreamt that a trapdoor appeared in the ceiling of the family room. A blue mist poured down out of the opening, and the next thing I knew, a young man with blond hair was standing over me. Then he just vanished."

I stared into my cup of tea, not daring to make eye contact with anyone. With a houseful of people for the past few days, I couldn't exactly sneak a quick trip to Amoran to let the Guardians know what had happened. When I didn't show up on Friday for my weekly visit, Ari must have come through the portal, seen George, and then disappeared. Ari could stay invisible for periods of time, so he'd probably hung around long enough to figure out what was up. Truth was, I'd barely thought about Amoran since Thursday night, almost as if I couldn't process two worlds at the same time right now.

"That is strange," Tom said. After a few moments, he added, "How about we get going on the memorial service."

Matt listened to the four of us describe what John was like, then suggested several secular readings and outlined a talk he could give on love that wouldn't refer to a higher power. Tom agreed to make the arrangements with the community center to hold the service on Saturday, two days after Thanksgiving.

The memorial service was beautiful. Kiley sang a song with Dave accompanying her on the guitar. Ryan performed the magic tricks that John had been teaching him, with Matt as his trusty assistant. Matt also had a love of magic and was well versed in the standard tricks of the trade. Those additions to the service provided just the right touch, lightening up the somber occasion in a way that John would have appreciated. It was the perfect sendoff.

The day after the service, George returned to his home in Maine. Kiley had arranged weeks ago to spend the day with a friend, and I encouraged her to keep that plan. Ryan was the last to leave, setting out at noon for Jake's house to pick up some of his things. He hadn't asked to attend church with the Hansens, and I wondered if their behavior the previous Saturday had something to do with that. For all their professed concern about us, the Hansens hadn't come to the memorial service, no surprise there.

Several people had recommended that I "put my grief behind me and get on with my life," as if not-grieving were a miracle cure. As if it were possible to not grieve. I knew their advice was faulty, and yet, right now I experienced an impatience to do just that. I'd cried so much in the past ten days I didn't think I could possibly have any tears left. But there were always more. I was sick and tired of crying, of feeling like the ground under me had turned to quicksand and I'd sunk so far down I could only breathe through a straw. And pretty soon the straw might go under, too.

After George, Kiley, and Ryan left, I dragged myself upstairs to take a shower. I entered my bedroom to get my robe and drew in a choked breath. One of the things John had done when we moved into our hundred-year-old house was to build us a "proper closet," complete with his and hers sections with folding doors. I'd closed off John's side of our closet that first night; the sight of his clothes, neatly hung and waiting for him, too much to bear.

It was open now. How, I don't know. Slack-jawed, I stared at John's pants, suits, shirts, then lurched forward and grabbed an armful of his clothes. Clutching them to me, inhaling his scent, I willed him to miraculously appear in them.

He didn't, of course. And when they slipped off their hangars, I slid to the floor with them.

"You said you would always be here for me," I shouted. "You promised me! How could you leave me like this?"

The grief of death is bad. The rage of death is much, much worse. How can you be mad at someone for dying? It didn't last long, though, before the immense sadness beneath the rage hurtled to the surface again. "Come back. Please, *please*, come back."

Strong fingers gripped my arm.

"John?"

Hands brushed the hair from my face.

"*Ashara?*" I whispered in disbelief.

She drew me into her arms and rocked me like a child. The sweetness of that gift elicited a fresh wave of crying. It took a while, but when my tears were once again spent, I smiled my appreciation at her. Ashara returned my smile as she settled back against the wall of my closet.

"Do you recall that before the Reparention I told you I lived one lifetime on Earth?"

I nodded, wondering where this was going.

"It was quite an undertaking. My Amoran body had to be put in a form of Light stasis so that my spirit could embody in human form. I chose to do so from birth. I wanted to know what the entire experience as an Earth person entailed. Birth. Love. Sex. Joy. Pain. Even death.

"Nearly every soul incarnating on Earth is born ignorant of who and what they truly are. But I knew why I was there. I knew my husband-to-be the instant I met him. I knew what my task was in living that life. And yet, while my knowledge may have been greater, I lived the same reality as any Earth dweller." She shook her head. "My parents died before my twelfth birthday. At sixteen, I married a man I loved deeply and gave birth to my first child within the year." She gazed at the remainder of John's clothing still hanging. "At the age of three, my beautiful little girl lay dead from influenza. On Amoran I could have saved her, but on Earth?"

"Oh, Ashara! I can't imagine what that's like."

She eyed me carefully. "You *were* that little girl. It was the second time I had to watch helpless as you died in my arms. But it was no less painful, I can assure you."

"That was . . . you were . . ." I stopped, trying to fathom what she was saying. "You mean, you were my mother once . . . on Earth?"

She smiled. "Twice. It was imperative that you were born into that specific genetic line, one that would eventually provide you in this lifetime with the best physical body for what you have set before you. Two years later, you were successfully embodied once again. Another little girl with dark, wavy hair and beautiful hazel eyes tinged with an emerald hue."

"That's not far from my appearance in this life."

"As was intended."

And that would make the tenth lifetime that I'd been missing.

Ashara sighed. "You had just turned eight when a raging wild boar gored your father to death. It was heading for you next, and I had only one shot before it reached you. It is nothing short of miraculous that I succeeded, as marksmanship was not a skill I had perfected."

Ashara paused in her recitation. The image of her toting a gun was hard to accept. But of course, she hadn't been Ashara in that life. Like me, she'd been another person entirely. Different body, different personality.

"Which lifetime was this?" I asked.

"Your name was Hannah."

"Hannah! That's the lifetime when Ari and I fell in love. Which means, you were the mother I watched waste away, dying of cancer. That's why I was going to take my own life. I didn't want to die the same way you had." A sob escaped me. "All this time . . . I've never known."

Ashara closed her eyes for a moment, then gazed at me with something akin to tenderness.

"I must leave you now, Meiri."

"No! You just got here. Can't you stay awhile? I can pass you off as a distant relative, and it wouldn't be a lie."

"Unlike you, I am not a Vibrational. It is not possible, in my Amoran body, to remain here much longer."

"I wish you were a Vibrational." Loneliness seeped into my bones. "I could really use your company."

She brushed my hair back again. "You have survived much worse throughout your lifetimes, and you will certainly survive this. Take the time you need to grieve your loss. Come back to Amoran when you are ready. You will know when that is."

"What about finding Ashi?" As the words left my mouth, a realization hit. Today was the anniversary of the Reparention. One year ago, I had suffered another devastating loss.

"I consulted the Foreseers about that." She grimaced. "They say that all is proceeding exactly as it should."

"Great," I said with sarcasm. "John's dead, Ashi's missing and possibly dead. Any other surprises in store for me that are 'meant to be' and 'happening as they should'?"

Ashara seemed to go far away for a moment. "One thing at a time." She kissed the center of my forehead, and a peaceful feeling spread throughout me. "That will last for a while. It will not take away your grief. It will simply offer you comfort alongside the sorrow."

And with that, she left.

Chapter 12

John left our family well provided for, something I learned within those first terrible days after he died. Without telling me, he'd upped his life insurance considerably and added an accident policy. I'd have enough to pay our bills for the next ten years and give our kids a head start on college costs.

"When did he make this change?" I'd asked our insurance agent.

"About a year ago," she'd replied. "It's not uncommon for people to think more seriously about their life insurance needs when they've faced a tragedy, or potential tragedy. He said your accident during the Big Storm got him thinking, and he never wanted you to worry about money if something happened to him."

Grateful beyond measure for the financial reprieve that afforded me, I followed Ashara's advice to take as long as I needed and stayed on Earth through the following summer so I could be with my kids while the schools were closed. That was the practical reason. The other reason? I was afraid to leave them, even though I knew that if something happened to me while I was on Amoran, Kiley and Ryan would be well cared for. With three sets of backup guardians—Tom and Dave, Nancy and Bob, and my parents, they would never lack for love and attention. However, the long-term arrangements weren't foremost in my mind. I hadn't a clue how I was going to resume weekly trips to Amoran when I couldn't tell a soul on Earth where I was. True, that had been the case before John died. But now, with him gone, it seemed different somehow. Riskier.

Once the kids were back in school, I began to feel restless, edgy. Then, on a Thursday in late September, I came home from the Tea Leaf Café to find a letter on my kitchen table.

Meiri,

Ashara said we need leave you alone until you are ready to return. Since you're still not here, I thought I'd let you know how we are.

Balthasarre tried to perform a transitional rebalancing of the vortex. According to him, the signatures on the Earth end needed strengthening. Ashara figured it was just an excuse, so she sealed the Amoran portal until he promised not to go back to Earth to check up on you.

As for the Master Healer, she's been extra cranky, dragging everyone out for nemestes gathering, sometimes late in the day when the glazzien are particularly nasty. Which they are most of the time now, as they wake from hibernation.

Eliasser is more circumspect than ever. When he is not in "meetings," he spends a lot of time at the Resting Stones, frowning as he stares out into the mist.

Here's the final nugget of gossip. Seems the Resting Stones aren't just for resting anymore. I saw Anders and Meilee kissing behind them yesterday.

Yes. Kissing! The energy here continues to shift in baffling ways.

If this letter seems like a thinly disguised attempt at enticing you back, then I've failed. It's an out and out plea for you to return. Ashara will be furious if she finds out what I've done, but as selfish as this is, we all miss you. Please come home soon.

—Your Very Most Favorite Elf Extraordinaire

I folded the letter and gazed out the window. Not one mention of John or my loss, just talk of Amoran—a fact I found inexplicably refreshing. I ached to go back, and knew it was time. But so much had happened in the past year, I wasn't sure how to pick up the pieces of my other life.

I did what I always do when the right course of action eludes me. I trekked up the path behind my house to the same place I'd counseled and cried with my kids after John's death. The unofficial lookout spot was used mostly by those of us who lived in our small neighborhood of two dozen homes built over a hundred years ago. Since the entrance to the park and main trails were on the other side of the mountain, access on this side was only through someone's back yard. The rest of the land, stretching two-thirds of the way up the mountain, was privately owned. The title holder lived in Australia and apparently had no interest in developing the area.

I walked to the far end of the clearing where the land dropped sharply away. It was this steep, nearly impassable hillside that John had struggled up the day he'd sent the borrowed soccer ball sailing over the edge. Which is why I was surprised to see a man making his way up through the brambles, not seeming taxed in the least.

I'd hiked these woods for years and always felt safe. Today, however, I experienced the uneasiness that came from being a woman alone in a deserted place. I had the strongest urge to turn tail and run home, away from the clearing, away from the man who could navigate the sheer rise like a mountain goat. I even tried, but it was as if my feet were planted in buckets of cement.

My mouth went dry and my heart started to pound as the man gained speed, head bent forward as he sprinted up the incline. With a sprightly hop, he leapt up next to me.

"Hello," he said, smiling as he tipped the brim of his English pea cap.

"Oh," I cried out. Finally unsticking my feet, I backed away.

Wire-rimmed glasses rested on a slightly beaked nose. He had a close-trimmed full beard and long, medium brown hair tied in a ponytail. Spectacles and ponytail aside, he vaguely resembled Ashi, except with lighter hair and a shade darker skin.

The mystery man tilted his head to the side. "I've frightened you. I didn't mean to."

He *had* frightened me, but it was his similarity to Ashi that left me speechless.

The man looked around at the expansive horizon. "There is always so much to see. So much to do. I like to take time now and then to remember the past, and what the past has brought me, instead of always fretting about the future." He met my gaze. "You worry about the future?"

My voice came out small and unsure sounding. "Sometimes. Especially about taking long trips away from my—" I snapped my mouth shut. Why was I telling this stranger my personal business? I fiddled with the loose button on my sweater to avoid his constant and unnerving stare.

He was silent for a moment, then stepped past me. I turned toward him and he caught my eye at the same time. "Most of us worry, don't we?" he said thoughtfully. "It's what we do with the worry that counts, I think." He glanced around. "I like to reflect on the past."

He seemed a little fixated on that point.

"I have a friend who believes in the power of now," I blurted out.

The mystery man gave me a small smile. "Truthfully, there *is* only now; only this perfect moment." He shrugged. "And the next. And the next." He took a step toward me again, holding up his index finger. "Consider this, though. If there is no such thing as time, as some physicists say, and if the past, the present, and the future are all happening at the same instant, then isn't our past also part of our now?"

The tension eased out of my body. I was starting to like this guy. "Which makes the future we worry about also part of our now, right?"

His smile widened. "Which is why the past, and what it held for us at one time, is so important to resolve. So we can enjoy our future, not worry about it."

I looked down, tears filling my eyes. Intuitively, I knew this wasn't about the Reparention, or Ashi, or John. It wasn't about sadness, either. It was more a sense of longing, an acute aching, for something very old from a long ago past. I swiped at my face and looked up, just as the man cut between some trees behind the stone bench where no known path existed.

I descended the mountain slowly as I considered my mystery man's advice. If I ever ran into him again, I owed him a big thank-you. Because by the time I reached my kitchen, I'd formulated a plan to help me not worry so much about the future.

I picked up the wall phone—we still had a landline—and dialed my mother. After explaining to her that I needed to take some time for myself, she agreed to be listed as the primary contact for Kiley and Ryan on Fridays.

And then, she blew my mind.

"So." She chuckled. "Going to your fairyland place?"

I nearly fainted. "I'm . . . sorry . . . what?"

"You know, the one you told me about last year."

"I . . . I told you about Amoran?"

"Hell, I don't remember what you called it. You were so serious, you scared me. I said you were several cards short of a full deck and needed to see a shrink."

Shoot. I *had* told her about Amoran, in a moment of weakness when I'd felt too alone and burdened by my secret life. I'd hoped she could be my confidante. She'd thought I was nuts and handed me a business card for a psychiatrist she and my dad had met on a photo safari in Africa. Realizing the mistake I'd made, I had given her a literal cover story—that I was just trying out an idea for the novel I was (supposedly) writing.

My nonexistent novel. It worked the first time. Why not now?

"That's right. I'm going to my fairyland."

"Good. It's about time you finished that story. When do you want to start?"

Why wait? "Tomorrow okay?"

"Sure. How about I surprise the kids and pick them up from school so they don't have to ride the bus?"

Something about that bothered me, although I couldn't pin down what it was. Not wanting to put Mom off, I ignored the warning heaviness in my midriff, and agreed.

I landed in the Main Chamber the following day, changed into a tunic in my room, then went in search of . . . well . . . anyone. The Mountain was unusually quiet. I hadn't seen a soul since I arrived. Then again, time of day rarely matched up between Amoran and Earth. For all I knew, it was the middle of the night.

Up ahead, out of sight around a corner, I caught a snatch of conversation between two Mountain residents as they discussed getting to

Midday Meal. Their voices faded away before I reached the T-intersection, but at least I knew what time it was.

Excited by the possibility of surprising everyone, I made my way to the Main Meal Room, opened the doorway, and skipped over the threshold. "Ta-da!"

No one was there.

Odd. I know I heard them right. They said Midday Meal. I tried the Guardian Meal Room, then several of the Meeting Rooms, even the Celebration Hall, just in case. All empty.

The silent Mountain made me nervous. Breathing hard, I ran to the only place I knew was hardly ever left unattended. I burst through the doorway of the Healing Room, nearly knocking Clarisanna off her feet.

Her eyes widened and her hand flew to her mouth. "Bless the Light, is it really you?"

"Where is everyone?" I demanded, nerves on high alert.

Clarisanna took a step back, studying me with concern. "At the Garrammon field. There is a tournament today."

"Oh." My shoulders began to relax. "That explains it." I ran my hand through my hair, pushing it back away from my face. "I'm sorry if I startled you."

"No, Meiri . . . I . . ." Clarisanna wouldn't meet my gaze now as she traced the edge of a healing stone with her finger. "We are not accustomed to death beneath the Mountain; it happens so rarely. I want to say something to you about your husband's return to the Light. I want to offer words of comfort, but none seem adequate. All of us beneath the Mountain miss Makashannar deeply, feel his absence every day—but for you, his Twin?" She shook her head. "Now you have lost the presence of another who filled you so completely with love. I cannot imagine the sadness you must feel. Whenever I do dwell on it, my heart feels a pain as though it somehow knows, understands, and wants to share the burden you carry."

Blinking back tears, I reached for her hands. "First, you say you have nothing to offer me. Then you present me with the most beautiful words I've heard since John died. You could give lessons to more than a few people on Earth. Thank you."

With a shy smile, she squeezed, then released, my hands. "I must gather a splint and poultice and return to the field. Vianna hurt her leg."

Before the Reparention, Vianna worked in the Healing Room. After Ashi went missing, she transferred to the school, to help out there in his absence. I'd never been able to get close to the reserved Assistant, although I deeply respected her skills. I also knew that she was an excellent Garrammon player, so this must hurt in more ways than one.

Clarisanna rummaged in the large cabinet. "Vianna is not the first to suffer injuries today."

"There were others?"

"Many. Never before have we run out of healing supplies during a tournament."

Clarisanna pulled items out of the cabinet and stacked them on a healing stone. As I watched her work, I considered the effect my arrival could have on others who might feel the need to offer me words of comfort. Was there some way I could make my return to Amoran easier for all concerned? What if I made such a splashdown on re-entry that the reason for my long absence would take a back seat?

"Will Vianna be able to continue playing?" I asked.

"No. And she is quite upset, as she made it to the final elimination round this time. Unless a replacement is found, her team will have to forfeit."

"Can't someone who played earlier fill in for her?"

Clarisanna put the poultice in a satchel. "Aside from the number of injured players, the rules are quite specific on this point. No one who has participated in the tournament and been eliminated is eligible."

Seemed like a weird condition. "Who's her unlucky partner?"

"Ari."

I smiled to myself as an outrageous idea took form. When I shared it with Clarisanna, she not only agreed to help, but embellished my plan with some dramatic touches of her own.

"This will be a wonderful surprise," she said. "The mood here of late has been . . . unpredictable. That is partly the reason for today's tournament—to cheer us up."

"Why do you need cheering up?"

"The weather is gloomy most days. Ashara used a word . . . infected?" I nodded. "It seems to have infected us. Some are irritable; some sad." She added the splint to the bag, and smiled. "I cannot wait to see the Master Guardian's expression when he learns you are here."

Neither could I.

Clarisanna assembled the outfit I'd need to pull off my charade, then we set off for the Garrammon field. There was a possibility that Ashara or Eliasser might sense me as I approached. But since they didn't know I was on Amoran, I hoped the excitement generated by a tournament would keep them distracted enough to provide me with adequate "energetic" cover.

We reached the last hill before the field as the first call-to-play sounded.

"I will deliver the healing supplies to Ashara, then inform Eliasser that there is a replacement available," Clarisanna said.

I crept up the slope, crawling on hands and knees as I neared the top to avoid being seen by the spectators on the opposite hill. While I waited, I adjusted the dark brown *pilea* I was wearing. The long-sleeved, floor-length cloak had an oversized hood that would shield my face if I kept my head down. As an added precaution, I had rolled my hair into a loose topknot and covered it with a silver cap that concealed my ears and forehead. But the pièce de résistance was what I wore under the pilea. Clarisanna insisted on loaning me one of her "old" dress tunics to wear. I protested that the emerald green garment, shimmering with gold and silver gossamer threads, was far too beautiful to play Garrammon in. But she had shaken her head emphatically. "I have not worn it for many years. Besides, it suits you." She was right. The form-fitting style—atypical for a tunic—flattered my otherwise average figure, and the color perfectly matched my eyes.

Then came the voice I'd longed to hear for the past year on Earth.

"While the excellent ministrations of the Master Healer will soon put Vianna to rights," Eliasser boomed, as if he were talking through a megaphone, "she will be unable to play in the final elimination match scheduled to begin now. Thanks to Clarisanna's visitor, Ari has a new teammate and will not have to forfeit."

So far, so good. Clarisanna's cover story was that she had cleared the visitor with Ashara while Eliasser was away recently, figuring that both Guardians would be too busy now to check that information with each other. It didn't make sense that a person who hadn't yet played in the tournament trumped the ones who already had. But it worked to my advantage, so I wasn't going to complain.

Shielded behind a bush, I peeked through the branches. Eliasser stood on the field, bent over in conversation with Clarisanna as the final call-to-play sounded. He straightened up and bellowed, "All players to the field," then seated himself in the front row as Ari and the other team took their places.

And there was my cue. I strode over the hill, down onto the field, and took my position on the same side as Ari. Head tilted forward to hide my face, I bowed long and low to the people in the "stands." But instead of the quick bow that was customary, I stayed bent over. And waited.

The spectators began to murmur. Eliasser cleared his throat, then politely called out, "It is time to begin. But surely you do not intend to play in a pilea."

No one in their right mind would play in the bulky garment. I shook my head, then rose up in as stately a manner as I could, considering I'd stepped on the pilea's hem. At an incremental pace that would make a snail cringe, I turned away from the crowd, undid the pilea clasp, removed my arms from the voluminous sleeves and grasped the garment by the shoulders.

And waited.

"Do you need assistance?" Eliasser asked with a hint of impatience.

Show time!

I waved the pilea like a matador's cape, flung it to the side, about-faced, and tore off the cap, undoing my topknot in the process. As my long dark hair cascaded past my shoulders, I looked up into Eliasser's astonished face and added my final touch.

"Hi, honey. I'm home."

The crowd was supposed to go wild. That's how Clarisanna and I had pictured it. But as my eyes locked on Eliasser's, the silence was deafening.

"Ari," Eliasser called out, his deep voice tremulous. "Is that really Meiri standing near you?"

Ari gaped at me. "I believe it is."

"Then I am not dreaming?"

"Not unless I am as well, Master Guardian."

"Thank you, Arrien." And with that, Eliasser closed the distance between us with several long strides and crushed me to him. Oh, boy. That was all it took to open the Kerrin floodgates. Crying, like hugging, was not common beneath the Mountain. But an even greater incongruity were the tears being shed now by the Master Guardian. The crowd stayed quiet, as though uncertain how to respond to this unusual behavior in their esteemed leader.

"I wanted to surprise you, Eliasser," I whispered. "I didn't mean to embarrass you."

He loosened his grip on me and smiled. "You did an admirable job of surprising me, my Meiri. As for embarrassing me . . ." He wiped his eyes with the sleeve of his aqua pilea, then turned back to the watchful crowd. "Meiri has brought us many wonderful gifts of expression from her experiences living on Earth. I have discovered tears to be one of the most precious."

The spectators inexplicably broke into applause.

Eliasser leaned in toward me. "Are you feeling all right being back? Energetically, I mean."

I nodded, unable to speak after the heartfelt—and public—admission he'd just made.

"Then, you should go break some legs."

I laughed. "No, it's . . . oh, never mind."

I didn't break any legs, and Ari and I didn't win the match. A betting official might have accused us of throwing the game, and it might have been true, although unintentional. Ari and I were just so damned happy to see each other, we played our worst game of Garrammon *ever.* His technique was even more atrocious than mine, if that can be imagined after almost a year with no practice on my part. By the time the round ended it had turned into a clown act rather than a Garrammon match.

The highlight was when Ari, after making a singularly poor attempt at fielding the ball, bowed low and long to the spectators just as I had done earlier. Even beginning players know you never turn your back on the field when a ball is in play. The opposing team managed to volley back just as Ari bobbed up from his bow, the ball heading straight for his head. I was laughing so hard, I couldn't spit out the word "duck" fast enough, so I simply shoved him out of the way. Falling into a heap, we kept right on laughing, until shouts of warning reached our ears. The ball continued its trajectory into the crowd, where Anders caught it and tossed it back to the field. It disappeared, then rematerialized directly over Ari and me on a new flight path—straight down. At the last second, Ari thrust his arm up and the ball smacked into his hand, saving us from a painful end.

And the crowd finally did go wild.

Chapter 13

One week after my surprise arrival on Amoran, the Master Guardian returned from one of his interminable meetings. He'd been summoned away the morning after the Garrammon tournament, which meant I'd barely had any time with him.

I was sitting in my usual seat when Eliasser walked into the Guardian Meal Room. The Guardians were once again taking their meals separate from the rest of the Mountain, although no one could tell me why. I'm not sure they knew.

The other Guardians exchanged welcome back greetings with Eliasser, however I couldn't seem to speak. As the mealtime chatter picked up again, Eliasser sat down to my right. But instead of filling his plate with nourishment, he folded his hands and looked sideways at me.

That's when I realized we were breathing in sync.

No, that wasn't quite right. It was as if we drew the same air into a single pair of lungs that belonged to both of us. This made no rational sense, but the experience of deep union filled me with awe. And a curious longing.

Our surreptitious gaze held. I touched my palm to my heart, then let the back of my hand rest on the table. Eliasser mimicked my gesture, allowing his palm to cover my upturned one. At the same moment, our fingers intertwined and our lungs pulled in deeply, filling us with air that seemed physically and emotionally charged. When Danaeus asked him a direct question, we finally released our hold on each other.

My eyes landed on Ashara, who had witnessed our interchange, her expression thoughtful.

Eliasser and I spent the afternoon together. After a long walk through the Outer Grounds, we settled ourselves side-by-side at the Resting Stones to watch what should be the evening mists—they now occurred late afternoon, another perplexing shift in our weather patterns—billow over the western side of the Mountain and sprawl across the plain beyond the stream. I'd just confronted Eliasser with the concerns Ari raised in his letter to me, minus the bit about Anders and Meilee kissing. Eliasser wasn't pleased about the violation of Ashara's orders to not contact me, but I pointed out that if Ari hadn't done so, I would still be on Earth thinking I couldn't make a go of my bi-dimensional life.

"Well?" I prompted, to get the discussion back on track. "What about the energy changes? I think it's time to stop kidding ourselves that what's happening is normal."

"I have nothing to say about Ari's perspective on things."

The tightness around Eliasser's eyes, the way his fingers curled into his palms, and his flat voice told another story. Eliasser had plenty to say, he was just unwilling to do so.

Instead of challenging him, I pried open one of his fists and intertwined our fingers. Using our joined hands as a conduit, I directed soothing energy from my heart to his. I wasn't sure why my ability to channel energy had increased since I'd returned, although I had my suspicions. Over the past seven days, I'd witnessed some of the things Ari mentioned in his letter. Normally, the energy in Guardian Lands was peaceful. It could be strong, even energizing at times, yet was always somehow serene. Now the air seemed charged with a restless feeling, the energy . . . ramped up somehow. Along with those changes came heightened emotions, and for me, an increase in abilities that had long lain dormant.

"You are the changed one," he said softly, giving my hand a squeeze.

"I'm probably affected by the same energy alterations you refuse to openly acknowledge. I've had help, though. Our Vortex Prayer intensive. Ashara's retraining. Heart Coalescence."

Eliasser frowned. "That was impulsive of me to do. I was struggling with a question the Foreseers had put to me. It caused me great discomfort to have to search my heart, my mind, and my soul so deeply for answers."

Once again, I experienced the confusion, fear, and pain he'd suffered that day. It was paired with something else, though, the nature of which eluded me. It almost felt like guilt, but I couldn't imagine what the Master Guardian—whose decisions and actions were always impeccable—had to be remorseful about.

I breathed deeply to control my own feelings so I could deal with his. Which reminded me that I had something else to tell him.

"Here's another thing that's different. I'm feeling what you're feeling right now. It didn't subside after our Heart Coalescence. If anything, it's growing stronger."

He withdrew his hand from mine, pressed his eyes shut and leaned his head back against the Resting Stone. "What I did that day was selfishly motivated. I wanted to be as close to you as I could be. Our hearts, Meiri, they are so—" He broke off and shook his head. "I initiated Heart Coalescence with you to ease my own pain, not for the deep, sacred sharing it is meant to be. Or for the way it might help you to locate Ashi."

I went breathless for a moment, remembering the exquisite sensation of our energies blending . . . growing . . . supporting each other. Regardless of the reason for it, we had both benefitted from coalescing our hearts. From Eliasser's point of view, I understood why he might have mixed feelings about it. I guess not *all* of his actions were impeccable, but as far as I was concerned, he needn't burden himself over this.

"You should know by now, my dear sweet king, that I would do anything to ease your pain, to help you. Anything at all. You asked my permission that day, not with words, but with your eyes and your feelings. And I said yes. Willingly. If it helps me locate Ashi, all the better."

Eliasser stared at his fingers, flexing them the same way I had done that day. "Your answer relieves me, but only in part. I hope you never regret it.

"Why would I—"

He held up his hand. "You may not have given that 'yes' as freely as you imagine. The Foreseers enlisted Ashara's aid to increase the effect of the Vortex Prayer."

I considered our first prayer session. "Ashara helped with the vibrational enhancement?"

"The Foreseers took care of that. Ashara's special talents were needed to further augment the prayer."

"But her primary skill is in potion making, not tweaking energy. I don't see how her expertise fits in."

And then, unfortunately, I did. I am not often a quick study, but in this case . . .

"She's been dosing us?"

Eliasser sighed. "Quite heavily."

"With what?"

"A reverse shielding draft that allows you and I to be more fully connected. My energy frequency, being nearly identical to Ashi's, can act as a beacon radiating through your Spirit. The more joined our Spirits can become, the greater will be your beacon."

Not that I minded being more fully connected to Eliasser, but I didn't like the part where we'd been manipulated. Why couldn't she just tell us what was going on? And whatever the Foreseers were haranguing Eliasser about was clearly upsetting him. And, by extension, me.

"I promise you, Eliasser, I will find Ashi, but I will do it without damaging your heart and your mind and your serenity in the process. For you to help me, I need you as you usually are. Whatever the Foreseers are putting you through, make them stop it. Right now."

Sadness framed Eliasser's beautiful aqua eyes as he directed his attention to the growing mist. "I am sorry, Meiri, for what this does to you. But I fear we cannot stop what is to come. I will do my best, but they have me . . . what is that silly saying you used before the Reparention? The one that makes no sense at all?"

"Caught between a rock and a hard place?"

He smiled. "Not that one, although it also makes little sense."

"Oh . . . they have you over a barrel?"

"Yes. But I am resisting them."

"Good. Keep at it." I sat up and adopted my best Ashara impression. "And now, you and I are not leaving the Resting Stones until we talk about these energy changes."

Eliasser and I had such a long discussion that the sun set, the mist cleared, and the stars came out before we returned to the Mountain. We arrived at the Guardian Meal Room, ravenous but at peace with each other. Evening Meal was long since over, but thanks to some kind soul who left food for us, we took our solitary repast at the empty table.

We weren't alone for long. One by one, the Guardians began to arrive.

I raised my eyebrows in question at Eliasser.

"Ashara," was his one-word explanation.

I'd suggested to Eliasser out at the Resting Stones—demanded, actually—that we have a meeting as soon as possible to go over all that he and I had discussed. I hadn't meant tonight.

"Did she listen in on our entire conversation?" I asked.

Eliasser managed a small smile as Ari entered and sat down. "You can be sure of it."

Danaeus and Anders took their places. Balthasarre arrived, followed by Clarisanna.

"She really did hear everything," I said, surprised by the Master Healer's speed and openness. For his part, Eliasser had objected—without good reason, in my opinion—to the request that a few non-Guardians attend.

When Meilee entered on the heels of Ashara, Eliasser sighed. "A student?"

"A very talented student." I smiled at Meilee, which she didn't catch because she'd shifted her gaze to Anders. They both reddened considerably as he set a chair for her next to him.

"They are heading for trouble," Ashara whispered as she plunked down next to Eliasser.

I looked from Meilee to Anders, then back to Ashara. "If this energy situation is to blame, then what they are feeling will probably go away when we fix it. And if their attraction remains afterward, where's the harm in it?"

Eliasser had his own take. In the interest of full disclosure, which I insisted we needed now, I'd finally told him about the kiss between Meilee and Anders.

"If they remain so afflicted," Eliasser said grimly, "our entire way of life is threatened."

Afflicted? Way of life *threatened*? I was so taken aback, I couldn't respond.

Mikellan, one of the Gossip Twins, as Ari and I had taken to calling them, came through the doorway carrying a tray with two carafes. Esteven, the snottier of the two, followed with another tray of goblets, and a third Assistant brought the Amoran equivalent of snacks. Apparently, this was going to be a long meeting. I would have preferred a good night's rest first, but I was impressed by the swiftness with which my suggestions had been acted on.

Ashara had them set another chair at the table. When that was accomplished, the three food Assistants headed back to the doorway.

Ashara whispered to Eliasser, who called out, "Would you please remain, Mikellan?"

"Certainly, Master Guardian," Mikellan replied, with a quick glance at Esteven. After an exchange of surprised looks, the other two left. Ashara closed the doorway, then pointed to the empty chair at the end of the table.

"Sit down, Mikellan."

"But . . ." Mikellan blinked several times. "How will I serve the fairybee wine?"

Ashara's expression was her version of an eye roll. "You will not be serving; we serve ourselves as you very well know. Now, sit!"

He perched on the edge of his seat like he expected to be booted out any minute.

"What is this about?" Balthasarre asked, glancing around the table at the extra bodies.

Mikellan wasn't the only one the Master Healer had blindsided. She had apparently called them all to a special meeting, in the Guardian Meal Room no less, without giving even the Guardians an explanation. And then, she ambushed me as well.

"Meiri. Say a blessing and begin your meeting. We have much to discuss."

"*My* meeting?" I froze, as all eyes focused on me. Some of these folks had been roused from their beds. I didn't think they'd appreciate a delay, but I was totally unprepared to lead a meeting. And a blessing? Not once since I returned to Amoran post-Reparention had I been called on to perform the blessing. Ashara had put me on the spot tonight, on two counts. But protocol and etiquette dictated that I do as she commanded.

"A minute please," I whispered to the group, self-consciousness warming my cheeks.

I placed my hands in my lap and stared down at them, avoiding eye contact as I tried to conjure up a standard blessing. But I was so nervous at that point, I couldn't recall a single one.

A full minute passed. My self-consciousness grew. My mind remained a complete blank.

Eliasser's hand closed over mine, gave a comforting squeeze, then withdrew. I appreciated his support, but my brain seemed to be taking a vacation.

There was only one thing left. Why I was reluctant to do this escaped me, but I handled my lack of words the same way I had addressed the Mountain community during my welcome back celebration a year ago.

One Light, please guide me. For that matter, guide us all.

Moments ticked by in a deafening silence as I awaited inspiration. Someone cleared their throat, followed by the rustle of people shifting in their seats. With my self-consciousness about to morph into mortification, I decided to turn the blessing over to Eliasser, whose sweetly chosen words always lifted us up. But when I opened my mouth to ask for his help, a strange thing happened. In quick succession, my jaw tightened and relaxed a half dozen times as my nerves tingled, head to toe. Then, every muscle in my body released a level of tension I didn't know I was holding. Next, a sense of peace, of sheer . . . serenity permeated me to my core, followed by even more intense nerve tingling that became so uncomfortable, I bolted to my feet with a gasp.

I don't know why standing helped ease the tingling, but as my nerves quieted, my eyes gently closed. And the necessary words finally came to me.

No. Not *to* me. Through me. Words poured through my Being with a force and passion I'd never experienced, my voice resounding off the walls of the room.

"The One Light guides us in all things. Every thought, feeling and insight comes to us from Its perfect Light, comes *through* us because we *are* that perfect Light."

My hands trembled; my arms shook as I allowed the energy now coursing through me to raise them up.

"I beseech all of us, command all of us, in the name of that Light-that-we-are, to accept, call forth and *become* our perfect guidance. Our perfect selves, united, connected, and acting as One."

My body shuddered with pure emotion as the One Light continued to use me as its vessel.

"And through this perfect guidance-that-we-are, we accept and fulfill the challenges set before us with right action, done in right timing, felt with right emotion, and conducted in right physicality. So be it!"

My direct connection with the One Light lessened, leaving me self-conscious once more. Channeling energy was commonplace here. Channeling the One Light? Not so much.

The first one to break the silence was unexpected. "It is true," Mikellan whispered. "You are the only one who can find Makashannar."

I opened my eyes and sank slowly back into my chair. Surprisingly, it was Balthasarre, not Eliasser or Ashara, who asked, "Has this ever happened to you before?"

I shook my head, blinked to forestall any tears that might come as an emotional aftermath, and looked to Ashara, hoping for guidance.

"About a mouthful will do," she said, handing me a soft-sided travel carafe.

I lifted my eyebrows in question as I unplugged the stopper and took a few sips.

"It is a special potion to normalize vibrations after a Speak-Through," Ashara explained. In all my time on Amoran, I'd never heard the term before. But the fact that she had come prepared with the potion told me that somehow, some way, the Master Healer suspected this might occur.

"I have only made this potion twice in all my years," Ashara continued. "Meiri has done exceedingly well for her first time channeling the One Light."

I struggled to keep from going weepy at the uncommon compliment.

Her gaze rested on me. "As precious as this moment is, we must move on. I am sure you will do equally well leading us in the journey to follow, which begins with this meeting."

My days chairing school committees came in handy. I had large sheets of the parchment-like paper common under the Mountain brought to the Guardian Meal Room, where Ari magically affixed them to the wall behind Eliasser and Ashara. Then we brainstormed, a concept I had to explain more than once until they got the hang of it. Using the "five Ws and one H" from a journalism class I'd had in college, we filled up ten sheets of paper with what, where, who, why, when, and how.

The "what" turned out to be the hardest part. Ari had noticed alterations in the energy and weather patterns soon after the Reparention. They'd been slight at first, the level of shifts that only an elven energy worker might notice. Then, the changes grew so gradually over time that the Mountain residents were able to acclimate without realizing things were different. That part was hard for me to fathom, but like people in a marriage that's been slowly going off the rails for years, this group was in serious denial. For my part, I'd noticed minor things easy enough to discount before John's death kept me away from Amoran for nearly a year. But when I returned a week ago? There was no way I could *not* see the changes, and how much they'd increased.

With an apologetic look at Anders and Meilee—who were probably the two most aware of the changes, but had the most to gain by keeping it to themselves—I had to confess that *some* Mountain residents were experiencing *certain* feelings. Putting it delicately got me nowhere. I finally had to bluntly say that some people had been witnessed kissing—in *that* way.

Meilee and Anders turned as red as vallius flowers.

"Who is kissing?" Danaeus demanded.

"That is not for me to share," I said in perfect imitation of Ashara.

"But . . ." Clarisanna said. "We should help them to *not* feel that."

I gave Ashara and Eliasser each a long, hard look. "Perhaps they like the way they feel. I believe the interested parties should have a say in what happens next."

"They are having parties?" Danaeus asked.

Ari and I shared a smile.

"No," Meilee answered. "We are not having parties. But we are kissing. And I am most definitely enjoying it."

Anders rose from his seat. "As am I. And, we have been kissing for quite some time now."

I thought Balthasarre was going to pass out. He swayed in his chair and his head dropped into his hands. "Oh, dear Light."

Ashara waved her hand and a potion cup appeared in front of him. "Drink quickly, my friend," she said. Then she flicked her fingers at the invisible doorway to admit a healing Assistant. He placed a tray containing an oversized carafe and ten small potion goblets in front of Ashara, then left.

"Reviving draft?" I asked her in surprise after taking a sip.

"You were expecting a shielding draft?"

"Frankly, yes." Ashi and I had needed to consume super-strength shielding drafts before the Reparention for two reasons: to keep us from spontaneously merging and to dampen our increasing physical attraction.

"It might surprise you to learn that I am in total agreement with you on this point."

It did, considering she'd thought Anders and Meilee were "heading for trouble." But I held my tongue. We had work to do.

We narrowed down our lists, settling on two possible causes for the energy changes: altered energy patterns spilling out of the vortex, or the time warp/energy anomaly thing that Ari and I had experienced. Needing a more succinct label for the latter, I dubbed it the Garrammon

Meadow Anomaly, then shortened it to just the Meadow Anomaly. The possible vortex spillage was about to be crossed off when I forced Eliasser's hand, making him admit that he accessed his meeting location from within the Seventh Vortex. That took an hour of discussion to parse out, especially with Eliasser still mum on where he went and what he did. But Balthasarre determined that whatever the Master Guardian was doing in the vortex was not causing a problem.

For the next two hours, we hashed out the Meadow Anomaly, with the technical folks—Anders, Balthasarre, and, surprisingly, Meilee—taking the lead. Eliasser was adamant that while the meadow was not the best place to take a stroll, the Foreseers had cleared it long ago.

"Long ago," Meilee repeated. "What about recently?"

"I think they would alert us if there was a problem," Clarisanna ventured. She'd been quiet so far, and I think she felt awkward.

"They didn't alert me the first time," I noted with asperity.

Ashara drew a sharp breath "No. They did not. You were with them just before you encountered the Meadow Anomaly, yet they said nothing."

Eliasser squeezed his eyes shut. "Dear Light. They allowed Meiri and Ari to be caught in it."

Silence prevailed as everyone digested that.

"Then the Meadow Anomaly must carry some significance, beyond it being a dangerous abnormality," Clarisanna said at length. She spread her hands out. "If we think of it like a dysfunction in the body, there should have been something the two of you"—she indicated Ari and me—"sensed beforehand."

Ari, who also had been extraordinarily quiet, said, "I felt absolutely nothing. It was Meiri who didn't think we should go in there."

I shook my head. "I didn't sense anything unusual. I did have a vague feeling that we shouldn't go in there, although that could have been guilt over disobeying Eliasser's request that I return directly to the Mountain. The fact that Ari couldn't detect anything until he literally fell into it is what has me curious."

Meilee looked at Ari. "Could it be something that you, even with your skill as an energy worker, had no reference point with which to identify? Perhaps you could not sense it because . . ." She paused, brow furrowing. "Because it did not exist until you encountered it."

"Impossible," Balthasarre exclaimed, eyeing Meilee with incredulity. "There is always a moment before even the slightest of anomalies when the vibration shifts enough to be noticed, certainly by an elven energy worker!"

Poor Balthasarre. He still hadn't recovered from the kissing revelation.

"Remember," I said. "We're considering all ideas, even the seemingly impossible ones."

Something nagged at me, but it was just out of my reach. I looked at Ari.

"You are the one who noticed the changes beneath the Mountain first. Did they increase after we encountered the Meadow anomaly?"

He nodded. "I believe so."

"Which also coincides with your return to Amoran," Mikellan offered, sliding a glance at me. He, too, had been mostly mum.

"And your point is?" I snapped. Was he blaming the insignificant Earth dweller for all their troubles? He was Ashara's choice for the meeting, not mine.

"I do believe we are tasked with considering the impossible," Ashara said evenly to me. "Even if it comes from an unexpected source."

Damn. She was right. However, I wasn't ready to give in totally, so I merely nodded.

"Go on," Ashara said to Mikellan. "What is your reason for making this connection?"

Mikellan blew out a sigh. Avoiding my stare, he said, "I am not an energy person, of course, but with food—as with potions, I imagine—you sometimes need the interaction of two substances to create a third, new one. Or, at the least, to enhance the original two, even if they are left in their original form."

"What does that have to do with anything?" Ari said. He wasn't a fan of Mikellan either.

I held up my hand to stave off another interruption and focused on the food Assistant.

"Are you suggesting that it was only when I returned to Amoran that the Meadow Anomaly could occur because it needed Ari's and my unique energy signatures to set it off?"

Mikellan nodded without meeting my eyes.

Shoot. He *was* useful. "Thank you, Mikellan."

Meilee, the boldest of the new arrivals, scanned the lists we'd made, then began to tick points off on her fingers.

"The Reparention occurs. Meiri stays on Earth for nearly a year. During that time, Ari notices some minor energy changes that worry him. No one else is concerned, and it is attributed to energy resettlement after the Reparention. He brings it up a second time and is still assured that nothing is wrong. Meiri returns."

"Her return would not have an effect," Eliasser grumbled. He had a problem with Meilee being here, but was it really just because she was still a student? He'd confided in me once that he suspected she might become Master Guardian someday.

"Remember. We're not discounting anything yet," I said. I nodded at Meilee to go on.

"Meiri and Eliasser perform the Vortex Prayer. Eliasser ethermoves from the Glen. Ari and Meiri take the Mindsail Lake to get back to the Mountain, but decide to go swimming first."

Everyone but Ari and I shuddered.

"They enter the meadow and are caught in the Meadow Anomaly for three days. Eliasser rescues them. The Foreseers advise that the Meadow Anomaly is over, and the meadow is safe."

"Nice recap. Thanks, Meilee." I turned to Ari. "How soon after that did you notice the changes increasing?"

"Not right away. The biggest shift came while you were on Earth after John died."

"Interesting," Balthasarre said. "Meiri could not be responsible for that increase."

Danaeus leaned forward. "What if the Meadow Anomaly was an initiating event?"

Ari looked thoughtful, then shook his head. "It might have intensified things, but I noticed Meilee and Anders going pink in the cheeks before then."

And there they go again, I thought, hiding my smile. My intuitive sensor picked up their affection, but it went beyond that. They were falling in love. What's more, I suddenly saw, as if in a vision, a pink mist surrounding them. The same kind I experienced with Eliasser and Ashi.

"I think Meilee and Anders are Twin Lights," I said in a hushed voice.

Eliasser looked at Ashara like she'd done something wrong.

"What?" she barked at him. "I know many things, but I am not omniscient."

"Why do you say that, Meiri?" Balthasarre asked.

"I can see it," I replied. "The sparkling pink aura of Twin Lights."

Gasps filled the air. Eliasser closed his eyes and hung his head, while Ashara shot me a look that said I'd just let the cat out of the bag. Their reactions didn't make sense—until I recalled the way the pink mist surrounded Eliasser and me during the Garrammon tournament.

"Does that mean you and the Master Guardian are Twin Lights?" Meilee asked. "I thought Makashannar is your Twin."

"And I did not know the pink mist was for that reason," Clarisanna added.

"Until now," Anders whispered. "It explains so many things that we see in our minds when we are together." He glanced at Meilee, who blushed.

Balthasarre cradled his head again. "Oh. Dear. Light."

I drew my lips between my teeth, thinking. I'd basically just broadcast our multi-twin relationships, which was not common knowledge and meant to be kept that way. There were three distinct directions this meeting could take, but I wanted to be sure we chose the right one for now. I knew what I wanted that to be, but there was a risk.

"Ashara?" I whispered.

After a moment's pause, she nodded. "It is time. And may the Light continue to guide us in the days to come."

Swallowing the lump that suddenly formed in my throat, I lifted my head and told the story that had never been divulged outside of the six of us who were not only Vortex Lights, but Twin Lights as well: Ashara and Asharren, Eliasser and Elianna, Makashannar and me.

"Ashara, and her Twin Light, Asharren," I began, "were created directly from the condensed energy of the Seventh Vortex as a single point of Light that then separated to become two distinct entities."

"Twin Lights. As are you and Makashannar," Clarisanna noted.

"True; Makashannar and I are Twin Lights. We are also Vortex Lights. But Ashi and I were not created directly from the vortex energy."

Silence permeated the room. Every pair of eyes riveted on me.

I drew in a breath. "Thousands of years ago, the Foreseers asked Ashara and Asharren to merge inside the vortex."

"And they did not return to the One Light?" Mikellan asked, shocked.

"Obviously," Ari snapped.

It was a valid question. The merging of a Twin Light pair is a rapturous experience which typically only happens when they are ready to return to the One Light for good.

I smiled at Mikellan. "The Foreseers assured them that they could safely merge without rejoining the One Light. They did, however, spend several bliss-filled days within the vortex as a reunited Light. When it was time for them to separate into their individual light-bodies, a miraculous thing occurred. As they lowered their vibrations, an inversion of energy pulled them back together, re-merging them for an instant before they completed the separation in a burst of Light. Only now, there were four: two other Beings in light-bodies had been produced. A new Twin Light pair. Eliasser and Elianna."

Meilee's brows furrowed. "*All four* emerged at the same exact time and from a single joined Light?" I nodded. "Then that would make each female a Twin to each male. That is . . . astounding." With a quick glance at the Master Guardian, she asked, "Did Eliasser and Elianna also merge in the vortex, producing yet another pair of Twin Lights?"

"Yes," I confirmed. "Ashi and me."

"Then you and Eliasser *are* Twin Lights, as he is also a Twin to Ashara, who is also a Twin to Makashannar. And Asharren." Her hazel eyes grew wider with each proclamation.

I smiled. "Yes. Male to female, we are all Twins to each other. However, there is a very slight variation in vibrational frequency with each generation, which is why we say that Eliasser is Ashara's Second

Twin, Ashi is her Third Twin, I am Eliasser's Second Twin, and so forth."

"Oh, my!" Tears sprang from her eyes. "This is wondrous! Why could we not have known this earlier?"

"Yeah," Ari said stiffly. "Why not, Meiri?"

Ashara shook her head. "Do not chastise your closest friend for something that was out of her control. The telling of this story is an extremely potent vibrational catalyst, a harbinger of tremendous import, and should never be divulged lightly or to those not affected." She squeezed her eyes shut, then slowly reopened them. "Except now, it would seem."

"What happens when this story is told?" Balthasarre asked.

Ashara sighed. "When Asharren and I left the vortex the day that Eliasser and Elianna were created, the Foreseers shared with us our birthright as a Sacred Point of Light created from the Living Vortex. Three days later, my Primary Twin Light left to assist the vortexes of the Fourth Universe. He never returned and has not been heard from since.

"Many years later, when Elianna and Eliasser merged in the vortex, having also created another pair of Twin Lights, I told them of their birthright as the Second Lights of Asharren and myself. Three days later, Elianna left Amoran to assist the Thirteenth Vortex. To this day, she remains trapped inside a dimensional variance."

Meilee was a quick study, but Mikellan and Clarisanna caught up. "What happened three days after Meiri and Ashi learned of their birthright?" Mikellan asked.

"The Reparention happened," I said.

"And we lost Ashi," Clarisanna added.

The room went quiet, and I was pretty sure it wasn't just me wondering what was going to happen in three days.

Ashara broke the heavy silence. "Meiri, when did you become able to see the aura of other Twin Lights?"

"Tonight. When I looked at Meilee and Anders and felt the love they have for each other."

I smiled as they both blushed again, but Ashara frowned, as she looked around the table.

"Who else sees, hears or feels things that are new for them?"

Every hand went up, even Danaeus's.

Clarisanna hunched forward, like she was folding into herself to not be seen.

"And what is that you are experiencing?" Ashara asked wearily.

Clarisanna barely lifted her head. "I have not *experienced* it, but I know about the Heart Coalescence of Meiri and the Master Guardian."

Another round of gasps at that disclosure. So much for Heart Coalescence being a private matter.

Ashara leaned forward, fascination warring with dismay. "How do you know this?"

"I saw the circle that enclosed both their hearts at the time. It still does, in fact." Her eyes grew misty. "It is . . . quite beautiful."

"Yes, it is," Ashara said dryly. "You are sitting here, a witness to Eliasser's and Meiri's Coalescence, and you did not think it important to tell us this until now?"

Eliasser held up his hand. "Enough. This has been a lot to take in. Let us reconvene at a later time."

Bleary-eyed, we trundled off to our rooms. We hadn't solved our problems, but we'd at least brought them out of the shadows. I still believed that finding Ashi was connected to all of this, but I couldn't figure out how.

I opened the doorway to my room and crawled under my sleep cover, not having the energy to change out of my tunic. I slept till late morning and woke up to find Ari at my bedside.

Chapter 14

"Time to get up," Ari said.

"Time to be left alone," I grumbled. I pulled the sleep cover over my head, then peeked over the top. "It's a little creepy to wake up and find you watching me like that."

A slow smile slid across Ari's face and he wiggled his eyebrows.

"Make that a lot creepy." I flung the cover aside and stomped to the ancillary.

"How much time do you have left on Amoran?" he called out as I changed into a fresh tunic.

I did the math. "Around ten days, give or take."

"Wait. You've only been back a week so far. Don't you have six Earth hours on Fridays? That should give you at least another three weeks here."

"Normally, that would be true. But because no one knew I was coming, I'd already been on Amoran for a couple of hours before Ashara initiated time-stretching. Besides, this is the first time my mother is 'watching the kids,' so to speak, and I don't want to be away that long."

"It would only be a couple more Earth hours," he groused, as I entered the room again. "And you need to make up to me how you held out about the First, Second, Third Lights thing."

"I do not." Ari blew me a raspberry, and I rolled my eyes. "I'm going in search of whatever breakfast leftovers I can find. Tag along if you want."

There was nothing to eat in the Main Meal Room. Mikellan, who looked inordinately perky for someone who had been up most of the night, told us that Eliasser and Balthasarre were in the Guardian Meeting Room with fresh plates of sharing food—Amoran for appetizers.

Me and Grumpy the Elf burst in on Eliasser and the Master Technician, who were huddled over the papers we'd drawn up last night.

"Can we crash this party?" I asked, pointing at the food.

Eliasser nodded impatiently and went back to his work.

"Grouchy Gus syndrome strikes again," I said, with a knowing look at Ari—who stuck his tongue out at me. "Juvenile."

We sat down and helped ourselves. Ari's mood finally got to me and we took to bickering about nonsense, and not in our usual good-natured way.

Frowning, Eliasser looked up. "You have been quarreling without let up. Therefore, I am assigning you both to—"

"I am not gathering nemestes today," Ari snapped.

"—an afternoon of Garrammon to work out these unresolved tensions."

Ari hung his head. "Oh. I thought . . ." He shrugged. "I'm sorry, Eliasser."

"Apology accepted. You may take Danaeus and Anders, if they are willing to put up with the two of you. Balthasarre will remain here, as I have need of his expertise."

When I located Danaeus and Anders, I didn't have to ask twice. They raced us to the field.

The exercise felt great. We were into our second round of games when Ari lobbed the ball out of bounds. It sailed past the field and came to a stop at the edge of the Garrammon Meadow. I ran to retrieve it, crossed the path, and almost tumbled into a deep hole.

"Holy cow. Where did this come from?"

Anders ran to my side, followed closely by Danaeus and Ari. Danaeus gasped as the opening doubled in size and began undulating like a snake.

"Everybody, move!" Ari shouted. We backed up to a safe distance and were gawking at the writhing crevice from four feet away when the hole quadrupled its dimensions.

This time, we ran. We stumbled onto the Garrammon field and had just turned around when the sky darkened, and the gaping chasm lit up with a blinding light.

"Get further back," Ari yelled. "I'm going for Eliasser." He vanished.

Danaeus pulled on my arm, but I couldn't seem to move. I stared transfixed as light pooled, then billowed above the opening, looking like low clouds of iridescent steam. I had the strangest compulsion to walk to the edge and let myself fall into the brilliant abyss.

"Meiri," Danaeus pleaded as Anders grabbed my hand.

I shook them both off. "No," I whispered. "I'm needed here."

Arms circled my waist. I clawed at the hands. "No!"

"Yes!" Eliasser pulled me backward.

A plume of light shot a hundred feet into the air, then dropped down like a spent geyser.

Eliasser pushed me at Ari. "Keep her here!"

Ari reached for my arms, but I gave him a death-glare. "Don't even think about it," I hissed.

Eliasser strode to the rim of the crevice and peered down. I hadn't been afraid for myself, but I was suddenly terrified for the Master Guardian's safety.

"Come away from there," I yelled to Eliasser.

"The plume has receded, Meiri," he said in his forced-calm voice. "It will not—"

"You're wrong!" My heart pounded against my rib cage as an even larger geyser of light soared from the cavernous depths into a false night sky. Eliasser snapped his head back, the bright light illuminating his stunned expression. I ran forward and yanked the back of his tunic as the rift widened. We teetered on the edge until hands dragged us to safety, where we collapsed onto the grass. The second "plume" sank into the ground, the fissure closed, the sky brightened, and the meadow returned to normal.

The five of us stayed where we were, shocked into silence. Eliasser stirred first, rose to his feet and pointed toward the Mountain. "Ari?

Go with Danaeus and Anders," he barked. "Gather the Guardians in our Meeting Room. I will be there shortly."

I made a move to get up, but Eliasser shouted, "Not you. You are to remain here with me, and you will listen and obey that command for a change."

Ari gave me a worried look, then did as he was told.

I hugged my knees. The plume had been beautiful. Terrifying, yet magnificent. And in that moment when I ran forward, I'd thought of nothing else but that Eliasser shouldn't die. Ever.

Eliasser regarded me for a long moment before reaching his hand down. I let him pull me to my feet where he gripped me by my arms, his expression distant, as if he were looking at me, but seeing something far off.

"In trying to save me," he said in a tightly controlled voice, "you put your own life in peril. I must now extract from you a firm promise, a vow if you will. No matter what happens in the future, you must never again try to save me."

"I won't promise that," I said, imitating his controlled tone.

His grip on me tightened. "Do not be heroic where I am concerned. You must—"

"I must *nothing*. If you want me to say the words, I will do so for your sake, but I will be lying and you will know it, so what is the point?"

His stern façade collapsed, and he hugged me to him. With his own heart pounding along with mine, and his emotions filled with desperation, he pleaded with me. "You do not understand what is at risk. Please, my Light. Promise to never save me again."

Fear and longing made me want to stay wrapped up in his arms. But I pulled away and stepped back from him, as if space could give me the courage I needed.

"I won't promise you that because I can't. I am neither heroic nor courageous. I am merely impulsive, and where you are concerned, single-minded. The instant I think you are in danger, something beyond my control drives me to protect you."

It was a strange thing to say; that I had to protect the Master Guardian of the Seventh Vortex, who had been alive for thousands of years without needing my help at all.

But he didn't react to that. Moving closer, he peered intently into my eyes before uttering the words that chilled my heart. "There may come a day when only one of us will be able to survive. If that happens, it is my life, not yours, which must be forfeit."

I felt sick thinking that such a time might ever arrive. Yet my answer was the same. "I'm sorry. I love you too much to ever let you die. I can't. I won't."

A flash of sadness crossed his beautiful face and I felt his heart twist in pain. But then his expression morphed into such a cold, hard look, I felt as though I were being tossed over a cliff. He grabbed my arms again, this time so roughly I was afraid I'd have a bruise. "Then, my beloved Light, I promise you this. If I must hurt you to keep you from saving me, I will. If I need to sacrifice my own life to make sure you do not sacrifice yours for my sake, I will. And by all the love of the Light within me, I can assure you that is a promise that I will never break."

I wrenched free and ran most of the way back to the Mountain. And since I am not a runner, by the time I got to the Resting Stones, I was physically ill from the exertion, as well as emotionally sick from what had just transpired. I fell to my knees, vomiting, like I was trying to purge myself of the words Eliasser had spoken. Because my newly honed intuition told me that Eliasser's prediction might very well come true. Someday, he might have to die to save my life.

By some force of will, I made my way to the Guardian Meeting Room. The closer I got, the slower I walked, as if something in me knew that this was a defining moment.

I thought I would be the last to arrive, but I took my place next to Balthasarre and waited with the rest of the Guardians for Eliasser to show up. Devastated that a beautiful Amoran day could turn so swiftly into a nightmare, I kept eyeing the doorway hoping Eliasser would breeze through saying it was all a misunderstanding.

It took nearly an hour before he showed up, and not the usual way. Materializing behind his chair, he yanked it back, sat down, and stared at Ashara. When he broke contact, Ashara squeezed her eyes shut. This did not bode well for our meeting.

Eliasser leaned forward studying each one of us in turn—except for me—then looked down at the table. Had I disappointed him so greatly that he couldn't even make eye contact with me?

"There are many reasons I wish with all my heart that Makashannar was here with us. His counsel at times like this was always insightful. More importantly, his answers might hold the key to the appearance of a planetary dimensional anomaly which *should not*"—Eliasser banged his fist down on the table, causing us all to jump—"be happening on Amoran, and most certainly not inside our Protected Lands." He shook his head as if trying to break free from troublesome inner thoughts, then threw his hands up in the air. "I need to ask Ashi what occurred during the destruction of the Mirror Vortex."

It's an extremely rare occurrence, but sometimes a vortex nearing extinction creates a duplicate of itself, a Mirror Vortex, but with one key difference: the exit portal shows up on an entirely different planet. Elvener's Mirror Vortex appeared on Amoran before the Fifth Vortex implosion, which is how we first made contact with the elves. With Elvener's fate sealed, we were making ready to bring their entire population to Amoran through the temporary link provided by the Mirror Vortex. But that's the problem with vortexes. Their energy patterns can shift without notice. We thought we had enough time. But we were dead wrong. And an entire planet perished because of it.

"Of even greater importance," Eliasser said with a sigh. "We need to know what really happened to Elvener when the Fifth Vortex collapsed."

"We already know what happened," I said, my voice wavering. I may not remember much of my life on Amoran before going to Earth, but the memories of Elvener's final moments remained painfully intact. "You, Ari, and I were there when the Mirror Vortex collapsed in on itself. We barely made it out, but we know what happened. When the Mirror Vortex imploded, so did the Fifth Vortex, taking Elvener along with it."

Eliasser cradled his head in his hands before glancing up at the group. "I did not sleep after our meeting last night. Balthasarre and I read over our notes and reviewed the cosmic energy charts. And now, after what just happened in the Garrammon Meadow, I think . . . it is only a possibility, mind you." He took in our small assembly, still avoiding my eyes. "The slimmest of possibilities exists that when the Fifth Vortex collapsed, parts of Elvener, instead of being crushed by the implosion were repelled outward where they may have encountered a dimensional variance of astronomic proportions."

The room erupted in shouts of disbelief and confusion, but Ari's strained voice rose above the rest. "What if it isn't just pieces of Elvener? What if my entire world was somehow spared?"

Eliasser and Ashara bowed their heads, waiting for us to settle down. When quiet was restored, Eliasser answered Ari's question with a heavy sadness I could feel in the pit of my stomach. "Whatever might exist of Elvener will most likely be in a form not recognizable to us. Pieces of it—" Eliasser broke off and shook his head. "As for the entire planet?"

Ari's eyes flashed. "You're lying. The same way you've been lying about where you go, who you see, and what you do."

Eliasser flinched at the accusation while the rest of us stared at Ari in shock. To speak to the Master Guardian like that? And to imply that he was lying to us?

But instead of a reprimand, Eliasser merely said, "I will not dignify that thoughtless outburst with a response. What I am trying to communicate to you all is that the changes we have been experiencing, and now the eruptions in the Garrammon Meadow, may be caused by this unidentified dimensional variance. No one I have consulted has been able to ascertain where this variance might be. But if it continues, its effects are potentially deadly, putting Amoran in grave peril—and by extension, Earth."

Eliasser held his hand up to stave off another round of exclamations. "Please let me finish. Locating this variance is crucial. Makashannar was inside the Mirror Vortex when it imploded, then he was miraculously released a few days later. We do not know where he was since he has never been able to recall that time. But if any part of Elvener survived decimation by being drawn into a dimensional variance, it is Makashannar—and Makashannar alone—who holds the key to its whereabouts."

I was trying to figure out how even part of a planet could be misplaced and why it fell to my missing Twin to find it, when I began to feel uneasy about the direction this was taking.

"Judging by what some of us just witnessed in the Garrammon Meadow," Eliasser continued, "we are running out of time. The fate of Amoran and Earth rests on Ashi's return."

I stared at Eliasser in disbelief, even as the eyes of my fellow Guardians practically burned holes in my skin. But I waited. Waited for the Master Guardian to take back the words he'd just dropped like deadweights onto the table. Waited in the pin-dropping quiet for him to look me in the eye. Which he finally did. And the apology I saw there, unspoken, but communicated to me just the same, pushed away my anger leaving only distress, despair, and discouragement.

"I have tried everything I can think of," I said, squeezing the words out. "We may be running out of time, but I am out of ideas. The Foreseers claim that I will lead Ashi out of darkness, but who will cure me of my apparent inner blindness so that I can see the way?" I stood up. "I've failed. Everyone sitting at this table knows it, including you, Eliasser."

I left the meeting, and a strong impulse sent me straight to the Glen. I'm not sure what I expected the Foreseers to do or say, or even if they would appear. Maybe I just wanted them to convince me that there was still hope.

The floral display that bordered the perimeter below the ring of trees had changed since I was last there. I squatted down, cradled a flower in my hand and sniffed the curly red, green, and gold petals, disappointed that they were scentless.

Red and green. Christmas colors. In a few months, the season of sharing and caring would arrive on Earth. My second Christmas without John; the third since Ashi disappeared. I was beginning to hate Christmas. Hell, I was beginning to hate myself.

I felt something wet in my clenched hand. Unable to recall making a fist, I opened my fingers. The Christmas flower lay crushed in my palm, staining my skin bloodred.

How fitting. I killed a pretty flower. Add that to my list of sins.

Self-pity and self-recrimination were vying for first place in my bankrupt consciousness, when the sweet voice sounded behind me.

"There is much conflict in you today, Daughter."

"You got that right. Although failure is more what I'm feeling."

"At what have you failed, dear one?"

I stood up. The pink Foreseer was inches from me. "Finding Makashannar. It seems that the fate of Earth, Amoran, and some disembodied parts of Elvener rest on his return."

"And who has made the judgment that you have failed?"

"I have," I answered readily. "And it's pretty obvious to the rest of them, too." I waved in the general direction of the Mountain.

"Well, then. That is serious," she said, but so lightly as to discount the sentiment. "Perhaps we should ask the Master Guardian to verify this unfortunate truth. Is that so, Eliasser? Do you believe Meirashannar has failed?"

I spun around. Eliasser stood a few feet away, at the entrance to the Glen, hands fisted at his sides as he glared at the Foreseer. "You should not have summoned me. I will not do this now."

"Do what?" I asked.

"Oh, my," the Foreseer said. "We are certain that now is precisely when you will do this."

"Do what?" I repeated.

Eliasser squeezed his eyes shut as five more Foreseers wafted through the aperture.

"Please . . . no," he whispered.

My mouth went dry. Had Eliasser just begged something of the Foreseers?

The pink Foreseer waved me toward the center of the Glen.

I folded my arms across my chest and refused to budge. "Do *what?*"

She smiled, first at me, then at Eliasser. "You and your Beloved Second Twin, the sweet king of your heart, are to merge today."

Chapter 15

"I think I heard you wrong. It sounded like you said—" My breath caught at the possibility that I hadn't heard wrong. I stared at the aperture, where the Elder was now making her appearance, then back at the pink Foreseer. "Eliasser and I are going to turn to light and merge?"

"Indeed. This energetic coupling is crucial and will aid you in locating Makashannar. We preferred it to be done when you first returned after the Reparention, however, there has been much resistance to our request." She glanced at Eliasser as the Elder wafted to my side.

"All things happen in their perfect right time," the Elder said. "This we accept."

Eliasser opened his eyes, but fixed them on the ground where my crushed flower lay, its crimson lifeblood marring the bright green grass. I took two steps toward him, then stopped, as I put together the bits and pieces I'd overheard the previous year.

"This isn't about timing, is it," I said, hurt and confused as the realization sank in. "You don't want to merge with me at all, not just now."

Eliasser shook his head. "Whether I want to or not is beside the point. It is the danger—"

The Elder cut him off. "You know better than to speak of danger in the Glen."

"That isn't allowed here?" I asked, unfamiliar with this rule.

"The occurrence of danger in the Glen is impossible, as the Master Guardian is well aware."

Eliasser glared at the Elder, his brilliant aqua eyes cold with anger. "You know very well what I mean. The danger is to—"

"I caution you again, Master Guardian; speak no more of your concerns. They are not relevant to the task at hand."

His voice rose an octave. "Not relevant?"

Uh oh. "What concerns?" I asked, apprehension lodging in my midriff. The Foreseers had a way of deciding what to tell or not tell about a situation. And the aftermath of those decisions sometimes had catastrophic consequences. Witness my violent demise the first time I was sent to stay on Earth a thousand years ago with their blessing. They hadn't been concerned then, either.

"Please," I beseeched her. "I need to know."

The Elder closed her eyes and shimmered for a few seconds before becoming as solid in body as I was. When she took my hands in hers, I felt warmth—human warmth. For some reason, that physical connection with her brought a lump to my throat.

"Beloved Daughter, the Master Guardian's fears have no bearing on what is to come."

"That simply is not true," Eliasser exclaimed. "Which *you* know very well."

"I know many things," the Elder commented mildly. She continued to look only at me, while speaking to the other Foreseers. "Prepare the Master Guardian for merging."

Eliasser's mouth set in a grim line as the blue and green Foreseers guided him toward the center of the Glen.

The Elder hadn't answered my question. I still didn't know what bothered Eliasser about our merging. And yet, he didn't protest further, didn't blurt out his worries or run out of the Glen refusing to merge, which is what I would have done in his place.

I didn't want to run, though. Quite the opposite. To be *required* to merge with Eliasser? Because it would help me find Ashi? To paraphrase an Earth saying, they had me at "merge."

But I did have my own concerns.

"Isn't that—" I bit back the word dangerous. "What if we return to the One Light forever?"

The involuntary wave of joy I experienced at the idea of returning to the One Light also filled me with embarrassment. I had a Twin to find, who apparently had a couple of planets to save. If Eliasser and I merged into the One Light forever, those plans would go down the drain. Not to mention the parentless family I would leave behind on Earth.

The Elder regarded me thoughtfully. Since she could read my mind as well as my emotions, there was no way of hiding what I had just experienced. "I'm sorry," I whispered.

"Dear One, be not afraid nor ashamed of the desire to merge into the One Light. It is what all life yearns to do. Indeed, it is what all life will one day do. But here in the Glen, you may shed all concerns. Today you will merely join as energy with your Beloved Second Twin."

Merely? My pulse began to pound in my ears as I remembered the exquisite bliss that Ashi and I experienced when we turned our physical bodies into light energy and merged in the vortex during the Reparention.

"While the Master Guardian is being prepared, it is time for your eyes to be partly opened."

The Elder pressed her warm palm to my forehead. The Glen rotated around us and we were sucked down a spiraling hole in the ground. When the spinning stopped, we were right back where we started. Except . . .

"It's different somehow," I said, looking around at the Glen.

"Yes. Even here, things change over time. You are about to witness the day you pledged your life in special service to the Light." She pointed at the entrance to the Glen where Eliasser and Ashara were making their way inside with—

"Is that me? I mean, my Amoran self? I look so young."

The Elder nodded. "You were the equivalent age of fifteen cycles on Earth. Of course, you had been on Amoran for many more years than that in your Vortex-created body."

Thousands, according to what I'd learned so far. Unimaginable to me.

The small entourage passed right by where we stood, apparently unaware of our presence. Eliasser had a slightly more youthful appearance than he did now, but the difference in Ashara was striking. Her hair was jet black, not gray, and tied back in a long ponytail that reached to her waist. Her face? Free of wrinkles, just like Eliasser's.

The Elder answered my unvoiced question. "That is what Ashara looked like before her body was put in stasis for her lifetime on Earth as your mother."

"Is that how she aged so much?"

The Elder nodded. "She knew that her physical body might be affected, even in stasis."

The impact of all that Ashara had done for me, and continued to do for me, struck home. The sacrifices she had made on my behalf were immeasurable.

"She made those sacrifices to help fulfill the promises you made on this day."

"Didn't Ashi also pledge his service to the Light? Where is he?" I asked. Then I remembered that, according to Ashi, his first time in the Glen was right before the Reparention.

"Many times has Makashannar been here," the Elder said. "He does not recall them."

Seven Foreseers formed a circle around Eliasser, Ashara, and my younger Amoran self.

"Where are you?" I asked the Elder.

"There." She indicated a misty purple Foreseer. "Before my color changed. Now . . . listen."

The "original" Meirashannar—I could only think of her in third person—pledged herself in service to the One Light until the Three Worlds of the Beginning Time had moved through their Planetary Cycles and Risen. I had no idea what that meant, but the other Meiri apparently did. She made her vows without hesitation, even as the Foreseers explained that this service would not be without pain and suffering and loss. I could feel from here, from twenty feet away, how clear and sure she was. For a moment, I wanted to be her again, to feel that confident.

Dizziness forced me to lean forward and deep breathe.

"We are advancing in time," the Elder said.

When I looked up, there were two additional people in the Glen. A man and a woman, both with waist-length hair the color of honey and wheat struck by moonbeams. They stood on either side of Meirashannar, pledging their aid and service to her when the time came. Then they kissed her in the center of her forehead and left the Glen accompanied by Ashara.

Only Eliasser and Meirashannar were left.

The purple-clad Elder, flanked on either side by three Foreseers, spoke to them, her words unintelligible, but the feeling behind them seemed to sear into my consciousness.

"Oh . . ." I gasped. "Oh . . . the Love. The Light."

The Elder beside me said, "Makashannar is your Primary Twin, yet it is to Eliasser's heart that you are bound, as he is to yours."

"I don't understand," I said, weeping now from the physical impact of that much Love energy flowing through my body.

"No, you do not. Nor will you for a long time." She gazed back at the younger versions of Eliasser and me. "And neither will your sweet king. The fear he experiences in your current time is because he does not understand what is to come. He fears that you and he will be parted again, and for that, he is correct. As to why, he is entirely incorrect."

"Why don't you tell him? Tell me? Why keep us in the dark?"

"Listen again. See with your Mind. Know with your Heart."

The purple-clad Elder became audible. "Blessed are you both for what you have, on this Day of Jubilation, agreed upon. Know you now, with all your Beingness, that you will prevail if you remain steadfast in your vows. Keep to your promises, follow the way laid out in your Hearts, and you will never stray from your true path. And now"—the purple Elder placed her palms flat on Eliasser's and Meirashannar's foreheads—"I take from you the memory of this time we have spent today, so that all may unfold in its right manner. Have no fear, Beloved Son and Beloved Daughter. All will be well in its right time, in fulfillment of your promises to the Light."

When she withdrew her palms, all seven Foreseers vanished.

Eliasser and Meirashannar collapsed onto the ground.

Ashara walked back into the Glen with the moonbeam-haired woman, who knelt beside the two prone figures. "They will sleep for some time," Moonbeam said. "I must return now. Allow them to awaken slowly and give them this when they are conscious." Two vials appeared in her hands, which she gave to Ashara. "Several drops mixed in fairybee wine."

Ashara nodded. "Will I see you again soon?"

Moonbeam shook her head. "The Council will not permit it at this time. We have too much to attend to with Earth." Moonbeam kissed Ashara on the forehead and then she, too, vanished.

Ashara sat down, crossed her legs, and placed one hand on Eliasser's shoulder, the other on Meirashannar's. Closing her eyes, she began to hum. The same tuneless humming I had done with Eliasser after our first Odyssey of Prayer in the Glen over a year ago.

White clouds swirled in from above, spiraling down around the Elder and me until we could no longer see the Glen of the past.

I turned to her. "Why the secrecy? Even if you couldn't let us have the memories, couldn't you have at least told us we had missing memories?"

"I just did," the Elder said with a smile. "Everything happens in its right time."

"Yes, yes, I know," I said, unable to keep the testiness out of my voice. "So you've said."

"And so you have believed, since long before you made these promises."

The white clouds spiraled up and away again, and we were in the current day Glen. The other six Foreseers surrounded Eliasser, humming a soothing melody in a chant-like fashion.

"He is prepared to merge now," the Elder said.

"But does he want to?" I couldn't help asking.

"Eliasser has wanted to since the day you made your promises." She turned to me, with something akin to bemusement. "And you, Meirashannar. Are you ready to merge with him?"

"Yes," I whispered, awed and humbled by the gift we were about to receive.

"Then know this. Your merging with Eliasser is as much to strengthen him as it is to bring you strength. And his frequency within you will be made richer, even as your signature within him will increase." She paused and glanced at Eliasser. "In all things, balance."

As the Elder led me into the circle of Foreseers, Eliasser watched my approach with the intensity of someone committing each step I took to memory.

A chill ran through me. "You're not going to take this memory away, are you? We'll remember this merging?"

"And more," she said cryptically, indicating I should stand directly in front of Eliasser.

"May I?" Eliasser asked her.

"Indeed. It will benefit you both."

"Meiri," he said, reaching for me. "Before we become nonphysical, I would like to—"

"Do this?" I folded myself into his arms.

The rumble of his laughter vibrated in my chest. "Yes, my Light."

He kissed the top of my head, then held my face between his hands. He brought his face so close to mine, that for a split second I thought he might kiss me on the lips. But he slowly backed away, and I found myself breathing a sigh of relief. Some lines just didn't feel right to cross.

The Elder stood behind me and raised my arms at a forty-five-degree angle. "Like this, Meirashannar. Place your palms out, facing your sweet king."

My face warmed at the Elder's use of my special endearment for Eliasser.

"Focus," the pink Foreseer said.

I jumped, startled to find her at my right side, inches from my ear. Only a moment ago, she'd been behind Eliasser. Had I somehow lost time?

"Is Meiri all right?" Eliasser asked.

"She is more than all right," the Elder said with calm assurance. "She is about to blend her heart and her Light into you, for whom no Love or Sacrifice is too great."

"Begin," the Blue Foreseer whispered into my left ear.

I started again, feeling as if time had once more moved forward, leaving me unaware of its passage. I stared at Eliasser for feedback, but his eyes were now closed.

"Focus, Meirashannar," the pink Foreseer repeated. "Use the word we gave you."

"What word?" I asked, but then I began chanting, "Peace, peace, peace . . ." under my breath. When had they instructed me to do that?

"Long ago, Beloved Daughter. Long ago," the Elder spoke to me privately.

"Peace . . . peace . . ." I continued. And then, I was no longer sure if I was speaking aloud, as the word began to echo inside my mind. *Peace . . . peace . . .*

"Know this with me, Beloved Lights," the Elder said. "What has been, will now be. What is to be, has already come. Be now more completely within each other's Heart."

I felt Eliasser's heart, then. Not his physical heart, but the energy of his Heart Center. It moved into my own Heart Center, and then that magnificent Love energy moved back into him.

"Heart Coalescence?" I may have cried it out loud, but I couldn't be sure, because all sound had taken on a hollow quality. Waves of energy pulsed up my spine. The six Foreseers sang and chanted as the Elder spoke.

"Light of the One Light. Into these two Souls, these two Lights, these two physical Beings, bring forth the vibration necessary for the merging of their Light forms. We seek, through the blending of their energy, to increase their Light and Love so that greater Love may be served."

The waves intensified. One wave entered my feet, traveled up my spine, then out the crown of my head. A companion wave moved through my crown, down my spine and into the ground beneath. As the energy grew in strength and the waves increased in frequency, my head spontaneously tilted backward. The Foreseers' singing came in clips, as though someone shut and opened a door. Time itself seemed to stretch, then collapse on itself, then stretch out again. The core of my body ignited with fire, but it was a cool fire. Nothing seemed to make sense anymore, and it didn't matter. The energy became all that mattered, all that existed.

The waves came so frequently now that they were almost indiscernible one from the other. The Foreseers moved us closer together until our bodies were touching. Our hands automatically clasped, our fingers intertwining, our movements involuntary. We pushed into each other as the perimeters of our bodies pulsed with Light and began to blur.

All the love I had ever held for Eliasser seemed to spill over into the space still occupied by his body, which had begun to waver in and out of focus. And his love for me pushed into the space where my physical body was pulsing in and out of physicality.

With one last push forward, we cried out as our bodies disappeared and our energy fully merged. Our joined Being responded with a vibrating ecstasy. We were One.

Our merging was only intended to last long enough for a quick blending of our energy, yet time continued to stretch and stretch and stretch . . .

Stars shone all around us, blinking in and out of focus.

Focus, focus . . .

The Star field brilliant, compelling, wondrous.

We want to remain . . .

Stars . . . more stars . . . so many . . .

We lay facing each other on the grass, our fingertips touching. Eliasser opened his eyes. Smiled, inched closer and wrapped his hand around mine. I brought our joined hands to my chest. His smile broadened, then he shut his eyes and sighed.

The next thing I knew, we were in each other arms, cheek pressed to cheek. Eliasser stroked my hair at the same instant I stroked his. Which made us laugh.

"We're still One," I whispered. "I think we'll always be One."

The Elder spoke from a few yards away.

"Vortex Lights. Your merging was a success."

"See? It worked," I said to Eliasser. "And we're fine. Nothing to worry about."

He smiled, closed his eyes, and held me close. I experienced his sigh of contentment, for I could feel his contentment even now, as if I had sighed myself. Then again, maybe I had. It was still hard to tell where I ended and he began, even though we were back in our physical bodies.

The Elder let us be for a few more minutes, then she quietly voiced, "Master Guardian? It has just begun."

That was odd. "What's begun?" I asked.

Eliasser's smile turned regretful. "I must go now, my Light."

"Now? No. We just merged."

"I am sorry," he whispered. "So very . . ." He backed away and stood up. "I must go."

"Meirashannar," the Elder said. I rolled over to face her. "You will remain here with me."

"But—" I turned back. Eliasser was already gone. He'd ethermoved out of the Glen.

To be so close to someone as to actually *be* that someone, and he to be you in the form of a joined entity. To exist, even for a short time, as one consciousness, one light-body, one heart, one mind. If only we had been able to remain in the Glen for a few hours, physically close, then slowly retreat. That would have been much kinder, far less painful, and I wouldn't have been sitting on the ground, suddenly sobbing.

"Why?" I asked the Elder between gulps for air.

"Let your grief spill out, Meirashannar, and then we will talk."

I left the Glen several hours later, having finally pulled myself together. I was surprised to learn that Eliasser and I had already had two full days to "reintegrate" from our merging, with moments of consciousness and lucidity which I now had no memory of. I wished I could remember those moments we'd shared together as we acclimated to our separate physical bodies. Mostly, we'd slept. But in our moments of wakefulness we'd eaten small amounts of food—all that could be tolerated after merging—and talked. *Pillow talk,* I'd thought when the Elder described it to me. Which, for some reason, made me even sadder.

Chapter 16

I barely spoke for the next three days, caught between the joy of our merging and the loneliness of having Eliasser physically gone. No one but Ashara was allowed to know what happened. Since I couldn't tell anyone, I kept to myself. To help me with my self-imposed isolation, Ashara cordoned off a private area in the Healing Room and encouraged me to work on more advanced potions. While I mixed and poured, I considered what Ashara said at our meeting about sharing the story of our birthright. Had we broken a cycle? Because as far as I could tell, the only thing that happened three days afterward this time was Eliasser leaving me in the Glen after merging. Hurtful to me, but not exactly momentous.

On the fifth day post-merging, I joined my companions for meals, then retreated to the Healing Room again. I could tell they were curious about my mood, especially since I'd disappeared for two days, then basically sequestered myself when I returned. What little I did offer was to announce that I would be returning to Earth in a few days.

The next morning, I woke to find Ari at my bedside, his graceful elven arms folded around a brown backpack perched on his lap.

"Sorry to startle you," he said when I gasped in surprise. "I don't know what's going on, but I'm guessing some friend time will help your mood. And selfishly? I really need you, Meiri. How about a day in the Outer Grounds?"

"Isn't the Outer Grounds off-limits again after that plume thing?"

"Ashara said that everything except the Garrammon Meadow is okay. She apparently got that word from the all-seeing Foreseers."

That was interesting. Ashara avoided the Foreseers at all costs. As for their endorsement?

"Ari, the Foreseers sometimes have their own agenda." *Sometimes?* "Them giving the okay doesn't mean that *we'll* be okay."

Ari held up a finger. "Got you there. Since everything is meant to be, or happens as it should or must or whatever, then we're still okay; even if we're not *okay* okay, if you get my drift. Besides, I have treats." He opened the backpack to show me the picnic he'd assembled.

I smiled. "Well, if you're offering to feed me."

"Just so you know, I didn't ask anyone's permission. I left Ashara a note for when she wakes up, so she won't panic wondering where we are."

Ashara panicked? Hard to picture. "What time is it?"

Ari grinned. "Get dressed. We're going to watch an Amoran sunrise."

We crept through the quiet Mountain corridors, out the Main Gate, then hung a left and continued to our favorite spot on the hill overlooking the Garrammon Lake. We'd just settled in with our food when the sun peeked over the trees lining the opposite shore.

"I never get tired of that sight," Ari whispered.

"Sunrise always fills me with hope," I said, hoping for Eliasser's swift return to me.

Ari munched on his solsatta, a kind of Amoran carrot stick, which he'd coated with a sweet, honey-like paste. "So, what was it like in the Glen?"

"What do you mean?" I choked out. Ari couldn't possibly know that Eliasser and I had merged.

"The sunrise. What was it like when you and Eliasser"—my heart leapt into my throat—"did your prayer sessions in the Glen?"

I blew out a relieved sigh, gave Ari a quick answer, then turned the topic around to a safer one—whatever was bothering him.

Ari began by unloading about Eliasser's frequent absences, the nature of which was still a big secret. It especially riled Ari that Eliasser wouldn't admit who he took counsel with now. "Who are these people Eliasser is consulting?" Ari shouted, punching the ground. "Why should we believe anything they say when we don't even know who they are?"

Ari moved on from there, the extent of his ire troubling to me. When he confessed that he felt most days like he was coming out of his skin, I made a mental note to inform Ashara and work up a potion for him before I went back to Earth. I let him vent, commiserating occasionally, until he wound himself down.

We sat in quiet reflection for a bit, then Ari said, "Your turn. What's up, Earth-girl?"

I shook my head. I'd have to come up with something, so I just said, "Not yet," to buy time.

"Okay. How about a swim?"

"Now you're talking!"

We played in the chilly Garrammon Lake, then dried off with Ari's drying dance. There was no pink mist this time as neither of my Twins was anywhere near me.

Next up was mindsailing. We went the long way to the Mindsail Lake, dutifully avoiding the Garrammon Meadow, then took turns sailing for the rest of the morning.

"Do you want to talk about it?" Ari asked at length.

I frowned. I wanted very much to confide in him.

"It's okay if you don't," he added.

I handed control of the mindsail back to Ari. I didn't have enough mental concentration to say more than a few words and sail at the same time.

"It's not that I don't want to, I'm not permitted to tell anyone," I said, feeling the weight of that secret like a concrete block in my midsection.

Ari did his magical mindsail preprogramming, then turned to face me. "That's good, because I'm not just anyone; I'm Arrien Etan, your Elf Extraordinaire!" He stuck his thumbs into imaginary suspenders and struck a pose.

I laughed. "You are that." I leaned over and let my fingers skim the cool water. "I think I'm hungry again," I said, surprised that it was true. I hadn't had much of an appetite lately.

Ari grinned. "That's better. Now I know you're all right, you bottomless pit."

I smiled. "How about we head to shore and eat our lunch on the beach? We can moor the boat, set out a resting cloth and take a nap afterward."

"Nah. I'm hungry, too. Let's eat here. We can let the mindsail drift for a bit."

We slipped off our shoes, rested our backs against the side of the boat and ate a leisurely lunch as the warm sun beat down on us.

"Why is it that a meal always tastes so good after exercise and sun?" I asked.

"That's easy for you to say. I'm the one who had to manifest over a hot backpack—" He broke off at the sardonic look I gave him. "I'll shut up. It's nap time anyway."

The day was growing warmer. Ari rolled out a resting pad on the boat bottom and we removed our tunic tops to cool off. Ashi's amulet rested on the outside of my tank top, as it usually did.

Ari's expression grew thoughtful. "Can I take a closer look at it?"

The request gave me a weird, unsettled feeling. I hesitated, unsure what my intuition was trying to tell me. It had something to do with the amulet and Ari, a sense of foreboding. But that thought had me doubting my intuition. This was my elven BFF, after all. Besides, Ashi and I had never been given any information regarding our amulets, other than that they were bestowed upon us right after our creation in the vortex. Since I couldn't think of a good reason not to, I removed the amulet, held it by the pendant, and offered it to Ari.

The instant our fingers connected around it, the amulet burned with a white, painful heat.

"Ouch!" we yelled, jerking our hands back. We must have been too close to the edge of the boat because the amulet dropped over the side and hit the water with a hissing *sploosh.*

I didn't think twice. Losing that amulet would be like losing Ashi all over again. I sucked in the biggest breath I could manage and dove in, thankful we were at the shallow end of the lake. I spied the still-glowing pendant as it disappeared between two rocks the size of basketballs. Tunneling through water that felt as thick as mud, I grabbed the still visible silver chain, and pulled.

The amulet didn't budge.

I clawed between the rocks with one hand, trying to liberate the pendant, but the stones were so close together all I did was scrape my fingers. Worse, the chain started sliding through my hand as though being pulled from below.

I kicked frantically at the rocks, hoping to dislodge one. But they barely wobbled and I nearly lost my grip as the amulet surged downward, bloodying my hands in the process. It had only been ten or fifteen seconds, but my lungs ached, and my eyes stung from being underwater.

Ari appeared at my side. He grabbed what little remained of the silver links and we yanked together. In a bizarre tug-of-war, we'd free up a few inches, then the amulet would seem to double in weight and sink further down. Strength failing, lungs burning, I was losing hope.

Ari caught my eye, stepped on one of the rocks and held up a finger. Then two fingers. I nodded my understanding. When he held up three fingers, we heaved with all our might. The amulet released with a slingshot effect that ripped the chain from my hands. Ari, still clutching the necklace, headed toward the surface, but I couldn't hold out any longer. Whether it was dumb luck or intuition, Ari glanced back at the same moment my lungs emptied in an explosion of air. In an instant, he grabbed me and ethermoved us to the boat.

When my gasping and choking finally settled into normal breathing, and my heart rate slowed from the ethermove, I sat up slowly. Ari held the amulet so tightly his knuckles were white. With trembling fingers, he held it out to me. The pendant portion looked perfectly normal now, but I shook my head and pointed to the bottom of the mindsail. I didn't know what had caused the amulet to freak out earlier, but I wasn't taking any chances.

As if it were made of explosives, Ari set it down gently and pulled his hands away. I scooped it up, secured the chain around my neck, and tucked the pendant beneath my tank top this time.

We rode in silence to the shore, moored the boat, then tried to dry off using Ari's drying dance. Several minutes later, we stood sopping wet and shivering, staring at each other in disbelief. The drying dance had never failed us.

"Something is terribly wrong," Ari said. "We need to get to the Mountain."

He tried to ethermove us again, but that failed, too, and we were forced to walk a cold, wet mile back to the Guardian Sanctuary. We arrived in the Main Chamber at the same moment Ashara entered from the opposite corridor. Eliasser must have just landed after a trip through the vortex, judging by the blue mist curling away from where he stood directly beneath the portal.

My entire Being exploded with joy at the sight of him. Thrilled that he had finally come home, I hurried across the tiled mandala. But as I drew closer to the Golden Circle, I could feel him struggling to shield himself, to control his emotions. Puzzled, I shook my head and held my hand over my heart, uncertain what to do, how to react. Merging with Eliasser had clearly done its job. I was more connected with him now than ever before. That meant I experienced his pain and conflict even more strongly.

"Where have you two been?" Eliasser demanded. "I gave clear instructions that no one was the leave the Mountain while I was gone."

Ashara met us in the middle. "Nice of you to drop in," she said to Eliasser, surprising me with the Earth phrase. "I knew where they were, and they had my blessing, unintentional though it may have been." She narrowed an eye at Ari. "I will speak with you later about that."

"And I will speak with *you* later," Eliasser snapped at Ashara. He turned on Ari. "I asked where you were!"

Elves are sensitive to the energy projected by others, and the Master Guardian was spewing discordance in spades. Ari put his arm around me—a gesture intended, I think, to comfort us both. "We spent a much-needed day in the Outer Grounds."

Eliasser's cheeks flamed red and he actually yelled at Ashara. "Does my leadership mean nothing to you? I said no one was to leave the Mountain while I was gone!" He thrust his arm straight out, pointing his finger at Ari and me. "Especially not these two!"

These two? Stunned at his harsh tone, my insides twisted into knots. What in the name of the Light was wrong with him?

Ashara stood her ground. "Then maybe you should have stayed here with your Beloved instead of running away and hiding. Where is your courage?"

Eliasser about-faced and stalked across the chamber. He hadn't looked at me once.

I opened my mouth, but couldn't form words, couldn't even think of any, as if my mind and lips had been injected with Novocain.

Ashara cleared her throat. "I am sorry. Neither of you should have heard that. Go now, both of you; change out of those wet clothes, then meet me in my quarters. Clearly, something has occurred that needs dealing with. Otherwise, he never would have been prompted to return."

Return from where? I moved my shocked gaze from Eliasser's retreating form to Ashara's sorrowful eyes and nodded. Ari pulled me closer to him, and I leaned on his shoulder as we left the Main Chamber.

Ashara, Eliasser, Ari and I sat on cushions at the low, Japanese-style table in Ashara's room. The fire-holder—Amoran's version of a fireplace—blazed in flames of blue, orange, and yellow. Even though I was dry, I couldn't seem to shake the chill of the Mindsail Lake. Under normal circumstances, I would have asked Eliasser to warm me up with the energy he could channel through his hands. But the wall he'd erected around himself now was insurmountable, his attitude made him unapproachable.

After tending to the cuts on my hand, Ashara poured a cup of strong, black tea for each of us, a taste of Earth she truly loved. Ari and I had already consumed a round of reviving draft. Eliasser periodically drank from a double-sized goblet Ashara had already refilled once.

"Now," she said, placing the ceramic teapot on a trivet, "it is best to begin at the start of your day in the Outer Grounds. Tell us everything you experienced."

Between sips of tea, Ari and I took turns providing Ashara and Eliasser with as complete an accounting of our time together as I could, declining to reveal the issues Ari had needed to get off his chest. Eliasser was already in bad temper and hearing Ari's complaints about him might only make things worse.

When we reached the point in our tale where the amulet wound up in the lake, Eliasser's attention sharpened. "Who was holding it then?"

"We both were. Like I said, it began to glow, then it burned our hands. We pulled away so fast, it flew into the water."

Ashara's eyes went wide. "It *flew*?"

"Well, not really. That's just an expression." Then, I paused, struck by something I hadn't had time to process before.

"It did fly!" Ari said. "We pulled our hands straight back, so the amulet should have fallen to the bottom of the boat. Instead, it was like it shot up and over the edge."

"I dove in after it," I continued. "It sank to the bottom and got tangled up in something."

"You entered the Mindsail Lake?" Eliasser exclaimed.

"Yes. But we saved the amulet, so it's all good," I added hastily, leaving out the part where I'd almost drowned.

"No. It is not 'all good,'" Eliasser thundered. "Nothing about this incident is in any way good. The water in the Mindsail Lake can be deadly if you are in it too long."

Ari drew in a breath. "Since when?"

Eliasser waved him off, which wasn't going to help Ari's growing irritation with the Master Guardian. Eliasser kept directing his comments—rants, really—to the center of the table. He hadn't looked at me once, and it was beginning to tick me off. Leaning forward, I tried without success to get Eliasser to meet my eyes.

"Here's a thought," I said. "Maybe if someone had told me not to enter the oh-so-dangerous Mindsail Lake"—I ladled on the sarcasm—"someone like you on the rare occasion you're here, I might have done things differently." I slapped my palm to my forehead. "What am I thinking? It wouldn't have made a damn bit of difference. Because if I hadn't jumped in to rescue the amulet, it would have disappeared through the bottom of the lake. And where would we be then? That amulet is part of how I will find Ashi."

Eliasser and Ashara both went still.

"You are certain of this?" Ashara asked. "How will it help?"

I shook my head. "I don't really know. But I keep thinking about something the Elder did during Ashi's and my Joining before the

Reparention." I reviewed the way she'd taken pea-sized stones, infused them with Light from the One Light, then put them inside our amulets. "I've already tried using Ashi's amulet to find him—meditating on it, sleeping with the pendant clutched in my hand, holding it and thinking about him. I even tried to remove the little stone, but it's like the amulet is welded shut. No matter what I've done, until now, it hasn't reacted at all." I pulled the pendant from beneath my tunic, kissed it, then let it rest on the outside now. "But today on the Mindsail Lake, something felt different. Like . . . it woke up when Ari and I touched it together." I shook my head again. "I was wearing Ashi's amulet when he pushed me to safety in the vortex during the Reparention. And he was wearing mine when the stabilizing explosion occurred. Maybe our amulets will call to each other. Seek each other out somehow."

Eliasser snorted. "You believe Ashi's amulet was *calling* to yours on the Mindsail Lake? Then where might Ashi be now, Meiri? *Inside* the lake bottom?"

Eliasser might as well have punched me in the stomach. Ashara's eyes went round before she narrowed them and let Eliasser have it. "If our beloved Ashi *is* inside the lake bottom, then that means he is most assuredly *dead.*"

Eliasser paled, pressed his lips together and ran his hand over his mouth.

"Good," Ashara said. "You can still be shocked back to your senses. Never speak to Meiri that way again. Due to the shielding you have placed around your heart and emotions, you cannot feel the pain you just inflicted on someone who would join her Twin at the bottom of that lake if it meant saving *your* life. Even now."

She turned to Ari. "Continue."

Ari told the rest of the story. When he finished, silence prevailed for a full minute, with all of us staring into the center of the table now.

Finally, Ashara spoke. "Something has been disrupted by this event. Something new has come. I do not know why it happened, or what caused it to happen, but we will need to proceed with great caution."

Without another word, Eliasser rose stiffly from the low table and left.

Later that evening, a soft vibration, called a beckoning, emanated from the wall containing my doorway. This was the Mountain equivalent of a doorbell. I tried to sense who was outside my room, but my brain was fried from too much thinking and my heart was weary from too much feeling. I gave an impatient wave of my hand and the opening appeared.

Eliasser stood on the threshold.

"May I come in?" he asked.

"You may always come in," I said, too surprised to see him to think of any other response.

He took the chair opposite me at my table. Our eyes met briefly, then he sighed and looked away. "I am sorry for leaving you so quickly in the Glen after we merged. And for taking out on you my frustrations with how things are."

"How *what* things are? What has upset you so much that you can't even look at me?"

Eliasser's jaw tightened. "The answer is complex and one I do not wish to share."

I touched his fingers. My heart sped up and my breath quickened at that simple contact. Our merging seemed to have a lasting physical effect on me.

"Maybe I can help. We've shared so much else."

Eliasser withdrew his hands and stood up. "I just wanted to offer you my apology. I will do my best to treat you with the kindness and respect you deserve."

The sting of withheld tears tightened my throat. "That's your apology? A little formal, don't you think? We became one Being in the Glen."

"Sleep well, Meirashannar." And, once again, he walked out on me.

It took me a long time to fall asleep. As far as I was concerned, the Master Guardian and I weren't finished with this discussion. I would corner him tomorrow and make him talk to me. At the very least, I needed him to explain why he was so angry with me. And after merging? Honestly, what was wrong with him?

When I arrived in the Guardian Meal Room the next morning, only Ashara, Danaeus, and Ari were present, and they were already halfway through their breakfast.

"Where's Eliasser?" I asked with a sinking feeling.

"Gone again," Ari said with a shrug. "What else did you expect?"

A goodbye might have been nice.

"I'm heading back early," I said, handing Ashara the potion recipe I'd written down to help Ari with his emotions. Something good came of my insomnia. "See you next time."

Without another word, I went straight to the Main Chamber, not bothering to stop by my room to change into my regular clothes. I craved the normalcy of my Earth life and an escape from my Amoran problems. I called the vortex and spun my way through the spiraling chamber of rainbow light, all the while unable to stop replaying Eliasser's apology last night. There was more to it, I was certain.

At the other end of the vortex, the blue mist deposited me gently down in my family room.

Right in front of my mother.

Chapter 17

"Mom!"

Her eyes rolled up into her head and her legs buckled. Just in time, I pushed her into a soft landing in the easy chair, hoping her fainting spell would buy me a minute to invent a plausible explanation for what she'd seen. But every thought that came to me went into an emotional shredder and exited as a useless pile of worry confetti.

Mom was already coming around.

"Stay here," I said, as her eyes fluttered open. "I'll get you some water."

I dashed into the kitchen and filled a glass while trying desperately to hatch a plan. Could I convince her that she'd hallucinated me dropping out of a hole in the ceiling? And just how terrible a daughter would that make me?

I heard movement in the next room, hurried out of the kitchen, and slammed into Mom. Good thing the water was still on the counter, or we both would have been soaked.

Mom's eyes were round and bright. "I don't want to be left alone with that . . . that . . . *thing.*"

Without thinking, I blurted out, "It won't come down on its own."

Ah, geez. Did I really just say that?

Mom staggered back a few steps and took in what I was wearing. "Oh my god. Your fairyland place wasn't just a story you made up? You were telling me the truth?"

I sighed. "I guess we need to talk."

Sensitive to Mom not wanting to be near "that thing," I steered us into the kitchen, helped her into a chair, and placed the water glass in front of her. She took tiny sips while I brewed some double-strength Scottish Breakfast tea. Her demeanor concerned me. Pale and quiet. Not a good sign for my usually mouthy parent.

I brought our tea mugs to the table and took a seat.

Mom wrapped her hands around the warm cup. "I didn't just imagine that?"

For a split second I considered letting her think she was nuts. But in the end, I knew it was time for the truth. "You didn't. However, what I'm about to share with you, you cannot tell another living soul."

I gave her a condensed version of the story from when I first returned to Amoran two years ago, to the Reparention and beyond, culminating in my current search for Ashi, my Twin Light. I had to explain what Twin Lights are (like soul mates, I said, to simplify things), but left out that Ashi and I had fallen in love and been gifted one special night together.

Rallying from her initial shock, her fear transformed into a growing fascination with Amoran, the Guardians, the Foreseers, and the vortex. By the time I was finished, she wanted to know when she could join me "on the other side," as she referred to it.

"I don't know if that's possible or allowed. I'll have to ask Ashara when I return." I cringed at the thought of telling the Master Healer, who would demand to know how I had let this happen. As if it were my fault that my mother showed up unannounced.

Come to think of it. "Mom, what were you doing in the family room?"

"I came by to get jackets for the kids. I wanted to take them apple picking after school, and the temperature is supposed to drop later. I knew you weren't going to be home, so I used my key to get in. I heard a strange sound in the family room and went to investigate." She shrugged. "That's when I saw you."

I leaned forward and placed my hand over hers. "I'm sorry you had to learn about it this way. But now that you know the truth, it might make my Friday trips easier on both of us."

"I was going to be your backup anyway, so I can certainly keep that up while you're on Amoran. It would help to know what time you leave and when you expect to be back. And"—she held up a finger—"I should probably stay here in your house while you're gone. You know, in case someone comes by while you're dropping out of the ceiling."

She didn't fool me one bit. "You can't go there unless I get their permission."

"You already said that." She grunted. "Doesn't the rest of what I'm saying make sense?"

It did. Now someone on Earth would know where I was if something happened. It was like a huge weight had been lifted from my shoulders. But I didn't care for the idea of her coming over every time I traveled to Amoran.

"We can try it once and see how it goes."

The week went by in a blur of our usual activities, punctuated by daily visits from Mom. I think she was worried I'd sneak off without telling her. The kids loved having Grandma around to pump for all those extras that their mean old mother always said "no" to. Truth was, I was glad to have her around for me, as well. It freed me up to process the aftermath of my merging with Eliasser. I would wake in the middle of the night, unable to get back to sleep, thinking about Eliasser's increasingly odd behavior. While it had grown more pronounced after our merging, he hadn't really been himself since I returned a year ago. Something was troubling him, something . . . deep. So deep that since our merging he needed to hide from me? I thought about the day at the Garrammon Lake when he'd coalesced our hearts. He'd left me then as well. Ashara had wanted him to remain with me after Heart Coalescence, but he went away . . . wherever he goes. Was he hiding from me then? Why had Ashara accused him of that now? *Hiding* from me? Whatever for? And why would he need courage? For the tasks ahead? To help me find Ashi?

And then, I'd come full circle in my ruminations, back to our merging, to the exquisite bliss of becoming One. One in energy, One in

Spirit, One in Light. Our merging was supposed to provide me with a closer connection to Ashi's energy signature. But if anything, that connection seemed to have lessened, as if the strength of Eliasser's energy blotted out all else.

My mother insisted on staying over Thursday night, which turned out to be a good thing. My sleeping patterns had become more disrupted as the week wore on. The night before I left, I barely slept, my dreams full of Ashi and Eliasser, fading in and out of each other. I woke the next morning, dizzy, disoriented, and slightly nauseous.

Mom cooked breakfast while I sat at the kitchen table staring out the back window in a daze. After Ryan and Kiley left, I changed into my tunic.

"It's backwards," Mom said, as I came downstairs.

"No it's . . . oh . . . you're right."

"Mother always knows best," she murmured, helping me to turn the top around. "You sure you're okay to go?"

I'd been wondering the same thing. "I sort of have to be," I said with a sigh as we walked into the family room.

"Hmph. Well, how about I stay with you until you're—" she pointed up at the ceiling.

I couldn't let my mother watch me open the portal. She was far too intrigued by Amoran, and I didn't trust her to stay on Earth if she ever figured out how to call the vortex on her own.

"We've already talked about this, Mom. I can travel between dimensions because I'm a Vibrational. You might die if you try to go through the vortex."

"Don't worry," she said, waving me off. "I won't watch."

"That's correct. Because you'll stay in the other room until I'm gone."

When I had her firmly ensconced in the kitchen, I called the vortex and stepped into the blue misty light. As I ascended, Mom ran in, hands on her hips and mouth in an "o" shape.

It wasn't hard to see where I got my stubbornness from.

When the second phase of vortex travel kicked in, I had all I could do to keep down what little breakfast I'd managed to eat. Relieved to finally land in the Golden Circle, I met another challenge. The mandala decorating the floor seemed to be moving—left, then right, left, then right—making it hard for me to find my way across the Main Chamber. Oddly unconcerned by this, I picked out the border of the Inner Circle and began to follow it, thinking in my lightheaded fashion that it would eventually lead me somewhere. I walked around it several times, doing that same tuneless humming that seemed to be peculiar to Ashara and me.

The humming turned into one long note, followed by the next long note, as if I were stretching out time itself. I continued for a while until it felt right to move on to the Outer Circle.

I walked that path, around and around, much like I'd seen people do at a labyrinth, although they walked ever closer to the innermost point, the center of the "maze," while I kept walking in circles. *I'm literally walking in circles.*

I tilted my head back and let out a full-throated belly laugh.

"Meiri?"

I turned slowly and my breath caught at the sight of him. Eliasser wasn't just physically beautiful, he had a beauty of spirit that radiated from him always—that is, when he wasn't in turmoil. I flushed with a mixture of pride, humility, and shyness. I had been privileged to share in that beautiful spirit.

"Yes, my sweet king?" I whispered.

The color in Eliasser's cheeks deepened. Was he experiencing the same sense of connection and gratitude? I placed my hand on his arm. "Do you feel it, too?"

His eyes narrowed. "Feel what?"

I couldn't answer him, because the music playing inside my head—like I had on the best earphones and highest quality music player—was so strange. And then, the people talking . . .

"Meiri," Eliasser said more insistently. "Are you all right?"

All at once, it was as if I'd split in half. I frowned as my vision clouded and an image pressed itself on the back of my retinas; two people in the middle of a gigantic galaxy of stars. And then the people were the stars, and the stars were the people, and . . .

"I found her like this," Eliasser said. "She has not moved or spoken for several minutes. I am afraid to touch her."

Why? Would I break?

I slowly drew my mind back out of the stars, but the loss was devastating. "It's too much," I murmured, a sob catching in my throat. "Too much loss."

"Meirashannar." It was a woman's voice, calm and assured and full of authority, much like the Foreseers. But the hands that shook me gently were decidedly physical. "Meiri!"

I breathed out, opened my eyes, and forced them to focus on the person standing before me.

So familiar. Where did I know her from?

Her sigh was full of relief. "Thank the Light you are here with us."

"But I want to be back in the stars," I whispered.

"The stars?" the woman asked. She stood very tall, with long, beautiful golden-white hair.

"Yes. With Eliasser. That is where we belong. That is where we are from."

Her eyebrows lifted as she glanced beyond me. "Was Meiri properly grounded after merging?"

"I believe we were grounded together," Eliasser said.

"But her physical body is from another world," the stranger said, exchanging a look with Ashara, who had come to stand beside her.

Now I recognized the newcomer. She had been there in the Glen when Eliasser and I made our promises to the One Light.

I stared at Moonbeam Hair. "I remember you."

Her expression remained neutral as she said to Ashara, "The grounding Meiri received may not have been sufficient for her Earth body."

"Which I am certain the Foreseers knew," came Ashara's caustic reply. "If Meiri was not properly grounded, you can be sure it was done on purpose."

"Then we will speak no more of this now. All things unfold in their true Light."

"What about Eliasser's grounding?" I asked. My gaze met his, and he quickly looked away. His emotions were placid enough, but I sensed something . . . off. "I think he is not all right."

Moonbeam Hair studied me thoughtfully. "You have great love for him, yes?"

"Of course, I do," I snapped, suddenly testy. I was tired of people telling me how much I loved Eliasser. "But really, just who are you?"

Ashara's eyes went round, a rarity for her. "Meiri! Mind who you are speaking to!"

"I would if I knew *who* I was speaking to!"

Moonbeam Hair didn't seem to mind. "I am Peliyama, Head of the Council of Light."

"Ohhh . . . I see." I folded my arms across my chest and made an intuitive leap. "Are you the one who keeps Eliasser away for ridiculous amounts of time?"

"Oh, dear Light," Eliasser wheezed out. "Forgive her, Peliyama. She does not—"

"Hey!" I cut him off. "I can speak for myself. And I'll apologize if I need to."

The corners of Peliyama's mouth turned up ever so slightly as she held up a hand to stave off another interruption.

"The entire Council is in agreement regarding our need for Eliasser," she said to me. "I know this has made things difficult for you. Unfortunately, that cannot be helped."

I planted my hands on my hips. "Okay. Then can I at least see where he goes?"

Peliyama gave me a full smile now. "You are asking to come see the Council of Light?"

I squared my shoulders. "Yes. I am." Then, my bravado faltered. "Is that all right?"

"It is more than all right; it is absolutely necessary. But not yet. You will have to be patient for now. Can you do that for me?"

I nodded, feeling like a small child with a kind, forbearing parent.

"Good. I will now ground you." Peliyama placed her hands on either side of my face and brought my forehead to touch hers. Warm, soothing energy spread from her hands throughout my body. The world came back into sharp focus and I felt like myself again. Which begged the question; if it was that simple to do, why hadn't the Foreseers seen to it?

Peliyama turned to Ashara. "I will not need Eliasser's assistance today after all. I believe it best that he remain here."

"Would it not be better for all concerned if I am absent?" Eliasser asked.

My jaw dropped, but before I could ask who "all concerned" was, and why they'd be better off if Eliasser was gone, Peliyama raised her hand again.

"You will remain here, Master Guardian," she said with finality, and I saw where that sense of authority could lead to if she was challenged in a way that did not suit her.

The portal opened and the blue mist rotated downward.

Peliyama glanced at Ashara. "I take my leave of you. May the Light guide you in these next days, particularly so now." She stepped into the mist and was gone.

I spun around to confront Ashara. "Tell me right now what's really going on or I'm heading back to Earth."

She pushed out a long, defeated sigh. "Come with me."

Eliasser walked the opposite way. Not a good sign. He and Ashara usually delivered distressing information as a bad news tag team.

"Aren't you joining us?" I called after him.

"Not this time, Meiri." And he hastened across the chamber and down a corridor.

I followed Ashara in the other direction, a sinking feeling in the pit of my stomach.

"He's *what*?" I screeched.

"Lower your voice, Meirashannar. You are not on the Garrammon field."

I headed straight for the potion table to fix myself a concoction of calming elixir and reviving draft. Ashara remained silent as I downed the brew in several gulps, grimacing at the taste. When I turned around, the look on her face—apology and dismay—said it all. "Oh my god. You knew this would happen. You didn't just think it might. You knew!"

Sweeping some stray leaves off the stone stool by the cabinet, she sat down.

"I would like to say I only suspected it might, that I was not certain. Or that I hoped he would be spared." She sighed again. "But I did know. Deep inside me, I knew."

"So did Eliasser, I'm guessing. That's why he didn't want to merge with me. He was afraid of this all along." I hunched over, hands on my thighs to better bear the pain twisting my solar plexus in a knot. "What am I going to do?"

"Why are you so afraid, my Light? This does not need to alter things."

"You're joking, right? Eliasser would rather be on an entirely different planet from me."

"You will both adjust." She met my frosty gaze with a steady one of her own. "He put off merging with you as long as he could. But in the end, the Foreseers won out."

"The Foreseers. How right you are. This was their doing!"

Ashara was cautioning me to stay put, but I was already halfway out the door. I didn't have to ask if the Foreseers knew this would happen. I planned on demanding to know why. Why they had allowed the Master Guardian of the Seventh Vortex to engage in an act that would awaken within him physical desires. And the sole object of those desires? Me.

I marched across the Glen, determination growing with each stomping step and planted myself in front of the aperture.

"Well?" I called into the opening. "What do you have to say for yourself?"

My legs shook, partly from anger, partly from recognition of the sheer audacity of my actions. But the gateway remained clear.

"Meirashannar, what is your wish?"

I spun around. The Elder stood barely two feet behind me.

"I . . . my wish?" She'd caught me off guard by arriving that way. Another stab of irritation brought me back to my purpose, if not my wish. "I don't wish for anything; But I do need answers."

She stared complacently at me for a moment, then turned and floated to the center of the Glen. Lifting her arms high into the air, she sang a praise to the One Light. I broke out in goose bumps at the beauty of her voice, and the gentle strength and love emanating from her. It was as if she had filled the Glen with her essence.

Be strong, Meiri. Get your answers.

I steeled myself and went to meet her. She closed her eyes and her ethereal presence turned as solid as my own. I'd only seen her do that twice—during Ashi's and my Joining ceremony, and most recently when Eliasser and I merged. Overcome by those memories, I couldn't speak. I would never win this battle. I'd lost it the moment I thought I could challenge her.

She tilted her head to the side and studied me again.

"Battle? Is that what you believe we are going to do now?"

I said nothing.

"My Light—my precious, precious Light. You persist in seeing things only through the veil of your limited human perception. Open up your Divine eye and see things as they truly are."

I sat down and cradled my head. "Humor me. Did you know this would happen?"

"The possibility was always present."

"Yes, I get that. But that isn't what I asked you." I lifted my gaze and stared at her. "Did you know, for a certainty, that this would happen?"

She smiled. "Very little can be said with certainty, Meiri."

This from a Foreseer! And she had never before used my fond-name, the one Ashi gave to me. I was sure it was designed to bring me back to the purpose of all this, finding my Twin.

She laughed. "Such a narrow perspective. While finding your Twin is of the utmost urgency in this moment of linear time, it is not the only purpose you have. When you pledged yourself in service to the Light in our Glen all those years ago, you had many purposes, many tasks laid out before you." She lowered herself to the ground and took my hands within her own warm, solid ones. "And you agreed to all of them.

Indeed, you were eager to help in this way. As Meirashannar. As Kerrin Scott. As the people you became in all the lifetimes you have lived. Each experience important. Each life informing who you are today. You have never wavered in this, your true purpose. To serve the Light in the way we requested of you. I invite you again to open your Divine eye and see rightly that which *is*, and that which *is not*."

I sighed. "Will you please give me a straight answer?"

"What do you wish to know, beloved Light?"

"You are a *Foreseer*, after all. Did you know, expect, believe, that instead of it just being a risk, that Eliasser would develop—" I didn't know what to call it that wouldn't make me uncomfortable. "That Eliasser would want to be with me in that way?"

She smiled again. "What way, my Light?"

Unbelievable. Every sentence that came out of her mouth was designed to push me. She wasn't going to answer until I said it out loud. Well, okay then. I'd give her what she wanted.

"That Eliasser would desire me sexually. It's just so wrong. He wasn't designed that way."

"You are uncomfortable that Eliasser desires you?" I nodded. "And knowing that he does is painful to you?" I nodded again. "We will not judge whether it is right or wrong for him to feel this way, what he feels just *is*. And how you feel in return, just *is*. There is no judgment on this."

"But I don't feel that way about him. I want my friend back. And Ashi . . ."

"Yes. Makashannar. You believe that Makashannar is the reason you are in this—predicament, you would call it—at the current time. But your "predicament" is part of a greater whole. Have you considered that?"

"I don't understand."

"No, you do not. Remember, my beloved Light; Makashannar is your Primary Twin, but it is to Eliasser's heart that you are bound, as he is to yours. So, accept that you are in this predicament. Accept it with grace. Find a way to be at peace with it. For the results of your merging with Eliasser and the consequences that will unfold over time, are indeed meant to be. And they are most certainly not wrong. Growth will occur on many levels—for you and for Eliasser. But most importantly, for Eliasser."

She reverted to her ethereal form and rose up, hovering as she contemplated me.

"Do you know why I sometimes take upon my energy self the shell of physicality?" I shook my head. "Because it feels good to have a physical form. Different from an energy form. Certainly not as intensely pleasurable as merging. But physical form is lovely in its own right. And it affords the Light an opportunity to be in this physical reality. The Light is enriched by it. Think about that, Daughter."

I stayed in the Glen long after she left, doing as she had asked.

It was with a sense of humility that I exited the Forest Portal into the narrow corridor that also contained Eliasser's quarters. I'd become clear on one thing. Eliasser and I needed to face this new development openly, no matter how uncomfortable it might be for us.

I was about to beckon his doorway when it opened anyway.

"Ari?" I said in surprise.

"One and the same. Ashara asked me to bring Eliasser's pilea to him." He stared at the aqua cloak in his arms. "She didn't say why he couldn't come get it himself. Evening Meal is about to start, but she told me to bring it to the Resting Stones."

"How about I bring it to him? I was going that way anyway."

"You were?" He squinted at me. "No, you weren't. But I won't ask . . . yet." He thrust the pilea into my arms.

"Thanks, Ari."

Eliasser was sitting with his back to a Resting Stone, his gaze fixed on the stream as it sparkled in the setting sun. I sat down beside him, my back to the adjacent stone, and placed the pilea in his lap. In the few moments of quiet before I spoke, I sensed something entirely unexpected radiating from him.

"Gratitude? For what?"

Eliasser picked up a flat stone and skipped it over the water, transforming the sparkling reflections into jagged spears. And said nothing.

Try as I might, I couldn't keep the anger from rising up within me. "You knew there was a risk of this happening, yet you didn't think to warn me?"

Eliasser sighed. "I know many things, Meiri. I knew you would come now to vent your anger. I knew you would want to talk about it and try to fix it. It is why I did not go far. We may as well have this conversation now and be done with it."

I didn't like the finality shrouding that statement. "What do you mean?"

He still wouldn't look at me. "We cannot change what has happened." He tossed another stone across the stream. "Whether I suspected it does not matter. I must now live with the consequence."

We both would have to live with the consequence, I thought grimly. And yet, what if I had suspected, or even known for sure, what the result of our merging would bring? Would I still have had gone through with it?

With a defeated sigh, I skipped a stone over the water. Yes. I would do anything I could to bring Ashi back.

Eliasser glanced at me. "As for the gratitude you sensed? I have never comprehended physical desire. But now, even as challenging as it may be, it is also a gift. It allows me greater understanding, and my compassion for others increases as a result." He smiled. "I see Anders and Meilee in an entirely different way now."

That was so like Eliasser to turn this nightmare into a learning experience, and a gift at that.

"Besides," Eliasser went on, "if Ashi could repress it so effectively, then I should be even more able to do so."

I debated how to remind Eliasser of the downside to Ashi's repression. The subliminal energy of his unacknowledged desire had affected me even more.

"Eliasser, those feelings Ashi thought he suppressed—"

"And therefore, did not feel."

"Not consciously. But he did feel them. Remember, because he repressed them, they made him ill. And because he repressed them, they made me even more . . . I grew more . . ."

Eliasser's jaw tightened and I couldn't finish the sentence. Couldn't even begin to imagine what would happen to my relationship with him if the unthinkable happened.

Eliasser's breathing became measured. In breath, out breath. In breath, out breath. I knew the signs. He was controlling his emotional reaction to what I'd said.

He looked down at his hands, which he turned palms-up. "Meiri," he said quietly. "Everything will be all right. Will you trust me?"

"I will try." I forced a smile, but I didn't say anything else. I fully trusted Eliasser. It was the Earth energy I'd inadvertently saddled him with that I didn't trust one bit.

Or maybe I did trust it. And that was the problem.

Eliasser left for the Council a few days later. I'd avoided him during that time to give us both some breathing room. As I worked with Ashara in the Healing Room, I confessed that I was having trouble adjusting to this new "situation." I didn't know how to act around him now, partly because I didn't want to make him uncomfortable.

Ashara stopped pouring the diluted valius into the pitcher and turned to me.

"This is not like when Ashi developed desires," she said. "The transition for Eliasser has been extremely difficult—not just physically, but emotionally and mentally as well. This does not excuse his behavior, but the turmoil he was in is why he was so harsh to you and Ari after you went into the Mindsail Lake. I am doing what I can to help with shielding potions, just as I did with you and Ashi, but with the energy changes affecting each of us differently, it is a greater challenge to get this right."

"Is there anything I can do?"

"Just what you are already doing."

"Avoiding him?"

She eyed me carefully. "You do not feel the same for him?"

I shook my head. "Not that way, thank the Light."

She nodded. "Then follow your heart."

I blinked. It seemed an incongruous and perhaps unnecessary thing to say; I usually follow my heart. But as I mixed up another batch of the shielding potion, I thought back to right before the Reparention. Aside from the risk of a spontaneous merging, Ashi and I weren't able to act on our feelings because of a vibrational discordance that made even a simple kiss painful. Which is why when the Foreseers gifted us our one night together, they'd had to move us into their realm.

"Ashara. When I find Ashi, will we still have the same vibrational difficulty as before?"

"No. Now that the vortex is in balance, you should be able to resume your intimate relationship with him."

The heat rose to my face as I considered something else.

"Does that mean that Eliasser and I could—" I cut myself off as my face grew even warmer. "I'm only asking because it helps to know if there are the same . . . restrictions."

I kept my gaze trained on the mixing bowl, so I would not have to witness her expression as her eyes bore into the side of my head.

"I see," she said quietly. "Since you do not have feelings for him that way, you should not need the aid of . . . restrictions."

She was right, of course. Why had I even asked that?

"And Meiri. Do not divulge Eliasser's . . . condition . . . to anyone, not even Ari."

It was hard for me to imagine a scenario where I would confide in someone that Eliasser was now capable of feeling that kind of desire. Unlike Heart Coalescence, this really did seem like a private matter.

I finished up the potion and left the Healing Room to meet Ari, Anders, and Danaeus at the Garrammon field. I'd put off telling Ashara that my mother had seen me descend out of the vortex. No one on Earth was supposed to have any knowledge of Amoran. What would happen when I confessed? Ashara would tell Eliasser, who'd fume over how I could have let that occur. His fuming I could handle. But Ashara would probably have to tell the Foreseers, too. If they could wipe memories from me, could they do that to Mom? *Would* they do it to her? I liked things the way they were. Loved having a confidant on Earth. And I wasn't about to give that up. Or have my mother's mind wiped!

Then the truth came to me in a head-slap moment. The Foreseers know all, which meant they were already aware of Mom's involvement. And apparently, they were okay with it.

I spent the remainder of that visit focused on the task of locating Ashi, even taking the mindsail to the spot on the lake where the amulet had flown overboard. But I didn't get so much as a flutter from the pendant. By the time I left Amoran, I'd made no great strides in finding my Twin. I arrived home to find my mother waking from a nap on the family room couch.

Opening one eye, she checked her watch. "Wish you could have been this prompt when you had to catch the bus."

"Hello to you, too, Mom."

She smiled and pointed to the kitchen. "I made cookies."

"Chocolate chip?"

"Is there any other kind worth baking?"

"Course not. Guess I'm a *chip* off the old block." I winced, waiting.

Mom stood up and hugged me. "Nice try, but you'll never be as *punny* as John."

"No one could be that bad," I said, with a laugh. And we settled in with tea, cookies, and conversation to await the kids' arrival home from school.

The next couple of months on Earth went by mostly without incident, except for the day I caught Mom hiding in the hallway, peering around the corner as I began to call the vortex. Thankfully, I hadn't gotten far. "This is not child's play," I'd said, soundly bawling her out. "For the umpteenth time, you could die trying to get there without proper training and help."

That was stretching things a bit. Moving between dimensions wasn't deadly for a non-Vibrational. But it was a lot harder on the body—even Ashara couldn't stay more than a couple of hours on Earth. But I wanted to dissuade Mom as much as I could from even trying.

She asked me once if anyone besides her had ever caught me traveling back and forth. I told her no, then shared the close call I'd had before the Reparention. Time had leapt forward, and I'd landed back on Earth six hours late, with John and Dan looking for me.

"I remember that," Mom said. Then she got a funny look on her face. "Could that happen again?"

I told her I honestly didn't know, but I didn't think so. We weren't going to the same extremes with time-stretching as we had back then.

On Amoran, Eliasser was gone as much as ever. When he was around, he assiduously avoided me. While I couldn't really blame him, the loss of his companionship, on top of John's death and Ashi's absence, was at times unbearable. But it proved a better alternative to the awkwardness that prevailed when we had to be in each other's presence. I wasn't sure if that awkwardness came from me, from him, or a combination of the two. To distract myself from this uncomfortable turn of events, I kept busy with Garrammon, potion making, and learning to ethermove. Or, more accurately, failing to learn to ethermove.

At least there were no new anomalies, and the Foreseers decreed that as long as we avoided the Garrammon Meadow, the Outer Grounds were safe, and we should resume our customary daily activities. The energy changes had shifted again in what was considered the positive direction. Most Mountain residents who previously had acquired new skills or abilities were nearly back to normal. The urgency surrounding the dimensional variance that might have eaten parts of Elvener subsided. And since Earth and Amoran weren't in the dire straits Eliasser had suggested back before we merged, I got a reprieve of sorts. I was still tasked with finding Ashi, however, the immediate pressure had lessened.

No one could explain why things had normalized. And, because everyone else felt better, no one seemed to mind. Except for me and Ari. The two of us felt like we were living Amoran's version of "hurry up and wait," counting breaths until the other shoe dropped.

It was at the beginning of a shortened visit in mid-November when things began to unravel. Mom made me promise to be back on Earth by noon, but she wouldn't say why. I'd argued with her that my Fridays on Amoran were important to maintain. In the end, I let her win this one. She was doing me a huge favor, and so far, had been very discreet about my other life.

By my second day back, Ari and I needed to get out of the Mountain in the worst way.

"Mindsailing?" I said after Morning Meal.

"Let's go," he answered, pulling me up by my hand.

An hour later, the sun warmed my face as the boat cut a path across the calm water of the Mindsail Lake. Giddy to have left behind the freezing dampness of Earth for a beautiful day on Amoran, I said to Ari, "Let's make it go faster."

"Faster? You want faster?" He burst out with a mischievous laugh.

"Oh, for god's sake, you dirty-minded elf." I giggled. Then I remembered just how long it had been since I'd had any. "Ari. Don't you wish we could, you know, take care of ourselves that way? Sort of like friends with benefits?"

Ari looked at me like I'd lost all my marbles. Instead of making the mindsail go faster, he brought it to an abrupt stop, nearly pitching me overboard. My eyes widened as I realized we were in the same place as when the amulet catapulted overboard.

"Yeah. Real fun," Ari said. "We'd only benefit once and then you'd be dead."

I sighed. "It's not really fair, is it?"

He rolled his eyes. "At least you can find someone to have 'benefits' with. You've got all of Earth, not to mention a few under the Mountain. I'm stuck."

"Oh, crap. Yeah. I'm sorry. I should learn to keep my mouth shut."

"Please, don't," he said, in earnest. "You're the only one I can have any real fun with. And that includes your stupid jokes and flirting."

My mouth dropped open. "I do not flirt. And my jokes are . . . okay, you're right on that count, but I don't flirt with you." I paused as he grinned at me. "Do I?"

"We flirt with each other. All the time." His smile vanished. "It's pathetic, really."

Something he'd said earlier sank in. "What do you mean I can choose from a few under the Mountain?" The boat, which Ari had brought to a complete standstill, began to rock side to side as the placid water abruptly turned choppy and gray as slate. "Hey. What's going on with—"

Ari cut me off. "Your aura lights up whenever you're near Eliasser."

I tore my gaze from the water and frowned, not sure where this was headed.

"I'm guessing my aura has lit up ever since I've known him."

Ari waved his hand impatiently. "Yes, yes. Your energy signature always shines in Eliasser's presence. But recently? It's more like when Ashi was around."

I couldn't meet Ari's eyes. "You must be mistaken. And since when do you see auras?"

The amulet began to pull at my neck like it contained a bag of rocks.

"I'm an elven energy worker. *Elven*, with all that implies. And what I'm trying to say is—" He raked his hand through his hair as the opaque water buffeted the mindsail like it was made of balsa wood. "What the heck?" We gripped the sides of the boat to steady ourselves, but our charged conversation kept us from doing the sensible thing—getting the hell off the lake.

"Eliasser's signature is different, too," he persisted. "The attraction between the two of you is so strong, it's mind-boggling."

"It's because of our complementary energy signatures. That's all!"

"It's not that type of attraction. It's sexual, and you know it. I ask you again, what happened to change that?"

A large swell of water nearly capsized the boat, but Ari refused to budge.

"Tell me. Now! It's important. We're not leaving here till you do!"

"Okay. *Okay!* The Foreseers made us merge. It's supposed to help me locate Ashi. Instead, it's made Eliasser have . . . those kinds of feelings for me. I hate it. I hate what it's done to us."

Ari's gaze softened. "Oh, Meiri. No, you don't. That's the problem. You're resisting it. Your aura says it all."

"Shut UP," I shouted. My shoulders ached from the increasing heaviness of the amulet.

Ari slammed his fist in his hand. "I knew it! I knew something important had changed. Don't you see what this means?"

I shook my head, clutching the outside of my tunic, trying to hold the pendant up so it wouldn't break my neck.

"It's working, Meiri! It will save us all!"

I don't know what concerned me more. The shifting water around us, the amulet that now felt like a bowling ball in my hand, or the crazed look in Ari's eyes.

Worried, I shook his arm. "What's working?!"

Beneath my tunic, the amulet grew hot and began to glow.

"The merging. We're closer to finding Ashi. But that's not all. I sense . . . I feel—"

"Ari!" I screamed. Dropping his arm, I pointed behind him.

He turned, then shouted, "Dive!" as a giant wave curled over the boat.

Too late. I only had time to hold my breath as the wall of water slammed the mindsail, tossing us into a maelstrom. I struggled toward the surface, but the amulet shot out from beneath my tunic, hell-bent on a different path. Since our last debacle with the amulet and the lake, I'd affixed a clasp around the chain close to my neck so I would never again risk losing it. Unfortunately, what I risked losing now was my life as the weight of pendant dragged me down.

Ari gripped my ankles and tried to yank me upward. The amulet countered with an increase in mass. Our descent sped up until the amulet disappeared through the muck at the bottom of the lake, taking Ari and me with it.

Chapter 18

"Ari?" I called into inky blackness. Unable to see a thing, I only knew that I was face down on a hard, dry surface. I rolled over, sat up, and felt down the length of my tunic. I'd just been dragged through churning water and mud, so it came as a shock that I wasn't the least bit wet.

"Ari!" Bile rose to my throat. Why does silence seem so deafening in absolute darkness?

"Don't move," he answered from a few feet away. "I'll come to you."

"Where are we?" My words echoed like I was in a large chamber.

"Best guess?" After some thudding, Ari reached me, grasped my hand, and held tight. "Another of these freaking freakish anomalies. I encountered something similar once. It's highly unusual and the name escapes me. But it's like a shifting channel-vent, one that could vanish at any moment, taking us with it into oblivion. Or we could fall into a chasm that appears with no warning. Either way, we have to be careful where we step."

Freakish anomalies? Channel-vents? *Oblivion?* "Do you make this shit up as you go?"

My wavering voice clued Ari to my true emotion. He squeezed my hand and brought it to his chest so I could feel the pounding of his heart.

"I wish I could, Meiri. I'd invent something much more to our liking, that's for sure. A nice grassy hill, good food. A swim in a pretty lake. More good food."

"I like your priorities. Considering we can't see, how can we be careful where we step?"

"We need to find a way. Staying put isn't an option."

I shivered, although not from being cold. "Okay. What's the plan?"

"Crawling is safest, but it will leave us too vulnerable. We have to walk, tapping our feet in front of us to make sure we're on solid ground. I'll go first, then you follow, but we'll stay connected." He squeezed my hand again. "That's all the plan I have at the moment."

Ari led the way with me right behind. Keeping our hands clasped together further slowed our progress as we inched our way through complete darkness. We were just getting the hang of it when a jagged line of vivid light etched its way over the ground to our right.

"Damn," Ari whispered. "That's the start of a fissure. Hold tight."

I clamped onto him. Partly blinded by the brightness, I tried to look away, but couldn't. Like ogling the aftermath of a car accident, I watched transfixed as the jagged line of light spread wider. The ground trembled, then a radiant plume of energy shot several yards into the air. Seconds later, the plume retreated and the fissure closed, consigning us once again to darkness.

"What do you make of that?" I asked. "Is that part of this channel-vent thing?"

"No. It looks more like a smaller version of what we've seen on the surface. Other than that, I don't know what to make of it. I'm now officially in the dark, pardon the pun." He sighed. "Let's keep going."

He tapped, then took a step.

"Ari, what if—"

"Shh. I hear something."

A fissure opened to our left and a massive plume soared hundreds of feet into the air. Its brilliance illuminated a large area, including a glowing half circle of white in the distance.

"We're in a tunnel," Ari exclaimed, as the heat from the plume nearly singed us. "Run while we have the light. We need to get to that opening!"

Ari tightened his grip on my hand and we raced ahead, my lungs burning with the effort. This plume took longer to expend itself. When it finally sank back into the ground, zero visibility brought us to an immediate halt. After our eyes adjusted to the darkness, the small half circle of light was much closer. We'd made good progress.

"Back to our tap-step?" I asked, gasping for air.

"Yes. But we can't go as slowly as before."

We picked up speed as we continued tapping, then stepping. After a few painstaking minutes, we seemed to come to a nonverbal decision and started walking as fast as we could. We were nearly to the exit when a plume exploded behind us.

We bolted forward and through the opening into sunlight. It took several moments for my eyes to adjust to the brightness before I could take in my surroundings. Then I stared dumbfounded at the vista before me.

"This looks like farmland on Earth. And . . . are those cornstalks?"

"It's not Earth. And that isn't corn. I think it's . . ." Ari sucked in a breath. "That can't be."

He was still staring at the cornstalk-like plants, so didn't see the woman approaching from our right. It was like she'd come out of nowhere.

"Um . . . Ari?" I said. "Someone's here."

Ari turned around. "Maya?"

I didn't recall what Ari's Eternal Companion looked like. This woman was a little taller than Ari, with light brown hair that fell in loose curls to her shoulders. Her sapphire blue eyes were saturated so deeply with the color that they seemed surreal. And strangely unfocused. If this was Maya, had we landed in some kind of afterlife?

"You know my name?" Maya asked.

"I . . ." Ari's voice went thick with emotion. "Maya, don't you recognize me?"

She stepped toward him. "Your voice. *Ari?* Is that you?"

Ari stood still while Maya read his face with her hands. She touched his hair, ran a finger across his lips. Then she kissed him briefly and pulled back.

Ari's expression was a mix of past grief and fresh wonder.

"It *is* you," Maya said, her tone part relief, part gentle reproach. "Where have you been?"

"Been?" Ari glanced at me. "I've been on Amoran."

"Are we dead?" I whispered to Ari.

Maya laughed gently. "That's what we thought at first.

We? "There are others?" I asked.

"A few. We can't seem to find our way out of here, though. We've walked as far as possible in all directions, but always come up against a wall of sorts, like an energy force."

Ari's expression turned guarded. "How long have you been here?"

She withdrew a notched stick from her pocket and counted out chips in the wood. "This is how I keep track of time since the implosion, when I lost the use of my physical sight."

"You remember the implosion?" I asked.

"I will never forget it," she said softly. "Only three of us made it through. Kylan and Haldoen, two brothers from the Vale Province were with me when the collapse began. We've been waiting for someone to rescue us for thirty days."

"Thirty days?" I exclaimed. "But it's been over—"

"Maya!" Ari cut me off and shot me a warning look. "Can you take us to the others?"

Pocketing the stick, Maya said to me, "I don't recognize your voice."

Ari and I shared another look and he shook his head. Unsure why he'd want to keep my identity a secret, I offered her a slice of truth. "I'm an energy helper from Amoran."

She nodded, the explanation seeming to satisfy her. Expertly navigating without use of a cane, Maya led us along a path toward a building up ahead that looked like a barn.

"Are you thinking what I'm thinking?" I whispered to Ari.

"A massive time warp," he whispered back. "Elvener's implosion happened eleven hundred years ago, yet Maya thinks she's only been here for thirty days."

Mental math is probably my only Earthly superpower. I did a rough set of calculations as we walked behind Maya, then said quietly to Ari, "I figure each day here equals about forty years. And each hour is a little less than two years."

Ari's mouth set in a grim line as we rounded a small group of trees. Two elves sat outside at a table, eating. They stood up, waving as we approached.

"Only three of you survived the implosion?" Ari asked.

"Yes. But a fourth person arrived right before you did."

"Right before . . ." I trailed off, my math mind working.

Maya hesitated, glancing around with unseeing eyes. "It seemed like only a few moments ago." She shook her head. "I've been confused today. No. It's been over an hour since he showed up. Maybe more. We had time to make our meal and begin to eat."

Over an hour since *he* arrived. That meant it was nearly two years ago in our time. Right around when the Reparention occurred.

I struggled to keep my voice even. "Where is this newcomer?"

Maya continued as if she hadn't heard me. "I tried to detect his energy signature, but all I perceive is . . . nothing." She shuddered. "I am told he is disheveled, mute, and stares ahead with eyes not blind, yet unseeing. He is . . . lost to us."

"Where is he?" I demanded, no longer hiding my emotions.

She seemed surprised at my outburst. "At the well. Behind the barn."

I ran, nearly tripping in my haste, cut around the barn, then stopped short and pushed my fist into my mouth to keep from crying out.

Next to the well sat a man in a tattered white tunic. Disheveled was putting it kindly. His clothes draped like rags about his thin body. One arm hung limp at his side, the other clutched his chest. Flies buzzed around his head. He didn't seem to notice them.

I could hear Ari coming up behind me, yelling to me to be careful, but it was too late. On legs that felt like wooden stumps, I stumbled the last few yards, knelt down, and tried to get Ashi to look at me. But the emerald green eyes, which had once gazed so intently into mine, stared vacantly ahead. Tears blurring my vision, I pushed the ragged hair away from his face and kissed him. His lips, cold as ice, offered no response.

Ari pulled me away, and we held onto each other, trembling. We both knew that what had happened to Ashi was worse than death. My Twin was indeed lost.

"We have to find a way out of this anomaly and fast," Ari breathed into my ear.

"Not without Ashi," I whispered. "Or the rest of them."

Ari gripped my arms. "If they believe it's only been a month, when in fact it's been over a thousand years, what do you think is happening in our time?"

I froze. I hadn't considered that. "Every minute we remain here—" I was too upset to do the math this time, but I knew it was bad. A week? Weeks?

Maya and the other elves caught up to us. She introduced Kylan and Haldoen to Ari, hesitating when it came to me. "Kerrin," I said. My Earth name would do for the moment.

Noting the position of the sun, which hung midpoint in the sky, Ari said, "We need to go back to Amoran to get help. We'll return before sunset to rescue you." Considering the time warp, it was a generous offer, giving a decade or so in our time to manage the feat.

"But how will you leave when no one has been able to do so yet?" Kylan asked.

Ari's eyes glazed over, his lips moving in silent speech. Without thinking, I grabbed his arms and shook him as if I needed to wake him up.

He blinked rapidly. "Thanks. I'm already being affected by this energy." He looked down, then stared in disbelief as a puddle next to the well rippled, formed little waves, then churned, all without apparent reason.

Ari's eyes lit up. "Water is the key."

"What do you mean?" Maya asked.

"No time to explain." Ari pointed at the puddle. "Did that water come from the well?"

"I spilled it earlier when I filled our cups," Kylan answered.

"Perfect. My friend and I need to drink from your well right now."

Haldoen ran back to the table and grabbed two goblets while Kylan pumped the spigot next to the well. When the water flowed freely, Haldoen filled the cups, then handed them to us.

"Drink it all," Ari said to me. "Then we'll ethermove."

Uh oh. "Ari? I haven't been able to ethermove yet."

He frowned. "Okay. I'll hold onto you and ethermove us both."

"If it's that simple, why couldn't they have done it?" I asked.

"Not only have they been here too long, but their entire reality needs to move. We don't have a way to do that now. Worse, the longer we stay, the more unstable we make it here."

We gulped the water down, then Ari grabbed me from behind.

"Think only of the mindsail, then take a deep breath and hold it."

A key part of ethermoving is setting the intention to become non-physical at the same moment you focus that intention on a location. I did the best I could, felt a massive hit of adrenaline, then cold water pressed against my skin as we broke through the surface of the Mindsail Lake into a moonless night.

"We missed the mindsail," Ari cried. "I can't find it in the dark."

"What do we do—argh." A wave knocked me over backward and my head went under just as I was taking a breath. I came up choking and gasping for air.

Ari wrapped his arms around my waist. "Hold tight. I've got to ethermove us again. Think only of the Main Chamber now."

The adrenaline hit was minimal and instead of disappearing instantly, our bodies slowly faded. A jet of white light shot up from the depths of the lake as we hovered above the water before rocketing through the air.

"Relax your muscles," Ari said. "I don't know if our atoms are—"

Too late. I had involuntarily braced myself for extreme pain when we crashed through the side of the Mountain. But instead of pain, I felt like lumpy gravy being pushed through a strainer.

We thudded onto the floor of the Main Chamber just outside the Golden Circle. I rolled over to push myself up, but all I could see was the tiled mandala where my hands and arms should be. What little experience I'd had with ethermoving, I knew this was wrong. Very wrong.

"Ari? Can you hear me?"

He grunted. "Get off my leg."

"Oh, is that your leg? I thought it was my leg."

"*Your* leg? We're invisible, Meiri, we didn't switch bodies."

A commotion sounded in one of the nearby passageways.

"I am sure I sensed them here," Eliasser bellowed as he burst into the Main Chamber.

Ashara raced in from behind him. "Could you have been mistaken?"

Without answering, Eliasser narrowed his gaze and scanned the room.

Ashara did likewise, then her eyes grew wide. "Oh, dear Light, they *are* here."

Eliasser nodded, his face white. "Caught."

"Ari, what is Eliasser talking about?"

"Caught. It means being stuck between physicality and non-physicality. Didn't Ashara explain this to you?" He didn't wait for an answer. "It rarely happens, and usually not to elves. The effect on our minds is a little like inhaling laughing gas on Earth. Judging by our inability to see each other and growing lack of mental coherence, I'd say we're already a Level Three."

"Is that bad?"

"Level Four is instant death."

Ashara and Eliasser were inching their way toward us, tiny tile by tiny tile. The sight of them mincing along would be enough to make anyone laugh, but thanks to the laughing gas effect, Ari and I lost it at that point.

"Why are they walking like demented ducks?" I chortled.

"Because if they touch us by accident, we'll disintegrate."

"Well, that's not good. When do we get to Level Four?"

He giggled. "About a minute."

I tried to stand up. Why, I don't know, but my legs wouldn't support my weight and I fell backwards. "What can we do to stop it?"

"Nothing." He laughed. "Not a God damned, Light blessed thing! Except . . ." Ari's hand groped for me in the invisibility, and landed on a strategic spot on the upper half of my body.

Hee-hee. "I didn't know you cared, Elfie."

I heard a thud as some part of his body fell against the tiled floor.

"You're going to have to do it Meiri," he said, all levity gone.

Like I'd been plunged into deep freeze, my mood went one-eighty. "What's wrong with us now?"

His voice came out in a whisper. "We're almost there Meiri. You have to do it, or we'll be gone soon."

"Do what?" My heart filled with dread. From mirth to misery in seven seconds.

Eliasser was now standing three feet from me. "You must ethermove again, Meiri."

"I can't ethermove!" I shouted, which, of course, Eliasser couldn't hear.

"You only need to go a few feet, but you must do it now. Hurry," Eliasser squeezed out.

Only a few feet? That was like miles to me!

I felt myself slipping out of reality, almost like a fadeout at the end of an old time TV show. Ari was right. I had to do it now or we'd be done for. I clamped my arms around him and focused on Eliasser, who was the right distance and provided the intense motivation I needed.

Adrenaline boost . . . wavering energy . . . wild spinning. Ari and I tumbled head over heels, bounced off the sides of the chamber, then shot straight up toward the ceiling.

No, no, no! Body . . . Disassemble! Atoms . . . get to Eliasser!

I filled every aspect of my vanished Being with the sight, sound and feel of my sweet king.

In a flash, Ari and I were back on the floor of the Main Chamber. This time, I could see the pale elf wedged beneath my body. Strong arms wrenched me free of the clutch hold I had on Ari's waist, then wrapped tightly around me.

"Thank the Light you are safe," Eliasser whispered. "We had nearly given up hope after finding the mindsail lodged in the tree roots across the lake." He brushed the wet hair back from my face. "Fissures are erupting everywhere. We were so afraid you had been drawn into one—" his voice broke.

"No. We were drawn into the lake," I said. "I have good—"

"For three weeks we have searched—"

"Never mind about that now! I have news . . . wait . . . we've been gone three weeks?"

"Do not speak, Meiri, until I can examine you," Ashara said, as she tended to Ari, who was only just rousing.

Balthasarre, Anders, and Danaeus came running toward us, but stopped at the sound of the portal opening. We all stared at the top of the Main Chamber as the blue mist rotated swiftly down to the Golden Circle. The stray rider had her back to us, but I knew who it was. She'd been watching me much more closely than I'd realized. Even so, I hadn't thought she could figure out how to open the portal. I was both dismayed and impressed.

Released by the mist, her knees buckled. She recovered quickly, then stomped across the mandala toward me. "Let go of her," she barked at Eliasser.

Eyes wide, he obeyed.

Mom took me by the arms. "I knew something was wrong. Are you all right, honey?"

Still in shock, I nodded. My mother had traversed the vortex for her first time and come straight through to the Main Chamber without any ill effects.

"But . . . are *you* all right?" I asked.

She shrugged. "I'm fine. I don't know why you make such a big deal out of it. Vortex travel is a piece of—" Her eyes rolled back in her head.

Chapter 19

Ashara insisted that Mom be carried to the Healing Room and assigned that task to Balthasarre. We all followed, Danaeus helping Ari while I leaned on Eliasser. With my mother temporarily indisposed, Eliasser returned to protective mode, his grip around my waist strong and uncompromising. I had missed contact with him so much that I let myself enjoy every moment of his attention.

As we walked, I tried to tell him that we'd found Ashi, but Ashara cut me off. "This is not an idle request. Until I have checked you for damage, you must conserve your strength. Do not speak. Not everyone survives being Caught."

That kept me quiet. The good news would have to wait.

When we reached the Healing Room, Mom roused just as Balthasarre placed her on a healing stone. He smiled down at her, and she fainted again. Meanwhile, Ari and I underwent a full examination. Other than some lingering dizziness, we were given a clean bill of health.

"I need to tell you all something," I said quietly, not sure how to proceed, not sure if the bad news outweighed the good news. Before I could go on, Mom woke again as Ashara put the finishing touches on a stabilizing draft for the three of us.

"That smells like a litter box," my mother grumbled.

Ashara smiled as she turned, tray in hand. "And I made it especially for you."

"Like hell, you did, shorty. I know you feed that crap to my daughter on a regular basis."

Ah, geez. *Shorty?* I couldn't even begin to figure out how to damage-control this mess. Ari laughed into his sleeve, Balthasarre blinked, and Eliasser's head swiveled back and forth between my mom and me. But Ashara's reaction was the most confusing as she set the tray down and handed Mom a goblet. "Nice to see you, Joanna. You are looking well."

Mom stared at Ashara, then narrowed her eyes. "Well, shit."

Ashara smiled.

My mother rubbed her hand over her face. "All of it?" she asked, subdued.

"All of it," Ashara confirmed. "Same request I always make when I give someone a potion."

My breath caught as my intuitive antennae pricked up.

Mom glared at Ashara, then impressed the hell out of me by chugging her stabilizing draft. She wiped her mouth with the back of her hand and gave the cup back to Ashara. They locked eyes in a visual standoff until Balthasarre broke the silence with an impatient request.

"In light of what is happening outside the Mountain, I would like to hear Meiri's news."

"Drink first," Ashara snapped at me. "Then talk."

I made a face at my cup, held my nose, and took a sip. "Gaagh. This is the worst yet!"

"Should have seen her with baby food vegetables," Mom mumbled.

Ashara laughed. "I have probably seen worse."

I shook my head at Ari. "Great. Now I've got two of them on my case."

Ari and I clinked goblets. Then we got brave and chugged the contents like my mother had. It took several moments for me to recover from the brew that did, in fact, smell like a cat box.

"Now, your news," Ashara said.

The declaration I was about to make felt oddly anticlimactic.

"We found Ashi."

"You . . . you found him?" Eliasser's eyes grew moist, then he turned on Ashara. "Next time, let them speak right away, for the love of the Light!"

Mom rolled her eyes at me and whispered, "Touchy."

I whispered back, "Not always."

Balthasarre was typically more laid back as a Guardian, but now he stepped up and took charge. And, I noted with mixed feelings, without any opposition from either the Master Guardian or the Master Healer.

"Danaeus?" Balthasarre called out.

"Here!" The dwarf jumped forward. I half expected him to salute.

"Find Meilee, Clarisanna, and Mikellan. Wake them from their sleeping stones if need be. Have them join the rest of us in the Guardian Meeting Room at once."

"What time is it?" I asked.

"Nearing dawn," Ashara answered.

"What about my mother?"

Ashara considered. "I need to keep her with someone until I am sure she is fit to travel back to Earth. How much time do you have left for this visit?"

"I . . . I'm not sure." Just thinking about it hurt my brain.

Mom caught my eye. "Another two Earth hours." She sighed. "The surprise I had planned for us can wait."

"Good," Ashara said. "Joanna will have ten days here to recuperate."

"What do we do with her now, though?" I asked.

"Hey! I'm in the room!" Mom wagged a finger at Ashara. "I'm staying with my daughter."

Ashara smiled. "Then you will make the eleventh member of our group today. Always an auspicious number, eleven."

Mom gave us a satisfied smile. Balthasarre helped her off the healing stone and led her from the room, followed by the rest of the group except for Ashara and me.

I stared at the Master Healer. "You're not surprised to see her, are you?"

"No. I knew this day would arrive. I just did not know when."

"Why was she able to go through the vortex like a pro?"

"You have not guessed?" I shook my head. "Your mother is also a Vibrational."

Mom . . . a Vibrational? I was oddly pleased. And proud.

Ashara's now unfocused gaze rested on the potions cabinet. She gave a vigorous shake of her head.

"I do not know what is happening to me lately." She met my eyes, then grasped my hands. "Promise me that you will take charge if Eliasser and I cannot perform our duties."

Shards of ice encased my spine. I had never seen the Master Healer this vulnerable. "Why would you—"

Ashara held her fingers to my lips. "Just . . . promise me."

Tears pricked at the back of my eyes, but I refused to allow them entrance. I couldn't speak and keep up my pseudo-stoic façade, so I merely nodded.

Ashara enveloped me in a warm embrace that bordered on clingy before exiting the room.

I sat, staring at the floor for so long that Danaeus was sent to come find me.

"You mother really let them have it," Danaeus said as we walked to the Guardian Meeting Room. "Is that the right phrase?"

I smiled and nodded. "You're turning into a regular Earth dweller. I'm almost afraid to ask, but how did she let them have it?"

"After she was introduced, Eliasser grumbled that she shouldn't have to be introduced, because she shouldn't be here to begin with. He was going on about Amoran needing to be kept a secret, and how 'Meiri should have told us about you,' when Joanna cut him off."

Danaeus continued, mimicking my mother's tone with remarkable accuracy. "'You people freak out about the strangest things. The damage was already done, and she didn't want to upset you. Especially you two,' she added, pointing at Ashara and Eliasser."

"Oh, god," I groaned.

Danaeus grinned. "She didn't stop there, though. She told them it's a miracle you hadn't been seen coming or going from the family room portal before, and how hard it is for you to juggle both worlds—you'll have to explain that one to me. And then she said, 'I have kept this stupid secret, and I will continue to keep this stupid secret. But I intend to help my daughter in any way I can. Just try and stop me!'"

Danaeus laughed. "I really like your mother." His smile lessened. "I don't remember my family too well, but I think our mothers would have enjoyed each other's company."

The comment surprised and saddened me. Danaeus had never mentioned a family or missing them. I'd asked him in the past about his homeworld, but he didn't like to talk about it.

"Someday, Danaeus, we will find a way to get you home."

He sighed and shook his head. "I don't think it's possible, but thanks for the offer."

We entered the Guardian Meeting Room and I took the empty seat between my mother and Ashara. The group had already been informed that Makashannar had been located. Now Ari and I finally got to tell the story of finding not just Ashi, but Maya, Kylan, and Haldoen. Because it was such an emotionally difficult tale for us to relate, we asked that questions be held until we were done.

There were exclamations of surprise and incredulity over the state of the Mindsail Lake, the strange tunnel with its plumes of flaming light, and the bucolic setting we arrived in. Cries of joy followed upon learning that not only had Makashannar somehow lived through the Reparention's balancing explosion, but three elves had survived the implosion of the Fifth Vortex. When we explained about the time warp, and how for Maya, Kylan, and Haldoen only one month had transpired since Elvener's destruction, everyone just looked stunned.

Then I broke the news about Ashi. Apart from Ari, who can't cry, there wasn't a dry eye in the place. Even Mom was a little teary-eyed, and she was the opposite of me when it came to that sort of emotional display. As for Eliasser? His heart broke right along with my own. After one long, wrenching sob, he covered his face with his hands.

Balthasarre cleared his throat. "I do not believe that Makashannar has survived two such incidents only to be beyond our reach now. Wherever his mind resides, we will bring him home—all the way home." Balthasarre glanced at Ari, then me. "We need to explore every aspect of your journey. How we proceed, what method we use to rescue our lost friends, will be found in the nuances of what you experienced."

Mom murmured, "And I thought meetings on Earth were long."

"We go all night, sometimes," I muttered back.

Ari and I launched into the details of our day. It got dicey when Balthasarre kept pressing us as to what we were arguing about right before the wave tossed us into the water.

"Just stuff," Ari finally shouted. "Why does it matter?"

Balthasarre leaned forward, scrutinizing Ari's face. This was something that usually fell to the Master Guardian or Master Healer. "What manner of 'stuff' may matter a great deal if it is what created waves in the lake. The water was calm until then, correct?"

Ari and I stared at each other. How could we tell the truth without telling the whole truth? No one was supposed to know that Eliasser and I had merged, let alone that he had now become capable of physical desires.

Ari crossed his arms. "We were discussing sexual energy. Who feels it. Who doesn't."

"I do not see the relevance," Balthasarre said with a frown. "You are both sexually able. Discussing other people should not cause heightened emotions."

Spoken like someone who doesn't feel desire.

Mom watched their continued interchange like a spectator at a tennis match. "A little clueless, isn't he?" she said so only I could hear.

"You don't know the half of it," I whispered back.

Balthasarre turned to me. "Meiri, you have made it clear that secret-keeping is a problem. I ask you again, who was the object of your idle chatter?"

His choice of words indicated how he felt about our conversation.

Ari gave the barest shake of his head, his way of telling me to keep quiet.

"If you must know," Ari snapped, "I accused Meiri of feeling that way about someone. She . . . disagreed. Her denial"—he tapped his heart—"caused unrest within me."

My heart skipped a beat as Eliasser narrowed his eyes and studied Ari, whose vague, but honest answer hit a little too close to home.

Balthasarre sighed. "Who was the recipient of your observation about Meiri?"

Ari waxed melodramatic. "I begged her to search her heart and accept the inevitable. To stop denying what is plain to me. Because it will hurt her, and hurt the object of her . . . affections."

The flush in my face probably wasn't missed by anyone. Damn Ari.

"And that person is?" Meilee prompted.

"Me!" He gave me his best Cheshire cat smile.

And I gave him my best evil eye. Except for who the object of my affections was, Ari not only told the truth, but he'd stuck it to me again about my supposed feelings for Eliasser.

No one gasped or seemed surprised. "I could have told you that ages ago," Danaeus said. "They're always teasing each other. It was only a matter of time."

"I *know*," Ari said with overblown emphasis. "Only a matter of time before she would have to acknowledge how she felt about a *certain someone*, right Meiri?" He hooked his thumbs in those imaginary suspenders he invoked from time to time. "After all, I am *to die* for!"

Mom whispered, "He is kind of cute."

"Not happening," I mumbled.

"Oh, come on. You could do worse."

"Not really," I hissed. "He meant 'die' in the literal sense of the word."

She shot a look across the table. Ari grinned and pretended to hang himself.

"Holy shit," Mom said, forgetting to lower her voice. When all eyes turned to her, my no-holds-barred parent turned a little pink. "Oh. Sorry. I'll keep quiet."

Ashara snorted out a laugh. "I give her five minutes."

"Enough," Balthasarre said, and brought the meeting back on track. "Thank you for your honesty, Arrien. Your interaction with Meiri out on the lake may have provided an opening for the anomalous energy to appear once more, although what its origin is, and why it comes at all is still a mystery. And as before, everyone here is being changed by it." He swept his hand around the table, stopped at my mother, and smiled. "Except for you, of course."

Mom smiled back and gave him a little salute, her cheeks flushed with color as their gaze held a few seconds.

"There is one thing I should mention now," Ari said. "When we left, there was an instability forming. I'm afraid that the place Ashi and the others are in does not have much longer to exist."

"How long before it collapses?" Ashara asked.

"A few days at most."

I groaned. "I thought we had a decade in our time. Did our interference bring this on?"

"Probably just made it happen faster," he said. "But if we hadn't gone there, we'd never know that Maya, Ashi, and the others are still alive."

There was that.

"About the wave," I said, as a thought came to me. "Maybe it wasn't what we were talking about that caused it to happen. Ari stopped the boat in the same place where the amulet went into the water the first time. The more we argued, the heavier the amulet became, and the choppier the water grew. But it was when I grabbed Ari's arm that it grew hot and started to glow."

Balthasarre stroked his beard. "What are you suggesting?"

"That the combination of Ari's and my energy, through physical contact, makes the amulet come alive."

Balthasarre nodded. "I am not sure what we can do with that information, but I am now moved to share this." With a wave of his hand, the wall behind Eliasser and Ashara came alive with a map of the area encompassing the Garrammon field, Garrammon Meadow, and the Mindsail and Garrammon Lakes.

"Where did that come from?" I asked.

"Anders and I created it with the help of our new ambient energy." Rising from his chair, he approached the map and smiled. "One good thing to come of the altered vibrational levels."

Balthasarre drew a large "x" with his finger in the center of the Garrammon Meadow, the letter appearing like fluorescent light. "This is where the portal to the Mirror Vortex was. It is also where we found Ashi several days after the Mirror Vortex collapsed. And here"—he made another "x" near the southwestern edge of the meadow—"is where Ari and Meiri were caught in the time warp last year, which we are now calling the Meadow Anomaly."

My peripheral vision caught my mother's head swivel. "I'll explain later," I whispered.

"A year from that event, the first plume of light erupted here." Another "x" went at the meadow's northern end. "Finally, this is where Ari and Meiri fell overboard and were drawn into what Ari thought might be a shifting channel-vent." He drew the last "x" in the Mindsail Lake, where it curved up along the eastern side of the meadow.

Ari shook his head. "I can't even say that for sure. I have never experienced anything like it. It seemed like a channel-vent, yet the area we found the survivors in had aspects of a dimensional variance. And underpinning it all—a time warp."

"Whatever this phenomenon is, it created havoc after Ari and Meiri went missing this last time. We searched the entirety of Guardian Lands for them. When the plumes of light began in earnest, we were forced to halt our efforts. For the three weeks they were gone, crevices opened and closed all over this area, spewing light high into the air." Balthasarre drew a large circle connecting the Xs at the northern, southwestern, and eastern edges of the Garrammon Meadow. "One thing stands out."

"The central point is where the Mirror Vortex portal was located," Meilee noticed.

"Yes, Meilee. I believe the Mirror Vortex is the key. Until we had contact with Elvener by way of the Mirror Vortex, the energy in our own vortex had been stable for over a thousand years. It was only after the Fifth Vortex implosion and Mirror Vortex collapse that unusual energy patterns appeared in the Seventh Vortex. Within the next hundred years, the currents grew stronger and the Darkness began to increase. That is when the Foreseers predicted the demise of our vortex without a radical repair effort."

"You are saying it was contact with Elvener and the Mirror Vortex that created the need for the Reparention in the first place?" Ashara asked.

"I believe so. Yes."

"When the Mirror Vortex collapsed," Anders said, "could it have created a dimensional variance that is located beneath the area encompassed by the circle?"

"Instead of on the surface. Interesting." Balthasarre tapped a finger to his chin. "Ari, where were Maya and her group when the Mirror Vortex collapse began?"

Ari thought for a moment. "They were supposed to enter the Mirror Vortex after I gave the signal. I didn't have time, though, because the implosion began right away at the Elvener end."

"Are you certain that Maya was not in the vortex yet?"

Ari sighed. "No. I just assumed. The collapse progressed too quickly. It was . . . chaos. I could barely see Ashi, who fought the vortex winds to come and rescue me. Still, I don't think Maya would have come in once it was clear that implosion was imminent."

"Why not?" I said to Ari. "I did it without a moment's hesitation." I closed my eyes, this being one memory I had obtained and held onto. "Ashi got you to our end, but you were both nearly paralyzed by dark energy. I entered the collapsing vortex and brought the two of you the rest of the way to the portal. I shoved you out, Ari, then turned around, wondering why Ashi wasn't behind me. That's when I saw that he'd been dragged back into the winds."

I shuddered. Contact with vortex winds during an upheaval was terrifying. "I wanted to rescue him, too, but Eliasser fought his way in through the narrowing portal and yanked me out. A second later the portal disintegrated." I swallowed hard. Every time I allowed myself this memory, I experienced all the feelings that went with it, including the loss of Ari's entire world.

"Meiri?" Balthasarre prodded gently.

I shook my head. "Sorry. Let's assume that Maya operates like I do where my loved ones are concerned. When the Mirror Vortex began its collapse, she wouldn't have wasted precious time debating whether it was the right or smart thing to do; she would have entered the Elvener portal to save her Eternal Companion. I'm also going to assume that she had no way of knowing that Ashi had already rescued Ari."

Balthasarre tilted his head. "So . . . if an anomaly was created when the Mirror Vortex collapsed—be it a dimensional variance, channel-vent, time warp, or all three combined—it may have taken Maya and her small group with it."

"Ashi was also in the Mirror Vortex when the implosion occurred," Meilee pointed out.

Ari leaned forward. "If the anomaly occurred at that moment, he might have been pulled within it temporarily, then released while the others remained trapped inside."

"Which means," Danaeus added, "based on the time warp component, he wasn't missing for several days, which was our experience of him being gone. For him, it would only have been a second or two."

We found Ashi a few days after the Mirror Vortex implosion, but it had taken months for him to regain consciousness. He'd never been able to tell us what happened after he rescued Ari. He didn't even remember me going in after him.

Clarisanna finally spoke. "If this place Maya is in, this dimensional variance or time warp or channel-vent, was created when the Mirror Vortex imploded, why is Makashannar there now?"

I pressed my palms to the table and took a stab at answering.

"What if, when the explosion to rebalance the Seventh Vortex finally detonated, it cut a temporary opening into this—whatever it is—and Ashi either fell through or got pushed into it?"

Meilee pointed to the map. "The Seventh Vortex is nowhere near the area defined by Balthasarre's circle. What opening could there have been?"

Eliasser sat forward in his chair. "A porthole."

Balthasarre squinted in concentration. "Yes. Quite rare, but that could explain it. Ari?"

"I agree, although why it didn't occur to me before this . . ." he trailed off and shook his head. "I don't think Amoran has ever seen one, and I'm sure we never had one on Elvener, so 'rare' is probably too generous a word."

I figured they weren't talking about a window on a ship, but Mikellan asked the question before I could.

"Forgive my ignorance, but I do not know what a porthole is."

Judging by the number of blank looks, I wasn't the only one in the dark. Balthasarre gave us a long, involved explanation which only succeeded in shifting the vacant stares to confusion.

Ari tried to simplify things. "It's like a quasi-controllable wormhole."

And . . . we were back to blank looks.

"Isn't that just an Earth term?" I asked.

"You're right. Boy, I am really off my game, speaking of Earth terms." He sighed. "Okay. Think of it as an interdimensional ether-moving device."

"Ah. Now I get it." As did everyone else except my mother.

"I'm still out of the loop, Ari," Mom said.

Ari turned to her and wiggled his eyebrows. "Beam me up, Scotty."

She laughed. "Got it." Then, she smirked at Ashara. "I win. I held my tongue for way more than five minutes, toots."

Ashara shook her head, but she was smiling. What the heck was up with these two?

"So, in the midst of a disaster, this . . . porthole . . . just appeared and transported Ashi to where Maya, Kylan, and Haldoen wound up a thousand years ago?" Meilee asked.

Ari tilted his head to the side. "The level of energy we were channeling during the Reparention, the intensity, then the explosion, could all have contributed to creating a spontaneous porthole. It would have been highly unstable—not controllable in the least, and it would have lasted barely long enough to get him out of the vortex. But it is a possibility."

"Question is," Anders said, "without imploding a vortex, collapsing a Mirror Vortex, or summoning up a porthole, how do we get back in there to rescue them?"

I rose and walked to the map. Balthasarre stepped to the side as I studied his handiwork up close. "Twice now, Ari and I have been drawn to this spot." I pointed to the "x" over the Mindsail Lake. "On two separate occasions, Ashi's amulet led us into the lake; the most recent time it brought us through the lake bottom and into—" I paused. We didn't really know what it was, and channel-vent/dimensional variance/time warp was a mouthful. "Let's call this whole thing—the tunnel of plumes and the place where the elves are now—the Elvener Anomaly, since it led us to Maya, Kylan, and Haldoen. Given all that, it's reasonable to assume that we could enter that way a third time to rescue them."

"I will not allow you to go into the Mindsail Lake again," Eliasser said firmly.

"I agree," Balthasarre said.

I let that slide.

"Ari, when we were in the . . . Elvener Anomaly . . . you said water was the key to getting us out. What did you mean by that?"

"I'm not sure. When the water at our feet started to shake with little waves, something about that seemed familiar, like a miniature version of what happened on the Mindsail Lake. It was an impulse to have us drink it, but I think it was the right move. I just don't know why."

Meilee slowly stood up, her gaze unfocused. "We must drink of life before our time, to set time right and bring back life. Water provides all that we need."

She gasped and slumped back in her chair, trembling.

"Someone help her," Anders cried out, pulling her into his arms.

"I am all right," Meilee whispered.

"Indeed, you are," Ashara said. "But you will need to rest. This type of contact with the Light can be difficult on the body. Meiri and I will make potions, first for you, Meilee, then for the rest of us. We will break now and return in three hours to make our plan."

Mom turned to me, her expression grim. "I had no idea. Not exactly a fairyland, is it?"

"It is usually," I said. "Except for times like this when it can be downright deadly."

Chapter 20

The difference in interdimensional energy finally got to my mother. She passed out on a healing stone while Ashara and I designed potions for our Rescue Team, as I had come to think of the ten of us. We had little time to spare, so the rest of the Mountain inhabitants would only get enhanced stabilizing drafts until we could do a person-by-person assessment. We left the actual potion production to a team of healing Assistants.

After helping Ashara, I managed to snag a few Zs before our next meeting. Then, for six hours we hatched plans, shot them down or remade them, only to scrap the revisions. By Evening Meal, which we ate while we worked, we were exhausted and cranky. Since we'd become unproductive at this point, we agreed to take a five-hour sleep break. Ashara promised special reviving drafts to keep us awake when we returned.

I grabbed Ari as we left the Guardian Meeting Room. "I think we're going about this all wrong."

"How so?" Ari's eyes were bloodshot. I'd never seen him so tired and overwrought.

"Meilee said water provides all. We were pulled into the Elvener Anomaly through water. Then, we had to drink water from the well to get back. Doesn't that strike you as important?"

"It strikes me that you and I take the most risks, do the most stupid things, and then have to bail each other out." He paused. "Pun intended."

I laughed. "Okay, that's true."

He gave me a weary smile as he linked his arm in mine. "Of course, that's what I love about our friendship."

I patted his arm. "Me too. And I think we need to get stupid one more time."

He froze. "You're not serious, are you?"

"I am. We need to access the Elvener Anomaly through the Mindsail Lake. Again."

The Rescue Team reconvened in the Guardian Meeting Room. My mother was still conked out, which didn't surprise me. I'd reacted the same way to my first long haul in another dimension.

During the past five hours, the fissures and plumes had completely abated. I hoped this would make my proposition more acceptable. I waited until everyone was settled with their individually tailored potions and reviving drafts, plus small plates of food, then laid out the plan Ari and I cooked up while we were supposed to be sleeping. Contrary to our usual seating arrangement, Ari and I were side-by-side, hoping to project together the strength and determination we knew would be necessary to sell the rest of the Guardians on our idea.

"I will get straight to the point," I said. "Ari and I need to use the amulet to guide us back to Ashi. If we focus on where he and the others are now and go intentionally into the Mindsail Lake, we hope to bypass the tunnel of plumes and end up where we need to be."

"Absolutely not!" Eliasser thundered.

Ari and I had anticipated this reaction. Ari took point now, arguing each objection that Eliasser brought up, countering it with logic. "But Meiri and I have never been hurt in the water. But we're the only ones who can swim. But our bodies, being from Earth and Elvener, are different; they can withstand the energy surges better. But we drank the water from the well with no ill effects. But we are the reason the plumes are coming in the first place!"

This was met with a shocked silence. Even Eliasser, who was becoming more agitated with each defense Ari offered, seemed taken aback.

Ari and I still weren't certain about the causal relationship, but there was definitely a correlation.

A thoughtful Balthasarre broke the silence. "Could it be?" he murmured, stroking his beard. "A year ago, Ari and Meiri experienced a unique dimensional time warp in the Garrammon Meadow. Twice now, they have had an altercation with an anomalous energy at the Mindsail Lake. Then there is the enormous surface plume that shot up from the edge of the meadow when they were playing Garrammon." He regarded Ari first, then me. "It does seem that when you two are present, things happen."

Ashara leaned forward. "There was also the day Ari summoned me to the Garrammon field when Meiri passed out at the edge of the meadow. They were together then as well."

Eliasser looked like he was about to come out of his skin. "I never heard about this!"

Ashara sighed. "You were gone. At the time, I only thought it odd that she heard a voice, not that she fainted."

Eliasser's eyebrows knitted together. "You heard a voice again? Male or female?"

"The same male voice I heard during the Meadow Anomaly," I said. "The one that called my name three times."

Eliasser folded his hands together and leaned his forehead against them like he was praying. Except he wasn't. He was trying to control himself, something I could sense even from here. I wanted to know why the voice bothered him, but this wasn't the place or the time. Especially not the time. We were swiftly running out of that commodity.

"We're not wild about doing this," I said. That was putting it mildly. We were terrified. "But we need to take advantage of a very important fact; the combination of Ari and I activates something in this anomalous energy."

"Is that because you are in love?" Meilee asked, blushing.

Ari and I guffawed, then quickly got control of ourselves.

"You are not in love?" Meilee perceptively asked.

Put so directly, I couldn't pretend. I stared at the food plate in front of me. My appetite gone, I had barely touched it. "Ari and I love each other very much, but we are not in love that way."

Balthasarre sounded crestfallen. "Why did you lie to us, Meiri?"

"She didn't." Ari placed his hand over my arm. "I lied. Meiri just went along with my ruse."

"Why would you do that, Meiri?" Eliasser asked, but with such gentleness that it threw me off guard. I met his gaze as he looked up from his folded hands and regarded me with an intensity that sent chills rolling up my spine. Sparks ignited in my brain. His aqua eyes bore into my emerald green ones, the connection seeming to hold me captive as every nerve ending in my body ignited with an inner fire. What was happening?

I stuttered to respond. "I . . . uh . . . because . . ."

Ari shot to a stand and slapped his palms on the table. "Because I was protecting her heart and our friendship. I did try to force Meiri to see the truth about someone, but the specifics of what we said will serve no purpose and may hurt others. That's all I'm going to say. Not every thought or feeling needs to be shared." As Ari lowered himself down again, he nodded in Eliasser's direction and whispered in my ear, "And if you could see what I see right now . . ."

Balthasarre sighed. "We should return to the matter at hand. I assume there is more to your plan. What will you do when the two of you make it back to Ashi?"

I dearly appreciated him saying "when" and not "if." Relieved to have something concrete to focus on instead of just sitting there with my nerve endings on fire, I said, "Bear with me, everyone. I know it didn't end well before, but Ari and I have gone over this several times, and we think that the only way we can bring the survivors home is by ethermoving them."

Eliasser opened his mouth in protest, but Balthasarre held his hand up. "How will you ethermove six people? And to what location?"

Ari and I traded a look. We hadn't worked any of that out yet.

"What about the Garrammon Meadow?" Meilee offered.

"The meadow . . ." Balthasarre drew his lower lip between his teeth, then released it as his eyes widened. "Dear Light. That is a brilliant suggestion."

Anders beamed and Meilee reddened as Balthasarre walked to the wall map and drew a tight circle around where the Mirror Vortex portal once was. "Meiri and Ari can use the trace energy that still emanates from the portal's location to amplify their ethermoving." He tapped the circle and looked at us both. "When you are in the Elvener Anomaly and ready to transport the survivors, concentrate on the Mirror Vortex portal as your landing point. We will wait here to receive you." He drew a circle around the perimeter of the Garrammon Meadow.

I looked at Ari. "You said their entire reality needs to move, not just the people."

"That is true," Balthasarre said. "The Elvener Anomaly, and all that it contains, needs to move into its own dimensional expression. Right now, it is in a slow-moving stasis."

"Time warp," I said, and he nodded.

"What about the plumes?" Eliasser asked, frowning. "When Ari and Meiri reach the survivors, the plumes will likely return, erupting through the surface of the meadow while we are waiting for them to ethermove."

Balthasarre set his mouth in a grim line. "That troubles me, too. With the time distortion, we will not know when they have reached the survivors, or when they are able to begin ethermoving. This also means we have no way of knowing when the plumes will arrive. It could possibly be as soon as Ari and Meiri leave us."

Anders said, "What if we envelop the meadow in a grounded energy circle?"

Ari whispered to me, "Like a force field."

"Good," Balthasarre said. "That might keep the plumes at bay. We will need to initiate it as soon as Ari and Meiri go into the lake. I fear we will not be able to hold it long, though."

Danaeus had an odd expression on his face. "But this is the right plan. I can feel it."

"How long will it take to work out the arrangements for the meadow?" I asked.

Anders gave Meilee's hand a squeeze. "We can have the patterns for the energy circle completed within six hours."

"With Clarisanna and Mikellan's help, I can have potions ready in about that time," Ashara said. "Dawn is approaching. When do you want to do this, Meiri?"

I felt the surety of the timing in my bones. "Today. Just before the sun sets." I waved Ari up from the table. "Let's get some sleep, Elf-boy. We've got a big night ahead of us."

"I'm really scared," I said quietly to Ari as we readied the boat at the Mindsail Lake.

"Me too. Now say your goodbye. It's time to go."

Eliasser, who had accompanied us this far, waited on the shore. Ari climbed into the mindsail and turned his back to us. The attempt at giving us privacy was sweet, but unnecessary.

I sighed, lifted my gaze from the sand, and met Eliasser's eyes. "Can I have a hug for good luck? I'll understand if you don't—"

Eliasser crushed me to his chest, my face pressed to his heart. I clung to him so tightly, my fingers hurt. At length, he loosened his grip and kissed the top of my head.

"Go now. Bring Ashi home. Bring them all back to us."

"I will," I promised him, and entered the mindsail.

Eliasser released the rope and gave the boat a push.

"May the Love of the Light guide you both," he called out.

His lone figure grew smaller, then disappeared from view as we sailed around a bend in the lake across calm and placid water. The place we needed to get to wasn't far.

"Ready?" Ari asked, when he'd brought the mindsail to a halt.

"As I'll ever be."

I pulled the amulet from beneath my tunic and held it out in front of me. Ari placed his fingers near mine, and we set our intention to go directly to the well, to where we'd left Ashi.

At the count of three, we grasped onto the pendant.

Bang! Flash!

A brilliant sphere of light radiated out from our joined hands, growing hotter and hotter until I could barely hold on to Ari or the pendant. Energy spiraled up through my body with a nauseating spinning. Ari and I had planned to transport directly to the well. The amulet had other ideas. Rotating at a feverish pace, we catapulted straight up into the air.

"Hold your breath," Ari screamed.

The energy flipped us over and plunged us head-down into the water. I figured we'd be pulled under the lake bottom, like before.

Again, the amulet surprised us.

Still spiraling at warp speed, we were dragged sideways through frigid water. Tightening our fingers, we struggled to stay connected as seconds that felt like hours ticked away.

Ari had better underwater skills than I did, but he was the first to lose them. In an explosive burst, he exhaled. Then, as if he couldn't stop himself, he sucked in a lungful of water and his face contorted in agony.

A moment later, the air rushed from my lungs. I forced my mouth closed and tried not to breathe in; tried to keep Ari's hand over the pendant; tried to keep our hands clasped together.

Tried to—

I convulsively inhaled. Water burned its way down my throat and hit my lungs like someone had scraped the insides of them with cut glass; the pain so excruciating, I prayed to pass out. Our trajectory pivoted ninety degrees and we hurtled down through the caustic water until I "fell" out of the lake bottom onto solid ground.

Rolling to my side, I threw up like I had food poisoning. My brain felt like it had been split in two. When I finally stopped retching, I wobbled up to a sitting position and held my aching head in my hands. Ari was several feet away, on the barn side of the well. I could only see his feet sticking beyond the rock wall. He was coughing so hard I thought his lungs would come up.

"Get him some water," Maya shouted.

"Where's Meiri?" Ari asked, before another coughing fit overtook him.

"Did Meiri come with you this time?"

It was an odd question, until I recalled that we hadn't told her who I was.

I tried to stand up, but my arms and legs felt like they had ten-pound weights strapped to my ankles and wrists. "I'm . . . here," I croaked through my parched throat, not sounding any better than Ari. How could I have sucked down that much water and still be thirsty?

"Keep him drinking," Maya commanded. Kneeling beside me, she felt my forehead and checked my eyes. That's when I noticed that hers were no longer vacant.

"You're feverish and dehydrated. I need water here!" she called out.

Haldoen thrust a cup into her hand, then returned to Ari.

Maya put her arm around my shoulder to keep me upright as I clumsily took some sips.

"Is that really you, Meiri?" she asked.

My body resembled the one I'd had when she knew me, but the energy I radiated was different now, so I understood her confusion.

"Yes," I rasped out. "Long story."

She offered me the cup again, and I gulped it down, the well water somehow restoring strength that the water from the Mindsail Lake had taken away.

Kaboom!

An earsplitting thunderclap tore through the air, the ground trembled, and the horizon turned blood orange. Black clouds that weren't there seconds ago dumped buckets of icy rain on us.

"He moved on his own!" Kylan shouted.

Lightning strikes zapped every which way—up, down, sideways. Each time one hit a solid object, the burning smell pinched inside my nose.

The sky went dark again as the rain continued to pound down.

"He did it again," Haldoen cried out. "Look!"

Ari was on his feet now. Maya helped me to mine, then pointed at the well. Ashi stood several feet back from the stone enclosure, drenched, but seemingly aware of his surroundings.

Fingers of light split the air once more, tearing a huge hole in the sky.

"This reality is coming apart," Ari yelled. "We've got to go now!"

Ashi stumbled around the well and pointed at Ari. "I . . . I know you, but I cannot recall why."

"We can deal with that later," Ari said. "We have to leave now, or we'll cease to exist."

Ashi nodded, his rain-covered face resolute. "What can I do?"

My raw throat tightened. That was so like Ashi. He may not have been in the Darkness, but he'd been in a type of darkness that was nearly as bad. And the first thing he did when he became conscious again? Offered to help.

A full-blown earthquake turned the well and the barn into piles of rubble.

"Everyone all right?" Ari called out, pushing himself up from the muddy ground. With varying degrees of success, we all lurched to our feet. Miraculously no one was hurt.

Ari clapped a hand on Ashi's shoulder. "We need to ethermove everyone out of here. I don't know if you will be able to help. You've been in this reality a long time."

Ashi flexed his fingers, as if testing their worthiness. "Where are we going?"

"The Garrammon Meadow, where the Mirror Vortex imploded."

Ashi squinted. "Garrammon Meadow. I think I remember that."

A jagged spear of light hit the ground where the barn had been.

"Gather around the well everyone, what's left of it," Ari said. "I'll take Maya and Kylan. Ashi and Haldoen, go with Meiri."

Ashi narrowed his eyes as he studied my muddy face. "That is not Meiri."

"Never mind that now," Ari snapped. "Just do as she says."

Ari and Maya wrapped themselves around Kylan and vanished.

I thrust Haldoen in front of me, then motioned Ashi into position. He hesitated for a moment, which was a really bad thing, because the ground below us began to disassemble. Ethermoving for me is a challenge to begin with, but that delay could cost us our lives.

I grabbed Ashi's hands, closed my eyes, invoked the Light's perfect unfoldment, and—

Through the melee of frantic voices, I picked one out.

"No one enter the meadow," Eliasser shouted. "They must come to us." His voice dropped as he pleaded, "Wake up, Meiri. Please . . . wake *up*."

I opened my eyes. I'd landed in the Garrammon Meadow with Ashi on top of me. Up above, more dark clouds whipped around in a twisting frenzy. Funnels formed, dipped to the ground, then snapped back up.

With a sudden slam of nausea, I rolled us both over, turned my head to the side and threw up. I was only clutching Ashi now, my fingers rigid and painful from gripping so tightly. Where was Haldoen?

"Meiri," Eliasser called out. "You must ethermove to me. Just like you did in the Main Chamber. Do it *now*!"

Ashi stared open-eyed at the sky, his expression blank. I shook him; once, twice. Nothing.

Tears blinded me. We'd come so far; I couldn't let him die now.

I threw myself on top of him, wrapped my arms around his back, focused on Eliasser and prayed. *By the One Light, by the Love of All—I claim one more ethermove.*

I barely felt the spinning and then Ashi was pried from my arms by Ashara, as Eliasser wrapped me up in his pilea like a baby in a blanket and ethermoved me to the Healing Room.

CHAPTER 21

"Kylan and Haldoen are gone?" I'd just been given a thorough checkup by Ashara and Peliyama, who had come from the Council of Light to lend her aid.

"They did not make it through to the meadow," Ashara said quietly, her gray eyes framed with sadness.

I turned away and covered my eyes with my hands. "I'd like to be alone now." I'm not usually uncomfortable crying in front of other people, but the wrenching upheaval I experienced over this news made me want to deal with my emotions in private.

"It is not only grief you are experiencing," Peliyama perceptively said. "You have traveled through multiple dimensional realities in one day. All aspects of your Being need time to adjust, not just your body. For you, tears are a necessary release. Shed as many as you must. Human bodies are made to be this way."

I appreciated the support, but I still wanted to be alone. The Guardians had seen me cry plenty of times, but this was more like when John died. Whatever the truth about my feelings, right now they were so over the top, I was embarrassed to have people see me. But what I heard next froze me to my core, effectively capping off those tears I so desperately needed to shed.

"I told you, she is not Meiri!" Ashi yelled from behind a privacy screen at the other end of the Healing Room.

"What's wrong with him?" I asked.

Ashara handed me a potion. "Drink."

I took the cup from her, downed the contents as fast as I could, then thrust it into her hands.

"Now will you tell me what the problem is?"

Ashara rarely looked sympathetic, so I knew I was in trouble whenever she did. "Ashi remembers nothing about the Reparention or the months you spent here with us beforehand."

"Nothing at all?"

"As far as he is concerned, you never came back to us." She drew her lips between her teeth, then added, "I am sorry to tell you this, but he is still waiting for his Twin Light to return."

"So am I." It was nothing short of miraculous that I ethermoved right off the healing stone to my room, landing on my sleeping stone. But that's what motivation will do for you. I sealed my doorway and had that whopping meltdown Peliyama was so certain would do me good.

"She knocked me out, plain and simple. Every time I woke up, she made me drink something else, and down I went for another twelve hours." Mom narrowed her eyes at me. "She admitted it, so don't go defending her."

"I won't. But did she tell you why?"

Mom waved her hand in the air like she was shooing away a fly. "Yeah, yeah. Some claptrap about interdimensional energy that would screw up my vibrations." She sighed and shrugged. "Sounded serious."

"It was . . . and still is. She did that to protect you. It's true about the energy. But she also didn't want you to worry about me." Or try to interfere.

Peliyama had gone back to whatever planet she was from. Mom and I were alone, finishing up our Evening Meal before I headed over to the "debriefing" meeting. Except for Ashi and Eliasser, the others were already there, listening to Ashara explain about Ashi's lack of memory. I stayed with Mom while they got that bad news out of the way. I didn't need to hear it twice. But it wasn't only a lack of memory that affected Ashi. When Ashara conducted a full health assessment on him, it seemed his ability to experience sexual desire was gone.

I asked Mom if she wanted to accompany me, but she declined. "No offense, but your meetings get a little longwinded. Vianna offered to show me around. I understand you've got quite the garden here."

"We do. You'll love it."

The garden is accessed through a portal located in the wall of the Main Chamber. I'm not sure if the garden is outdoors somewhere, or just appears to be outdoors, like an illusion. But it's full of exotic plants and flowers, with a fountain at the center and rose bushes galore. As lovely as the garden is, I'd only been there a few times since I returned after the Reparention, preferring the true outdoors of the Outer Grounds. Now? I'd rather be going for a garden stroll than to a meeting with Ashi in his present state.

Mom and I parted ways, and I made it to the Guardian Meeting Room just after Eliasser got Ashi settled in his usual seat. Ashi shot me a look and frowned. I resisted the urge to frown back, knowing it was childish and I was just upset. It wasn't his fault he didn't know who I was.

Eliasser had insisted that attending a Guardian meeting might help bring back Ashi's memory, but all it seemed to do was agitate him more. In his confused state of mind, he recalled some things, but not others. Accepted some things, but not others. He remembered Ari and the rest of the Guardians, but not me—although he remarked how much like "his Twin" I looked. He now recognized Maya from when the four of us—Maya, Ari, Ashi, and I—were part of the Transition Team tasked with leading the entire elven population through the Mirror Vortex to Amoran. In his mixed-up mind, he accepted Maya's presence without question, even though we'd all thought she had died along with the rest of Elvener over a thousand years ago. But when we explained the presence of Meilee, Mikellan, and Clarisanna, Ashi shook his head like he couldn't comprehend why all these people were necessary. "When Meiri returns from Earth, we will once again make eight, the proper number for the Reparention."

The room went quiet for a few moments. Ashara had warned us not to force the issue with Ashi. We'd reverted to using my Earth name, Kerrin, to avoid further disturbing him. For some reason, he didn't connect that with his Twin.

Ari and I detailed our rescue of the survivors from the Elvener Anomaly, with input from Maya. Her eyes had begun to heal right after Ari and I left the first time. Anders suggested it might have been a result of the decaying anomaly and the speeded-up time frame after Ari and I disrupted the energetic "status quo."

The next hour was devoted to the tale of the Garrammon Meadow contingent. In a similar fashion to how we'd enacted the Reparention, the group on the surface channeled energy in a circular rotation, setting up a force field to keep the plumes at bay. The only thing we hadn't counted on was time inside the Elvener Anomaly collapsing, bringing it closer to our time. The group was only doing a practice run when several plumes appeared. They immediately strengthened the force field, and not a moment too soon. A gigantic opening appeared in the center of the meadow, and Meilee had cried out that she could see us in the anomaly, could see what was happening. Everyone held position as the winds grew and fissures erupted outside of the force field. Moments later, Ari and Maya rematerialized above the enormous chasm. A heartbeat later, the chasm closed, Ari and Maya fell to the ground, and the Garrammon Meadow grew silent.

A full five minutes passed with the Garrammon Meadow looking much as it always did. As each minute ticked by, it became harder for them to believe that Ashi and I had survived. Just as the grief of this wrenching loss set in, one long, jagged bolt of lightning hit the meadow with a deafening explosion, scorching the grass and sending a cloud of smoke spreading across the circle. When the air cleared, Ashi and I lay where the bolt had struck. Crevices formed around us, creeping closer, growing wider. I'd been so focused on Ashi, I hadn't noticed.

"That explains why no one entered the meadow to assist us," I said.

Anders picked up the narrative. "Not entirely. Something happened after we rescued Maya and Ari from the center of the meadow. The ground changed its physical property to become more like liquid. Only it still looked like grass."

Anders removed his hand from beneath the table. I had assumed he and Meilee were merely holding hands until I saw the bandage that encased his lower arm.

"Oh, Anders," I cried out. "What happened?"

He shrugged. "I sensed something different and reached down to touch the grass with the tip of my fingers. The 'grass' rippled like water, and then a tremendous force sucked me forward." He glanced at Meilee, who grimaced.

"I had a vision that Anders would be pulled inside," Meilee said with a shudder. "And I Saw what would become of him. He would still exist, but he would no longer be Anders. He would become a shadow of himself."

Like what happened to Ashi, I thought.

"It had only taken my arm when Meilee pulled me back," Anders supplied. "Ashara tells me it will take time, but in a few months, I will be completely healed."

With that, the story of what happened in the Garrammon Meadow was complete. I'd never seen Eliasser look so haggard, but that was the only way to describe him now. What he must have gone through during those five minutes, believing that both Ashi and I were dead.

"Thank you, everyone," I said quietly. "Without your effort on the surface, we would never have made it through. I only wish our plan had worked to save the other elves."

Eliasser sighed. "With the Elvener Anomaly gone, it appears that energy is returning to normal in Guardian Lands. Within a few weeks, the upheavals we experienced may become just another story that we tell. Bless all of you for your patience, love, and caring for each other. We have endured so much these past few years. Joy and grief. Success and failure. Through it all, you have remained steadfast in your commitment to each other, to our promises, and to the Light. I am honored to serve alongside you. Let us join now in grateful thanksgiving."

We clasped hands around the table. Eliasser spoke a beautiful blessing, which I only half-heard. Instead of keeping his eyes closed, Ashi stared at me.

I knew this because I was watching him, too.

Our ambient energy continued to normalize. Meilee stopped having visions. Even Eliasser claimed to be feeling better, although he and I had no close contact, so it was hard for me to tell. I was one of the few unsettled, something I attributed to being around Ashi the Amnesiac, who only seemed to grow more upset and confused in my presence. At least I didn't have to encounter him near my room now. In order to keep watch over him, Ashara had him staying in the room he'd occupied whenever I visited before the Reparention, which was located near Eliasser's and Ashara's quarters. Even so, when Ashara gave my mother a clean bill of health a few days later, I decided to cut my visit short.

When Mom and I landed in the family room, I told her we should do a meditation to help switch our energy patterns back to Earth, but she blew me off and headed to the kitchen. I did a quickie version of the meditation, then joined her as she placed two cups of steaming tea on the table along with a plate of fresh-baked chocolate chip cookies. Well, fresh-baked before she snuck through the vortex an Earth hour ago.

I sat down opposite her, grabbed two cookies, and began dunking. "What's the surprise?"

Mom blinked, then her face registered understanding. "Right. That seems like ages ago."

"Welcome to my world."

She smiled. "I scheduled the two of us for a massage at that new spa in town. I called before I went"—she pointed a finger at the ceiling and twirled it in a circle—"and told them I'd rebook."

"Thanks. That's so sweet of you."

Mom folded her arms across her chest. "What's up with you and Ashi?"

I folded my arms in imitation of her. "What's up with you and Ashara?"

Mom's face crumpled. A part of me wanted to tell her to forget it, no big deal. Keep whatever secret she and the Master Healer shared. But I didn't. I'd gotten the distinct impression that they knew each other. I needed to know how and why.

Mom leaned forward and stared into her mug of tea while she talked.

"Still hard for me to believe I was only nineteen when I got pregnant with you." She shook her head. "So young. So stupid. My life was a wreck. I was a big-time partier in those days. A friend dared me to go a full week without getting high. She thoroughly pissed me off with that. It's not like I was a substance abuser. I just liked to have fun!" She shook her head. "That's what I thought, anyway. But I was pissed off enough to prove I didn't have a problem, so I went a few days without taking a thing. Then Friday night rolled around. I was weakening by the minute when I walked into a party and met this amazing guy. Wham! Like I'd been hit with a ton of bricks. I didn't partake that night—not even a single drink—but I was higher than a kite. Like . . . a natural high." She shrugged. "Anyway, I took him back to my place."

"Grandma's house?" I blurted out.

Mom finally met my eyes. "My mother threw me out when I was eighteen, and before you think ill of her, she had damn good reason. I was crashing with a different friend than the one who challenged me to get clean. My temporary roommate was gone for the weekend, so I had the place to myself. I don't think you need to me to elaborate what I did for those forty-eight hours, but I guess you could say I traded one way of getting high for another."

Ugh. "I can do without the visuals."

"A month later, I peed on a stick. Your father offered to marry me. I said no."

"But you did marry him."

She looked down again, fiddling with her mug. "That weekend changed me. I'd lost all interest in getting high, but still—I was in no shape to become a mother. A few days after he asked me, I started spotting and cramping." She sighed. "I'm sorry, honey, there's no nice way to put this. I was praying for a miscarriage. But then, an old woman visited me."

"Ashara."

Mom now looked me dead in the eyes, her stare almost as riveting as one by the Master Healer herself. "She said I had a choice. Without her help, I was going to lose the baby. But should I decide to keep the incredibly special child I had been gifted with, she would help me.

"It's weird, Kerrin. My whole psyche did a U-turn. I knew I had to do anything I could to keep you safe. I agreed to her terms, including that I 'marry that young fool willing to take you on—he will make you happier than you can imagine.'"

One thing I had always known growing up—my parents loved each other and loved us. Like all kids, my siblings and I thought our parents were weird, a source of embarrassment at times, who gave us too many rules and not enough allowance. In other words, my parents were *parents.*

Mom looked away. "I'm sorry. I never wanted to tell you this. To finish it out, though, Ashara visited me once a month, brought me a special 'tea' that would ease my pregnancy. And it worked. Wish I'd had her around for the other two!"

It was an attempt at humor, but I wasn't in the mood.

"Okay," she said. "Your turn. I want the details about Ashi."

We had a half hour before the bus arrived. I'd already told her about how important Ashi and I were to the Reparention. Now I gave her the rest of our story. How a mishap during a healing ritual had caused Ashi to be able to have sex; how we had fallen in love and finally been given one special night together by the Foreseers.

When I finished, she sat back in her chair and nibbled on a cookie. "Do you think he'll get his 'desires' back?" She rolled her eyes. "I can't believe those people call it that."

"I know, right? I just follow their lead on that one. As for Ashi getting them back? I'm trying to not have expectations in that area."

The front door opened with a bang. Mom leaned closer. "I hope for your sake, he does. You could use a little action, my dear. You are hella tense!"

That was so like my Mom.

"Hey there, sport," Mom greeted my daughter as she came into the kitchen.

"Grandma!" Kiley threw her arms around my mother.

Mom patted her hand. "Is she still beating you?"

"Every night, twice on Sunday! I have Social Services on speed dial."

"Cute," I said.

Mom smiled at me as she got up to leave. Kiley did her pouting frowny-face as Mom grabbed her sweater from the back of the chair. "You can't leave now, Grandma. I just got here," Kiley whined like a three-year-old. Such an actress!

I stared from Kiley to my mother and back again. And just like that, I knew my Earth life, as routine as it was, needed to change.

I waved Mom back down. "You and the ball and chain have plans tonight?"

She gave me a palms-up. "Do we ever?"

This from the woman who'd been globetrotting with her husband for the past several years since my dad took early retirement. A photo safari to Africa, hiking through India, pyramids in Egypt, not to mention annual trips to Disneyworld. My dad's health had slowed down their travel plans, but they were still active locally.

I picked up the phone and dialed my parents' home number. Like me, they still had a landline. "Dad? Head on over here. We're going to do a family game night."

"Yay!" Kiley yelled from two feet away, killing what was left of my hearing.

"Dinner's included," I said to my dad. "Yes, right now would be good."

An hour later, Ryan, Kiley, Mom, Dad, and I were just sitting down to an early dinner, when I had to get up to answer a knock at the front door.

"Matt," I said, surprised to see him. Having struck up a friendship after John's memorial, we now met once a week in the afternoon. Alternating between the Beanie Roast and the Tea Leaf Café, we debated life, love, and spirituality. Matt, a confirmed coffee addict, was trying to get me to love the beverage I considered "tar with milk and sugar," while he was resistant to liking "dishwater with a side of moldy lemon."

"Hey. I know it's not our usual day," he said, "but I wanted you to try this."

He handed me a travel mug. I made a face, then took a tentative sip.

"It's tea! And it's great!"

"It's a proprietary blend from an online tea shop. Two sugars and two percent, right?"

"I should deny that, but it's perfect."

"Well, here's the kicker. I actually like this swill!"

I laughed, then swung the door open. "Come on in. We're just about to have dinner."

His eyebrows lifted. "At five o'clock on a Friday afternoon?"

"Leaves more time for game night. Can you stay? You'd make six, and that's a perfect number for the game I have in mind."

"So . . ." Matt stepped inside. "You're really just using me."

"Of course."

He smiled. "As long as we're clear."

We played until ten, then started a Netflix series. At midnight, Mom and Dad called it quits. Matt left soon after, and Kiley and Ryan trundled up the stairs, arguing about something, as always. I went back into the family room and stared up at the ceiling, thinking.

I spent the next several days in reflection about Amoran and my life there. Ashi and Maya had been rescued, the Elvener Anomaly was gone and the heightened energy was on the wane. The job I'd been tasked with—finding Ashi—had been accomplished. Any promises I had yet to fulfill were somewhere in the future, which meant there was no pressing need for me to return to Amoran. With this realization, my decision came easily enough.

I headed to Amoran on Thursday, instead of the usual Friday. I left Mom a cryptic note on the kitchen table with enough coded detail so she'd know my plans in case she showed up unexpectedly. Since I arrived a day early, I wasn't surprised that no one greeted me when I landed in the Main Chamber. I ran into an Assistant who let me know that the Guardians were at Evening Meal in the Guardian Meal Room.

I walked through the open doorway and stopped short. Mikellan, Clarisanna, and Meilee were absent, most likely they'd gone back to dining in the Main Meal Room. That left only the usual eight seats. With Maya present, all of them were in use. Including mine. I knew the Guardians hadn't expected me, yet seeing all the chairs occupied gave me an odd, hollow feeling.

Eliasser's eyes lit up at the sight of me as Ari exclaimed, "Earth-girl!"

"Ari! Watch your words," Ashara snapped before turning to me. "You are early, *Kerrin*."

Balthasarre hopped up, dragged over one of the chairs kept to the side for the musicians, and placed it at the end of the table.

"Thank you," I said quietly, sitting down.

"Welcome, *friend*," Eliasser said. "We are glad to have you back from *your other world*."

My other world? So that's what Ashara meant when she admonished Ari to watch his words. But . . . *friend?* I thought my eyes were going to fall out of their sockets. I stared at Eliasser, who shook his head in warning. The tension in the room was palpable. Had something changed in the week I'd been gone?

Ashi narrowed his eyes as he studied my face. "Have I seen you before?"

Apparently, something had changed, and not for the better.

"You most certainly have seen me before," I said defiantly, irked by the way they were placating him. "Quite recently, in fact. I'm *Kerrin*. From *Earth*."

Ashara groaned, but Ashi smiled. "My Twin Light is on Earth now. Her name is also Kerrin. Do you know her?"

"Let it alone," Ashara said to me.

I looked down at the food I normally enjoyed, then at the people I'd grown so close to, been through so much with. Ari shifted in his seat. Balthasarre seemed pensive. Eliasser frowned, while Maya regarded me with a combination of sympathy and concern. Danaeus and Anders kept their heads down. I hadn't been sure until this moment that I'd go through with my plan. But now? The decision I'd made back on Earth held.

I stood up. "Tomorrow is the first anniversary of my husband's death."

"Oh, my Light," Eliasser said. "I am sorry that we did not remember."

"It's okay. I know you don't mark events that way. I came today for one reason; to tell you all that I need time away from Amoran. I want to do normal things for a change—have family game nights, eat lasagna with meat sauce, maybe even go on a date." Not that I couldn't do those things anyway, but splitting myself between two worlds often meant I didn't experience either one as fully as I could.

In deference to Ashara's request that I "let it alone," I added, "I'll stay on *my other world* through our holiday season. Then, who knows?" I met Eliasser's gaze again. "I have to figure out where I fit in now."

"Where you have always fit in," Eliasser replied, his expression hovering between hurt and disappointment. "By my side. Where I need you, now more than ever."

Ashi, his face a mask of confusion, stared from me to Eliasser, then back to me, probably trying to figure out who this stranger from another world was and why she was so important to the Master Guardian.

"Someone else needs you more right now," I said to Eliasser, my heart filling with compassion for Ashi's plight. Then, in self-defense, I steadied my emotions and forced myself to view him as a stranger, the same way he saw me. I couldn't allow myself to feel the loss of the man I had loved so well, and who had returned that love so thoroughly. "For his sake, Eliasser, as well as mine, I need to be on Earth." I'd let the planetary reference slip out again. But having to walk on eggshells while I was on Amoran was just another reason to take a break. A long one.

Ashi's expression turned from mixed up to pleased. "You are going to Earth?"

There didn't seem to be much point in denying it now. "Yes," I replied.

"If you see Kerrin, would you tell her I am waiting for her?"

I didn't bother to answer.

Did I miss Amoran over the next few months? I did indeed. Immensely. However, I stood by my decision. Ashara had told me once that an important aspect of intuition is discerning what is true so you can make correct choices. However, it doesn't guarantee that those choices will feel good; they may even bring you grief.

November slid into December. The holidays came and went. January blasted in with frigid temperatures and tons of snow. Schools were closed several times and we made the most of it with movie marathons and game nights. Matt and I continued to meet weekly alternating between coffee and tea—I finally discovered a latte I could live with—and lots of spirited conversation. I even invited him to my newest social endeavor.

I am usually all thumbs when it comes to crafts, but I tossed caution to the wind and started a twice-monthly get-together that I uncreatively dubbed "Creativity Night." Megan brought her quilting, Rebecca was into scrapbooking, and John's sister, Nancy, was knitting dog sweaters as part of her new pet-sitting business. Mom joined us and started crocheting another patchwork afghan like she'd given me a few years back, but she wouldn't say who this one was for. She even got me to try knitting again, and the striped scarf I was working on wasn't half bad. Matt didn't say what his project was, but it involved a laptop, some writing reference books, and lots of furrowed brow action on his part.

And then came Valentine's Day. I'd never put much stock in that manufactured holiday, but John had loved it, making feel like a queen for a day.

This year I couldn't shake a bad case of feeling lonely. I tried to walk the trail behind my house, but the cold and the snow meant I couldn't go much further than the first few hundred yards. Dejected, I headed home, suddenly missing Amoran with a vengeance.

I opened the back door to the aroma of orange spice, Ari's favorite tea. He was slumped in a chair, his energy subdued.

I hung up my jacket, toed off my boots, and slid into the chair next to him.

He poured us each a cup from the teapot. "Already has sugar," he said quietly. "Here's the milk." He pushed the little pitcher toward me.

I placed my hand over his arm. "Are you okay?"

He shook his head. "It's bad, Meiri. It came back and it's bad. Worse than before."

"What has?" I asked, already suspecting the answer.

"The weird energy. A week ago. Like a tidal wave of disruption."

"You too?"

He nodded. "It's possible that the Elvener Anomaly didn't fully disintegrate, or move to a new dimensional expression, but is now lodged inside Amoran." He sipped his tea, then hugged the warm cup to his face. “Please come back.” He set his mug down and laid his cheek on my arm, his shoulders trembling.

I rested my head on top of Ari’s and pulled out my cell phone. “Hey, Siri? Call Mom.”

Chapter 22

"What is that stranger from Earth doing here?" Ashi yelled. "You said Meiri was coming!"

I stood in the Guardian Meeting Room doorway, trying not to appear shocked by Ashi's wild-eyed glare. Ari had warned me that Ashi's condition began deteriorating as soon as the energy disruption resumed a week ago, threatening to undo what little progress they'd made with him in my absence. While he still couldn't recall the year leading up to the Reparention, the Guardians had finally gotten him to accept that the Reparention had in fact occurred and that he had suffered greatly during the explosion.

Balthasarre took me aside as chairs were shuffled around. Aside from Balthasarre and Ashi, Eliasser and Ashara were the only other Guardians present. "We need to push him to remember who you are."

Push him? He looked like he was at his breaking point.

"Shouldn't we be focusing on the disruption?" I asked.

"The Foreseers say Ashi is key to what happens next. We must cure him of this amnesia."

I glanced at my Twin, who was being calmed by a potion from Ashara and an energy feeding from the Master Guardian. Eliasser finished, then stumbled back to his seat and pulled long and hard from an enormous goblet. My hand flew to my mouth as I stifled a gasp. Ari had also clued me in to Eliasser's state—he was inexplicably growing weaker each day. But witnessing it was another story. My heart hurt just to see him like this.

Balthasarre continued quietly, "We want you to sit next to Ashi. Close physical contact may prompt him to remember."

I had my doubts about what close physical contact might prompt Ashi to do. "What if pushing him brings on *pentuma*? That's what happened to me when I recovered the memory of my first Earth death." Before the Reparention, I'd not only recalled, but relived the violent death I experienced soon after Ashara brought me to live on Earth.

Balthasarre nodded. "I am aware of that. But we have to risk it, Meiri. Whatever is causing this disruption is growing so fast, we may all be in danger of pentuma."

That was a terrifying prospect. Brought on by an accumulation of energy in the brain—typically otherworld energy—pentuma was excruciating and deadly. If not caught and treated within minutes, the energy essentially ripped a person's brain apart. The merciful aspect? Death came so quickly a person didn't suffer long.

I lowered myself into the seat next to Ashi. Fortified by the potion and calmed by Eliasser's energy, Ashi merely grimaced at me, then looked straight ahead.

Balthasarre placed a goblet of fairybee wine in front of me. Bless him.

"It is time for the truth," Ashara said to me. "Begin with the first communication you received from us before the Reparention. Recount everything you remember about that time. Leave nothing out, even if it takes all day."

I took a long drink of wine, then began with the day a little over two years ago when I'd found an odd pink letter. Because the dimensional differences between Earth and Amoran severely limit interaction between the two worlds, what contact does occur has to be handled with great care. That letter, embedded with an energy key designed to bridge the divide between the two dimensions, was the only safe way the Guardians could transfer certain energy values, knowledge, and memories to me while I was on Earth in an Earth body. But I never got to read more than a few lines before the letter was destroyed in a freak accident. Which is why I arrived on Amoran with no memory of my previous life there, or my role as a Vortex Guardian.

"I made that letter," Ashi said, sounding surprised. "How did you get it?"

Eliasser pointed to a pile of paper in the center of the table. "It would help if you do not comment, Ashi. Write down any questions you have. We will take breaks to supply you with answers. Will that be all right with you?"

Eliasser spoke as one would to a small child. Ashi gave several rapid nods, pulled a piece of paper in front of him and grabbed a writing stick so tightly his knuckles went white. He reminded me of my kids—when they were about four years old. Where was the Ashi I knew, so sure of himself his confidence bordered on arrogance?

I steadied my breath and continued with the letter's destruction before I could read it. Ashi's brow furrowed and he scribbled on the paper. Then, my first visit to Amoran, when Eliasser initiated some of the changes the letter was supposed to have begun. My second visit, when I nearly died in the vortex. How Ashi had healed me using the Integration Link.

"No!" Ashi slammed his fist down. "I would never have performed the Integration Link without the Master Guardian's approval."

Eliasser's lips parted and his gaze met mine, and I wondered if we were thinking the same thing. Before the Reparention, Eliasser made clear that had Ashi sought Eliasser's approval—which he apparently should have—Eliasser would have denied that approval and performed the Integration Link himself. In which case, Ashi might never have become sexually imbued. Eliasser would have, instead.

I turned to Ashi, phrasing my question as carefully as I could. "Is there any instance where you might have performed that healing without waiting for approval?"

He shook his head. "It would not be necessary."

"Even if someone was in danger of dying?"

"I can summon Eliasser like that"—he snapped his fingers—"and he will be at my side."

Interesting. At the time, I thought it was my fault that Ashi developed physical desires, that I'd infected him with my Earth energy. But it seemed he had brought that on himself by breaking protocol. He couldn't have known what would happen as a result—we'd already ascertained that before the Reparention. Was there some underlying reason he went against standard procedure?

Ashara waved her hand impatiently. "We may have all day, but I prefer to end this before Evening Meal."

"Ashi." Balthasarre pointed at the paper.

"I will try," Ashi said. "But this is very frustrating."

I ran through the months after that second, fateful visit. The Guardians' inability to accept me at first, then finally embracing me as Meiri, even though I wasn't like the Meiri who had left them to live on Earth. Reparention training. Garrammon. The intimate celebration dinner after a highly successful Reparention practice.

I looked to Ashara at this point. She pressed her lips together and nodded.

And so, I told my Primary Twin how I had really died one thousand years ago during what was to be a temporary sequester on Earth. I glanced at Eliasser, then had to look away from the grief I saw there, sorry beyond measure that he had to hear this story again. With how much he loved that Meiri—innocent Meiri in her Amoran body—to know that she had been sexually assaulted, beaten, then left to die on the dirt floor of a hovel, was too much for him.

By the time I finished, Ashi's face was devoid of color as he let out a carefully measured breath. "While I am sorry for your pain, I am grateful that you are not Meiri, because to think that she—" He broke off, shaking his head.

Ashara nodded at me to go on. I explained how I started to go pentuma after relating that story at the celebration dinner. How he and Eliasser saved me. How Ashi and I began to grow closer. The visit to the Foreseers where we momentarily left our bodies. Then, how I kissed him.

He reared back in disgust. "Why would you do such a thing?"

I'd forgotten an important event. It was also at the celebration dinner that I realized I was in love with him, Earth style. I filled in that gap, then decided to skip forward to the moment when I learned the Integration Link had caused major changes within him. He'd suppressed those changes so well that none of us, Ashi included, knew what was really going on with him. Finally, he needed a healing, which I performed. It was during that healing that I detected what he had been repressing all that time.

I reached for my cup to take a drink, but it was empty. Rather than pass a carafe around the table, Eliasser brought the pitcher to me, leaned over my shoulder, and whispered in my ear as he poured my wine. "This may be difficult for him."

I nearly laughed. It was difficult for him back then, but at least he'd accepted me as Meiri.

Eliasser added wine to Ashi's goblet, then returned to his seat.

"Well?" Ashi sounded impatient. "What was I suppressing?"

Struck by an impulse, I grabbed his arm, spun him to face me and delivered the blow.

"Sexual desire. For me. Meiri. Your Twin."

Ashi jerked away like he'd touched a hot stove. Then, he laughed. Long, hard, and loud.

"Now I know you are trying to deceive me."

I'd had enough. "It's true. And you know what else?"

Eliasser leaned forward, hands on the table. "Not now, Meiri."

"Her name is not Meiri!" Ashi yelled.

"Yes, it is," I shouted back. I pushed my face right in front of Ashi's. He flinched, but I didn't move. "Everything I've told you is true. And here's the rest of this story. Before the Reparention, we made love, Ashi. Lots of it. Passionate, wonderful, exciting love."

He grimaced. "Impossible. I am not able to do such a thing."

"Maybe not now, but you were then." I decided to pull out the stops. "We had sex. Lots and lots of sex. And you loved every minute of it."

Ashi's expression went blank, then turned so calm, the sudden change worried me.

"Hear me now," he said in a controlled voice. "I have no memory of you or anything you have told me. I do not know who you are, or why you persist in wanting to take the place of *my Twin!*" He beat his fist against his chest. "*My Twin* would never speak so to me. And as for performing that . . . that *act* so common to Earth people?" He shook his head. "I would never . . . could never . . . do such a thing. Aside from finding it repulsive, I am not made that way."

Eliasser and I shared another look, then I said to Ashara, "I need a break. I'm going to get some air. I won't be long."

Time is a relative thing. The Guardians can stretch it like a rubber band. Sometimes it can even shoot forward. In this case, I should have defined "long."

I walked fast until I reached the Main Gate, then broke into a jog. I wanted to keep going, keep running, forever if necessary. I wouldn't, of course. Aside from the fact that I am not a runner, we had once again been warned away from the Garrammon Meadow. A strange, pulsing vibration had been detected right in the center of the meadow where the Mirror Vortex portal had once been. The Foreseers deemed it toxic, possibly lethal.

I was already out of breath, but the exertion felt great. Promising myself to turn around well before I reached the meadow, I was about to veer left toward the Garrammon field when Eliasser appeared ten yards ahead. If I'd had any wind left, I would have run right by him. But I was heaving air in and out of my lungs so fast and hard, I was in danger of passing out. I slowed to a stop a few feet before him and bent over, hands on my knees. When he came closer, I gasped out, "Give me . . . a minute."

Eliasser didn't listen. He pressed his hand to my back. Warmth spread throughout my torso. My breath came more easily. The pounding of my heart calmed. Finally, I straightened up.

"Are you all right?" he asked.

He was directly in front of me now. So . . . close.

Too close. I stepped back. To protect him from my energy. But those brilliant aqua eyes drew me in. Concern, question, love . . . all reflected there. I tried to stop myself, but I couldn't seem to help what happened next, as I fell forward and wrapped my arms around him. Pressed my face to his chest. Heard and felt his heartbeat, rapid and strong.

"Oh, god. How I miss you, Eliasser. I miss us . . . like this . . . the way we were before . . ." I trailed off. "I'm sorry. So sorry if this is . . . I don't want to make things difficult for you."

His arms were around me now, holding me, stroking my hair. "We will get through this, Meiri, I promise. I know things are different for you, but—" He took a deep breath. "I must keep my distance. When this is all over, I am convinced we will be as we once were."

"How can you be sure?"

"I just am." He sighed. "I have to be. Because if I did not believe what I have just told you, I would lose all hope." He pulled his head back and smiled at me. "And the Master Guardian must never be without hope. Remember that when you are Master Guardian someday."

I laughed. "Like that's ever going to happen."

Lifting his eyebrows, he mimicked a Foreseer. "You doubt me, Daughter of the Vortex?"

The paraphrase of something the Elder said to him during our first Odyssey of Prayer made us both laugh. Tension eased out of me as we shared a precious moment of uncensored emotional closeness. The way we were supposed to be. And in that moment of closeness, I let my guard down, not realizing how thick a wall I'd built around myself. Around my heart. And, I realized with a mixture of dismay and relief, around my body. I'd been fighting it for so long, denying it to myself. No more.

I curled the front of Eliasser's tunic in my fingers and held tight. But I wouldn't look at him, couldn't meet his gaze as I whispered, "Things aren't different for me."

He started to protest, but I silenced him with my finger to his lips. Felt the shiver run through him at that intimate contact. Acknowledged the thrill that ran through me in return.

Time for truth and right action.

"Let me get this out, Eliasser, and then let me gracefully walk away. I have always loved you beyond measure, beyond reason. You are, without a doubt, the Being I love most in the entire cosmos. It has always been so. It will always be so." I pressed my palms to his chest, felt his heart beating faster. He was trying to control his breathing, but was losing the battle.

"Now? I love you even more. With a fullness that leaves me breathless."

I closed my eyes and stepped back. But I didn't walk gracefully away because I wasn't sure my legs would support me. Instead, I took the coward's way out and ethermoved, not caring where I ended up. As long as I didn't have to face Eliasser after my confession.

I should have been more precise, though. Should have cared where I ended up. Because when the spinning stopped and I opened my eyes, I was in the center of the Garrammon Meadow. The potentially lethal center of the Garrammon Meadow. Right where the Mirror Vortex portal had once been.

I let out the breath I was holding. Nothing *seemed* out of the ordinary. No pulsing energy.

Afraid to move, I waited to a count of ten before twisting my head left, then right.

Nothing amiss. So far, so good.

I rotated slowly in a circle, checking the environment, feeling for odd vibrational currents.

Still nothing. The Garrammon Meadow seemed like any other area of Guardian Lands. The grass was just . . . grass. Not a caustic liquid that would burn me to a crisp if I sank within it.

I considered ethermoving out. Hesitated. Checked my intuition again. Things seemed so normal that I questioned my senses.

Too normal? I should leave quickly. So why was I waiting? What was keeping me here?

"Meiri!"

I turned around. Eliasser stood just outside the meadow, but then he took a step forward.

"Stay back!" I called out, my words reverberating like I was on a loudspeaker.

Eliasser halted, seeming as surprised as I was by my megaphone voice. Then he got that determined look on his face. There would be no stopping him now. He would try to rescue me.

"No!" I shouted, thrusting my hand out.

Energy exploded from my palm and formed a translucent wall around him. Inside, he appeared to be frozen in place.

Oh, god. What had I just done? And how had I done it?

"I'm sorry," I called out.

Eliasser didn't move.

"I didn't mean to—" To what, Meiri? Turn him into a statue? "I'll come—"

Wild pulsing vibrations rammed up through my body, nearly knocking me off my feet. Struggling to keep my balance, I pivoted at the sound of a strange hissing sound behind me. With a deafening crack, the ground before me split open and light erupted from the fissure, soaring into the air like a geyser.

I didn't spare it a thought or question. Like I'd been waiting for this moment, I walked straight into that geyser of Light. But instead of being carried up on the plume, I dropped down through a brilliant chasm, landing like a feather on blue-green grass. All around me were trees with orange and pink leaves. An enormous golden sun hung in a mango sky.

Energy continued pulsing up my spine, softer now, swaying me side to side.

Voices . . . to my left. I tried to turn, but my feet were stuck into the ground. *Completely* into the ground, I realized looking down. Where had they gone?

Kylan and Haldoen appeared. Although their mouths moved, the words they spoke echoed inside my head. "*We are all right, Meiri. We are home.*"

My reply came directly out of my mind. "*With the One Light?*"

They laughed and vanished.

The energy pulsing through my body now throbbed insistently. Faster. *Faster.* My aching head felt like it was going to explode.

A smiling woman approached. She placed leaves and fragrant berries into my outstretched hand. When had I thrust my arm out?

"For the journey back," she said into my mind.

"Am I dead?" I asked. She shook her head.

The pounding vibrations made my brain ache. I looked around again. "*Where am I?*"

The woman held out her hand. A tiny planet hovered above her palm.

Her smile faded. *"Hurry, Meiri. There isn't much time before the Rising."*

"Rising?"

Lightning flashed inside my mind and I was back in the Garrammon Meadow. It was dark out now, a hazy, moonless night. Eliasser lifted me in his arms. His reserve of strength always amazes me, but now? When he was getting so much weaker? Astounding.

"I can think of no one who could survive being inside a plume or descending into a fissure," he whispered softly.

"I'm all right," I said. "Just need sleep."

I experienced the adrenaline rush and spinning of ethermoving. I thought he'd take me to the Healing Room, but instead he set me down on my sleeping stone.

"Stay with me," I whispered, a sense of dread slithering through me.

"I will not leave you, my Meiri. Ever."

My fingers relaxed. Leaves and berries fell out onto my sleep cover.

Eliasser gasped. "Where did you get those?"

I was falling again . . . down . . . down . . . into a sleep so deep it felt like I'd be out for days.

"The lady gave it to me," I mumbled.

Down . . . down . . . down . . .

Eliasser shook me gently. "What lady?"

"Pink trees . . . blue-green grass . . . Haldoen was there . . ."

I fell beyond Eliasser's reach.

I woke groggy in my empty room. What a crazy dream I'd had!

Flexing my fingers, I stared in surprise at the violet stains covering them. I brought my hand to my face and sniffed. My skin smelled sweet. Like fruit. Like—*berries?*

Images burst to the surface of my mind. A woman holding an entire world in the palm of her hand. Kylan and Haldoen, saying they were fine. Pink trees . . . blue-green grass . . . the plume of Light . . . the bolt of energy that froze Eliasser.

Wait. I *had* frozen Eliasser. Then . . . it wasn't a dream? I'd really seen Kylan and Haldoen? They said they were home, but where was home? And the woman . . . she was an elf, too! Her ears were pointed! It hadn't registered at the time, I'd been so taken with everything, not to mention the energy that pounded my body. I was sure glad that was gone.

My doorway opened. Eliasser must be returning. He said he'd never leave me. I knew those were just words spoken in the moment, but I was going to tease him about it anyway.

I pushed myself up, but dizziness forced my eyes shut. When the spinning passed, I opened my eyes to greet my sweet king and gasped.

Ashi hovered next to me—his expression, blank; his gaze, vague; his energy—

"Oh!" I reeled from the blast of pure malice that rushed out of Ashi, hitting me full force in the chest. Heart pounding, I slid off the opposite side of the sleeping stone and backed away, trying to summon Eliasser or Ashara. But I'd never learned that trick, and all I could manage was to cry out mentally, *Help me!*

The only effect my telepathic pleading seemed to have was on Ashi. His eyes snapped into focus as one long finger traced the edge of my sleep cover. "You won't escape this time," he whispered in a voice that made my skin crawl.

I tried to ethermove, but collapsed instead, seized by waves of nausea.

Ashi yanked me to my feet, hands gripping my arms, fingers digging into my flesh.

"Stop," I cried. "You're hurting me."

"I'll do worse than that, you slut. Just like your whore of a mother."

Joanna? That didn't make sense. Ashi didn't know anything about my mother, and while she may have been a partier, she certainly wasn't a slut or a whore. That concept didn't exist on Amoran, just on Earth where—

I went cold with terror as recognition dawned where I'd heard those words before. From the father who'd abused me in my clay pot life.

I tried to relax, to act normal, to keep Ashi calm. "Listen, I—"

He shoved me against the wall and rammed his arm into my throat.

"Don't bother crying for help. No one cares about a little bitch like you."

Ashi had caught me on an outbreath, cutting off my air supply, leaving me with no reserves. He kept talking and pressing, but I couldn't make out words over the roaring in my ears. Dots blinked in and out as they swirled an inch from my face. My vision darkened and the roaring turned into a long, painful buzz.

And then—I was free! I slumped to the floor, still unable to breathe. When a hand touched my shoulders, I struck at it, whimpering.

"Let me do this," Eliasser said. Reaching around from behind me, he covered the front of my neck with his palms. Soothing warmth seeped into my throat, then washed over my entire body. I finally gasped in a lungful of air and began to sob.

Eliasser pulled me to my feet and pressed our hearts together, feeding me energy the same way he'd fed Ashi during our meeting. As Eliasser's peaceful essence permeated me, my cries dwindled to muffled hiccups. Eventually, I swiveled my head to look down at my Primary Twin, who lay in a heap on the floor, twitching.

"Did you do that to him?" I asked.

"No. I believe Earnie came to your rescue. A blue light disappeared through the wall as I entered the room. He must have compromised Ashi's energy somehow."

Compromised? Ashi looked like he'd been hit with a Taser.

"Earnie did this? Is that even possible?"

I faced Eliasser again, took in those magnificent eyes regarding me with such love, concern, and—oh, dear Light—something I was afraid to acknowledge for the longing it elicited in me.

Fight it, Meiri. You are stronger than this!

But I couldn't. And I wasn't. My entire body went white-hot as the pulsing vibrations from the Garrammon Meadow returned. That strange, foreign energy rocked up my spine and swirled around us both. The air grew thick with untapped potency. I could almost see the vibrational waves—like heat off pavement on a sweltering day.

Eliasser gasped, his eyes wide. "Meiri . . . I . . ."

Sheer wanting rose up within me, so strong I thought I would come apart at the seams.

Oh god, oh god, oh god. You know what to do. Walk away. Walk away now.

"I need you," I blurted out, surprised and terrified by the admission I'd just made. But I couldn't stop myself. The words just kept pouring out.

"I don't just want you, Eliasser." I blushed furiously. "I need you . . . that way . . ."

Breathing hard, Eliasser grasped my arms. "You are not thinking clearly."

I laughed—a strange, hollow sound. I wasn't thinking at all. I was way past thinking. That was the point. "You don't understand. It's beyond our control!"

Eliasser attempted to prove me wrong. Tried to slow his breathing, to calm himself. When that failed, he snapped out in frustration, "We always have control."

But he didn't let me go. His hands moved up my arms. His touch electrified me, but it was the foreign energy rocking my body that sealed the deal. I had to relieve the building pressure and I could think of only one way to do that. To make the intense vibrations go away. To make my head stop aching like it did when I fell through the fissure.

The fissure. Where an elven woman held a world in the palm of her hand and asked me to hurry. Where Haldoen and Kylan told me they were home. If they weren't dead, and they weren't with the One Light, then only one explanation made sense to my half-crazed mind.

They were on Elvener.

"I think I know what this is," I exclaimed. "It's not like before. Not like with Ashi." Energy surged up me in waves, stimulating every nerve cell in my body. I let out a small cry.

Eliasser pushed my hair off my shoulders, his expression conflicted. "Meiri, I—" He drew in a breath, tried to let it out slowly, but failed.

"Not our fault," I gasped out. Whatever desire we felt for one another was magnified tenfold by the elven energy coursing through us. The vibrations continued to magnify. Unstoppable. Bodies can only withstand so much. We had to relieve it.

Like reaching the eye of a hurricane, the pulsing energy ebbed, replaced by a welcome calm. In a moment of insight, I understood why Eliasser had been getting weaker. The same thing had happened to Ashi when he repressed his desire.

I pulled in a ragged breath. "You are fighting it too much. It's going to kill you." I sucked in another breath. "I will give myself to you right now, if for no other reason than to save your life."

His fingers graced my face so tenderly I couldn't bear it. The desire in me so strong, I thought I would catapult out of my skin. Then . . . he shook his head.

Oh, god.

I grabbed his hand and kissed his palm. "For your sake, my sweet king, *I will do this.*"

I was still too embarrassed to name what "this" was, the act I was so willing to do.

But Eliasser understood. He squeezed his eyes shut. Shook his head again.

"For your sake, my sweet Meiri, I will not."

I felt like I was dying a thousand painful deaths. But it wasn't about rejection. It was about pure need, which exploded as the eye of the storm passed and the pulsing returned full bore. I cried out as energy pounded up my spine. Judging by the sudden, intense longing on Eliasser's face, the energy was drumming up and down his body as well. "Don't you see?" I grasped onto his tunic. "It's not just for you. We both need this!" I yanked him forward and tried to kiss him.

He reared his head back. "No, Meiri! We would regret—"

An agonizing cry split the air. Ashi's back arched at an impossible angle as he screamed again and again. I'd never seen it on another person, but I'd felt it myself. *Pentuma.*

Eliasser threw himself on top of Ashi and both my Twin Lights vanished.

Chapter 23

"Thank you," Eliasser said, as Clarisanna handed him a goblet of shielding draft.

I was next. I accepted the cup from her and raised it at the Master Guardian. With a smile, he tapped the rim of my goblet—a little Earth custom I'd brought to Amoran. Then we downed our special potions to keep the rampant ambient energy from making us physically crazy.

It had been a week since Ashi nearly killed me, Earnie nearly killed Ashi, and I nearly killed my friendship with Eliasser by trying to get him to sleep with me. He and I had talked it all out, agreeing that a monumental influx of elven energy was to blame for my insistent behavior. Eliasser didn't hold it against me. I was trying hard not to hold it against myself.

But truthfully? I think we were both hiding behind elven energy as an excuse. Ari was right. The potential for me to be drawn physically to Eliasser had always been there. And, as had been true for Ashi, once Eliasser became infected with Earth energy—in our case when we merged—it was only a matter of time before it would affect us both.

Ashi was recovering in the Healing Room. Eliasser and Ashara had gotten to him in time, heading off the devastating effects of pentuma. At first, they thought that the onslaught of otherworld energy—elven energy—was the cause of his pentuma. But when Ashara found the doorway to Ashi's regular room wide open, the artifacts uncovered, and the clay pot smashed on the floor, she arrived at another possibility. He had somehow broken through the energy seals she had placed on his room, then "channeled" the memory of that particular past life, making his absorption of otherworld energy two-fold. He'd had those artifacts all along, so it seemed odd that they would affect him that way now. But Ashara wasn't taking any chances, and had removed them from his room.

Now Ashi was in a potion-induced coma to complete the healing. The prognosis was good that he'd wake up soon. What his state of mind would be when he did was another story.

I was worried about Earnie, and hoped he'd made it back safely to his realm. He'd saved my life, and I wanted to thank him. I just wasn't sure how to do that with a sentient ball of light.

Clarisanna moved on to the rest of the group gathered at the meeting table, which once again included Clarisanna, Meilee, and Mikellan. Our team was a bit fractured at the moment. We'd been arguing for the past week over the details of what I experienced out in the Garrammon Meadow. Eliasser and I had tried to convince the others that a new, more potent form of elven energy, and not remnants of the Elvener Anomaly, was at the root of our current problems. However, it was when I suggested why the elven energy was here that I really lost them. Oddly, the most intractable were Ari and Maya—the two who had the most to gain if I was right.

I'd told and retold what happened when I entered the plume and descended into a fissure, yet the resistance persisted. Balthasarre, along with Ari and Maya, eventually conceded that vibrational echoes—that was a new one on me—of the destroyed planet *might* be affecting us. This, they assured me, accounted for what I interpreted as elven energy. And as for what I saw? I'd merely had a vision, because it is *impossible* to enter a plume or survive falling through a fissure. Eliasser was adamant that he saw me do exactly that. But the other three claimed that when I "froze" Eliasser energetically, he could not have seen anything at all. Therefore, what he witnessed must have also been a vision.

I'd rolled my eyes on that one. Denial runs deep, and not just on Earth.

It was late afternoon on Day Eight of the Great Debate, as I'd dubbed it mentally. Ashara was tending to Ashi—there had been some movement in his healing in the past two days—and Anders was running an errand for me. Everyone else was present, and when we'd finished imbibing our potions, I stood up and placed my palms on the table.

"Whether or not you believe I descended into a fissure, or that what I had was merely a vision, I need you to see what I witnessed when I was there. Or here." I tapped my head, which earned me a few laughs. "My attempts to share it verbally have failed. With the help of Balthasarre's multi-media device, I hope to give you a clear picture of what I encountered."

I walked around the meeting table and waved my hand to turn on the "wall." I smiled despite the seriousness of what I was proposing. It was like doing a slide show presentation on Earth. A picture is worth a thousand words, as the saying goes. I'd had Anders help me with this, because I thought it might be the only way to prove my point. He was busy gathering some information and would join us soon, hopefully before I made my wildest pronouncement.

"Here is the location where I fell into a fissure." I pointed to the large "x" in the center of the Garrammon Meadow that marked where the Mirror Vortex portal had been. "And here is what I saw." I flicked my fingers at the "screen" and a different image appeared.

Maya and Ari stared, then began a kind of measured breathing. Eliasser's face softened as he blinked several times. Besides our two resident elves, who grew up there, only Ashara, Eliasser, and Ashi knew firsthand what Elvener looked like. I had once; but whatever time I spent there during our plan to move Elvener's population to Amoran was lost to me, along with most of my other pre-Earth Amoran memories.

"It is beautiful," Meilee said, the first to break the silence. "So different from Amoran, and yet, so wondrous."

I love Earth's and Amoran's green forests and blue skies. But the mango elven sky, blue-green grass, and pink and orange trees were amazing. They didn't exactly sparkle, but that was somehow the impression they gave. The artist I'd had render them had done a remarkable job of capturing what I'd seen.

I flicked to the next "screen."

"That is Omanien," Maya cried out. "Head of the Elven High Council."

"Omanien," I repeated, rolling the name around on my tongue. It didn't just sound familiar, it felt familiar, which I found confusing. "This is the woman who gave me berries and leaves. But she also showed me this." I pointed at the "screen" and another image appeared—Omanien holding a planet in the palm of her hand.

"That does look like Elvener," Maya said thoughtfully.

Ari shook his head. "Meiri could have recreated this, along with Omanien's likeness, out of a buried memory from when she was on Elvener as part of the Transition Team."

"But she could not have recreated this!" a familiar voice boomed.

Ashi strode into the room like nothing had happened to him, flicked his hand at the screen, and the image changed.

No one paid attention to the wall. Some bolted from their chairs, others exclaimed from where they sat, "Are you all right?"

Ashi smiled, and in that instant, I knew that he was okay. I stayed where I was, waiting while the others crowded around him. When he finally looked at me and our eyes met, Danaeus asked, "Do you remember everything now?" at the same moment Meilee inquired, "Are you fully restored?"

Keeping his eyes locked on mine, Ashi answered Danaeus's question first.

"I recall everything up to the explosion during the Reparention. The rest is gone, and it is probably best that it remain so."

"So . . ." Mikellan started hesitantly as he pointed at me. "You know who she is?"

Ashi's smile wavered a bit. "I know very well who she is. And I owe her a great debt. I may not remember past the Reparention, but Ashara has told me what transpired during my rescue and the months that followed." My tears were already forming as he moved toward me. "At our Joining, the Elder said my greatest challenge lay before me, but that next to me stood the Love that would guide me out of darkness." He held his hands to my face and brushed the tears from my cheeks. "Thank you, my Twin, for my rescue from darkness."

One thing was certainly different about Ashi. He would never have committed such a public display of affection before. I gazed into those mesmerizing emerald eyes and felt. . . hesitation. What was that about? My forehead wrinkled and my lips parted in question.

Ashi shook his head and whispered, “Not now,” before turning to the group. “All right. Seats, everyone. We have work to do.”

That was so like Ashi. Take charge. The width of my smile actually hurt my facial muscles.

Ashi indicated the “screen,” which now pictured a beautiful rendering of Amoran, blue and green and lovely as it would be seen from miles above the planet. He must have manifested it, which impressed me no end. With everything he'd been through, Ashi's skills only seemed to have improved.

Then Ashi's face tightened as he put up the next “slide.”

Everyone gasped.

Amoran was still there, but huge chunks of it were flying into space. In the center, where the molten heart of the planet should be, was another world. Since we'd just seen its tiny likeness a few minutes ago, cradled in the palm of Omanien, head of the Elven High Council, no one needed to ask which planet was tearing Amoran apart.

Anders came breathlessly into the room. “I think you are right, Meiri. I have the . . . Ashi? Ashi!” Anders made a beeline for my Twin, then stopped short as he caught sight of the image on the wall. “Oh, dear Light. You *are* right.”

Ashi drew in a deep breath, nodded to a grim-faced Ashara as she entered the Guardian Meeting Room, then addressed us all. “I do not recall my time in the Elvener Anomaly; however, I seem to have absorbed information while I dwelt there in darkness. I ask your trust to accept what I now tell you, something I know with a certainty that I feel in here.” He tapped his chest. “When the Fifth Vortex imploded, the entire elven world was drawn intact into an astronomical dimensional variance. There, it went into stasis. Time did not pass for them until recently, when Elvener began to rise in frequency. It was most likely our Reparention that initiated the process of waking it up. Unless we can change its energetic course, in ten days Elvener will increase in vibration to the point where it will transcend its current location and become physical for a brief time in our dimension." He pointed at the screen. "Right in the center of Amoran."

With that depressing confirmation of my crazy notion that Elvener still existed, we finally did get down to work. Ashi was truly back, running the meeting with Balthasarre as his co-anchor. Eliasser was strangely quiet, once again seeming to abdicate his role as Master Guardian. Ashara also remained silent for much of the proceedings, which, like our wrangling with what to do to rescue the refugees from the Elvener Anomaly, involved a lot of plans hatched, then rejected. We finally called it quits near midnight, agreeing to reconvene in the morning to continue our brainstorming.

Ashi left the room with Eliasser, arm in arm, heads bowed, deep in conversation. Figuring I could wait to talk to Ashi alone, I headed to my room, hoping to log in a few hours of shut-eye.

The climate changes wrought by the increasing elven energy had permeated the Mountain, and the temperature inside my quarters was uncomfortably warm for me. I removed my tunic top, and was about to doff my leggings, planning to sleep in underpants and my ever-present tank top, when someone requested entrance to my room. I looked down, decided the leggings and tank top covered enough, and opened the doorway.

At the sight of Ashi, my face grow even warmer.

"May I come in?" he asked.

"Certainly," I said, smiling. I waved him toward the table, and we sat across from each other making awkward small talk while Ashi looked around my room, avoiding my gaze. My heart grew heavy as I realized my Twin was keeping something from me.

"Ashi? It's late. I need to sleep. What is it?"

He sighed. "Whatever plan we devise to help Elvener may cost you and I our lives."

Well, at least it wasn't small talk. "And?"

He looked at me in surprise. I hadn't meant to sound cavalier, but I'd come to terms before the Reparention with what my role as a Vortex Light and Guardian meant. Not that I wasn't fearful at the same time, but Ashi was telling me something we both already knew and accepted.

However, he clearly had something to say, and I was pretty sure I wasn't going to like it.

"When Meilee asked me if I am completely restored, I did not answer."

I'd been so stunned to see him upright and coherent, I hadn't thought about him neglecting to respond to her.

"I did not want to lie to Meilee," he continued. "Or to you." Keeping his emotional guard up, he partially dropped the energetic defense he'd placed around his physical body.

"Oh, dear Light," I whispered. "You aren't completely restored."

"I am not."

He reached for my hands, but I put them firmly in my lap and shielded my heart. Now I understood his earlier hesitation.

"When did you find out?"

His gaze wandered to the banners on the wall. "Ashara's potions kept me unconscious while I healed, but I was still able to dream—at least, what I thought were dreams. When I woke, confused by what I'd seen, I shared them with her. She told me they were not dreams at all, but memories." He tilted his head to the side. "I do not comprehend how I can remember all that we did, what we physically shared, and yet feel nothing now. The elven energy should make me—" He shrugged. "I am sorry that I cannot . . ." Trailing off, he curled his fingers into fists and shook his head. "But those feelings did not return. I can no longer relate to you that way. I can only think that, in order to help Elvener rise, I must be devoid of that energy."

He still hadn't made eye contact, which was good, because the surge of anger I experienced must have clearly shown on my face. He could have said anything else, made any other supposition as to why he no longer felt physical desire. But that he *had* to be free of it? That it was *necessary*? This was the same crap I'd put up with when I'd first returned to Amoran before the Reparention. That somehow, Earth energy was "less than." And that physical desire, in particular, was suspect. I was tired of "that energy" being maligned, no matter how obliquely.

I took a deep breath to steady myself. "You believe this is meant to be. That not regaining your desire for me has a purpose."

Ashi's eyes finally met mine. "Yes," he said sadly. But his emotional defenses slipped, and how he really felt about losing physical desire hit me like a slap in the face. Ashi professed to feel sorry that he was devoid of *that energy*, but mostly, he was relieved. While I hated to admit it, it made sense, in a way. Recalling what we shared was now an intellectual exercise for him. Not being able to *feel* what we shared was like being told chocolate tasted amazing, but never allowing a piece to melt on your tongue.

Still . . . I dropped the shielding around my heart so he could tell that I knew how he really felt, and that it was his *dishonesty* that hurt me the most.

He squeezed his eyes shut and lowered his face, but he didn't offer an apology.

I stood up and waved the doorway open again. "See you in the morning."

"Meiri . . . please. Can we talk about this? I am still your Twin. I love you."

"I know you do. I love you, too."

Rising from the chair, he moved toward me. "I just cannot love you that—"

"Got it!" I backed away. "Please go. Now."

I climbed onto my sleeping stone and turned away from him. I waited until he left, then I sealed my room and erected a thick wall in my consciousness so I could physically, emotionally, and telepathically shut him out.

I'd been in and out of a fitful sleep for several hours when I packed it in and went for a walk, ending up in the Main Chamber. Needing some nature, I opened the portal to the garden, headed to the fountain, then hung a right and continued down the path.

Balthasarre was on his knees, a row of potted plants lined up next to him as he cleared a new area adjacent to the vortex roses. He glanced up, smiled, and went back to digging.

I parked myself on the bench across from the rose bed and watched him work. He finished planting one of the roses, brushed his hands off on his tunic, then came and sat beside me.

"Trouble sleeping?" he asked.

"You could say that."

"I just did."

I turned to him, thinking he'd done the Danaeus thing of taking me literally. But he was smiling again. "Oh, you were joking," I said, laughing at myself. "And you?"

He looked back at the bed he'd been working on. Vortex roses usually held no fragrance, however, the one he'd just put in the ground permeated the air with a lovely perfume.

"I did not even try. I am so energized these days that I came here instead. Gardening brings me pleasure and calms my otherwise troubled spirit."

I placed my hand on his arm. "Aside from the possibility of Amoran being ripped into pieces, is anything else bothering you?"

I sensed something was, but my intuitive feelers couldn't tell what.

"I am conflicted about the effect elven energy is having on those of us beneath the Mountain. It is disruptive, overstimulating, and changing us in ways that are not always to our benefit. And yet, I was once a part of this type of energy, although much reduced."

"Ari mentioned that you came from another part of Amoran when Anders was a baby."

"Yes, but did he also tell you why?"

I shook my head.

"My wife and I were naturally skilled energy workers with an incredible affinity for interdimensional energy. The Guardians asked that we assist them with a problem in the vortex two thousand years ago. We were quite young at the time, and for Amorans, adventurous as well. We welcomed the opportunity to work in the Seventh Vortex.

"Rosanna and I were only to be here for a short while. Then, an accident occurred in the vortex, much like the one I suffered before the Reparention. Except Rosanna did not survive it."

"Ashara told me once that your wife died in a similar way. I don't recall Rosanna, though, I'm sorry to say."

He nodded. "Eliasser asked me to stay on beneath the Mountain as the Master Technician. Anders could grow up here and attend the school with the knowledge on my part that he would one day be a Guardian. I am proud to say, he is the youngest appointed Guardian yet."

"He's a great person and an amazing resource. We're lucky to have him."

"We are, indeed. When I decided to stay beneath the Mountain, Anders received a great gift. But he was also denied the right to choose. Had I gone back to Amoran proper and allowed Anders to develop, to discover his own path as all Amoran children do, he might have had the opportunity to fall in love, marry, perhaps have a child. All the things I was able to do."

"Considering how things are beneath the Mountain at the moment, maybe he still will."

Balthasarre shook his head. "I believe that once we restore Elvener to her new dimensional frequency, our Guardian Lands will again become the settled way they have always been."

I turned to him, surprised by his choice of wording. "Would you rather the energy didn't entirely leave?"

He just stared off at the rose bed.

"Balthasarre, how else has the elven energy affected you?"

He sighed. "In a way, I have already answered that question. I remember how it felt to fall in love. To become a father. I miss it . . . the feelings, the sensations. Even though sexual desire is much subdued beyond Guardian Lands, it does exist. Elven energy has reminded me, in a physical way, what life outside the Mountain is like."

We sat quietly for a few moments. Then, I decided to venture a far more personal question.

"Is there someone that you are interested in?"

He smiled, then grimaced, seeming embarrassed. "I hope you will not think less of me for this, but I find this woman exceptionally intriguing." He sighed. "There are reasons I could never . . ." He paused. "For one thing, she is married."

That narrowed the field quite a bit. "It can't be anyone under the Mountain, none of us are married. And it can't be anyone outside of Guardian Lands, because no one has been allowed to leave since the energy ramped up. In fact, the only married person who has been around lately is"—I gulped—"*my mother?*"

His light brown cheeks tinged with red. "I am sorry if that bothers you."

"Not in the least. It's just . . . aside from her being married, not to mention from Earth, aren't you a little young for her?"

Balthasarre caught my eye. "Age should not matter at all. If it did, then in truth, I would be too old for her by several thousand years."

"Good point," I said, and left it at that. I wasn't being ageist, at least not in the typical sense. Mom would turn sixty in a couple years, while Balthasarre appeared to be midforties. Not a huge gap. But with the age repression under the Mountain, he was likely to remain in his forties for decades. And where would Mom be then?

He took my hand and changed the subject. "Now. What troubles you, my friend?"

I threw all caution aside and told Balthasarre everything, including the things I was supposed to keep to myself. I told him about Eliasser and I merging, and the Master Guardian's subsequent development of desires. Balthasarre's eyebrows raised up high at that disclosure, but he didn't interrupt, just let me talk.

And talk I did. He heard it all. How things were for me when John died. How hard it was to go on after that. How I missed that type of closeness with someone so much that I couldn't breathe properly at times. How when Eliasser and I merged, it set in motion what felt to me like the destruction of our relationship. How I'd almost kissed Eliasser, and how he'd refused.

Then I got to Ashi. Since Balthasarre had been present at the meeting where I'd confronted Ashi about our lovemaking he already knew that Ashi and I had surpassed a platonic relationship. Now I told him about Ashi's "incomplete" restoration. I left out Ashi's subsequent dishonesty. That was between Ashi and me.

"Oh, dear," Balthasarre said. "That must have hurt terribly."

"Yes. It did. And as much as Ashi may have thought he wanted to talk about it—"

"He would not have been able to speak to your heart, your emotions. He would only have been speaking from his mind. Sometimes, that attempt at compassion hurts even more."

Balthasarre and I sat together, each with our own thoughts and feelings. Oddly enough, I, who love physical contact, was grateful that he didn't try to hug me, or make placating "I'm so sorry for you" type statements. Like after John died, I needed to share with someone the pain in my heart and have them hear it. Really hear it. Hear me.

At length, Balthasarre cleared his throat. "When Rosanna died? That is when I began gardening. Would you like to help me plant the remaining roses?" He stood up and stretched.

"I would love to."

We had just put the last rose into its hole when Eliasser rounded the bend several yards away and headed slowly down the path toward us.

Balthasarre spoke softly as we pushed loose dirt around the lovely red and pink plant. "Life is a strange thing, Meiri. I feel for a woman whom I cannot possibly have, while you love two men who are free to return your feelings. But one can no longer physically do so. And the other?" He shook his head. "Apparently too 'noble' to share that love."

He tamped down the dirt and looked at me.

I grabbed onto his arm. "Thank you. I am more made whole in these moments shared with you, than with all the potions and conversations I have had."

"What are friends for?" he replied.

I burst out laughing. "Where did you get that phrase?"

He gave me a palms-up gesture. "Meilee. She writes down every saying you use and practices them with Anders."

"Well, I'll be."

"What will you be?" Eliasser, who had reached us, asked.

Balthasarre and I shared a look and another laugh. "You had to be there," I answered.

"She uses that one, too," Balthasarre said.

"Did either of you get any sleep?" Eliasser asked.

We shook our heads.

"Neither did I," he said, and we walked in silence to our meeting to figure out how to achieve the impossible.

Chapter 24

"That's impossible!" Danaeus crossed his arms and frowned.

"We know," Meilee said. "But the impossible is what we are called to do now, correct?"

"Agreed." Eliasser regarded her with an odd intensity. "If Mikellan's idea will not work, it is not because we deem it to be impossible, but because it is not the correct impossible choice."

At that ridiculous statement, we all laughed. We'd been going like this for hours and were, to put it in Earth terms, fried.

Ashi grasped my hand and smiled. Before the meeting, he had explained why he'd basically lied about preferring to not have physical desires. Guessing I'd be upset about the change in our relationship, he thought it would hurt me less if I believed he was equally sad. "I am so sorry, my Twin," he'd said. "I could feel what I did to you . . . in here." He tapped his heart. "Can you forgive me?"

"I already have," I'd replied, surprised to discover that it was true.

Now, after hours of nonstop processing, I said, "I need a break. I'm going to the Resting Stones."

"Too far," Ashara said.

I shrugged. "What's the worst that can happen? Maybe a fissure will suck me inside and the folks at the other end of the rainbow will provide me with some answers this time."

"Rainbow," Ashi whispered. He was staring at the center of the table, but seemed to be viewing something miles away.

"Are there rainbows inside a fissure?" Anders asked me, taking my statement literally.

I smiled. "No, but—"

"—there are colors," Ashi cut in, smacking his palms down. "Why did I not think of that?"

We all turned to him. "You have been inside a fissure?" Eliasser asked.

Ashi shook his head. "Not like Meiri has. But I have ridden a rainbow to its source."

Ashara and Eliasser traded a look, probably worried that Ashi's mental state might be deteriorating again.

"What do you mean?" Balthasarre asked.

"I am not sure. Something about color is significant. I . . . I believe I am having a memory. About the Reparention." Ashi rubbed his hand over his face, then began speaking so rapidly I struggled to keep up with his thoughts. "When the explosion occurred during the Reparention, there was an arc of white light which split into seven colors. Something about that light . . . and the colors it split into. Seven colors. Seven stars. Seven people working to—" He shook his head again and closed his eyes.

Eliasser rose from his chair as Ashara grabbed the potion carafe.

I waved them back down. While Ashi may not be able to "relate to me" that way, as he'd put it last night, we were still intricately linked. I sensed him reaching out to me, his feelings coming more in tune with my own.

"You said seven people, Ashi," I voiced. "Do you mean the Foreseers?"

Ashi opened his eyes. "Their colors are not reflective of the rainbow. Why is that?"

Ashara snapped, "I do not see the point of—"

"We're brainstorming," I cut in. "I'm curious, too. Why aren't they all in rainbow colors?"

Ashara sighed. "They do not remain the same color for the entire time they are Foreseers."

That didn't answer the question. Eliasser remained standing, still not seeming convinced about Ashi's mental health.

Ashara flicked her fingers at the wall, activating the "screen." Likenesses of the seven Foreseers appeared, the first five in rainbow order:

red, orange, yellow, green, blue, followed by pink, and the Elder's unique shimmering silver.

"To mimic the rainbow, those last two should be indigo and violet," I said.

"What is indigo?" Meilee asked.

"What we on Earth call a purplish blue."

Meilee stared at the images on the screen. "Yet here we have pink and silver."

"The red and blue Foreseers blend together when necessary to form violet," Ashara said.

I still felt like we were missing something. "That gives us one more rainbow hue, although there was a violet Foreseer once. That was the Elder's previous color."

"And just how do you know that?" Ashara demanded, eyes narrowing.

Clarisanna didn't give me a chance to answer. "But pink? Why pink and not indigo?"

Ashi bolted out of his chair like he'd been pricked by a nemestes thorn. "Because the Foreseers were never intended to mirror the colors of the rainbow," he exclaimed, seeming to pull the information from somewhere deep inside him. "That is what the Ether Lights do!"

"Ether Lights? You mean, these guys?" I moved to the screen and waved my hand, hoping to manifest images of the Ether Lights. In my case, manifesting anything would be a miracle.

Instead, I apparently broke the wall TV. The screen went blank, the room went dark, and a blue light no bigger than a pea pulsed above the table. With each beat, it grew larger until it was as big as the table, scattering the rest of the group from their chairs, backing them into the wall.

Except for me and Ashi. "Earnie?" I whispered.

What happened next took mere seconds.

He pulsed twice, then dropped back down to Ether Light size and moved into my chest. Ashi threw his arms around me from behind, and Earnie expanded so he was inside us both. In the span of a few brief moments, Earnie imprinted into our hearts, minds, and emotions who the Ether Lights really are. And what they needed us to do to save Elvener and Amoran.

The blue light extinguished and the room returned to normal. Ashi and I stumbled backward, caught by Eliasser and Ashara who broke our fall.

"Drafts!" Ashara called out. Mikellan and Clarisanna sloshed reviving draft into goblets and pushed them at us. Ashi and I gulped the liquid down, feeling restored almost before reaching the bottom. Our contact with Earnie had enriched us, not depleted our energy; but when he left, our physical bodies had to adjust to his absence.

"Well?" Danaeus said impatiently when we all were seated again.

Ashi's voice was husky with emotion. "What we call Ether Lights were created when the One Light came into Being. Never having become embodied, or transformed into stars, planets, vortexes, or any of the other components of our universe, Ether Lights are able to work in all cosmic, physical, and energetic manifestations of existence. As such, they can bridge different realms of reality to act as conduits for the elevation and transformation of not just whole worlds, but entire dimensions."

Ashi hesitated, then met my eyes. I nodded, understanding his nonverbal request. Contact with Earnie had affected him emotionally far more than me. I placed my palm over Ashi's heart and channeled what peace, love, and serenity I could into him. Gratified as he relaxed under my ministration, I hoped this was one thing that wouldn't leave me when Elvener was restored. I had never realized how personally uplifting it can be to channel energy this way.

"Thank you," Ashi thought to me. *"Can you—?"*

"Certainly." And I took over the recitation.

"There are millions of Ether Lights throughout all the universes," I said. "Their color expression can be infinite, either by blending together to form new hues or by changing their individual color when needed. But in their purest form, they do in fact mirror the colors we know of as the rainbow. Because of their uniqueness, they are the only ones who can aid Elvener to rise to her proper dimensional expression."

I stopped, and thought to Ashi, *"This next part is yours, my Twin."*

"I will try . . . "

With an appreciative glance my way, he said, "When the explosion to rebalance the Seventh Vortex occurred, I experienced pain so excruciating, I"—he drew in a shaky breath and squeezed my hand hard—"I wished to die. But a moment later, a brilliant white light engulfed me, then split into seven rays of color. The rainbow light pulled me forward, each ray taking a turn at holding me steady as we descended through a luminous chasm. It seemed like it took forever to reach the bottom, but there I fell into a waking dreamless sleep."

"How—" Anders began, but Ashi held up his hand.

"I do not know how one can be awake and asleep, but I was. Seeing nothing. Feeling nothing. Still aware, but being . . . *nothing.*"

"And the Elvener Anomaly? How did it come to be there?" Maya asked.

"Right as the Mirror Vortex folded in on itself, a small portion of Elvener and a small portion of Amoran from the Garrammon Meadow combined to form the Elvener Anomaly, taking Maya, Kylan, and Haldoen with it."

Meilee frowned. "I do not understand. If everything happens as it should, then *someone* must have considered this as a possibility."

Ashara grunted. "You can be sure they did, Meilee."

I was also certain the Foreseers knew, but we would accomplish nothing constructive now by sidetracking onto that topic. Ignoring both comments, I said, "Ashi was also caught up in the forming of the Elvener Anomaly during the Mirror Vortex collapse, but he was ejected from that time-distorted realm before he could become stuck there."

"The first time," Balthasarre clarified.

"Yes. And it's a good thing he was, as Ashi had other tasks ahead of him."

"Like the Reparention," Clarisanna said.

"And the saving of Elvener now," Mikellan added, gazing at Ashi with unabashed awe.

"Glad you two finally woke up," Ashara said.

"Ashara!" I snapped at her, but I couldn't help laughing as I added, "What is up with you?"

"You. Earth phrases. Joanna. Getting older."

I shook my head. Had I dropped into an alternate universe? Since when did Ashara, who had been in existence for thousands of years, worry about aging? But our interchange did what nothing else had been able to do. Lightened the mood in the room from somber and awed to . . . well . . . just lighter. Which was a good thing, because now Ashi needed to tell everyone what the Ether Lights needed us to do.

This was where my Twin excelled. Ashi's explanation about energy circles, vibrational lifting, and temporarily breaking open the dimensional divide went over my head. The bottom line? With the twelve of us working in concert with the Ether Lights, Elvener and Amoran would straddle both dimensions until Elvener rose in vibration to assume its new place in the cosmos, in its own dimension. Or, as Earnie had communicated to us, Elvener's rightful place as one of the Three Worlds of the Beginning Time."

Ashi paused and squeezed my hand again. His silence was interpreted as the time to ask questions, which some of them did—all at once.

Meilee: "What do you mean . . . the Three Worlds of the Beginning Time?"

Anders: "How do we make these energy circles?"

Balthasarre: "Can we work without harm in two dimensions?"

Mikellan: "Why have the Ether Lights waited this long?"

"That is a good question, Mikellan," Ashi said, causing the food Assistant to turn bright red. "The answer is similar to why we had to wait to perform the Reparention. Energy levels within Guardian Lands, particularly the Garrammon Meadow, needed to increase to where combining our energy with the Ether Lights is possible."

Clarisanna's eyes went wide. "We are going to combine with them? Like you two just did?"

Ashi tilted his head. "I believe so. The Ether Lights will help us to make the energy circle—we can discuss how later," he said to Anders. Then to Balthasarre he added, "And if we are careful, no harm will come to us. The Ether Lights can help us form a protective barrier between the dimensions, but we will still be exposed." He hesitated. "As to the Three Worlds of the Beginning Time, I must admit, I have never heard of this."

"I have," I said, remembering where I'd encountered that expression before. Eliasser and Ashara regarded me with surprise. Since I couldn't bring up my merging with Eliasser, I merely stated, "The Elder Foreseer once showed me a vision of my younger Amoran self. I pledged myself in service to the One Light"—I closed my eyes, trying to recall the exact words—"until the Three Worlds of the Beginning Time have moved through their Planetary Cycles and Risen." Opening my eyes, I admitted, "I still don't know what that means, but when I fell into the fissure, Omanien said there wasn't much time before the Rising. She must be referring to the increase in vibration Elvener needs to make it into the next dimension."

"And the Ether Lights can do this?" Ari sounded incredulous.

"It's who they are," I said simply.

The room was quiet for several more moments, as the group digested what we'd told them.

Eliasser finally spoke. "All this time, I thought I was the one bringing them forth from their dimension. Using them as entertainment." He shook his head. "I am humbled beyond measure. And chastised by my arrogance, ignorance, and assumptions." He looked at Mikellan, Meilee, and Clarisanna. "I objected to your presence at these meetings, as you well know, because your presence was not of my choosing. And not done in the manner we are accustomed to." He turned to me. "The apology I owe you, Meiri, runs even deeper. You have brought to us a mirror for our selves. With your different ways from Earth, which we have all objected to at one time or another, you have shown us where we are blinded by our complacence and assurance in the way things have always been. But things change. It is the nature of life. We may have forgotten that. I most certainly did."

He paused and pressed his palms to the table. "I pray for the One Light to guide us in these next days, to keep us safe. And should the energy disruption—" He stopped and looked away. "No. What I mean to say is, should the energy *changes* we have experienced remain with us in any way, may we all have the grace and sweetness of heart to accept them as a gift from the One Light Itself." He met my eyes again, his expression soft with feeling. "I know I will do so, and with a grateful heart."

I forced myself to breathe. The baring of Eliasser's soul, so raw and vulnerable, left everyone speechless. Did he know about Ashi's changed condition? If so, I tried not to think about what Eliasser's last admission might portend for me personally.

Meilee rose from her chair, her eyes unfocused as she channeled a message. "Two become one, always One. It is the way of Life. The torch passes to the next, and then the next, and then the next. But always, one remains One."

And on that ambiguous note, we took a much-needed break for a long overdue meal.

Wanting some time alone, I ate quickly, then slipped away while the rest of group was still talking about Ether Lights. I passed through the courtyard to the Main Gate, noting how bright the evening sky was. How different that was from the last time I'd been outdoors at night, when Eliasser ethermoved me from the Garrammon Meadow. How long ago was that, anyway? Two weeks? It felt longer.

I sighed. Like an eternity.

I creaked open the gate and went straight ahead to the Resting Stones where I stared into the distance without focusing on any one thing. When thoughts or fears or concerns . . . or sadness . . . crept in, I pushed them gently to the side. Closing my eyes, I let the Love I had been privileged to experience throughout all my lifetimes on Earth and Amoran saturate my Being. I let go, as much as I was humanly capable, of my attachment to outcome—any outcome, whether with Ashi, Eliasser, or the "impossible" miracle we were called to perform. And then, I gave thanks to the One Light as I committed every cell and fiber of my Being to all that I had promised to do—even the tasks that were blocked from my awareness, apparently by my own agreement.

I opened my eyes to a soft blue glow inches from my face and smiled. "And, of course, I am thankful to you, Earnie, for showing us how silly we are. We have all made assumptions and let prejudice rule our judgment." I cupped my hands in front of me and he settled in my palms. He was his normal (normal? Was that another assumption of mine?) size and color. And the name I'd given him? Earnie? Sheesh. He must have a true name, an original name. For those of us in bodies, it would be our Spirit or Soul Name.

I snuggled him to my cheek, feeling the kiss of his vibrating energy like a feather touch on my skin. Regardless of who my soul was, or what my origin was, I lived each day on Earth now as an average woman. Yet here I was, cuddling with a life form who predated all of us. How did I get to be so blessed?

"Earnie, if it is possible to love a sentient Light, I do love you."

"More than possible," Eliasser said, sitting down beside me.

Surprised I hadn't felt his presence as he approached, I scooted to the side to make room for him and we both leaned back against the stone.

"Anything we can imagine can become real, Meiri. It is the nature of manifesting."

Earnie brushed Eliasser's cheek, then slowly faded from view.

My heart at peace, I took Eliasser's hand, intertwined our fingers, rested my head on his shoulder, and promptly fell into a deep, contented sleep.

Chapter 25

"It is time," Balthasarre said.

His statement was met with somber nods. It had taken us a full week to iron out the details and prepare for another rescue mission.

"Let us review the basic steps," Ashi said. "Then we can make our way to the meadow."

We'd gone over the scenario so many times, I didn't think a review was necessary. It wasn't the plan we needed to come to terms with. It was the unknowns that had us second-guessing ourselves, the unexpected twists and turns that were part of dealing with astronomical energy fields. I kept quiet, though, suspecting that the constant verbal rehearsing gave us some small feeling of control over what was to come.

"When the sun sets, we will begin our unifying meditation," Ashi began. "When the moon rises, Meiri will summon the Ether Lights."

I'd stopped correcting Ashi on this point. I didn't know how to call the Ether Lights, not in the way that Eliasser could. I just knew that I would think of Earnie at the right time—because Earnie would inspire that in me—and the Ether Lights would come when they were needed.

"This is where we must be fully open," Ashi continued. "Accept what the Ether Lights lead us to do, which may seem at odds with what we believe we know to be true. Meiri?"

"Well said, Ashi. Remember; this manner of communication is different than mindspeak. Trust what you feel. That is your best guidance." I pushed up from my chair, signaling the end of the meeting. "I think we are as ready as we will ever be. Let's go."

The twelve of us headed to the Garrammon Meadow. Anders and Meilee led the way, holding hands. Ari and Maya followed, arm in arm. Balthasarre and I walked together, with Ashi and Eliasser right behind us. Ashara brought up the rear with Clarisanna, Danaeus, and Mikellan, the latter lagging farther behind with each hesitant step. By the time we reached the meadow, Mikellan looked like he wanted to bolt.

I left Balthasarre's side and took Mikellan by the hand. "Frightened?"

He blushed. "Of course not. That would not be right."

"May I?" I held my hands a few inches from his heart. My ability to impart energy had improved even more over the past week, and now included people other than Eliasser and Ashi.

Mikellan nodded, then sighed with relief after I fed him a hefty dose of energy.

"You must always be honest with yourself about how you feel," I advised him. "Those of us who have been Guardians for a while may be used to this sort of thing, but we are still scared."

He raised a dubious eyebrow. "All of you?"

"Even Makashannar, whom I know you admire greatly."

Mikellan's blush deepened as he glanced to where Ashi was checking the position of the sun. It seemed to be rushing to the horizon. "He does not seem frightened."

"It's an act," I said. "He's terrified."

"No!"

"Yes! Remember, as his Twin, I can feel what he feels."

"You are ruining my reputation," Ashi said into my mind.

"For a good cause," I replied. *"And it's not as if I'm lying."*

I felt, rather than saw, Ashi's smile in return. I'd told the truth. He was as nervous as I was.

Ashi guided everyone into their proper location: four male/female pairs equally spaced in a circle inside the meadow with Ashi and me opposite Maya and Ari, and Eliasser and Ashara across from Anders and Meilee. The remaining four Guardians took their places, one between each pair. We'd debated arrangements and positioning ad nauseum, finally settling on this configuration to balance the energy of those who had spent time in the Elvener Anomaly (Ashi and Maya) with Ari and I, who had spent more time "above ground" as we now thought of it. We would have checked in with Earnie about the layout, but after visiting Eliasser and me at the Resting Stones, the Ether Light had been absent for the past seven days. I could only hope he was off somewhere getting super-charged for the ordeal ahead.

With everyone situated, we began the unifying meditation. Something didn't feel right, but since I'd never done anything like this, I held my tongue. We were about halfway through the meditation when Maya called out, "This is wrong. Ari and I radiate too much elven energy together. I should be opposite Ari, with Meiri across from Ashi."

Ashi closed his eyes and held his arms out, palms facing the center of the meadow.

"Maya is correct," he shouted. "Meiri, switch places with her."

"No," I said as loudly as I could. "Something about that isn't right either."

Balthasarre raised his voice. "We agreed to this ahead of time and we should stick with our plan. Everyone—stay where you are. Continue the meditation. Then we can decide if—"

He broke off as a small plume rose out of the ground, then sank back.

"Hurry," Danaeus yelled. "It's beginning! Sooner than we thought. I can feel it."

"Yes," Meilee shouted back. "The time to set all time right has arrived. Be at peace with your solution, for dissolution is the key."

Oh, how I wish these channelings came with translations!

Ari and Ashi called back and forth, trying to figure out what to do. I seemed to be the only one who noticed the small blob of blue light push up out of the ground where the plume had descended.

"*Earnie?*" I called to him mentally.

Suddenly, he was inside me. I felt that same warm tickle in my heart as when he helped me view my past life artifacts. "*Show me what to do, Earnie.*"

Bless my little blue friend, he did just that. Images rolled quickly through my mind.

"Meiri."

My eyes flew open, startled by an actual voice. "Come," Eliasser said, guiding me several yards to my left. "Beside me. We stand together."

Earnie's tickle increased. "Earnie confirms this," I called out loudly, so there would be no debate. "But we must achieve balance." Following the path Earnie had laid out in my mind, I shouted, "Ashi, stand beside Ashara. I will stay with Eliasser. Maya? Next to Ari. Your elven energy is needed together. I think it was the rest of our configuration that threw it off." Earnie pulsed me a resounding *yes.* "Earnie confirms it." I waited for more. I got a clear picture of each of the four male/female pairs at a specific compass point. "Ashi and Ashara—stand on West; Ari and Maya—you are East; Meilee and Anders—South; Eliasser and I are already on North."

Balthasarre objected. "The rest of us are supposed to be at those locations, on what you called the cardinal points."

"I was wrong. You need to stand on the ordinals." I'd have to thank the Girl Scouts for their wilderness training.

Earnie pulsed his confirmation so forcefully, I went a little woozy.

"Easy there, friend," I whispered aloud to him. "I'm only human."

The tap-tap-tap he played on my heart was soft and sweet.

"Oh!" Ari cried out. "I get it. It's an elven thing about time, distance, direction, and vibration. Meiri is right. The directional term is from Earth, but the position is correct. Danaeus? You are between Meilee and me."

Southeast, in other words.

"Mikellan? You are opposite Danaeus."

Northwest.

"Balthasarre? Between Meilee and Ashi with Clarisanna directly across from you."

Southwest and Northeast, respectively. As the group took their new positions, Eliasser and I stared at each other for a long moment, then I pulled him to me. "You are my One. There is no doubt in my mind or heart." Eliasser's eyes clouded with worry and fatigue. "Whatever happens," I added, "I will always be by your side. In whatever way I can be." And before he could stop me, my hands were over his heart, and I gave him a massive dose of energy.

"Sometimes I think you love me too much, honor me too much."

I smiled at my sweet king. "It was Earnie's idea. I'm just following his orders."

Eliasser didn't return my smile. "Keep your promise."

"Meiri!" Danaeus's frantic cry derailed my thoughts. "I sense they are coming, and the moon hasn't risen. What do we do?"

I broke free from Eliasser's penetrating gaze. "Accept them," I called out. "Let them guide you. Just like we discussed."

All at once, light shown over the valley. The silvery light of a full moon.

"It should be a crescent," Maya exclaimed. "Has time moved forward?"

"How can it have?" Balthasarre called to her. "We would have seen it. Felt it."

"Get ready," I shouted as a fissure opened and a stream of Ether Lights launched out of the ground. I'd been right about not needing to call them.

Just as Ashi had done when Earnie first appeared to us in the Guardian Meeting Room, Eliasser stood at my back and wrapped his arms around me, holding tight. Earnie, already in the center of my chest, expanded to include Eliasser, who sighed with delight. Then Earnie enlarged his energy field until Eliasser and I were secured in a bubble of shimmering blue light. Through the haze, I could barely discern the other eleven Ether Lights as each one spiraled up into the air, then merged with its intended host.

I checked to see if I still had mind communication with my Primary Twin. *"Ashi?"*

"Oh . . . it is so . . ." I felt him sigh. *"Nice."*

"They are amazing, aren't they?"

What he said next surprised me. *"When the time comes, keep that promise to Eliasser. Do not stop to save . . ."* The rest was static, like an un-tuned radio station signal.

Keep my promise? Do not stop to save . . . Eliasser? Was that what Ashi was trying to tell me? If so, he had wasted his breath.

The air cleared, and for a moment, I saw my companions in all their glowing glory. We made a rainbow ring of Light: Meilee/Red, Anders/Orange; Ashi/Yellow, Ashara/Green. Eliasser and I were both blue, Ari/Indigo, Maya/Violet. Those standing on the ordinal points were a blend of the colors on either side. Beautiful!

Eliasser reached for my hands and I held tight. Earnie pulsed faster and faster, until I could no longer think rationally. Whatever mind communication we had hoped to maintain as a group was gone, lost in the intense throbbing of the Ether Lights' frequencies.

With a deafening crack of thunder, a magnificent column of Ether Lights, hundreds of them, rocketed out of the crevice, circled several times in the air, then dropped to ground level and began speeding along the circumference behind us.

Brilliant plumes soared out of the fissure, so high they blotted out the moon. I tried to raise my arms to shield my eyes, but my muscles wouldn't respond. It wasn't that I *couldn't* move, but that any action my mind told my body to take would take eons to register. Fear knifed through me as I realized that time was slowing down, but only for the twelve of us on the circle's perimeter. This wasn't part of our plan.

"Earnie? Help us!"

Earnie bathed me in a warm, comforting energy as time continued to decelerate for those of us in human form until it essentially stopped. Frozen, unable to participate beyond hosting our Ether Lights, we could only watch what happened next.

The Ether Lights circling behind us were still pulsing, spinning, jetting around the perimeter, their speed increasing until they became a multicolored blur. Then, like a cosmic camera flash, they transformed into a single ring of pulsing white brilliance.

Dozens more plumes erupted from the ground, splitting the crevice wide open as they rose into the sky. The circling ring of pulsing Ether Lights behind us lifted into the air and whirled around the plumes, shaping them into radiant clouds that formed a sparkling dome high above the Garrammon Meadow. Magnificent!

The widening crevice snapped shut, shaking the ground, threatening to tumble us from our positions like statues in an earthquake. Earnie strengthened his hold on Eliasser and me, keeping us in place. It made no logical sense that I could still think, could process, could even feel fear as my body remained lodged in a single moment of time while time sped up around us.

The ring of pulsing Ether Lights now joined with the sparkling dome of transformed plumes. Then—*Boom!* The crevice reappeared, spreading wider, until it became a giant chasm bearing down on us as it consumed the floor of the meadow. Almost to our feet, now. Near enough that we could see down inside it, at the small planet rising up through smoky levels of rainbow-colored light. Red. Then orange. Yellow. Green. The higher Elvener rose, and the nearer the planet got to surface, the larger it appeared, until I was sure it would tear us all apart.

Elvener reached the violet level. The Ether Lights still inside of us catapulted out and soared above the chasm, crashing into each other with a thunderous *boom.* The "soundwave" knocked us several feet back from the chasm's edge. Stunned by the impact, it took me a moment to realize that normal time had been restored. I scrambled to my feet, but stumbled forward. Eliasser pulled me back, wrapping his arms around me again, this time to keep me in place.

The Ether Lights we had hosted were now a chaotic ball of swirling, rotating, gyrating rainbow light; light that expanded downward, acting like a tractor beam.

I stared transfixed as Elvener rose out of the chasm. I was so close, I could almost reach out and touch its oceans, its land. My brain bent sideways trying to comprehend that I had an up close view of a planet.

When Elvener's southern pole cleared the chasm's edge, the rainbow Ether Lights acting as a tractor beam merged into the iridescent dome. The dome then shimmied and poured itself, like a liquid, over Elvener, covering it completely. When the last "drop" was in place, the meadow shook so violently, I thought Amoran was coming apart.

The covered planet rose higher; the ground beneath us shaking; the chasm spitting fire and light; until in a burst of light like a nuclear bomb, Elvener and its shroud vanished.

"Keep your positions until this is completely over," Balthasarre shouted. It took a while for the shaking and the plumes to dissipate, but the huge hole in the Garrammon Meadow remained. We hadn't counted on that.

"Stay where you are until the chasm closes," Balthasarre called out again. "Everyone, think of something we can do to help that occur. In its current state, the meadow is highly dangerous. Any movement could have toxic consequences."

Eliasser was still holding me from behind when I had that same strange feeling I'd experienced previously when confronted with the crevices in the Garrammon Meadow. Like something wasn't finished. Like . . . I had a task to perform. I struggled out of Eliasser's arms and inched forward.

"Meiri!" he exclaimed, grabbing for me. "We must stay put."

"I know what I am doing."

Did I? I felt like I'd slipped into a dream state.

I should have known it was too much to ask. Eliasser clamped down on my wrists. With a violent twist, I yanked free. Caught off guard, he fell to the ground, slamming his head on a rock. Eyes rolling back in his head, his breath came in labored gasps.

"Eliasser!" I exclaimed, kneeling beside him. Dear god, what had I done?

"Go, Meiri," Ashi shouted, waving me forward as he ran toward us. "I will help Eliasser."

"DO NOT MOVE!" Balthasarre's usually calm voice was nearly hysterical with fear.

Torn between Eliasser and the magnetic pull of the chasm, I hesitated.

"Go!" Ashi yelled. "Do not save Eliasser! You have other promises to keep!"

A flush of warmth moved through my body, followed by a sense of purpose that felt, for lack of a better word, ancient. Sacred. Holy.

Trancelike, I turned away from my sweet king and reached the rim in a few steps. Inches from the massive opening, I executed an elaborate set of hand movements that I had no idea I knew, while speaking words in a language I had never heard before.

A single plume of light rose slowly to the top. I had turned my back—literally—on Eliasser. I had done what he requested. I hadn't saved him. Now, in order to fulfill a different promise, one I sensed but did not remember, I had to step into that soaring plume of energy.

Had to. And did.

This time, I didn't descend. I rose up like the Ether Lights had. Ethereal voices called to me as the plume I traveled within grew brighter until it was blindingly intense. Squeezing my eyes shut against the painful brilliance, I lifted my hands into the air and spoke more words I didn't understand. Yet what came out of my mouth was not what I heard in my head. It felt as if the real words, the ones in my mind, transformed into something else.

"Mosha elior anwar kiran!" I said them in my normal voice, but the air shook with the sound's vibration.

"*Again, Meirashannar*," a Voice spoke into my mind. The same Voice I had heard during the Reparention, whose counsel gave me the insight to help myself so I could do my part to save Earth and Amoran.

"Mosha elior anwar kiran!"

A thunderclap split the air.

"*Again, Meirashannar!*" the Voice repeated. The same Voice that had spoken my name in the Garrammon Meadow.

"Mosha elior anwar kiran! So be it."

"And so the Light comes . . ." the Voice said softly.

And it did. With an explosion of Light, the plume descended, far more rapidly than it had risen. Caught unaware, I lost my balance, fell out of the plume and into the chasm. I tried to ethermove, but nothing happened. All around me, the ground was closing in. In a few moments, the chasm would be gone, and me along with it. There was only one way this could end.

I offered up a quick prayer to the One Light—to take care of my children, my family, my friends, my two Twin Lights, and—

Severe spinning cut off my last request, followed by nausea, then pain as I landed hard on solid ground. Stunned, I lay there for a moment. Had I reached the bottom of the chasm? Was it possible to survive this? Had I fallen into a dimensional variance?

Lifting my head, I took in Ashi's stricken expression as he ran forward, his eyes trained beyond me. I was in the Garrammon Meadow, and with a sick heart, I knew who had saved me. Just as he had vowed to.

I pushed to my knees and turned. Eliasser gripped the chasm's edge. It was nearly gone.

"No," I screamed, scrambling toward him as he dug his fingers into the ground.

A bolt of energy hit me square in the chest and I couldn't move. Could only watch as Eliasser slipped over the edge. A second bolt of energy and Ashi, also on his way to save Eliasser, froze mid-stride.

Danaeus approached, shaking his hand, which still glowed from the effort of turning Ashi and me into statues. "I didn't think it would feel like that," he said calmly. He smiled at us, then leapt into the pit.

"Danaeus," I yelled. *Oh, Danaeus. Now we've lost you both?*

But we hadn't. Danaeus rose up on a plume, carrying Eliasser over his shoulder. Placing him gently on the ground, Danaeus said, "I'm going back. I have finally found a way home, to my world." He turned around to enter the plume that seemed to be almost waiting for him, then called over his shoulder, "Thank Earnie for me, Meiri. This was his doing. I'm going to miss you all." He unfroze Ashi and me, melded into the plume and vanished.

Ashi and I dragged Eliasser back from the edge, and just in time. The chasm expanded, heaved out one last plume of light, then closed up with a final thunderclap.

The remaining Guardians broke position and hurried toward us. Eliasser's body was alarmingly still, his pulse weak, his breathing shallow. Ashi and I pressed our hands over his chest and began feeding him energy. By the time the rest of the group reached us, Eliasser was still unconscious, but breathing normally.

Ashara checked his energy pulse. "He will recover, but we should get him back to the Mountain. He needs a complete assessment, as do we all. Especially you," she added, looking at me. "What possessed you to walk into the plume like that?"

"You can blame that intuition you worked so hard for me to hone. And I'm fine. See?" I flexed my arms, muscle man style. "Just a little dizzy." I tried to stand up, but it was like I'd been frozen again. "I'm sorry. I can't seem to move at all."

Ashara jammed her hand over my chest, got a horrified expression on her face, then pulled me to her. The first adrenaline hit of ethermoving made me so sick and hurt so much that I actually screamed. Then, mercifully, the world turned to cotton candy and faded away.

CHAPTER 26

Crash!

I bolted upright, then held my hands to my face, cradling my throbbing head. "Ohhh . . ."

"She is awake," a voice pronounced.

"You made enough noise," another voice said. "How could she not be?"

I peeked between my fingers. I was in a private nook in the Healing Room with two blue-gowned elves as my attendants. One of them presented me with a goblet. I took a sip, then gulped like I hadn't had liquid in weeks.

"Not too fast," a deeper woman's voice said. Peliyama came into view and peered into my eyes while Omanien took my energy pulse.

Omanien? "Is Elvener okay?" I croaked out.

She smiled. "Our world is fully restored and Amoran is no longer in danger."

"Is everyone else all right?"

"Your group came through a grueling experience with very little damage," Peliyama said. "You sustained the most injuries due to your time in the plume of light."

"Eliasser?"

"He is now in perfect health."

"Ashi?"

Omanien laughed. "Before you make us recite each person's status, all are fine."

I took a few more sips from the goblet, then handed it to one of the elven attendants. The drumming in my mind was lessening, my thoughts clearing. "What about Danaeus?"

"Let your heart rest easy where Danaeus is concerned," Omanien said. "As Elvener rose in vibration, it disrupted other dimensional variances, some of which had been stuck in place for more time than I have been alive. Danaeus is back on his homeworld."

I shook my head. "I'm going to miss him, but I think he always felt like the odd man out here." Something I could relate to. "How long have I been asleep?"

"We placed you in stasis three months ago," Omanien said.

My mouth went dry again. "Months?" I tried to climb off the healing stone.

"Be still," Peliyama said, gently pushing me back.

"But my kids. How many days have I been gone from Earth?"

"Lingering energy from Elvener's rising have allowed us to manipulate time for more days than usual without damaging time itself. However, it takes a greater number of Earth hours to accomplish that, and the effect is only temporary. To answer your question, I believe it has been nearly one Earth week since you left that world."

"Oh my god. Does my mom know?"

Omanien smiled. "Your mother has been quite helpful in that respect. I have already sent someone to Earth to inform her that you are awakened."

It was crazy, but I suddenly wanted my *mommy* like I hadn't since I fell off a pony at a carnival when I was ten. "Can she come here?" Before they could answer, I said, "Oh. Probably not. She must be looking after . . . after—" I stopped, suddenly breathless.

Peliyama nodded at Omanien, and the two women climbed onto the stone with me, Omanien at my back, Peliyama in front. Pressing their hands to my Heart Center, they began to hum. As if I'd been awake for days, and desperately needed sleep, my eyelids felt too heavy to hold up.

Clarisanna's soft voice prompted me awake. "Meiri. It is time to be up."

When I opened my eyes, a face pushed into view. "Mom!"

My mother climbed onto the stone and drew me into her arms. Between gulps of air and sobs, I squeezed out, "Kids?"

"They're fine. I don't know how these people do it, but not even a week has passed on Earth." She stroked my cheek, brushing away my tears. "You owe me big time, kid."

I laughed—a choking, half hysterical sound. "Mom. I love you so much." Sob, gulp. "I know I was a pain as a teenager, and I'm sorry for all the—"

"Oh, zip it. I got my revenge. There is Kiley, after all."

Mention of my daughter's name brought a fresh round of crying. But it wasn't just me. Mom had gone quiet. I pulled back, surprised by the tears spilling over onto her cheeks.

"The looks on their faces when they came to Earth to tell me what happened?" She sniffled. "I was sure I'd lost you. They thought I'd feel better knowing they put you in some sort of induced coma to heal. As if. Then they laid the time frame on me. Three months—they hoped! I told them not to take any longer or they were in big trouble."

I smiled. "And to whom did you deliver that order?"

"The hot dark-haired one, the extra hot white-haired one, and the supremely hot gardener."

I laughed. She'd gone back to joking to protect herself from her feelings. But that was my mom. I'd learned the same trick from her, but I'd always been too emotional for it to work for me as well as it did for her.

"I'm guessing you mean Ashi, Eliasser, and Balthasarre?"

"Yep. The three Stud-keteers."

"Ugh. That's enough. Even I can't joke about them that way."

"I'll tell you what isn't a joke. Covering for your absence. I told everyone, including your job—do you know how much unused paid time off you have?—that I demanded you stop whining about that book you never get around to writing and forced you into a week's vacation at a retreat, paid for by me. Happy early birthday, by the way."

Ashara came in and handed me another goblet. "Joanna will have to leave now."

Mom sighed. "I never get to have any fun."

Ashara smiled and shook her head at me.

"We have a saying on Earth," I told her. "The apple doesn't fall far from the tree."

"That's my girl," Mom said, and we bumped fists.

Mom slid off the healing stone. "How much longer?"

"One more Earth day should do it," Ashara said. "As long as our current time-stretching holds, that will give her three weeks here to fully recover now that she is out of stasis."

Mom did an elaborate fake bow, complete with hand curls. "Yes, your highness."

"At least you know your place," Ashara said, and the two of them left the room, arm in arm.

I sat there, alone with my thoughts as I consumed what smelled and tasted like reviving draft with a little something extra added in. Three months in stasis. Hard to wrap my brain around it.

Clarisanna returned, relieved me of the goblet, then guided me off the healing stone. "Normally, we would take several days to get you walking on your own again, but there is an important meeting today and the Guardians are hoping you can attend. The potion you consumed is a special draft of Peliyama's which should bring back your muscle tone more quickly."

I nodded, took a step and my knees buckled. Grabbing onto the side of the healing stone, I wound up laughing as I straightened up.

Clarisanna narrowed her eyes at me, but I reassured her. "I'm fine. Just wobbly."

Leaning on her arm, I tried again. And down I went, this time all the way to the floor.

"Meiri!" she exclaimed, reaching for my hands.

I waved her off. "I don't know what's in that potion, but moving tickles."

Clarisanna backed away. "This reaction is not correct. I will bring help."

"Okay, but I'll stay here on the floor. I'd rather not move again, if it's all right with you." I leaned against the healing stone as tiny, ticklish electrical impulses zinged through my nervous system. Looking more worried than ever, Clarisanna left the room.

I wasn't concerned about my response to Peliyama's special draft. Regardless of how much time I spent on Amoran, the energetic makeup of my Earth body meant unusual side-effects were not uncommon. Tilting my head back, I allowed my eyes to close a moment as I pondered what the "important meeting" was about. I hoped it wasn't some other problem we'd have to deal with. I may have been knocked out for several months, but I needed a long vacation, nonetheless.

"Meiri."

I opened my eyes. "Eliasser?"

I was close, but the face smiling down at me didn't belong to the Master Guardian.

"Elianna?" I whispered.

Strong hands gripped mine, lifting me to my feet like I weighed no more than a fairybee. Eliasser's Primary Twin pressed her palm over my breastbone and channeled a river of strengthening energy that rippled its way throughout my body in mere seconds. When she removed her hand, I stood on my own, the tickling energy gone.

"How did you do that?" I asked, awed at the power she possessed. I had never experienced anything like that, not even from Eliasser.

Still smiling, she shook her head. "That explanation will have to wait. I do not have much time, Meiri. I came to heal you and to give you a message."

"A message? I don't understand. Does Eliasser know you're here?"

"He does not. I am not actually here. My body is in stasis on Elvener, in a special healing chamber. I will not be able to return to Amoran physically for some time. If at all." A hint of sadness framed her beautiful aqua eyes, a perfect match to Eliasser's.

"Then, how—"

"You must listen, Meiri. I cannot maintain this physical projection much longer. There are things to come which will seem undoable to you. In some ways, wrong. You will need to look deep into your heart to find the truth in all things." She began to shift in and out of focus.

"Don't go yet! Let me get Eliasser."

Her image became solid again for a moment. "He cannot know I was here. No one can. This is a secret you must keep. Here." She pointed to my heart. "Keep me here, as I always am."

"Oh, Elianna. I can't keep this from him."

Wavering in and out of physicality again, she said, "You must. You will. Remember . . . what seems right may be wrong. What appears to be wrong could be right. Promise me that you will follow your heart."

"I promise."

Her fading image snapped out of sight as Clarisanna came around the cloth partition, followed by Peliyama.

"Meiri? Are you all right now?" Clarisanna asked.

I turned away and composed myself as best I could. "Yes."

Clarisanna placed a formal yellow tunic on the healing stone, an unusual color for Amoran, then left. I peeled off the Healing Room caftan and tugged on the yellow leggings.

Peliyama helped me pull the tunic top over my head. "You healed quickly, Meiri," she said, fixing me with the same calculating gaze that was usually Ashara's purview.

She knew something was up. But I'd just made a promise to Elianna that I had no intention of breaking. And so, I obfuscated. The Foreseers had taught me well.

"Yes, I did, didn't I? I guess what just happened to me is another impossible miracle."

We locked eyes for a long moment. "I see," Peliyama said quietly.

I didn't know if the Head of the Council of Light could read minds or see the future like the Foreseers. But she didn't challenge me, and we made our way to the "important meeting."

When we stopped outside the open doorway to the Celebration Hall, I looked in and smiled. So, it was *that* kind of meeting. The large room was packed with people seated at tables crammed in every which way. A buffet table lined one wall. Along the opposite wall was another long table. There, from left to right, were Eliasser, Ashara, Omanien, an elf I didn't know, three unoccupied chairs, a man sporting the same moonbeam hair as Peliyama, then Ashi. Peliyama led me to the empty seat beside my Twin, then sat on the other side of Moonbeam Man.

Ashi folded his hand over mine and smiled. "I am grateful beyond measure that you are healed and whole."

I blinked, staring at my Twin, wondering why his energy was so shielded that I could barely sense anything from him at all. Or was I the one doing the shielding? Keeping my defenses up in order to guard Elianna's secret? Either way, the blockage threw me. All I could manage in response was "thank you."

Ashi tilted his head to the side, his expression quizzical. I was spared having to answer his unspoken question when Omanien and Peliyama rose together, held their goblets high, and toasted the Guardians for their role in restoring Elvener and saving both Elvener and Amoran from destruction. That wasn't all, though. Our effort had resulted in a different form of balance to the Seventh Vortex. Unheard of in the history of the spinning energy giants, the Seventh Vortex now boasted four access points or portals: Earth, Amoran, Elvener and the planet that housed the Council of Light, whose name, curiously, never seemed to be mentioned. I smiled, thinking how convenient it would be now for Ari to visit his world. And, of course, to take me with him. I longed to see Elvener again in all her glory.

As the toast continued, Eliasser's attention shifted from Omanien to me, his intense gaze seeming to bore into my soul. Unsettled, I broke eye contact and turned to Ashi, shocked to find he was breathing hard, his hands clenched in front of him.

"What's wrong?" I whispered.

He shook his head. "It is as if Elvener is rising again, only this time, inside of me."

Alarmed at the possible implications, I waved as discreetly as I could, beckoning Ashara to me. Ashi seemed unable to speak, so I relayed to the Master Healer what he'd told me.

She nodded. "He will be all right, Meiri. I know what this is. Come with me, Ashi. We should be back before the closing ceremony."

Peliyama sat down, but Omanien remained standing.

"Today, I have one more honor to bestow," she said, nodding at the doorway to the Celebration Room. Maya and Ari entered, wended their way to the long table and took the seats at the very center. The place of honor.

Omanien raised her goblet once more. "Imryss and I are privileged to present Arrien Etan and Amaya Nitri, who will one day assume the roles of Heads of the Elven High Council."

Ari gave a sheepish grin and Maya seemed outright embarrassed. But they both stood and bravely received the thunderous applause. Caught off guard by the proclamation, I didn't remember to clap until it was almost too late. My heart clenched. Did this mean they would both be living on Elvener permanently now?

Peliyama's companion, Moonbeam Man, gazed at the empty space between us. "Why not move over, Meiri? I think it will be some time before Ashi is able to join us again."

"Do you know what's wrong with him?" I asked, taking Ashi's deserted chair.

"I have some idea." He smiled. "We have not been introduced. I am Panimore of the Council of Light."

"Ah," was my brilliant response. I thought he looked familiar. Panimore was Peliyama's companion in the vision the Elder had shown me.

Panimore filled my goblet with fairybee wine. "Drink up, Meirashannar. Stasis can be quite hard on a physical being. I appreciate that you are even able to be here now."

"Thank you. I am glad to be here."

Panimore regarded me thoughtfully. "While you were in stasis, we determined that Ashi's contact with the mementos from your past lives was responsible for his violent behavior."

I nodded, not really wanting to be reminded of the day my Twin had almost killed me. Or what happened with Eliasser afterward.

"Ashi asked me to destroy them." Panimore drummed his fingers on the table. "However, it was not the artifacts which caused the problem, but the way they were imbued—perhaps imprinted is a better word—with the emotions of each lifetime. Those emotions will now always be too much for Ashi to take in."

"But he had those objects, in some cases, for hundreds of years without them affecting him."

Panimore riveted his gaze on me. "Until you viewed them."

That caught me up short. "You mean, I'm the one who imprinted them with emotion?"

He nodded. "And you did so while Elvener's energy patterns were infusing everyone and everything in the Guardian Sanctuary. Those artifacts are powerfully energized now."

Poor Ashi. It was my fault he'd had such a hard time. Then again, it was Earnie's idea in the first place that I view them, so there must have been a good reason for the way things unfolded.

"To safeguard Ashi and ease his concerns, I have transferred all but two of the artifacts to the Council headquarters where I will keep them for you."

"Are you sure that's a good idea?" I was with Ashi on this one. Destroying them seemed a better option.

Panimore's gaze intensified. "I am quite certain you will need them someday."

The back of my neck prickled, which told me my next statement was most likely moot.

"Honestly? I don't think I ever want to see any of them again."

"Indulge me if you will. I took charge of the remaining two. When you go to your room tonight, one of them will be resting on your sleeping stone. And here is the other one." Panimore opened his hand, revealing the small, polished stone paperweight from the lifetime I'd been spoiled rotten.

I grimaced, remembering who I'd been then. "I wasn't the nicest person in that life."

"No, you were not. Because the man who parented you was quite deficient in that area. Earth is a difficult environment to incarnate into. And some of us, even when we have only one lifetime to experience, are not well equipped for the task."

He placed the stone in my palm and closed his fingers over mine.

Recognition flooded me. "You were the father who spoiled me?"

"One life to live, and I could not get it right," he said ruefully, withdrawing his hand.

"In that case, I wish I could have given you a better experience. From what I understand, this past life stuff works two ways. I can be handed a challenge or an easy life. Good parents or—" I cringed, thinking of the abusive father from my clay pot life. "Not so good. What I make of those challenges is up to me."

His expression softened, and I thought I detected a hint of sadness. "Remember that when it comes time for your next tasks. You will have choices to make. Choose well, Meiri."

Massive chills consumed my spine. Ashara had said the same thing to me just before we all entered the vortex to perform the Reparention: *Choose well, Meiri.* The choice I made? To forfeit my own life to save Eliasser, which made Ashi risk his life so that I wouldn't lose mine. Those choices set in motion a series of events that led to the successful rising of Elvener. I shook my head, in awe of how much we don't know, even when we act from intuition.

I reflected on Elianna's warning that right and wrong might masquerade as each other. Panimore's caution made even more sense now. Presented with options that disguised their true nature, I would have to choose well. Would have to dig deep to unmask the truth.

I don't know how long I sat there pondering right, wrong, truth, and choice. I tuned back in when Omanien and Imryss requested room be made for dancing. I glanced around at the tables, where empty plates were the norm. I hadn't eaten, when had they? I didn't seem to have full control of my experience of time yet. I finished my food and my fairybee wine. Then, with a word to Panimore about where I was going, and the request to offer my apologies to anyone who asked for me—something I didn't think was likely with all the merrymaking going on—I tucked the stone paperweight into the pocket of the unusual yellow tunic and went to my room.

The other artifact Panimore left for me was on my sleeping stone. It was the pillowcase from the only lifetime I had taken a woman as my lover. I held the fabric to my face, feeling the deeply spiritual Love it represented.

A note had been left under the pillowcase. The penmanship was impeccable, but it wasn't Ashi's careful lettering.

Meiri,

Love arrives in many forms and in many ways. The soul you shared this Love and this life with has incarnated and been with you in each of your Earth lives, as male and female equally.

That meant it couldn't be Ari. He hadn't needed to incarnate on Earth.

This soul is in your life now.

Which also left out John.

When the time is right, you will recognize each other. Keep each other safe. He is part of your final task, and has a special place, as do you, in the hearts of the Council of Light.

He? That eliminated fifty percent of the people I knew.

Many blessings I send you, my daughter. Be at peace during these next few years. You have earned the rest.

With Love and Light, Panimore

I reread the note several times, then stored it in one of my drawers along with the paperweight. I left the pillowcase on my sleeping stone, brought a fresh tunic into the ancillary, and took an energy shower. There must have been a way to keep me clean when I was in stasis, but I needed a fresh start. Hot water would have been preferable, but I had to work with what was available. I took my time getting dressed, thinking about the last two years, the task we'd all accomplished, and the many ways that task had changed us. Life certainly was strange, full of unexpected twists and turns.

Fully dressed now, I tucked Ashi's amulet beneath my tunic top and exited the ancillary.

And drew in a sharp breath.

Ashi was leaning against my sleeping stone, the pillowslip pressed to his cheek. The last time he had contact with one of the artifacts, it hadn't gone so well.

"Such Love emanates from this," Ashi said. He looked up and must have read something in my expression. "Ah. There is nothing to fear, Meiri. Panimore removed the ones that caused me trouble, and as you know, I was cured of that difficulty anyway."

So much so that he'd asked Panimore to destroy them?

I crossed to the sleeping stone and took the pillowcase from Ashi. Before I could stop him, he held my hand and probed my mind, my heart, and my emotions. I tried to back up and shutter myself, but he grabbed me by the wrist. "Don't," he said. "Let me sense you."

A sliver of fear shot through me. Ashi had used a contraction. I don't know why Amorans didn't use that form of speech, but except for those of us who hailed from off-world, it was universal. Its appearance now felt wrong, especially since the only other time Ashi had used a contraction was when he attacked me.

I pulled away and hastened to the back counter. I added the pillowslip to the same drawer as the paperweight and Panimore's note, closed the drawer with my knee, and turned around.

"Ashi!" I gasped.

He was directly in front of me, blocking my way. Clasping his hands on my shoulders, he breathed out, "Read me, Meiri. Read my heart. Then my mind. Then my feelings."

Scared to do what he asked, but afraid not to, I closed my eyes, shielding my own inner world as best I could. Among other concerns, like Elianna's secret, I didn't want to reawaken my attraction to Ashi when nothing could be done about it.

I probed his Heart. His spiritual Love for me as his Twin was profound . . . and beautiful.

I searched his mind next, relieved to find his thoughts clear, without conflict or confusion.

Then, I opened myself up to his emotional center, where more personal love resided.

Ashi's feelings for me were pure and good.

I opened my eyes and smiled.

He smiled back. "So, Dr. Meiri. Do I have a clean bill of health?"

I laughed. "Dr. Meiri? Clean bill of health? Where did you get that from?"

He pulled a scrap of parchment out of his pocket and waved it in the air. "Ari."

"Ari. Of course." Between the mischievous elf and the Anders/Meilee duo, the entire Mountain would be slinging slang from Earth in no time.

"Now," Ashi said, "tear down that thick stone wall you have built to keep me out and allow me deeper into your psyche."

I shook my head. "I'm sorry, Ashi. You seem fine, but I am still the same as I always have been. And being around you without my 'thick stone wall' as you put it is hurtful for me."

"Because of the physical relationship you want to have with me," he stated.

I sighed. "Yes."

We were still standing at my back counter. Opening a large drawer, he withdrew a carafe and two goblets and carried them to the table. "I stashed this away earlier."

"Shielding draft?" I asked hopefully, as I followed him.

He didn't answer. Just uncapped the bottle and began to pour. "While you were in healing stasis, I visited the Foreseers. I let them know I was quite perturbed with them."

I had to smile at that.

"I asked them to explain why the way I am"—he tapped his heart—"keeps changing. Do you know what they said?"

I shook my head, trying not to chuckle at the idea of Ashi taking on the Foreseers.

"They told me that change is the nature of the universe!"

I bit my lip.

Ashi frowned while he finished filling the goblets. "I told them I already *knew* that. However, I did not seem to be the one making the *choice* as to how I was changed. They replied, in that way of theirs, that *of course* I was the one making each choice, and that I had agreed to each change many hundreds of years ago."

Ashi handed me one of the goblets. "I told them I found their vague response annoying."

I gave it up and laughed. "Oh, boy. How did they react to that?"

He smiled. "Just like you did now."

"I'll bet," I said. "They never take anything personally."

Ashi picked up his cup. "I propose we celebrate ourselves. To us, Meiri. To Twin Lights. To whatever the future holds. To whatever choices we have made."

He tapped the rim of my goblet, then chugged what must have been half the contents of his cup. Surprised by that, and still a little wary, I took a small sip. It was sweet, delicious, and instantly relaxing. If it was a shielding draft, it was a new one on me. Either way, I took a few gulps. I needed to relax, big time.

"And," Ashi said, holding his cup high, "to whatever tasks we have yet to do, and the changes we have consented to have thrust upon us, whether we are happy with them or not."

"Like the way you developed physical desires before the Reparention?"

Ashi emptied his goblet, set it down, then removed mine from my clenched fingers.

"Like the way physical desires were taken from me after the Reparention."

That surprised me. He'd seemed glad about that before.

"When I asked the Elder about it," Ashi went on, "she claimed it was a choice I had made to enable me to help effect the rising of Elvener without becoming . . . distracted."

There was that word again. I frowned and bit my lip for a different reason.

Ashi moved closer, lifted a lock of my hair with his fingers and tucked it behind my ear.

Talk about distracting. Shivers ran through me. He'd done something like that after he'd acknowledged his desire for me before the Reparention..

"What did you say to her then?" I asked, barely able to get my voice above a whisper.

His smile turned sly. "I told them I wanted to make a new choice. That when you awoke from stasis, I would very much like to be *distracted.*"

My heart began to pulse in my throat. "Can . . . can the Foreseers do that?"

"They cannot."

My spirits sank. "Oh. Then you are still—"

"*They* cannot. Apparently, the power to change resides with me. They said I had to choose to be . . . distracted . . . with full intention, knowing that this path will have more challenges for me. And for you."

Ashi's arms circled around me; his fingers traced a line down my backbone.

My heart was thrumming so rapidly now, I felt lightheaded.

"Tell me, my Twin," Ashi breathed into my ear, "what choice do you think I made?"

"One way to find out," I whispered. I kissed him, long and hard. Every inch of my flesh quivered as Ashi returned my kiss with all the passion and skill I remembered.

"Okay then," I said breathlessly when we finally came up air. "Want to spend an hour being completely distracted?"

He guided me toward the sleeping stone. "I was hoping for all night."

Chapter 27

Ashi and I took Morning Meal the next day in the Guardian Meal Room. When we showed up late, Balthasarre tipped his goblet at us, then set to work catching me up on the past several months. I'd had too many other things occupying me last night to care about being brought up to date on Mountain happenings.

Clarisanna and Meilee were now official Guardians, taking the chairs vacated by Danaeus and Ari. This brought our Guardian complement back to the accustomed—but not mandatory—eight. They tried to get Mikellan to stay, but he claimed he'd had enough excitement for the next hundred years or so, and wanted to focus on his research with potions, food chemistry, and something that sounded like alchemy.

For the most part, things were back to normal in Guardian Lands. Energy changes had eased away. Tempers returned to normal. No new illnesses were reported. And two of the people who had experienced physical desires in some form—Eliasser and Balthasarre—had slowly lost them. Meilee and Anders were another story. The elven energy seemed to have affected them more directly, perhaps because of their age. They would retain their libidos, but their aging process would speed up now as a result, something they didn't seem bothered by.

I broached the subject of birth control to Ashara, and not just for the teenage lovebirds. I was pretty confident that I could no longer conceive due to something that no one other than my sister-in-law Nancy knew about; I'd never even told John. But I wasn't willing to risk finding out I was wrong by "accident." A pregnancy at this point would be hard to explain to my Earth family and friends.

"You do not know?" Ashara said.

"Know what?"

"It is impossible for anyone living in Guardian Lands to conceive."

"But I'm not from Guardian Lands."

"But Ashi is. And you are affected as well when you are here."

"And you are sure that nothing will happen?"

Ashara crossed her arms. "If Ashi could conceive a child, it would be a bigger miracle than the raising of Elvener."

I didn't point out that raising Elvener was a miracle we had accomplished. She was so certain, though, that I decided to trust her wisdom. With that question settled, I went back to getting "distracted" with Ashi every chance I could for the next three weeks.

Ari and Maya were gone now, getting re-acclimated to their homeworld. I missed them both, but in Ari's case, I'd lost one of my best friends. Which is why I was thrilled when Ashi and I were permitted to make one trip to Elvener as a private thank-you from the Elven High Council. It was supposed to be an informal visit, but quickly turned into a lively celebration as only the elves can do. We spent most of our time indoors, as the energy outside the domed buildings was considered too volatile for the two of us.

I stuffed myself with every elven delicacy possible, then had to waddle down the hall to use the bathroom. I had just exited after doing my business, when Ashi, Ari, and Maya caught me up by my arms and pulled me toward the door to the outer world.

"I thought we couldn't do this," I said.

Maya handed me a flask. "This will give you an hour or so. Ashi drank his already."

Eager to see more of Elvener, I chugged mine down, and we left the building. The main thoroughfare was paved with a blue, crystal-like substance. After several quick turns, the road opened onto a vast grassy field.

I stopped short. Blue-green grass, pink and orange trees, mango sky.

"This is it," I exclaimed. "This is where I was when I entered the plume the first time."

"We know," Ari said. "Maya and I figured it out."

Ari ran ahead, then turned around, pulled something out of his shoulder bag, and tossed it to Ashi. Maya ran in front of Ashi and grabbed the round object before Ashi could.

"Is that a Garrammon ball?" I asked.

"Deactivated," Ari said. "We're just going to play catch."

Even with Maya's tonic, the exercise left me breathing hard. Yet it also seemed to activate memories of my time on Elvener when the four of us formed the core of the Vortex Transition Team. I'd spent a fair amount of time here as we prepared to ferry Elvener's population through the Mirror Vortex to its new home on Amoran. Not for the first time, I wondered what would have happened if we had been successful. And if I'd never had to leave Amoran.

"I remember being here," I said, as we stopped playing and settled on the grass.

Ari manifested drinks and his amazing elven cake. "We thought you might," he said. "It didn't seem right that you should be without those memories, especially since you and Ashi won't be able to return."

"Why not? We spent months here during our Transition Team days."

"Your Vortex-created bodies protected you. Now, yours is from Earth, and Ashi's contains Earth energy. Until our world fully settles into its new dimensional patterns, elven energy would eventually consume you if you remained here too long."

"But you can come to Amoran and Earth. Hardly seems fair," I said, pouting.

Ari smiled. "Omanien left a present for you on Amoran. Ashi knows where it is."

Ashi tossed the ball to Ari, who returned it to his satchel with a sigh. "Time for you to go."

Ari and Maya would remain on Elvener for the next several months. When we arrived at the elven portal, my heart heavy with that knowledge, I hugged them both.

Maya called the vortex and the blue mist descended, wrapping around Ashi and me.

Ari called out, "Love you, Earth-girl."

I waved goodbye through the thickening mist. "Back atcha, Elf-boy!"

Maya and Ari disappeared from view as Ashi and I soared upward.

"Just a little farther," Ashi said as he led me across the plain east of the Garrammon Lake to see Omanien's gift to us.

Suddenly, as if it popped up out of nowhere, we came to a mini forest of tightly packed trees tucked up against a steep hill. Ashi closed his eyes, steepled his hands and bowed. An opening appeared between the trees revealing a shaded path. It wound inward for forty yards or so, then took one last tight curve.

"It's beautiful," I exclaimed, gazing in wonder at a two-story high waterfall. Water, aqua-green and shimmering in the early morning sunlight, cascaded over a rock precipice into a pool below. Steam rose from the surface into the cool air of dawn. The part of the pool not backed by the waterfall was bordered by trees—luxurious *green* trees—that grew right up to the water's edge, with one exception. To the right of where we stood was a grassy area about fifteen by twenty feet—a perfect space to picnic on after a swim.

Ashi led me toward the water and kicked off his shoes.

"Hold on," I said. "You hate water."

Ashi smiled as he bent over to remove my shoes for me, then drew us both in up to our chests. I would have thought the water would be chilly, like the Garrammon and Mindsail Lakes. But this water was as warm as a bathtub. Sheer heaven. "Okay, Twin-boy. What gives?"

He tsked. "Your Earth speech is so imprecise."

I mock-glared at him. "Water? You? Since when?"

"Ari convinced me."

"How?"

"By suggesting that since you love swimming, I should learn to love it, too." He planted a kiss on my nose, and I giggled. "As it turns out, not only do I like this water, but the area can be sealed for privacy." He waved his hand in the general direction of the entrance.

"Is that what you just did? Lock us in?"

Ashi planted littles kisses in a circle around my face. "What do you think?"

Selfishly, we waited a few days before telling anyone else about the Steaming Falls, as we'd named the elven retreat. The reactions were a mixed bag. Meilee and Anders asked for swimming lessons. Balthasarre forbade them to go anywhere near the water. Clarisanna wanted to see the falls, but not to swim. Eliasser shook his head in disgust at the whole idea, and Ashara left the room.

"Where are you going?" Eliasser called after the Master Healer.

"To pack what Meiri calls a picnic lunch. And yes, Meilee and Anders will learn to swim."

On the day I returned to Earth, I arrived in my family room at precisely twelve noon. The mouthwatering aroma of mac and cheese baked from scratch, and hot dogs convinced me to forgo the reintegration meditation and head to the kitchen.

"I wasn't sure what you'd want to eat," Mom said, her tone subdued. "The mac and cheese just came out of the oven, and the hot dogs are done."

"How did you know when I'd be back?"

She grinned, then bent to remove the hot dogs from the broiler. "The hunky one came through and let me know."

Oy. "Hunky one?"

"Balthasarre. What a weird name, huh? Like from ancient times."

Like biblical, to be exact. And yes, weird.

"It gave me a chance to give him his gift."

"Gift?"

"Yup. I finished the afghan while you were gone. Gave me something to do while I was biting my nails at three in the morning worrying about you." She rolled her eyes.

I rolled mine right back. "You slept like a baby on my new mattress, didn't you."

She smiled at that. "Actually, I used the pull-out in the den." She whipped out her phone, tapped a few times, then handed it to me. "That's what I gave him."

Speechless, I stared at the gorgeous creation. This was no crazy patchwork blanket like the one she'd crocheted for me many years ago.

"The design's my own," she said, peering over my shoulder. "Those are vortexes roses spiraling out of the center. The ones around the edge are Earth roses. Roses are beautiful on both worlds." She sighed. "When I was on Amoran the first time, he gave me his own tour of the garden, and told me how he took up gardening after his wife died. I told him we were birds of a feather . . . sort of. I took up gardening to keep from killing my husband."

"You didn't!" I exclaimed.

"Kill your father? Of course not."

"You know what I mean." It felt awkward talking to her about Balthasarre, knowing how he had felt about her. I wondered if she had any indication. Then, taking in her flushed cheeks and averted eyes, I wondered if my mother had feelings for the Master Technician as well.

Truly awkward.

I spooned some mac and cheese onto two plates and brought them to the table. Mom added a hot dog to each one, and we sat down to eat.

She asked me about everyone on Amoran, except for Balthasarre because she had just seen him. I had her fill me in on what the kids were up to. But underneath it all, I could sense something was bothering her.

"What is it, Mom?"

She didn't answer right away. I held my tongue, giving her space while she cleared our plates, then filled my new electric teakettle. My Mom is not the silent type, so the fact that she said nothing until she brought the doctored mugs of tea to the table made me nervous.

Leaning over her cup, she stirred idly.

I sipped and waited.

"I'm having trouble keeping this from your father," she said at last. "I don't like lying to him about something so big. I don't know how you did this while John was alive. To think it almost broke up your marriage." She met my eyes. "And I'm worried about you. Have you counted how many times you almost died? Or did die?" She shook her head. "I want to be okay with this. I just don't know how."

What could I say? It had taken me many time-stretched months on Amoran before the Reparention to come to terms with my "destiny," at least what I knew of it back then. I still didn't know what dangers—or joys—lay ahead. But after helping bring a planet back from the brink of destruction, as well as the planet it would have taken down with it, there was no doubt in my mind that I would try to do whatever was requested of me.

I'd looked up the word "destiny" once. One of the meanings was "to decide ahead of time." That's what I'd done in the Glen of Foreseers more than a thousand years ago. I'd been a different person then, but I'd made a promise at the soul level. Several promises, as it turns out.

To decide ahead of time. I wasn't mindlessly following someone else's predetermined plan. I was choosing to follow a path I'd laid out for myself, or at least had agreed to. And yet, how would I feel about the promises I'd made but didn't remember—because of an amnesia I'd agreed to—when my next task was revealed?

I couldn't answer that now. Would I object? Possibly. Would I run from it? Maybe. But as I sat across from my mother, I knew one thing. All our lives are interconnected in ways we can't always see and can't imagine. Mom stumbled onto Amoran for a reason. It seemed we both needed to come to terms with that now.

I reached out and we clasped hands. "I've lived a double life now for nearly two and a half years. Has it been hard? You bet. And it's not just John I had to hide from. It's everyone in my life, Ryan and Kiley included. But this is all so much bigger than I am, Mom. It's why, except for that one time I broke down and tried to get you to believe me, I haven't breathed a word about Amoran to anyone.

"The Foreseers like to say that everything has a reason or is meant to be. So, I think there's a reason you caught me dropping out of the portal that day. I think you're a part of my Amoran journey. That makes you subject to the same restrictions that I am. And because we can't tell anyone about Amoran, we have to lie to people we love. That said, I can't force you to abide by that restriction. If you feel you need to tell Dad, tell him."

Her serious expression dissolved into a smile, then a laugh. "How could I? He'd think I was nuts." She grew thoughtful. "Except, if I showed him the portal in the ceiling . . ."

I shook my head. "You know what Dad is like. What do you think would happen if you called the vortex in front of him?"

She sighed. "You're right. Except for his occasional bouts of religious guilt about not going to church regularly, he's so rational, I think it would destroy him."

I wouldn't go that far, but I kept quiet. Mom had just given herself a reason to be okay with lying to her husband; it was for his own good.

"Come on, fellow Vibrational," I said. "Let's walk off that mac and cheese."

"Fellow Vibrational," Mom mused. "I like that."

I went back to my Friday Amoran visits, with Mom once again acting as my backup. The Earth months rolled by and winter blew itself out into the gentlest spring we'd had in years.

One morning in late May, Eliasser inquired what I would like for my birthday.

"My birthday?" Once again, I wondered if I had dropped into an alternate universe. "My birthday isn't for several months yet. Besides, I didn't think you celebrated birthdays here."

"We do not as a rule. But Ari says that this birthday is considered somewhat momentous."

"Not really. I'm turning thirty-nine, not forty."

"Perhaps he added in the extra time you have spent here with us."

Thanks a lot, Elf-boy. I wasn't about to do the math, but it would probably make me more than forty. "I'll be sure to give Ari his payback next time he's here," I grumbled.

Eliasser looked thoughtful. "Does that mean you do not want to celebrate? Or receive a gift? I still think I would like to give one to you," he continued, not waiting for my answer. "It is a nice Earth custom—recognizing someone's first arrival on the planet."

I didn't say a word, hoping this would go away. Being with Eliasser was gift enough for me.

"Well? What do you wish for, my Meiri? Or should it be a surprise?" He had a determined look on his face. "I will get you a present no matter what you say."

And just like that, I knew what I wanted from Eliasser. I might have to thank the obstreperous elf after all. "Would you like to know what I want most in all our world?"

"Of course." He beamed his solar smile at me.

"Come swimming with me at the Steaming Falls."

The smile vanished. "Oh, I do not think that is a good idea."

Now I was the one smiling. "Just once. It will be the best gift you could ever give me."

"Then I will have to give you the second-best gift, because I will do no such thing."

Time wore on, and I forgot about Eliasser's offer of a birthday present. My birthday was still a month away the day I hurried to the Resting Stones to meet up with Ashi, Ari, and Maya; the latter two were on an extended visit from Elvener. We had an early morning Garrammon match planned, and I was itching to get to the field.

But the only one at the Resting Stones was Eliasser. I'd been delayed leaving by a request from Ashara that "simply could not wait." I knew I was running behind, but had the others gone on without me?

"Come, Meiri. Let us walk," Eliasser said.

"Can we head toward the Garrammon field? I'm late for my match."

"Certainly."

We took the path that meandered around low rolling hills until we reached the Garrammon field. Which was empty.

"Meiri," Eliasser said. "Will you trust me now?"

"Um . . . sure. I always trust you."

"Ashi, Ari, and Maya are not coming to play Garrammon."

"They're not?"

"No. I am going to ethermove us now. Will you allow that?"

"Okay. Where—"

But he'd already wrapped his arms around me. After an adrenaline-fed ride, I opened my eyes and gasped. We were at the Steaming

Falls. A basket overflowing with food and two carafes rested in the grassy area. "You brought me here for a picnic?"

"Yes. After you have"—he shuddered—"brought me into the water."

My mouth fell open. "You're serious?"

Eliasser smiled. "Happy birthday, Meiri."

He removed his shoes and shrugged out of his pilea. Underneath, he wore a standard issue Guardian tunic. "Best to get it over with so I can get out as soon as possible."

"Oh, no. If you're going to get in, you have to let me show how much fun we can have."

I slipped off my shoes, reached for his hands, and led him slowly to the water's edge.

"I will not submerge my head or engage in those antics that you and Ari do."

I stopped and looked him squarely in the eyes. "Don't continue if you truly don't want to. But if you do continue, you must follow my lead and do exactly as I say. Will you trust *me* now?"

He surprised me by laughing. "I cannot believe I doing this."

"That's more like it! Come on, one step at a time."

I learned two charming facts as we inched into the water. Eliasser was ticklish and Eliasser giggled. "Why are you laughing?" I asked, but I didn't really want him to stop. I'd never heard anything so engaging as the Master Guardian giggling.

"The water . . ." he gasped. "It tickles."

"It does? Not to me." The water did have a tingly feel to it today, but I loved it. Eliasser was clearly uncomfortable, though. I held my hand to his heart and infused him with soothing energy, an ability I had retained.

"Thank you," he said, and he stopped giggling.

I inched us further in, halting when the water reached our waists. "So, what do you think?"

Eliasser gave my query the same ample consideration he'd given the question about hugging when I'd first asked him about that several years ago.

"Now that the water is not tickling me, it feels rather . . ."

"Nice?" I offered hopefully.

He let out a long, deep, soulful sigh. And nodded.

"Yahoo! I knew it! I knew if I could just get you in here—"

"Meiri! Look!" Hands on my shoulders, he turned me around. Morning sunlight made a thousand tiny rainbows explode in the mist above the cascading water. The whole day seemed to have absorbed a kind of electricity, because the rainbows began to glow, then radiated a sparkly light all their own. I turned to face Eliasser, who was still staring, transfixed, above my head.

It began as a small, innocuous sensation in my chest.

Then it grew exponentially.

Eliasser's gaze moved rapidly downward. "Meiri, are you—"

I shook my head. "I thought you were."

"No." He probed my mind, then exclaimed in wonder. "If I am not, and you are not, then who—?"

Those were the last words either of us spoke as the full embrace of Heart Coalescence engulfed us. Like magnets pulled together, we found ourselves heart-to-heart, our hands clutching each other's shoulders.

In an explosion of light and sound and feeling, the energy circling around and between us magnified. The only communication we could manage was the simultaneous tightening of our grip on each other—an involuntary reaction when a person realizes they are about to relinquish their physical body. The body isn't always quite ready for that, which is why the customary position for merging is one of open acceptance, hands clasped and out to the sides in supplication to the good graces of the universe and the Light. Nonetheless, Eliasser and I were merging, right there in the Steaming Falls, with no one around to guide us through it.

In a second explosion of Light, our bodies began to leave the physical state. But the atoms which made us up were still present when they moved rapidly into each other. For one odd, exhilarating moment, Eliasser and I were somehow physical and merged at the same time.

The third explosion of Light came so fast we were pushed up and out of the physical and fully merged before we grasped that it had happened.

Where are we? we thought together.

Stars dropped, one by one, into the center of us.

Who are we?

Epilogue

Ashara and Eliasser kept their eyes on the Garrammon match in progress. By their side were Peliyama and Panimore, who had arrived earlier following an urgent call from the Guardians.

"Has Meiri inquired about her next task?" Peliyama asked.

"She says she does not want to know what is coming," Ashara replied.

Peliyama watched as Meiri leapt high to field a tricky play. "That is just as well. She has at least two Earth years before she will be called."

Panimore touched Eliasser on the arm. "Come. Let us walk for a bit."

Eliasser sighed. Once again, he would be questioned about what had occurred at the Steaming Falls. And once again, he would have no answers.

The two women waited for the men to disappear around the curve in the path.

"Tell me again what happened. And exactly how you found them," Peliyama said.

From anyone else, Ashara would have resented the request to repeat what had already been told. But it was Peliyama who asked, and she was no more a fan of idle words than was the Master Healer. However, this was their first opportunity to discuss the matter in private. There was always the possibility that something had been missed.

"I felt them leave physicality as though an earthquake struck the core of my Being. I consulted the Foreseers at once. They would not divulge how or why it happened, or where Eliasser and Meiri were." Ashara shook her head, still amazed by what had occurred. "It was three days until I sensed them reenter physicality in the Old Clearing. I ethermoved at once. They were lying unconscious, not on the stone, but on the grass before it, in front of the three flowers."

"And they remember nothing beyond what you have already told me?"

"Apparently not. It is an odd thing, Peliyama. They were completely merged, yet they also seemed to have had an experience as separate entities. Meiri's only memory is of a field of stars that resembled flowers made of light. She picked one of the star-flowers and ate it."

"And Eliasser?" Peliyama continued to watch the game as though it interested her.

"He recalls instead that they each picked a star-flower and fed it to the other."

"Oh dear. I keep hoping that part will change. But it is clear it will not, so we must proceed with what we have." Peliyama's brow furrowed. "And they did not require grounding?"

Ashara threw her hands up. "None at all. Their energy signatures were perfectly balanced. It confounds me."

"Who could have seen to that if Meiri and Eliasser were not with the Foreseers?"

As though driven by a baseball bat, the Garrammon ball rocketed straight toward Peliyama. She held her arm out and the ball froze a few inches from her hand. It took Meiri and Ari a while to come get it as they kept pulling on each other's tunics to prevent the other from reaching the ball first.

"Are they always like this?" Peliyama asked.

Ashara grumbled, "I sometimes think they will make me *pentuma* before my service is complete. And yet," she added with a sigh, "I miss their antics. Meiri is happier when Ari visits."

Ari was first to reach the women. Seeing the floating ball held hostage in mid-air, he grinned. "I bet you'd be great at Garrammon. Would you like to play?"

"It would be unfair," Peliyama said, "as I will always know where the ball is."

Meiri caught up, took in the frozen ball and Ari's open-mouthed stare.

"Then you would always win," Ari said. "We could use you on our team."

"What benefit would that be, Arrien? To always know you are going to win?"

Peliyama released the ball and Meiri snapped it up. "Thank you," she said softly, then turned to follow Ari back to the field.

"Meirashannar. Why will you not look at me?"

Meiri turned around, but still would not meet Peliyama's gaze. "I'm sorry. I mean no disrespect, but your Light is too bright for my eyes."

Peliyama hid her surprise. "How long have you been able to see my Light?"

"Since . . . a few days ago."

"When you and Eliasser merged."

"Yes."

"Thank you, Meiri. I can shield it if necessary and will do so now. Will you permit me the honor of seeing into you?"

The younger woman reluctantly lifted her face.

Interesting, thought Peliyama. *She aches for me to do this, and yet she resists as well. What could she be afraid of?*

The probing was so gentle that Meiri barely felt a thing. When it was over, Meiri turned to Ashara. "You should have her give you lessons. Her eye drilling doesn't hurt."

Peliyama waited for Meiri to leave. What she had discovered had shaken her. It was not the anticipated discomfort of mind probing that struck fear in Meiri.

"Watch her carefully, Ashara. She will move fast now, much faster than Eliasser is able to."

"Her Earth body?"

Peliyama nodded. "She still believes she is held back by it, but I tell you in warning, what appeared to hold her back will now propel her forward."

Ashara sighed again. "Did she initiate it?"

"No. But neither did Eliasser, I can feel the truth in his heart even from here. Panimore will merely confirm that for me. And yet, somehow, they both did."

The look the Council Head favored Ashara with was fraught with meaning.

The Master Healer's eyes clouded over. "You do not mean . . ."

"Watch her. Watch them both. They will need to be protected until it is time. But for now? They must be separated."

"They will object."

"It cannot be helped."

Ashara returned her focus to the field where Meiri played; unknowing, innocent.

It promised to be a long two years.

Author's Note

Cootie makes a brief, off-page appearance in *Elvener's Legacy.* In much earlier drafts of both the first and second books, Cootie (and our shenanigans) figured more prominently. Sadly, in the interest of moving the story forward, those scenes wound up on the "cutting room floor."

The adult version of the children's game is, like Bunco, played with paper, pencil, and dice. Food is present, as is wine and plenty of chocolate. But it's the friendship and support of twelve women that have met monthly (or as nearly as we could) since 2003 that mean the most to me—and I wanted to honor something that is such an important part of my life.

And if you'd like to start your own Cootie Group, the directions are on my website: www.debrakoehler.net

Acknowledgements

I remain ever grateful for the crazy contest formerly known as National Novel Writing Month. The spirit of NaNoWriMo lives on in programs that have stepped up to fill the gap left by the closing of its parent organization—including NaNo2.org hosted by a team of volunteers that includes NaNoWriMo founder, Chris Baty.

Raquel Brown (RaquelBrown.com) is an amazing and encouraging editor to work with. As before, any mistakes are mine alone, as I am prone to nonstop tinkering with the text until I am finally forced to hit PUBLISH.

The gratitude I owe Marlene Cullen—good friend, fellow writer, and sounding board—is boundless. Check out her inspiring website at TheWriteSpot.us.

Many thanks to the Redwood Writers branch of the California Writers Club as well as the Authors Guild forums for the wealth of information and support offered there.

For my Cootie Group. We began as friends with kids in the same school, volunteering on school committees, but over the past twenty-three years have evolved into so much more. You ladies are my rock. And I never laugh harder than when I'm with you!

To my readers. I am so gratified that you love this story as much as I do. I hope you enjoyed this second installment of the Amoran Chronicles. The third book is in the works.

Finally, to my family. Even when I'm not pounding out the beginnings of another novel during November, they still suffer the occasional frozen meal when I am too distracted to stop writing and feed them a proper dinner!

About the Author

In addition to *Amoran* and *Elvener's Legacy*—Debra Koehler has been published in the anthology *Vintage Voices* and the poetry anthology *And the Beats Go On*. She has also given presentations on Honoring Your Unique Writer's Journey, and Paths to Publishing, and is a member of the California Writers Club, the Authors Guild, and the Alliance of Independent Authors (ALLi).

Debra lives in Northern California with her husband, daughter, and three rescue cats, one of whom bangs on her bedroom door at five every morning demanding to be fed. The early start gives her plenty of time for writing cozy/epic fantasies with humor and a touch of romance.

The third book of The Amoran Chronicles, *The Amelea Variance*, is in the works! To receive information about release dates—or just to say hello—visit Debra at www.debrakoehler.net

Made in the USA
Las Vegas, NV
24 May 2026

47009850R00194